EMERGENCY SURGERY

The nearest-object indicator showed something moving toward the Med Ship. There was a small object headed toward the planet from empty space. Calhoun put on double acceleration to intercept it.

The spacephone growled: *"Med Ship! What do you think you're doing?"*

"Getting in trouble," said Calhoun briefly.

"Med Ship!" the voice rasped. *"Keep out of the way of our missile! It's a megaton bomb!"*

Calhoun said irrelevantly: "Those who in quarrels interpose, must often wipe a bloody nose." He added, "I know what it is."

Calhoun aimed his ship. He knew the capacities of his ship as only a man who'd handled one for a long time could. He knew quite exactly what it could do.

The rocket from remoteness—the megaton-bomb missile—came smoking furiously from the stars. Calhoun seemed to throw his ship into a collision course.

The rocket swerved to avoid him, though guided from many thousands of miles away. There was a trivial time-lag between the time its scanners picked up a picture and transmitted it, and the controlling impulse reached the missile in response. Calhoun counted on that. But he wasn't trying for a collision. He was forcing evasive action.

He secured it. The rocket slanted itself to dart aside. Calhoun threw_____ and slashed the mis_____ flame. . . .

MED SHIP

+ + +

MURRAY LEINSTER

EDITED BY
ERIC FLINT & GUY GORDON

MED SHIP

This is a work of fiction. All the characters and events portrayed in this book are fictional, and any resemblance to real people or incidents is purely coincidental.

"Med Ship Man" was first published in *Galaxy*, October 1963, and was later reissued in *Doctor to the Stars* (Pyramid 1964). "Plague on Kryder II" was first published in *Analog*, December 1964, and was later reissued in *S.O.S. From Three Worlds* (Ace 1967). "The Mutant Weapon" was first published under the title "Med Service" in *Astounding*, August 1957. It was reissued as a novel under the current title by Ace in 1959. "Ribbon in the Sky" was first published in *Astounding*, October 1957, and was later reissued as part of *S.O.S. From Three Worlds*. "Tallien Three" was first published under the title "The Hate Disease" in *Analog*, August 1963, and was later reissued as part of *Doctor to the Stars*. "Quarantine World" was first published in *Analog*, November 1966, and was later reissued as part of *S.O.S. From Three Worlds*. "The Grandfathers' War" was first published in *Astounding*, October 1957, and was later reissued as part of *Doctor to the Stars*. "Pariah Planet" was first published in *Amazing*, July 1961, and was reissued as a novel by Ace under the title *This World is Taboo*.

All rights reserved, including the right to reproduce this book or portions thereof in any form.

A Baen Books Original

Baen Publishing Enterprises
P.O. Box 1403
Riverdale, NY 10471
www.baen.com

ISBN: 0-7434-3555-9

Cover art by Bob Eggleton

First printing, August 2002

Distributed by Simon & Schuster
1230 Avenue of the Americas
New York, NY 10020

Production by Windhaven Press, Auburn, NH
Printed in the United States of America

CONTENTS

MED SHIP MAN

I

Calhoun regarded the communicator with something like exasperation as his taped voice repeated a standard approach-call for the twentieth time. But no answer came, which had become irritating a long time ago. This was a new Med Service sector for Calhoun. He'd been assigned to another man's tour of duty because the other man had been taken down with romance. He'd gotten married, which ruled him out for Med Ship duty. So now Calhoun listened to his own voice endlessly repeating a call that should have been answered immediately.

Murgatroyd the *tormal* watched with beady, interested eyes. The planet Maya lay off to port of the Med Ship *Aesclipus Twenty*. Its almost-circular disk showed full-size on a vision-screen beside the ship's controlboard. There was an ice-cap in view. There were continents. There were seas. The cloud-system of a considerable cyclonic disturbance could be noted off at one side, and the continents looked reasonably as

3

they should, and the seas were of that muddy, indescribable tint which indicates deep water.

Calhoun's own voice, taped half an hour earlier,
sounded in a speaker as it went again to the communicator and then to the extremely visible world a
hundred thousand miles away.

"Calling ground," said Calhoun's recorded voice.
"Med Ship Aesclipus Twenty *calling ground to report
arrival and ask coordinates for landing. Our mass is
fifty standard tons. Repeat, five-oh tons. Purpose of
landing, planetary health inspection."*

The recorded voice stopped. There was silence
except for those also-taped random noises which kept
the inside of the ship from feeling like the inside of
a tomb.

Murgatroyd said:

"Chee?"

Calhoun said ironically:

"Undoubtedly, Murgatroyd! Undoubtedly! Whoever's
on duty at the spaceport stepped out for a moment,
or dropped dead, or did something equally inconvenient. We have to wait until he gets back or somebody else takes over!"

Murgatroyd said *"Chee!"* again and began to lick his
whiskers. He knew that when Calhoun called on the
communicator, another human voice should reply. Then
there should be conversation, and shortly the force-
fields of a landing-grid should take hold of the Med
Ship and draw it planetward. In time it ought to touch
ground in a space-port with a gigantic, silvery landing-
grid rising skyward all about it. Then there should be
people greeting Calhoun cordially and welcoming
Murgatroyd with smiles and pettings.

"Calling ground," said the recorded voice yet again.
"Med Ship Aesclipus Twenty—"

It went on through the formal notice of arrival.

Murgatroyd waited in pleasurable anticipation. When the Med Ship arrived at a port of call humans gave him sweets and cakes, and they thought it charming that he drank coffee just like a human, only with more gusto. Aground, Murgatroyd moved zestfully in society while Calhoun worked. Calhoun's work was conferences with planetary health officials, politely receiving such information as they thought important, and tactfully telling them about the most recent developments in medical science as known to the Interstellar Medical Service.

"Somebody," said Calhoun darkly, "is going to catch the devil for this!"

The communicator loud-speaker spoke abruptly.

"Calling Med Ship," said a voice. *"Calling Med Ship* Aesclipus Twenty! *Liner* Candida *calling. Have you had an answer from ground?"*

"Not yet. I've been calling all of half an hour, too!"

"We've been in orbit twelve hours," said the voice from emptiness. *"Calling all the while. No answer. We don't like it."*

Calhoun flipped a switch that threw a vision-screen into circuit with the ship's electron telescope. A starfield appeared and shifted wildly. Then a bright dot centered itself. He raised the magnification. The bright dot swelled and became a chubby commercial ship, with the false ports that passengers like to believe they look through when in space. Two relatively large cargo-ports on each side showed that it carried heavy freight in addition to passengers. It was one of those work-horse intra-cluster ships that distribute the freight and passengers the long-haul liners dump off only at established transshipping ports.

Murgatroyd padded across the Med Ship's cabin and examined the image with a fine air of wisdom. It did not mean anything to him, but he said, *"Chee!"* as if making an observation of profound significance. He went back to the cushion on which he'd been curled up.

"We don't see anything wrong aground," the liner's voice complained, *"but they don't answer calls! We don't get any scatter-signals either. We went down to two diameters and couldn't pick up a thing. And we have a passenger to land! He insists on it!"*

Ordinarily, communications between different places on a planet's surface use frequencies the ion-layers of the atmosphere either reflect or refract down past the horizon. But there is usually some small leakage to space, and line-of-sight frequencies are generally abundant. It is one of the annoyances of a ship coming in to port that space near most planets is usually full of local signals.

"I'll check," said Calhoun curtly. "Stand by."

The *Candida* would have arrived off Maya as the Med Ship had done, and called down as Calhoun had been doing. It was very probably a ship on schedule and the grid operator at the space-port should have expected it. Space-commerce was important to any planet, comparing more or less with the export-import business of an industrial nation in ancient times on Earth. Planets had elaborate traffic-aid systems for the cargo-carriers which moved between solar systems as they'd once moved between continents on Earth. Such traffic aids were very carefully maintained. Certainly for a space-port landing-grid not to respond to calls for twelve hours running seemed ominous.

"We've been wondering," said the *Candida* querulously, *"if there could be something radically wrong below. Sickness, for example."*

The word "sickness" was a substitute for a more alarming word. But a plague had nearly wiped out the population of Dorset, once upon a time, and the first

ships to arrive after it had broken out most incautiously
went down to ground, and so carried the plague to
their next two ports of call. Nowadays quarantine
regulations were enforced very strictly indeed.

"I'll try to find out what's the matter," said Calhoun.

"We've got a passenger," repeated the *Candida*
aggrievedly, *"who insists that we land him by spaceboat if we don't make a ship-landing. He says he has
important business aground."*

Calhoun did not answer. The rights of passengers
were extravagantly protected, these days. To fail to
deliver a passenger to his destination entitled him to
punitive damages which no space-line could afford.
So the Med Ship would seem heaven-sent to the
Candida's skipper. Calhoun could relieve him of
responsibility.

The telescope screen winked, and showed the surface of the planet a hundred thousand miles away.
Calhoun glanced at the image on the port screen and
guided the telescope to the space-port city—Maya City.
He saw highways and blocks of buildings. He saw the
space-port and its landing-grid. He could see no
motion, of course. He raised the magnification. He
raised it again. Still no motion. He upped the magnification until the lattice-pattern of the telescope's
amplifying crystal began to show. But at the ship's
distance from the planet, a ground-car would repre-
sent only the fortieth of a second of arc. There was
atmosphere, too, with thermals. Anything the size of
a ground-car simply couldn't be seen.

But the city showed quite clearly. Nothing massive
had happened to it. No large-scale physical disaster
had occurred. It simply did not answer calls from
space.

Calhoun flipped off the screen.

"I think," he said irritably into the communicator

microphone, "I suspect I'll have to make an emergency landing. It could be something as trivial as a power failure"—but he knew that was wildly improbable—"or it could be—anything. I'll land on rockets and tell you what I find."

The voice from the *Candida* said hopefully:

"Can you authorize us to refuse to land our passenger for his own protection? He's raising the devil! He insists that his business demands that he be landed."

A word from Calhoun as a Med Service man would protect the space-liner from a claim for damages. But Calhoun didn't like the look of things. He realized, distastefully, that he might find practically anything down below. He might find that he had to quarantine the planet and himself with it. In such a case he'd need the *Candida* to carry word of the quarantine to other planets and get word to Med Service sector headquarters.

"We've lost a lot of time," insisted the *Candida*. *"Can you authorize us—"*

"Not yet," said Calhoun. "I'll tell you when I land."

"But—"

"I'm signing off for the moment," said Calhoun. "Stand by."

He headed the little ship downward and as it gathered velocity he went over the briefing-sheets covering this particular world. He'd never touched ground here before. His occupation, of course, was seeing to the dissemination of medical science as it developed under the Med Service. The Service itself was neither political nor administrative, but it was important. Every human-occupied world was supposed to have a Med Ship visit at least once in four years. Such visits verified the state of public health. Med Ship men like Calhoun offered advice on public-health problems. When something out of the ordinary turned up, the Med Service had a staff of researchers who hadn't been wholly baffled yet. There were great ships which could carry the ultimate in laboratory equipment and specialized personnel to any place where they were needed. Not less than a dozen inhabited worlds in this sector alone owed the survival of their populations to the Med Service, and the number of those which couldn't have been colonized without Med Service help was legion.

Calhoun re-read the briefing. Maya was one of four planets in this general area whose life-systems seemed to have had a common origin, suggesting that the Arrhenius theory of space-traveling spores was true in some limited sense. A genus of ground-cover plants with motile stems and leaves, and cannibalistic tendencies, was considered strong evidence of common origin.

The planet had been colonized for two centuries, now, and produced organic compounds of great value from indigenous plants. They were used in textile manufacture. There were no local endemic infections to which men were susceptible. A number of human-use crops were grown. Cereals, grasses and grains, however, could not be grown because of the native ground-cover motile-stem plants. All wheat and cereal food had to be imported, and the fact severely limited Maya's population. There were about two million on the planet, settled on a peninsula in the Yucatan Sea and a small area of mainland. Public-health surveys had shown such-and-such, and such-and-such, and thus-and-so. There was no mention of anything to account for the failure of the space-port to respond to arrival-calls from space. Naturally!

The Med Ship drove on down. The planet revolved beneath it. As Maya's sunlit hemisphere enlarged, Calhoun kept the telescope's field wide. He saw cities and vast areas of cleared land where native plants were grown as raw materials for the organics' manufactures. He saw little true chlorophyll green, though. Mayan foliage tended to a dark, olive-green.

At fifty miles he was sure that the city streets were empty even of ground-car traffic. There was no space-ship aground in the landing-grid. There were no ground-cars in motion on the splendid, multiple-lane highways.

At thirty miles altitude there were still no signals in the atmosphere, though when he tried amplitude-modulation reception he picked up static. But there was no normally modulated signal on the air at any frequency. At twenty miles, no. At fifteen miles broad-cast power was available, which proved that the landing-grid was working as usual, tapping the upper atmosphere for electric charges to furnish power for all the planet's needs.

From ten miles down to ground-touch, Calhoun was busy. It is not too difficult to land a ship on rockets, with reasonably level ground to land on. But landing at a specific spot is something else. Calhoun juggled the ship to descend inside the grid aground. His rock-ets burned out pencil-thin holes through the clay and stone beneath the tarmac. He cut them off.

Silence. Stillness. The Med Ship's outside micro-phones picked up small noises of wind blowing over the city. There was no other sound at all.

—No. There was a singularly deliberate clicking sound, not loud and not fast. Perhaps a click—a double-click—every two seconds. That was all.

Calhoun went into the airlock with Murgatroyd frisking a little in the expectation of great social suc-cess among the people of this world. Calhoun cracked the outer airlock door. He smelled something. It was a faintly sour, astringent odor that had the quality of decay in it. But it was no kind of decay he recognized. Again stillness and silence. No traffic-noise. Not even the almost inaudible murmur that every city has in all its ways at all hours. The buildings looked as buildings should look at daybreak, except that the doors and windows were open. It was somehow shocking.

A ruined city is dramatic. An abandoned city is pathetic. This was neither. It was something new. It felt as if everybody had walked away, out of sight, within the past few minutes.

Calhoun headed for the space-port building with Murgatroyd ambling puzzledly at his side. Murgatroyd was disturbed. There should be people here! They should welcome Calhoun and admire him— Murgatroyd—and he should be a social lion with all the sweets he could eat and all the coffee he could put into his expandable belly. But nothing happened. Nothing at all.

"Chee?" he asked anxiously. *"Chee-chee?"*

"They've gone away," growled Calhoun. "They probably left in ground-cars. There's not a one in sight."

There wasn't. Calhoun could look out through the grid foundations and see long, sunlit, and absolutely empty streets. He arrived at the space-port building. There was—there had been—a green space about the base of the structure. There was not a living plant left. Leaves were wilted and limp. There was almost a jelly of collapsed stems and blossoms, of dark olive-green. The plants were dead, but not long enough to have dried up. They might have wilted two days before. Possibly three.

Calhoun went in the building. The space-port log lay open on a desk. It recorded the arrival of freight to be shipped away—undoubtedly—on the *Candida* now uneasily in orbit somewhere aloft. There was no sign of disorder. It was exactly as if the people here had walked out to look at something interesting, and hadn't come back.

Calhoun trudged out of the space-port and to the streets and buildings of the city proper. It was incredible! Doors were opened or unlocked. Merchandise in the shops lay on display, exactly as it had been spread out to interest customers. There was no sign of confusion anywhere. Even in a restaurant there were dishes and flatware on the tables. The food in the plates was stale, as if three days old, but it hadn't yet begun to spoil. The appearance of everything was as if people at their meals had simply, at some signal, gotten up and walked out without any panic or disturbance.

Calhoun made a wry face. He'd remembered something. Among the tales that had been carried from Earth to the other worlds of the galaxy there was a completely unimportant mystery-story which people still sometimes tried to write an ending to. It was the story of an ancient sailing-ship called the *Marie Celeste*, which was found sailing aimlessly in the middle of the ocean. There was food on the cabin table and the galley stove was still warm, and there was no sign of any trouble, or terror, or disturbance which might cause the ship to be abandoned. But there was not a living soul on board. Nobody had ever been able to contrive a believable explanation.

"Only," said Calhoun to Murgatroyd, "this is on a larger scale. The people of this city walked out about three days ago, and didn't come back. Maybe all the people on the planet did the same, since there's not a communicator in operation anywhere. To make the understatement of the century, Murgatroyd, I don't like this! I don't like it a bit!"

II

On the way back to the Med Ship, Calhoun stopped at another place where, on a grass-growing planet, there would have been green sward. There were Earth-type trees, and some native ones, and between them there should have been a lawn. The trees were thriving, but the ground-cover plants were collapsed and rotting. Calhoun picked up a bit of the semi-slime and smelled it. It had a faintly sour and astringent smell, the same he'd noticed when he opened the airlock door. He threw the stuff away and brushed off his hands. Something had killed the ground-cover plants which had the habit of killing Earth-type grass when planted here.

He listened. Everywhere that humans live, there are insects and birds and other tiny creatures which are essential parts of the ecological system to which the human race is adjusted. They have to be carried to and established upon every new world that mankind hopes to occupy. But there was no sound of such living creatures here. It was probable that the bellowing roar

of the Med Ship's emergency rockets was the only real
noise the city had heard since its people went away.

The stillness bothered Murgatroyd. He said, *"Chee!"*
in a subdued tone and stayed close to Calhoun.
Calhoun shook his head. Then he said abruptly:

"Come along, Murgatroyd!"

He went back to the grid and the building hous-
ing its controls. He didn't look at the space-port log
this time. He went to the instruments recording the
second function of a landing-grid. In addition to lifting up and letting down ships of space, a landing-grid
drew down power from the ions of the upper atmosphere, and broadcast it. It provided all the energy that
humans on a world could need. It was solar power,
in a way, absorbed and stored by a layer of ions miles
high, which then could be drawn on and distributed
by the grid. During his descent Calhoun had noted
that broadcast power was still available. Now he looked
at what the instruments said.

The needle on the dial showing power-drain moved
slowly back and forth. It was a rhythmic movement,
going from maximum to minimum power-use, and
then back again. Approximately six million kilowatts
was being taken out of the broadcast every two
seconds for half of one second. Then the drain cut
off for a second and a half, and went on again—for
half a second.

Frowning, Calhoun raised his eyes to a very fine
color photograph on the wall above the power dials.
It was a picture of the human-occupied part of Maya,
taken four thousand miles out in space. It had been
enlarged to four feet by six, and Maya City could be
seen as an irregular group of squares and triangles
measuring a little more than half an inch by three-
quarters. The detail was perfect. It was possible to see
perfectly straight, infinitely thin lines moving out from

the city. They were multiple-lane highways, mathematically straight from one city to another, and then mathematically straight—even though at a new angle—until the next. Calhoun stared thoughtfully at them.

"The people left the city in a hurry," he told Murgatroyd, "and there was little confusion, if any. So they knew in advance that they might have to go, and were ready for it. If they took anything, they had it ready-packed in their cars. But they hadn't been sure they'd have to go because they were going about their businesses as usual. All the shops were open and people were eating in restaurants, and so on."

Murgatroyd said, *"Chee!"* as if in full agreement.

"Now," demanded Calhoun, "where did they go? The question's really that of where they could go! There were about eight hundred thousand people in this city. There'd be cars for everyone, of course, and two hundred thousand cars would take everybody. But that's a lot of ground-cars! Put 'em two hundred feet apart on a highway, and that's twenty-six cars to the mile on each lane . . . Run them at a hundred miles an hour on a twelve-lane road—using all lanes one way—and that's twenty-six hundred cars per lane per hour, and that's thirty-one thousand . . . Two highways make sixty-two . . . Three highways . . . With two highways they could empty the city in under three hours, and with three highways close to two . . . Since there's no sign of panic, that's what they must have done. Must have worked it out in advance, too. Maybe they'd done it before. . . ."

He searched the photograph which was so much more detailed than a map. There were mountains to the north of Maya City, but only one highway led north. There were more mountains to the west. One highway went into them, but not through. To the south there was sea, which curved around some three

hundred miles from Maya City and made the human
colony on Maya into a peninsula. It was a small fraction of the planet, but grains wouldn't grow there. The
planet could grow native plants for raw material for
organic chemicals, but it couldn't grow all its own food
so its population was limited.

"They went east," said Calhoun presently. He traced
lines with his finger. "Three highways go east. There's
the only way they could go, quickly. They hadn't been
sure they'd have to go but they knew where to go
when they did. So when they got their warning, they
left. On three highways, to the east. And we'll follow
them and ask what the hell they ran away from.
Nothing's visible here!"

He went back to the Med Ship, Murgatroyd skipping with him. As the airlock door closed behind
them, he heard a click from the outside-microphone
speakers. He listened. It was the doubled clicking,
as of something turned on and almost at once turned
off again. There was a two-second cycle—the same
as that of the power-drain. Something drawing six
million kilowatts went on and immediately off again
every two seconds. It made a sound in speakers
linked to outside microphones, but it didn't make a
noise in the air. The microphone clicks were induction; pick-up; like cross-talk on defective telephone
cables.

Calhoun shrugged his shoulders almost up to his
ears. He went to the communicator.

"Calling *Candida*—" he began, and the answer
almost leaped down his throat.

"*Candida to Med Ship. Come in! Come in! What's
happened down there?*"

"The city's deserted without any sign of panic," said
Calhoun, "and there's power and nothing seems to be
broken down. But it's as if somebody had said,

'Everybody clear out' and they did. That doesn't happen on a whim! What's your next port of call?"

The *Candida*'s voice told him, hopefully.

"Take a report," commanded Calhoun. "Deliver it to the public-health office immediately after you land. They'll get it to Med Service sector headquarters. I'm going to stay here and find out what's been going on."

He dictated, growing irritated as he did so because he couldn't explain what he reported. Something serious had taken place, but there was no clue as to what it was. Strictly speaking, it wasn't certainly a public-health affair. But any emergency the size of this one involved public-health factors.

"I'm remaining aground to investigate," finished Calhoun. "I will report further when or if it is possible. Message ends."

"What about our passenger?"

"To the devil with your passenger!" said Calhoun peevishly. "Do as you please!"

He cut off the communicator and prepared for activity outside the ship. Presently he and Murgatroyd went to look for transportation. The Med Ship couldn't be used for a search operation. It didn't carry enough rocket-fuel. They'd have to use a ground vehicle.

It was again shocking to note that nothing had moved but sun-shadows. Again it seemed that everybody had simply walked out of some door or other and failed to come back. Calhoun saw the windows of jewellers' shops. Treasures lay unguarded in plain view. He saw a florist's shop. Here there were Earth-type flowers apparently thriving, and some strangely beautiful flowers with olive green foliage which throve as well as the Earth-plants. There was a cage in which a plant had grown, and that plant was wilting and about to rot. But a plant that had to be grown in a cage . . .

He found a ground-car agency, perhaps for imported

cars, perhaps for those built on Maya. He went in.
There were cars on display. He chose one—an elaborate sports car. He turned its key and it hummed. He
drove it carefully out into the empty street. Murgatroyd
sat interestedly beside him.

"This is luxury, Murgatroyd," said Calhoun. "Also
it's grand theft. We medical characters can't usually
afford such things or have an excuse to steal them. But
these are parlous times. We take a chance."

"*Chee!*" said Murgatroyd.

"We want to find a fugitive population and ask what
they ran away from. As of the moment, it seems that
they ran away from nothing. They may be pleased to
know they can come back."

Murgatroyd again said, "*Chee!*"

Calhoun drove through vacant ways. It was somehow nerve-racking. He felt as if someone should pop
out and say, "Boo!" at any instant. He discovered an
elevated highway and a ramp leading up to it. It ran
west to east. He drove eastward, watching sharply for
any sign of life. There was none.

He was nearly out of the city when he felt the chest-
impact of a sonic boom, and then heard a trailing-away
growling sound which seemed to come from farther
away as it died out. It was the result of something traveling faster than sound, so that the noise it made far
away had to catch up with the sound it emitted nearby.

He stared up. He saw a parachute blossom as a bare
speck against the blue. Then he heard the even deeper-
toned roaring of a supersonic craft climbing skyward.
It could be a spaceliner's lifeboat, descended into
atmosphere and going out again. It was. It had left a
parachute behind and now went back to space to
rendezvous with its parent ship.

"That," said Calhoun impatiently, "will be the
Candida's passenger. If he was insistent enough—"

He scowled. The *Candida*'s voice had said its passenger demanded to be landed for business reasons. And Calhoun had a prejudice against some kinds of business men who would think their own affairs more important than anything else. Two standard years before, he'd made a planetary health inspection on Texia II, in another galactic sector. It was a llano planet and a single giant business enterprise. Illimitable prairies had been sown with an Earth-type grass which destroyed the native ground-cover—the reverse of the ground-cover situation here—and the entire planet was a monstrous range for beef-cattle. Dotted about were gigantic slaughter-houses, and cattle in masses of tens of thousands were shifted here and there by ground-induction fields which acted as fences. Ultimately the cattle were driven by these same induction-fences to the slaughter-houses and actually into the chutes where their throats were slit. Every imaginable fraction of a credit profit was extracted from their carcasses, and Calhoun had found it appalling. He was not sentimental about cattle, but the complete cold-bloodedness of the entire operation sickened him. The same cold-bloodedness was practiced toward the human employees who ran the place. Their living-quarters were sub-marginal. The air stank of cattle-murder. Men worked for the Texia Company or they did not work. If they did not work they did not eat. If they worked and ate—Calhoun could see nothing satisfying in being alive on a world like that! His report to Med Service had been biting. He'd been prejudiced against business men ever since.

But a parachute descended, blowing away from the city. It would land not too far from the highway he followed. And it didn't occur to Calhoun not to help the unknown chutist. He saw a small figure dangling below the chute. He slowed the ground-car. He estimated where the parachute would land.

He was off the twelve-land highway and on a feeder-road when the chute was a hundred feet high. He was racing across a field of olive-green plants—the field went all the way to the horizon—when the parachute actually touched ground. There was a considerable wind. The man in the harness bounced. He didn't know how to spill the air. The chute dragged him.

Calhoun sped ahead, swerved, and ran into the chute. He stopped the car and the chute stopped with it. He got out.

The man lay in a helpless tangle of cordage. He thrust unskillfully at it. When Calhoun came up he said suspiciously:

"Have you a knife?"

Calhoun offered a knife, politely opening its blade. The man slashed at the cords. He freed himself. There was an attaché-case lashed to his chute-harness. He cut at those cords. The attaché-case not only came clear, but opened. It dumped out an incredible mass of brand-new, tightly-packed interstellar credit certificates. Calhoun could see that the denominations were one-thousand and ten-thousand credits. The man from the chute reached under his armpit and drew out a blaster. It was not a service weapon. It was elaborate. It was practically a toy. With a dour glance at Calhoun he put it in a side pocket and gathered up the scattered money. It was an enormous sum, but he packed it back. He stood up.

"My name is Allison," he said in an authoritative voice. "Arthur Allison. I'm much obliged. Now I'll get you to take me to Maya City."

"No," said Calhoun politely. "I just left there. It's deserted. I'm not going back. There's nobody there."

"But I've important bus—" The other man stared. "It's deserted? But that's impossible!"

"Quite," agreed Calhoun, "but it's true. It's

abandoned. It's uninhabited. Everybody's left it. There's none there at all."

The man who called himself Allison blinked unbelievingly. He swore. Then he raged profanely. But he was not bewildered by the news. Which, upon consideration, was itself almost bewildering. But then his eyes grew shrewd. He looked about him.

"My name is Allison," he repeated, as if there were some sort of magic in the word. "Arthur Allison. No matter what's happened, I've some business to do here. Where have the people gone? I need to find—"

"I need to find them too," said Calhoun. "I'll take you with me, if you like."

"You've heard of me." It was a statement, confidently made.

"Never," said Calhoun politely. "If you're not hurt, suppose you get in the car? I'm as anxious as you are to find out what's happened. I'm Med Service."

Allison moved toward the car.

"Med Service, eh? I don't think much of the Med Service! You people try to meddle in things that are none of your business!"

Calhoun did not answer. The muddy man, clutching the attaché-case tightly, waded through the olive-green plants to the car and climbed in. Murgatroyd said cordially: *"Chee-chee!"* but Allison viewed him with distaste.

"What's this?"

"He's Murgatroyd," said Calhoun. He's a *tormal*. He's Med Service personnel."

"I don't like beasts," said Allison coldly.

"He's much more important to me than you are," said Calhoun, "if the matter should come to a test."

Allison stared at him as if expecting him to cringe. Calhoun did not. Allison showed every sign of being an important man who expected his importance to be recognized and catered to. When Calhoun stirred impatiently he got into the car and growled a little. Calhoun took his place. The ground-car hummed. It rose on the six columns of air which took the place of wheels. It went across the field of dark-green plants, leaving the parachute deflated across a number of rows, and a trail of crushed-down plants where it had moved.

It reached the highway again. Calhoun ran the car up on the highway's shoulder, and then suddenly checked. He'd noticed something. He stopped the car and got out. Where the ploughed field ended, and before the coated surface of the highway began, there was a space where on another world one would expect to see green grass. On this planet grass did not grow. But there would normally be some sort of self-planted vegetation where there was soil and sunshine and moisture. There had been such vegetation here, but now there was only a thin, repellant mass of slimy and decaying foliage. Calhoun bent down to it. It had a sour, faintly astringent smell of decay. These were the ground-cover plants of Maya of which Calhoun had read. They had motile stems and leaves and flowers. They had cannibalistic tendencies. They were dead. But they were the local weeds which made it impossible to grow grain for human use upon this world.

Calhoun straightened up and returned to the car. Plants like this were wilted at the base of the space-port building, and on another place where there should have been sward. Calhoun had seen a large dead member of the genus in a florist's. It had been growing in a cage before it died. There was a singular coincidence, here. Humans ran away from something, and something caused the death of a particular genus of cannibal weeds.

It did not exactly add up to anything in particular, and certainly wasn't evidence for anything at all. But

Calhoun drove on in a vaguely puzzled mood. The germ of a guess was forming in his mind. He couldn't pretend to himself that it was likely, but it was surely no more unlikely than most of two million human beings abandoning their homes at a moment's notice.

III

They came to the turn-off for a town called
Tenochitlan, some forty miles from Maya City. Calhoun
swung off the highway to go through it. Whoever had
chosen the name Maya for this planet had been interested in the legends of Yucatan, back on Earth. There
were many instances of such hobbies in a Med Ship's
list of ports of call. Calhoun touched ground regularly
on planets named for counties and towns when men
first roamed the stars and nostalgically christened their
discoveries with names suggested by homesickness.
There was a Tralee, and a Dorset, and an Eire. Colonists not infrequently took their world's given name
as a pattern and chose related names for seas and
peninsulas and mountain-chains. Calhoun had even
visited a world called Texia where the landing-grid rose
near a town called Corral and the principal meat-
packing settlement was named Roundup.

Whatever the name Tenochitlan would have suggested, though, was denied by the town itself. It was
a small town. It had a pleasing local type of

architecture. There were shops and some factories, and many strictly private homes, some clustered close together and others in the middle of considerable gardens. In those gardens also there was wilt and decay among the cannibal plants. There was no grass, because such plants prevented it, but now the plants preventing grasses themselves were dead. Except for the one class of killed growing things, however, vegetation was luxuriant.

But the little city was deserted. Its streets were empty. Its houses were untenanted. Some houses were apparently locked up, here, though, and Calhoun saw three or four shops whose stock-in-trade had been covered over before the owners departed. He guessed that either this town had been warned earlier than the space-port city, or else they knew they had time to get in motion before the highways were filled with the cars from the west.

Allison looked at the houses with keen, evaluating eyes. He did not seem to notice the absence of people. When Calhoun swung back on the great road beyond the little city, Allison regarded the endless fields of dark-green plants with much the same sort of interest.

"Interesting," he said abruptly when Tenochitlan fell behind and dwindled to a speck. "Very interesting. I'm interested in land. Real property. That's my business. I've a land-owning corporation on Thanet Three. I've some holdings on Dorset, too. And elsewhere. It just occurred to me. What's all this land and the cities worth with the people all run away?"

"What," asked Calhoun, "are the people worth who've run?"

Allison paid no attention. He looked shrewd. Thoughtful.

"I came here to buy land," he said. "I'd arranged to buy some hundreds of square miles. I'd buy more if the price were right. But—as things are, it looks like the price of land ought to go down quite a bit. Quite a bit!"

"It depends," said Calhoun, "on whether there's anybody left alive to sell it to you, and what sort of thing has happened."

Allison looked at him sharply.

"Ridiculous!" he said authoritatively. "There's no question of their being alive!"

"They thought there might be," observed Calhoun. "That's why they ran away. They hoped they'd be safe where they ran to. I hope they are."

Allison ignored the comment. His eyes remained intent and shrewd. He was not bewildered by the flight of the people of Maya. His mind was busy with contemplation of that flight from the standpoint of a man of business.

The car went racing onward. The endless fields of dark green rushed past to the rear. The highway was deserted. There were three strips of surfaced road, mathematically straight, going on to the horizon. They went on by tens and scores of miles. Each strip was wide enough to allow four ground-cars to run side by side. The highway was intended to allow all the produce of all these fields to be taken to market or a processing plant at the highest possible speed and in any imaginable quantity. The same roads had allowed the cities to be deserted instantly the warning— whatever the warning was—arrived.

Fifty miles beyond Tenochitlan there was a mile-long strip of sheds. They contained agricultural machinery for crop-culture and trucks to carry the crops to where they belonged. There was no sign of life about the machinery. There was no sign of life in a further hour's run to westward.

Then there was a city visible to the left. But it was

not served by this particular highway, but another. There was no sign of any movement in its streets. It moved along the horizon to the left and rear. Presently it disappeared.

Half an hour later still, Murgatroyd said:

"*Chee!*"

He stirred uneasily. A moment later he said, "*Chee!*" again.

Calhoun turned his eyes from the road. Murgatroyd looked unhappy. Calhoun ran his hand over the *tormal's* furry body. Murgatroyd pressed against him. The car raced on. Murgatroyd whimpered a little. Calhoun's fingers felt the little animal's muscles tense sharply, and then relax, and after a little tense again. Murgatroyd said almost hysterically:

"*Chee-chee-chee-chee!*"

Calhoun stopped the car, but Murgatroyd did not seem to be relieved. Allison impatiently:

"What's the matter?"

"That's what I'm trying to find out," said Calhoun.

He felt Murgatroyd's pulse, and timed it with his sweep-second watch. He timed the muscular spasms that Murgatroyd displayed. They coincided with disturbances in his heart-beat. They came at approximately two-second intervals, and the tautening of the muscles lasted just about half a second.

"But I don't feel it!" said Calhoun.

Murgatroyd whimpered again and said, "*Chee-chee!*"

"What's going on?" demanded Allison, with the impatience of a very important man indeed. "If the beast's sick, he's sick! I've got to find—"

Calhoun opened his med kit and went carefully through it. He found what he needed. He put a pill into Murgatroyd's mouth.

"Swallow it!" he commanded.

Murgatroyd resisted, but the pill went down.

Calhoun watched him sharply. Murgatroyd's digestive system was delicate, but it was dependable. Anything that might be poisonous, Murgatroyd's stomach rejected instantly. But the pill stayed down.

"Look!" said Allison indignantly. "I've got business to do! In this attaché-case I have some millions of interstellar credits, in cash, to pay down on purchases of land and factories! I ought to make some damned good deals! And I figure that that's as important as anything else you can think of! It's a damned sight more important than a beast with a belly-ache!"

Calhoun looked at him coldly.

"Do you own land on Texia?" he asked.

Allison's mouth dropped open. Extreme suspicion and unease appeared on his face. As a sign of the unease, his hand went to the side coat pocket in which he'd put a blaster. He didn't pluck it out. Calhoun's left fist swung around and landed. He took Allison's elaborate pocket-blaster and threw it away among the monotonous rows of olive-green plants. He returned to absorbed observation of Murgatroyd.

In five minutes the muscular spasms diminished. In ten, Murgatroyd frisked. But he seemed to think that Calhoun had done something remarkable. In the warmest of tones he said:

"Chee!"

"Very good," said Calhoun. "We'll go ahead. I suspect you'll do as well as we do—for a while."

The car lifted the few inches the air-columns sustained it above the ground. It went on, still to the eastward. But Calhoun drove more slowly, now.

"Something was giving Murgatroyd rhythmic muscular spasms," he said coldly. "I gave him medication to stop them. He's more sensitive than we are so he reacted to a stimulus we haven't noticed yet. But I think we'll notice it presently."

Allison seemed to be dazed at the affront given him. It appeared to be unthinkable that anybody might lay hands on him.

"What the devil has that to do with me?" he demanded angrily. "And what did you hit me for? You're going to pay for this!"

"Until I do," Calhoun told him, "you'll be quiet. And it does have the devil to do with you. There was a Med Service gadget, once—a tricky little device to produce contraction of chosen muscles. It was useful for restarting stopped hearts without the need of an operation. It regulated the beat of hearts that were too slow or dangerously irregular. But some business man had a bright idea and got a tame researcher to link that gadget to ground induction currents. I suspect you know that business man!"

"I don't know what you're talking about," snapped Allison. But he was singularly tense.

"I do," said Calhoun unpleasantly. "I made a public-health inspection on Texia a couple of years ago. The whole planet is a single, gigantic, cattle-raising enterprise. They don't use metal fences. The herds are too big to be stopped by such things. They don't use cowboys. They cost money. On Texia they use ground-induction and the Med Service gadget linked together to serve as cattle fences. They act like fences, though they're projected through the ground. Cattle become uncomfortable when they try to cross them. So they draw back. So men control them. They move them from place to place by changing the cattle-fences which are currents induced in the ground. The cattle have to keep moving or be punished by the moving fence. They're even driven into the slaughterhouse chutes by ground-induction fields! That's the trick on Texia, where induction fields herd cattle. I think it's the trick on Maya, where people are herded like cattle and driven out of their cities so the value of their fields and factories will drop—so a land-buyer can find bargains!"

"You're insane!" snapped Allison. "I just landed on this planet. You saw me land! I don't know what happened before I got here. How could I?"

"You might have arranged it," said Calhoun.

Allison assumed an air of offended and superior dignity. Calhoun drove the car onward at very much less than the headlong pace he'd been keeping to. Presently he looked down at his hands on the steering-wheel. Now and then the tendons to his fingers seemed to twitch. At rhythmic intervals, the skin crawled on the back of his hands. He glanced at Allison. Allison's hands were tightly clenched.

"There's a ground-induction fence in action, all right," said Calhoun calmly. "You notice? It's a cattle-fence and we're running into it. If we were cattle, now, we'd turn around and move away."

"I don't know what you're talking about!" said Allison But his hands stayed clenched. Calhoun slowed the car still more. He began to feel, all over his body, that every muscle tended to twitch at the same time. It was a horrible sensation. His heart-muscles tended to contract too, simultaneously with the rest, but one's heart has its own beat-rate. Sometimes the normal beat coincided with the twitch. Then his heart pounded violently—so violently that it was painful. But equally often the imposed contraction of the heart-muscles came just after a normal contraction, and then it stayed tightly knotted for half a second. It missed a beat, and the feeling was agony. No animal would have pressed forward in the face of such sensations. It would have turned back long ago.

Calhoun stopped the car. He looked at Murgatroyd. Murgatroyd was completely himself. He looked inquiringly at Calhoun. Calhoun nodded to him, but he spoke—with some difficulty—to Allison.

"We'll see—if this thing—builds up. You know that it's the Texia—trick. A ground—induction unit set up—here. It drove people—like cattle. Now we've—run into it. It's holding people—like cattle."

He panted. His chest-muscles contracted with the rest, so that his breathing was interfered with. But Murgatroyd, who'd been made uneasy and uncomfortable before Calhoun noticed anything wrong, was now bright and frisky. Medication had desensitized his muscles to outside stimuli. He would be able to take a considerable electric shock without responding to it. But he could be killed by one that was strong enough.

A savage anger filled Calhoun. Everything fitted together. Allison had put his hand convenient to his blaster when Calhoun mentioned Texia. It meant that Calhoun suspected what Allison knew to be true. A cattle-fence unit had been set up on Maya, and it was holding—like cattle—the people it had previously driven like cattle. Calhoun could even deduce with some precision exactly what had been done. The first experience of Maya with the cattle-fence would have been with a very mild version of it. It would have been low-power and cause just enough uneasiness to be noticed. It would have been moved from west to east, slowly, and it would have reached a certain spot and there faded out. And it would have been a mystery and an uncomfortable thing, and nobody would understand it on Maya. In a week it would almost be forgotten. But then there'd come a stronger disturbance. And it would travel like the first one; down the length of the peninsula on which the colony lay, but stopping at the same spot as before, and then fading away to nothingness. And this also would have seemed mysterious but nobody would suspect humans of causing it.

There'd be theorizing and much questioning, but it would be considered an unfamiliar natural event.

Probably the third use of the cattle-fence would be most disturbing. This time it would be acutely painful. But it would move into the cities and through them and past them—and it would go down the peninsula to where it had stopped and faded on two previous occasions. And the people of Maya would be disturbed and scared. But they considered that they knew it began to the westward of Maya City, and moved toward the east at such-and-such a speed, and it went so far and no farther. And they would organize themselves to apply this carefully-worked-out information. And it would not occur to any of them that they had learned how to be driven like cattle.

Calhoun, of course, could only reason that this must have happened. But nothing else could have taken place. Perhaps there were more than three uses of the moving cattle-fence to get the people prepared to move past the known place at which it always faded to nothingness. They might have been days apart, or weeks apart, or months. There might have been stronger manifestations followed by weaker ones and then stronger ones again. But there was a cattle-fence—an inductive cattle-fence—across the highway here. Calhoun had driven into it. Every two seconds the muscles of his body tensed. Sometimes his heart missed a beat at the time that his breathing stopped, and sometimes it pounded violently. It seemed that the symptoms became more and more unbearable.

He got out his med kit, with hands that spasmodically jerked uncontrollably. He fumbled out the same medication he'd given Murgatroyd. He took two of the pellets.

"In reason," he said coldly, "I ought to let you take what this damned thing would give you. But—here!"

Allison had panicked. The idea of a cattle-fence suggested discomfort, of course. But it did not imply danger. The experience of a cattle-fence, designed for huge hoofed beasts instead of men, was terrifying. Allison gasped. He made convulsive movements. Calhoun himself moved erratically. For one and a half seconds out of two, he could control his muscles. For half a second at a time, he could not. But he poked a pill into Allison's mouth.

"Swallow it!" he commanded. "Swallow!"

The ground-car rested tranquilly on the highway, which here went on for a mile and then dipped in a gentle incline and then rose once more. The totally level fields to right and left came to an end, here. Native trees grew, trailing preposterously long fronds. Brushwood hid much of the ground. That looked normal. But the lower, ground-covering vegetation was wilted and rotting.

Allison choked upon the pellet. Calhoun forced a second upon him. Murgatroyd looked inquisitively at first one and then the other of the two men. He said:

"Chee? Chee?"

Calhoun lay back in his seat, breathing carefully to keep alive. But he couldn't do anything about his heart-beat. The sun shone brightly, though now it was low, toward the horizon. There were clouds in the reddened sky. A gentle breeze blew. Everything, to outward appearance, was peaceful and tranquil and commonplace upon this small world. But in the area that human beings had taken over there were cities which were still and silent and deserted, and somewhere— somewhere!—the population of the planet waited uneasily for the latest of a series of increasingly terri- fying phenomena to come to an end. Up to this time the strange, creeping, universal affliction had begun at one place, and moved slowly to another, and then diminished and ceased to be. But this was the greatest and worst of the torments. And it hadn't ended. It hadn't diminished. After three days it continued at full strength at the place where previously it had stopped and died away.

The people of Maya were frightened. They couldn't return to their homes. They couldn't go anywhere. They hadn't prepared for an emergency to last for days. They hadn't brought supplies of food.

It began to look as if they were going to starve.

IV

Calhoun was in very bad shape when the sports car came to the end of the highway. First, all the multiple roadways of the route that had brought him here were joined by triple ribbons of road-surface from the north. For a space there were twenty-four lanes available to traffic. They flowed together, and then there were twelve. Here there was evidence of an enormous traffic concentration at some time now past. Brush and small trees were crushed and broken where cars had been forced to travel off the hard-surface roadways and through undergrowth. The twelve lanes dwindled to six, and the unpaved area on either side showed that innumerable cars had been forced to travel off the highway altogether. Then there were three lanes, and then two, and finally only a single ribbon of pavement where no more than two cars could run side by side. The devastation on either hand was astounding. All visible vegetation for half a mile to right and left was crushed and tangled. And then the narrow surfaced road ceased to be completely straight. It curved around a hillock—and here the ground was no longer perfectly flat—and came to an end. And Calhoun saw all the ground-cars of the planet gathered and parked together.

There were no buildings. There were no streets. There was nothing of civilization but tens and scores of thousands of ground-cars. They were extraordinary to look at, stopped at random, their fronts pointed in all directions, their air-column tubes thrusting into the ground so that there might be trouble getting them clear again.

Parked bumper to bumper and in closely-placed lines, in theory twenty-five thousand cars could be parked on a square mile of ground. But there were very many times that number of cars here, and some places were unsuitable for parking, and there were lanes placed at random and there'd been no special effort to put the maximum number of cars in the smallest place. So the surface transportation system of the planet Maya spread out over some fifty sprawling square miles. Here, cars were crowded closely. There, there was much room between them. But it seemed that as far as one could see in the twilight there were glistening vehicles gathered confusedly, so there was nothing else to be seen but an occasional large tree rising from among them.

Calhoun came to the end of the surfaced road. He'd waited for the pellets he'd taken and given to Allison to have the effect they'd had on Murgatroyd. That had come about. He'd driven on. But the strength of the inductor-field had increased to the intolerable. When he stopped the sports-car he showed the effects of what he'd been through.

Figures on foot converged upon him, instantly. There were eager calls.

"It's stopped? You got through? We can go back?"

Calhoun shook his head. It was just past sunset and

many brilliant colorings showed in the western sky, but they couldn't put color into Calhoun's face. His cheeks were grayish and his eyes were deep-sunk, and he looked like someone in the last stages of exhaustion. He said heavily:

"It's still there. We came through. I'm Med Service. Have you got a government here? I need to talk to somebody who can give orders."

If he'd asked two days earlier there would have been no answer, because the fugitives were only waiting for a disaster to come to an end. One day earlier, he might have found men with authority busily trying to arrange for drinking-water for something like two millions of people, in the entire absence of wells or pumps or ways of making either. And if he'd been a day later, it is rather likely that he'd have found savage disorder. But he arrived at sundown three days after the flight from the cities. There was no food to speak of, and water was drastically short, and the fugitives were only beginning to suspect that they would never be able to leave this place, and that they might die here.

Men left the growing crowd about the sports-car to find individuals who could give orders. Calhoun stayed in the car, resting from the unbearable strain he'd undergone. The ground-inductor cattle-fence had been ten miles deep. One mile was not bad. Only Murgatroyd had noticed it. After two miles Calhoun and Allison suffered. But the medication strengthened them to take it. But there'd been a long, long way in the center of the induction-field in which existence was pure torment. Calhoun's muscles defied him for part of every two-second cycle, and his heart and lungs seemed constantly about to give up even the pretense of working. In that part of the cattle-fence field, he'd hardly dared drive faster than a crawl, in order to keep control of the car when his own body was uncontrollable. But presently the field-strength lessened and ultimately ended.

Now Murgatroyd looked cordially at the figures who clustered about the car. He'd hardly suffered at all. He'd had half as much of the medication as Calhoun himself, and his body-weight was only a tenth of Calhoun's. He'd made out all right. Now he looked expectantly at what became a jammed mass of crowding men about the vehicle that had come through the invisible barrier across the highway. They hoped desperately for news to produce hope. But Murgatroyd waited zestfully for somebody to welcome him and offer him cakes and sweets, and undoubtedly presently a cup of coffee. But nobody did.

It was a long time before there was a stirring at the edge of the crowd. Night had fully fallen then, and for miles and miles in all directions lights in the ground-cars of Maya's inhabitants glowed brightly. They drew upon broadcast power, naturally, for their motors and their lights. Somewhere, men shouted. Calhoun turned on his headlights for a guide. More shoutings. A knot of men struggled to get through the crowd. With difficulty, presently, they reached the car.

"They say you got through," panted a tall man, "but you can't get back. They say—"

Calhoun roused himself. Allison, beside him, stirred. The tall man panted again:

"I'm the planetary president. What can we do?"

"First, listen," said Calhoun tiredly.

He'd had a little rest. Not much, but some. The actual work he'd done in driving three-hundred-odd miles from Maya City was trivial. But the continuous and lately violent spasms of his heart and breathing muscles had been exhausting. He heard Murgatroyd say ingratiatingly, *"Chee-chee-chee-chee,"* and put his hand on the little animal to quiet him.

"The thing you ran away from," said Calhoun effortfully, "is a type of ground-induction field using broadcast power from the grid. It's used on Texia to confine cattle to their pastures and to move them where they're wanted to be. But it was designed for cattle. It's a cattle-fence. It could kill humans."

He went on, his voice gaining strength and steadiness as he spoke. He explained, precisely, how a ground-induction field was projected in a line at a right angle to its source. It could be moved by adjustments of the apparatus by which it was projected. It had been designed to produce the effects they'd experienced on cattle, but now it was being used on men.

"But—but if it uses broadcast power," the planetary president said urgently, "then if the power broadcast is cut off it has to stop! If you got through it coming here, tell us how to get through going back and we'll cut off the power-broadcast ourselves! We've got to do something immediately! The whole planet's here! There's no food! There's no water! Something has to be done before we begin to die!"

"But," said Calhoun, "if you cut off the power you'll die anyway. You've got a couple of million people here. You're a hundred miles from places where there's food. Without power you couldn't get to food or bring it here. Cut the power and you're still stranded here. Without power you'll die as soon as with it."

There was a sound from the listening men around. It was partly a growl and partly a groan.

"I've just found this out," said Calhoun. "I didn't know until the last ten miles exactly what the situation was, and I had to come here to be sure. Now I need some people to help me. It won't be pleasant. I may have enough medication to get a dozen people back through. It'll be safer if I take only six. Get a doctor to pick me six men. Good heart action. Sound lungs. Two should be electronics engineers. The others should be good shots. If you get them ready, I'll give them the same stuff that got us through. It's desensitizing medication, but it will do only so much. Try and find some weapons for them."

Voices murmured all around. Men hastily explained to other men what Calhoun had said. The creeping disaster before which they'd all fled—it was not a natural catastrophe, but an artificial one! Men had made it! They'd been herded here and their wives and children were hungry because of something men had done!

A low-pitched, buzzing, humming sound came from the crowd about the sports car. For the moment, nobody asked what could be the motive for men to do what had been done. Pure fury filled the mob. Calhoun leaned closer to Allison.

"I wouldn't get out of the car if I were you," he said in a low tone. "I certainly wouldn't try to buy any real property at a low price!"

Allison shivered. There was a vast, vast stirring as the explanation passed from man to man. Figures moved away in the darkness. Lighted car-windows winked as they moved through the obscurity. The population of Maya was spread out over very many square miles of what had been wilderness, and there was no elaborate communication system by which information could be spread quickly. But long before dawn there'd be nobody who didn't know that they'd fled from a man-made danger and were held here like cattle, behind a cattle-fence, apparently to die.

Allison's teeth chattered. He was a business man and up to now he'd thought as one. He'd made decisions in offices, with attorneys and secretaries and clerks to make the decisions practical and safe, but without anybody to point out any consequences other than financial ones. But he saw possible consequences to himself, here and now. He'd landed on Maya because he considered the matter too important to trust to anybody else. Even riding with Calhoun on the way here, he'd only been elated and astonished at the success of the intended coup. He'd raised his aim. For a while he'd believed that he'd end as the sole proprietor of the colony on Maya, with every plant growing for his profit, and every factory earning money for him, and every inhabitant his employee. It had been the most grandiose possible dream. The details and the maneuvers needed to complete it flowed into his mind.

But now his teeth chattered. At ten words from Calhoun he would literally be torn to pieces by the raging men about him. His attaché-case with millions of credits in cash— It would be proof of whatever Calhoun chose to say. Allison knew terror down to the bottom of his soul. But he dared not move from Calhoun's side. A single sentence in the calmest of voices would destroy him. And he'd never faced actual, understood, physical danger before.

Presently men came, one by one, to take orders from Calhoun. They were able-bodied and grim-faced men. Two were electronics engineers, as he'd specified. One was a policeman. There were two mechanics and a doctor who was also amateur tennis champion of the planet. Calhoun doled out to them the pellets that reduced the sensitiveness of muscles to eternally applied stimuli. He gave instructions. They'd go as far into the cattle-fence as they could reasonably endure. Then they'd swallow the pellets and let them act. Then they'd go on. His stock of pellets was limited. He could give three to each man.

Murgatroyd squirmed disappointedly as this briefing went on. Obviously, he wasn't to make a social success here. He was annoyed. He needed more space.

Calhoun tossed Allison's attaché-case behind the front-seat backs. Allison was too terrified to protest. It still did not increase the space left on the front seat between Calhoun and Allison.

Four humming ground-cars lifted eight inches from the ground and hovered there on columns of rushing air. Calhoun took the lead. His headlights moved down the single-lane road to which two joining twelve-lane highways had shrunk. Behind him, other headlights moved into line. Calhoun's car moved away into the darkness. The others followed.

Brilliant stars shone overhead. A cluster of a thousand suns, two thousand light-years away, made a center of illumination that gave Maya's night the quality of a vivid if diffused moonlight. The cars went on. Presently Calhoun felt the twitchings of minor muscular spasms. The road became two, and then four, and then eight lanes wide. Then four lanes swirled off to one side, and the remaining four presently doubled, and then widened again, and it was the twelve-lane turnpike that had brought Calhoun here from Maya City.

But the rhythmic interference with his body grew stronger. Allison had spoken not one word while Calhoun conferred with the people of Maya beyond the highway. His teeth chattered as they started back. He didn't attempt to speak during the beginning of the ride through the cattle-fence field. His teeth chattered, and stopped, and chattered again, and at long last he panted despairingly:

"Are you going to let the thing kill me?"

Calhoun stopped. The cars behind him stopped. He gave Allison two pellets and took two himself. With Murgatroyd insistently accompanying him, he went along the cars which trailed him. He made sure the six men he'd asked for took their pellets and that they had an adequate effect. He went back to the sports car.

Allison whimpered a little when he and Murgatroyd got back in.

"I thought," said Calhoun conversationally, "that you might try to take off by yourself, just now. It would solve a problem for me—of course it wouldn't solve any for you. But I don't think your problems have any solution, now."

He started the car up again. It moved forward. The other cars trailed dutifully. They went on through the starlit night. Calhoun noted that the effect of the cattle-fence was less than it had been before. The first desensitizing pellets had not wholly lost their effect when he added more. But he kept his speed low until he was certain the other drivers had endured the anguish of passing through the cattle-fence field.

Presently he was confident that the cattle-field was past. He sent his car up to eighty miles an hour. The other cars followed faithfully. To a hundred. They did not drop behind. The car hummed through the night at top speed—a hundred and twenty, a hundred and thirty miles an hour. The three other cars' headlights faithfully kept pace with him.

Allison said desperately:

"Look! I—don't understand what's happened. You talk as if I'd planned all this. I—did have advance notice of a—a research project here. But it shouldn't have held the people there for days! Something went wrong! I only believed that people would want to leave Maya. I'd only planned to buy as much acreage as I could, and control of as many factories as possible. That's all! It was business! Only business!"

Calhoun did not answer. Allison might be telling the truth. Some business men would think it only intelligent to frighten people into selling their holdings below a true value. Something of the sort happened every day in stock exchanges. But the people of Maya could have died!

For that matter, they still might. They couldn't return to their homes and food so long as broadcast power kept the cattle-fence in existence. But they couldn't return to their homes and food supplies if the power-broadcast was cut off, either.

V

Calhoun considered coldly. They were beyond what had been the farthest small city on the multiple highway. They would go on past now starlit fields of plants native to Maya, passing many places where trucks loaded with the plants climbed up to the roadway and headed for the factories which made use of them. The fields ran for scores of miles along the highway's length. They reached out beyond the horizon—perhaps scores of miles in that direction, too. There were thousands upon thousands of square miles devoted to the growing of dark-green vegetation which supplied the raw materials for Maya's space-exports. Some hundred-odd miles ahead, the small town of Tenochitlan lay huddled in the light of a distant star-cluster. Beyond that, more highway and Maya City. Beyond that—

Calhoun reasoned that the projector to make the induction cattle-fence would be beyond Maya City, somewhere in the mountains the space-photograph in the spaceport building showed. A large highway went into those mountains for a limited distance only. A ground-inductor projector field always formed at a right angle to the projector which was its source. It could be adjusted—the process was analogous to focusing—to come into actual being at any distance desired, and the distance could be changed. To drive the people of Maya City eastward, the projector of a cattle-fence would need to be west of the people to be driven. Logically, it would belong in the mountains. Practically, it would be concealed. Drawing on broadcast power to do its work, there would be no large power-source needed to give it the six million kilowatts it required. It should be quite easy to hide beyond any quick or easy discovery. Hunting it out might require days or weeks of searching. But the people beyond the end of the highway couldn't wait. They had no food, and holes scrabbled down to ground-water by men digging with their bare hands simply would not be adequate. The cattle-fence had to be cut off immediately. The broadcast of power had to be continued.

Calhoun made an abrupt grunting noise. Phrasing the thing that needed to be done was practically a blue-print of how to do it. Simple! He'd need the two electronics engineers, of course. But that would be the trick . . .

He drove on at a hundred and thirty miles an hour with his lips set wryly. The three other cars came behind him. Murgatroyd watched the way ahead. Mile after mile, half-minute after half-minute, the headlights cast brilliantly blinding beams before the cars. Murgatroyd grew bored. He said, *"Chee!"* in a discontented fashion and tried to curl up between Allison and Calhoun. There wasn't room. He crawled over the seatback. He moved about, back there. There were rustling sounds. He settled down. Presently there was silence. Undoubtedly he had draped his furry tail across his nose and gone soundly off to sleep.

Allison spoke suddenly. He'd had time to think, but he had no practice in various ways of thinking.

"How much money have you got?" he asked.

"Not much," said Calhoun. "Why?"

"I—haven't done anything illegal," said Allison, with an unconvincing air of confidence, "but I could be put to some inconvenience if you were to accuse me before others of what you've accused me personally. You seem to think that I planned a highly criminal act. That the action I know of—the research project I'd heard of—that it became—that it got out of hand is likely. But I am entirely in the clear. I did nothing in which I did not have the advice of counsel. I am legally unassailable. My lawyers—"

"That's none of my business," Calhoun told him. "I'm a medical man. I landed here in the middle of what seemed to be a serious public-health situation. I went to see what had happened. I've found out. I still haven't the answer—not the whole answer anyway. But the human population of Maya is in a state of some privation, not to say danger. I hope to end it. But I've nothing to do with anybody's guilt or innocence of crime or criminal intent or anything else."

Allison swallowed. Then he said with smooth confidence:

"But you could cause me inconvenience. I would appreciate it if you would—would—"

"Cover up what you've done?" asked Calhoun.

"No. I've done nothing wrong. But you could simply use discretion. I landed by parachute to complete some business deals I'd arranged months ago. I will go through with them. I will leave on the next ship. That's perfectly open and above-board. Strictly business. But you could make a—an unpleasing public image of me. Yet I have done nothing any other business man wouldn't do. I did happen to know of a research project—"

"I think," said Calhoun without heat, "that you sent men here with a cattle-fence device from Texia to frighten the people on Maya. They wouldn't know what was going on. They'd be scared. They'd want to get away. So you'd be able to buy up practically all the colony for the equivalent of peanuts. I can't prove that," he conceded, "but that's my opinion. But you want me not to state it. Is that right?"

"Exactly!" said Allison. He'd been shaken to the core, but he managed the tone and the air of a dignified man of business discussing an unpleasant subject with fine candor. "I assure you you are mistaken. You agree that you can't prove your suspicions. If you can't prove them, you shouldn't state them. That is simple ethics. You agree to that!"

Calhoun looked at him curiously.

"Are you waiting for me to tell you my price?"

"I'm waiting," said Allison reprovingly, "for you to agree not to cause me embarrassment. I won't be ungrateful. After all, I'm a person of some influence. I could do a great deal to your benefit. I'd be glad—"

"Are you working around to guess at a price I'll take?" asked Calhoun with the same air of curiosity.

He seemed much more curious than indignant, and much more amused than curious. Allison sweated suddenly. Calhoun didn't appear to be bribable. But Allison knew desperation.

"If you want to put it that way—yes," he said harshly. "You can name your own figure. I mean it!"

"I won't say a word about you," said Calhoun. "I won't need to. The characters who're operating your cattle-fence will do all the talking that's necessary. Things all fit together—except for one item. They've been dropping into place all the while we've been driving down this road."

"I said you can name your own figure!" Allison's voice was shrill. "I mean it! Any figure! Any!"

Calhoun shrugged.

"What would a Med Ship man do with money? Forget it!"

He drove on. The highway turn-off to Tenochitlan appeared. Calhoun went steadily past it. The other connection with the road through the town appeared. He left it behind.

Allison's teeth chattered again.

The buildings of Maya City began to appear, some twenty minutes later. Calhoun slowed and the other cars closed up. He opened a window and called:

"We want to go to the landing-grid first. Somebody lead the way!"

A car went past and guided the rest assuredly to a ramp down from the now-elevated road, and through utterly dark streets, of which some were narrow and winding, and came out abruptly where the landing-grid rose skyward. At the bottom its massive girders looked huge and cyclopean in the starlight, but the higher courses looked like silver lace against the stars.

They went to the control-building. Calhoun got out. Murgatroyd hopped out after him. A bit of paper clung to his fur. He shook himself, and a five-thousand-credit interstellar credit certificate fell to the ground. Murgatroyd had made a soft place for sleeping out of the contents of Allison's attaché case. It was assuredly the most expensive if not the most comfortable sleeping-cushion a *tormal* ever had. Allison sat still as if numbed. He did not even pick up the certificate.

"I need you two electronics men," said Calhoun. Then he said apologetically to the others: "I only figured out something on the way here. I'd believed we might have to take some drastic action, come daybreak. But now I doubt it. I do suggest, though, that you turn off the car headlights and get set to do some shooting if anybody turns up. I don't know whether they will or not."

He led the way inside. He turned on lights. He went to the place where dials showed the amount of power actually being used of the enormous amount available. Those dials now showed an extremely small power-drain, considering that the cities of a planet depended on the grid. But the cities were dark and empty of people. The demand-needle wavered back and forth rhythmically. Every two seconds the demand for power went up by six million kilowatts, approximately. The demand lasted for half a second, and stopped. For a second and a half the power in use was reduced by six million kilowatts. During this period only automatic pumps and ventilators and freezing equipment drew on the broadcast-power for energy. Then the six-million-kilowatt demand came again. For half a second.

"The cattle-fence," said Calhoun, "works for half a second out of every two seconds. It's intermittent or it would simply paralyze animals that wandered into it. Or people. Being intermittent, it drives them out instead. There'll be tools and parts for equipment here, in case something needs repair. I want you to make something new."

The two electronics technicians asked questions.

"We need," said Calhoun, "an interruptor that will cut off the power-broadcast for the half-second the ground-induction field is supposed to be on. Then it should turn on the broadcast power for the second and a half the cattle-fence is supposed to be off. That will stop the cattle-fence effect, and I think a ground-car should be able to work with power that's available for three half-seconds out of four."

The electronics men blinked at him. Then they grinned. They set to work. Calhoun went exploring.

He found a lunch-box in a desk. It had three very stale sandwiches in it. He offered them around. It appeared that nobody wanted to eat while their families—at the end of the highway—were still hungry.

The electronics men called on the two mechanics to held build something. They explained absorbedly to Calhoun that they were making a cut-off which would adjust to any sudden six-million-kilowatt demand, no matter what time-interval was involved. A change in the tempo of the cattle-fence cycle wouldn't bring it back on.

"That's fine!" said Calhoun. "I wouldn't have thought of that."

He bit into a stale sandwich and went outside. Allison sat limply, despairingly, in his seat in the car.

"The cattle-fence is going off," said Calhoun without triumph. "The people of the city will probably begin to get here around sunrise."

"I—I did nothing legally wrong!" said Allison, dry-throated. "Nothing! They'd have to prove that I knew what the—consequences of the research-project would be. That couldn't be proved! It couldn't! So I've done nothing legally wrong . . ."

Calhoun went inside, observing that the doctor who was also tennis champion, and the policeman who'd come to help him, were keeping keen eyes on the city and the foundations of the grid and all other places from which trouble might come.

There was a fine atmosphere of achievement in the power-control room. The power, itself, did not pass through these instruments. But relays here controlled buried massive conductors which supplied the world with power. And one of the relays had been modified. When the cattle-fence projector closed its circuit, the power went off. When the ground-inductor went off, the power went on. There was no longer a barrier

across the highways leading to the east. It was more
than probable that ground-cars could run on current
supplied for one and a half seconds out of every two.
They might run jerkily, but they would run.

Half an hour later, the amount of power drawn from
the broadcast began to rise smoothly and gradually. It
could only mean that cars were beginning to move.

Forty-five minutes later still, Calhoun heard stirrings
outside. He went out. The two men on guard gazed
off into the city. Something moved there. It was a
ground-car, running slowly and without lights. Calhoun
said undisturbedly:

"Whoever was running the cattle-fence found out
their gadget wasn't working. Their lights flickered, too.
They came to see what was the matter at the landing-
grid. But they've seen the lighted windows. Got your
blasters handy?"

But the unlighted car turned. It raced away. Calhoun
shrugged.

"They haven't a prayer," he said. "We'll take over
their apparatus as soon as it's light. It'll be too big to
destroy, and there'll be fingerprints and such to identify
them as the men who ran it. And they're not natives.
When the police start to look for the strangers who
were living where the cattle-fence projector was set
up . . . They can go into the jungles where there's
nothing to eat, or they can give themselves up."

He moved toward the door of the control-building,
once more. Allison said somehow desperately:

"They'll have hidden their equipment. You'll never
be able to find it!"

Calhoun shook his head in the starlight.

"Anything that can fly can spot it in minutes. Even
on the ground one can walk almost straight to it. You
see, something happened they didn't count on. That's
why they've left it turned on at full power. The earlier,

teasing uses of the cattle-fence were low-power. Annoying, to start with, and uncomfortable the second time, and maybe somewhat painful the third. But the last time it was full power."

He shrugged. He didn't feel like a long oration. But it was obvious. Something had killed the plants of a certain genus of which small species were weeds that destroyed Earth-type grasses. The ground-cover plants—and there were larger ones; Calhoun had seen one plant decaying in a florist's shop which had had to be grown in a cage—the ground-cover plants had motile stems and leaves and blossoms. They were cannibals. They could move their stems to reach, and their leaves to enclose, and their flowers to devour other plants. Perhaps small animals. The point, though, was that they had some limited power of motion. Earth-style sensitive plants and fly-catcher plants had primitive muscular tissues. The local ground-cover plants had them too. And the cattle-fence field made those tissues contract spasmodically. Powerfully. Violently. Repeatedly. Until they died of exhaustion. The full-power cattle-fence field had exterminated Mayan ground-cover plants all the way to the end of the east-bound highway. And inevitably—and very conveniently—also up to the exact spot where the cattle-fence field had begun to be projected. There would be an arrow-shaped narrowing of the wiped-out ground-cover plants where the cattle-field had been projected. It would narrow to a point which pointed precisely to the cattle-fence projector.

"Your friends," said Calhoun, "will probably give themselves up and ask for mercy. There's not much else they can do."

Then he said:

"They might even get it. D'you know, there's an interesting side effect of the cattle-fence. It kills the plants that have kept Earth-type grasses from growing here. Wheat can be grown here now, whenever and as much as the people please. It should make this a pretty prosperous planet, not having to import all its bread."

The ground-cars of the inhabitants of Maya City did begin to arrive at sunrise. Within an hour after daybreak, very savagely intent persons found the projector of ground-induction and hence cattle-fence fields. They turned it off. It was a very bulky piece of equipment, and it had been set up underground. It should have been difficult to find. But it wasn't.

By noon there was still some anger on the faces of the people of Maya, but there'd been little or no damage, and life took up its normal course again. Murgatroyd appreciated the fact that things went back to normal. For him it was normal to be welcomed and petted when the Med Ship *Aesclipus Twenty* touched ground. It was normal for him to move zestfully in admiring human society, and to drink coffee with great gusto, and to be stuffed with cakes and sweets to the full capacity of his expandable belly.

And while Murgatroyd moved in human society, enjoying himself hugely, Calhoun went about his business. Which, of course, was conferences with planetary health officials, politely receiving such information as they thought important, and tactfully telling them about the most recent developments in medical science as known to the Interstellar Medical Service.

PLAGUE ON KRYDER II

After Calhoun and Murgatroyd the *tormal* were established on board, the Med Ship *Aesclipus Twenty* allowed itself to be lifted off from Med Service Headquarters and thrust swiftly out to space. The headquarters landing grid did the lifting. Some five planetary diameters out, the grid's force fields let go and Calhoun busied himself with aiming the ship for his destination, which was a very long way off. Presently he pushed a button. The result was exactly the one to be expected. The Med Ship did something equivalent to making a hole, crawling into it, and then pulling the hole in after itself. In fact, it went into overdrive.

There were the usual sensations of dizziness, nausea, and a contracting spiral fall. Then there was no cosmos, there was no galaxy, and there were no stars. The *Aesclipus Twenty* had formed a cocoon of highly stressed space about itself which was practically a private sub-cosmos. As long as it existed the Med Ship was completely independent of all creation outside. However, the cocoon was active. It went hurtling through emptiness at many times the speed of light. The *Aesclipus Twenty* rode inside it. When the overdrive field—the cocoon—collapsed and the ship returned to normal space, it would find itself very far from its starting point. For every hour spent in overdrive, the ship should break out somewhat more than a light-year of distance farther away from Med Service Headquarters.

The background tape began to make its unobtrusive sounds. In overdrive, of course, the Med Ship was wholly isolated from the normal universe of galaxies and stars. There was, in theory, only one conceivable way in which it could be affected by anything outside its own overdrive field, and that had never happened yet. So there could have been a sepulchral, nerve-racking silence in the small spacecraft but for such sounds as the background tape provided.

Those were trivial, those sounds. One had to pay close attention to hear them. There was the sound of rain, and of traffic, and of wind in treetops and voices too faint for the words to be distinguished, and almost inaudible music—and sometimes laughter. The background tape carried no information; only the assurance that there were still worlds with clouds and people and creatures moving about on them.

But sensory assurance of the existence of a real cosmos is as essential to a man's subjective health as hormones and enzymes to his body. Calhoun would have suffered from the lack of such noises if they'd stopped, but he paid no attention to them when they began.

On this occasion the Med Ship stayed in overdrive for three long weeks, while the overdrive field hurtled toward the planet Kryder II. Calhoun was supposed to make a special public health visit there. Some cases of what the planetary government called a plague had turned up. The government was in a panic because plagues of similar type had appeared on two other worlds previously and done great damage. In both other cases a Med Ship man had arrived in time to check and stop the pestilence. In both cases the plague was not a new one, but a pestilence of familiar diseases. In both forerunners of this third plague, the arriving Med Ship's *tormal* had succumbed to the infection. So the government of Kryder II had called for help, and Calhoun and Murgatroyd answered the call. They were on the way to take charge.

Calhoun was singularly suspicious of this assignment. The report on the contagion was tricky. Typically, a patient was admitted to hospital with a case of—say— typhoid fever. It was a sporadic case, untraceable to any previous clinical one. The proper antibiotic was administered. With suitable promptness, the patient ceased to have typhoid fever. But he was weakened, and immediately developed another infectious disease. It might be meningitis. That yielded to treatment, but something else followed, perhaps a virus infection. The series went on until he died. Sometimes a patient survived a dozen such contagions, to die of a thirteenth. Sometimes he remained alive, emaciated and weak. No amount of care could prevent a succession of totally unrelated illnesses. Exposure or non-exposure seemed to make no difference. And the cause of this plague of plagues was undetectable.

It shouldn't be impossible to work out such a problem, of course. Both previous plagues had been checked. Calhoun read and reread the reports on them and wasn't satisfied. The Med Ship man who'd handled both plagues was reported dead, not of sickness, but because his ship had blown itself to bits on the Castor IV spaceport. Such things didn't happen. *Tormals* had died in each pestilence, and *tormals* did not die of infectious diseases.

Murgatroyd was the *tormal* member of the *Aesclipus Twenty*'s crew. During three weeks of overdrive travel he was his normal self. He was a furry, companionable small animal who adored Calhoun, coffee, and pretending to be human, in that order. Calhoun traveled among the stars on professional errands, and Murgatroyd was perfectly happy to be with him. His tribe had been discovered on one of the Deneb planets; their charming personalities made them prized as pets. A long while ago it had been noticed that they were never sick. Then it developed that if they were exposed to any specific disease, they instantly manufactured overwhelming quantities of antibody for that infection.

It was the remarkable talent of *tormals*—all *tormals*—that they could not be infected by any microorganism. They could not ordinarily contract any ailment at all. Their digestive systems rejected any substance that would impair their health, and they had a dynamic reaction to infective material. When their normal defenses were bypassed and pathogenic material was put into their bloodstream, they produced antibodies, their structure could be determined and they could be synthesized in any desire quantity. So whatever infection a new planet might offer, it could be brought under control.

Now it was standard Med Service procedure to call on them for this special gift. When a new strain or a novel variety of disease-producing germ appeared, a *tormal* was exposed to it. They immediately made a suitable antibody, the Med Service isolated it, analyzed its molecular structure, and synthesized it. So far there hadn't been a single failure. So *tormals* were highly valued members of Med Ship crews.

Now two of them had died in epidemics of the kind now reported from Kryder II. Calhoun was suspicious

and somehow resentful of the fact. The official reports
didn't explain it. They dodged it. Calhoun fumbled
irritably with it. One report was from the Med Service man now dead. He should have explained! The
other was from doctors on Castor II after the Med
Ship blew up. Nothing explained the explosion of the
ship and nothing explained how *tormals* could die of
an infection.

Perhaps Calhoun disliked the idea that Murgatroyd
could be called on to give his life for Med Service.
Murgatroyd worshiped him. Murgatroyd was a *tormal*,
but he was also a friend.

So Calhoun studied the reports and tried to make
sense of them while the *Aesclipus Twenty* traveled at
a very high multiple of the speed of light. Its cocoon
made it utterly safe. It required no attention. There
was a control-central unit below decks which compe-
tently ran it, which monitored all instruments and kept
track of their functioning. It labored conscientiously
for three full weeks and a few hours over. Then it notified Calhoun that breakout from overdrive was just one
hour away.

He doggedly continued his studies. He still had the
reports of the earlier plagues on his desk when the
control-central speaker said briskly, *"When the gong
sounds, breakout will be five seconds off."*

There followed a solemn tick, tock, tick, tock like
a slow swaying metronome. Calhoun tucked the reports
under a paperweight and went to the pilot's chair. He
strapped himself in. Murgatroyd recognized the action.
He went padding under another chair and prepared
to hold fast to its rungs with all four paws and prehensile tail. The gong sounded. The voice said, *"Five—
four—three—two—one."*

The ship came out of overdrive. There was a sensation of intense dizziness, a desire to upchuck which

vanished before one could act on it. Calhoun held onto his chair during that unhappy final sensation of falling in a narrowing spiral. Then the Med Ship was back in normal space. Its vision screens swirled.

They should have cleared to picture ten thousand myriads of suns of every imaginable tint and degree of brilliance, from faint phosphorescence to glaring stars of first magnitude or greater. There should have been no familiar constellations, of course. The Milky Way should be recognizable though subtly changed. The Horse's Head and Coalsack dark nebulas should have been visible with their outlines modified by the new angle from which they were seen. There should have been a Sol-type sun relatively near, probably with a perceptible disk. It ought to be the sun Kryder, from whose second planet had come a frightened demand for help. The *Aesclipus Twenty* ought to be near enough to pick out Kryder's planets with an electron telescope. Normally well conducted journeys in overdrive ended like that. Calhoun had made hundreds of such sun-falls. Murgatroyd had seen almost as many.

But there was never a breakout like this!

The Med Ship was back in normal space. Certainly. It was light-centuries from its staring point. Positively. Somehow, there were no stars. There was no Milky Way. There were no nebulas, dark or otherwise. There was absolutely nothing of any kind to match up with reasonable expectations, considering what had led up to this moment.

The screens showed the Med Ship surrounded by buildings on a planet's surface, with a blue and sunlit sky overhead. The screens, in fact, showed the buildings of the Interstellar Medical Service as surrounding the Med Ship. They said that Calhoun had traveled three weeks in overdrive and landed exactly back at the spot from which he'd been lifted to begin his journey.

Murgatroyd, also, saw the buildings on the vision screens. It is not likely that he recognized them, but when the *Aesclipus Twenty* landed, it was the custom for Calhoun to go about his business and for Murgatroyd to be admired, petted, and stuffed to repletion with sweets and coffee by the local population. He approved of the practice.

Therefore when he saw buildings on the vision screens he said, *"Chee!"* in a tone of vast satisfaction. He waited for Calhoun to take him aground and introduce him to people who would spoil him.

Calhoun sat perfectly still, staring. He gazed unbelievingly at the screens. They said, uncompromisingly, that the Med Ship was aground inside the Med Service Headquarters landing grid. The buildings were outside it. The screens showed the sky, with clouds. They showed trees. They showed everything that should be visible to a ship aground where ships receive their final checkover before being lifted out to space.

Murgatroyd said, *"Chee-chee!"* with a pleased urgency in his tone. He was impatient for the social success that came to him on every land-on planet. Calhoun turned his eyes to the outside pressure dial. It said there was seven hundred thirty millimeters of gas-pressure—air-pressure—outside. This was complete agreement with the screens.

"The devil!" said Calhoun.

The logical thing to do, of course, would be to go to the air-lock, enter it, and then open the outer door to demand hotly what the hell was going on. Calhoun stirred in the pilot's chair to do exactly that. Then he clamped his jaws tightly.

He checked the nearest-object meter. Its reading was what it should be if the Med Ship were aground at headquarters. He checked the hull temperature. Its reading was just what it should be if the ship had been aground for a long time. He checked the screens again. He checked the magnetometer, which gave rather unlikely indications in overdrive, but in normal empty space recorded only the Med Ship's own magnetic field. It now registered a plausible Gauss-strength for a planet like the one on which headquarters was built.

He swore. Absurdly enough, he flipped the switch for the electron telescope. It filled a screen with dazzle, as if there were too much light. He could not use it.

Murgatroyd said impatiently, *"Chee! Chee! Chee!"*

Calhoun snapped at him. This was completely impossible: It simply could not be! A little while ago, he'd known the sensations of breakout from overdrive. He'd been dizzy, he'd been nauseated, he'd felt the usual horrible sensation of falling in a tightening spiral. That experience was real. There could be no doubt about it.

Instruments could be gimmicked to give false reports. In the course of a Med Ship man's training, he went through training voyages in ships which never left ground, but whose instruments meticulously reacted as they would in a real voyage. In such training exercises, vision screens showed blackness when the mock-up ship was theoretically in overdrive, and star-systems when it theoretically came out. A student Med Ship man went through illusory "voyages" that included even contact with theoretic planets; everything that could happen in a spaceship, including emergencies, was included in such mock-up trips. No training unit could simulate the sensation of going into overdrive or coming out of it, and he'd felt them. This was no mock-up trip.

Growling a little, Calhoun threw the communicator-switch. The speaker gave out the confused murmur of ground level signals, like those a space-type communicator picks up in atmosphere. Through it, vaguely, he could hear the whispering, faintly crackling Jansky radiation which can be received absolutely anywhere. He stared again at the vision screens. Their images were infinitely convincing. Overwhelming evidence insisted that he should go to the air-lock and out of it and hunt up somebody to explain this absurdity. It was inconceivable that a ship should travel for three weeks vastly faster than light and then find itself peacefully aground in its home port. It couldn't happen!

Murgatroyd said impatiently, *"Chee!"*

Calhoun slowly unbuckled the seat-belt intended to help him meet any possible emergency at breakout, but a seat-belt wouldn't help him decide what was reality. He got cagily to his feet. He moved toward the airlock's inner door. Murgatroyd padded zestfully with him. Calhoun didn't go into the lock. He checked the dials, and from inside the ship he opened the outside lock door. From inside the ship he closed it again. Then he opened the inner lock door.

He heard a hissing that rose to a shout, and stopped.

He swore violently. Every instrument said the ship was aground, in atmosphere, at Interstellar Medical Service Headquarters, but he opened the outer lock door. If there was air there, nothing would happen. If there was no air outside, the air in the lock would escape and leave a vacuum behind it. He'd closed the outer door and opened the inner one. If there was air inside the lock, nothing could happen, but air had rushed into it with a noise like a shout.

So there'd been a vacuum inside the air-lock; so there was emptiness outside. So the *Aesclipus Twenty* was not back at home. It was not aground. Hence, the appearance of Med Service Headquarters outside was illusion and the sound of ground-level communication signals was deception.

The Med Ship *Aesclipus Twenty* was lying to the

man it had been built to serve. It had tried to lure him into walking out of an air-lock to empty space. It was trying to kill him.

II

Actually, outside the ship there was nothing even faintly corresponding to the look of things from within. The small vessel of space actually floated in nothingness. Its hull glittered with that total reflection coating which was so nearly a non-radiating surface and was therefore so effective in conserving the heat supply of the ship. There was a glaring yellow star before the ship's nose. There were other white-hot stars off to port and starboard. There were blue and pink and greenish flecks of light elsewhere, and all the universe was specked with uncountable suns of every conceivable shade. Askew against the firmament, the Milky Way seemed to meander across a strictly spherical sky. From outside the Med Ship, its nature was self-evident. Everywhere, suns shone steadily, becoming more and more remote until they were no longer resolvable into stars but were only luminosity. That luminosity was many times brighter where the Milky Way shone. It was the Milky Way.

Minutes went by. The *Aesclipus Twenty* continued

to float in emptiness. Then, after a certain interval, the outside airlock door swung open again and remained that way. Then a radiated signal spread again through the vacancy all about. It had begun before, when the outer door was opened, and cut off when it shut. Now it began to fill a vast spherical space with a message. It traveled, of course, no faster than the speed of light, but in one minute its outermost parts were eleven million miles away. In an hour, they would fill a globe two light-hours in diameter—sixty times as big. In four or five hours, it should be detectable on the planets of that nearby yellow star.

Calhoun regarded the light on the ship's control-board which said that a signal was being transmitted. He hadn't sent it. He hadn't ordered it. The ship had sent it off itself, as of itself, it had tried to lure him out to the vacuum beyond the air-lock.

But the ship was not alive. It could not plan anything. It could not want anything. It had been given orders to lie to him, and the lies should have caused his death. But a man would have had to invent the lies. Calhoun could even estimate exactly how the orders had been given—but not by whom—and where they'd been stored until this instant and how they'd been brought into action. He had no idea why.

The Med Ship was inevitably a highly complex assemblage of devices. It was impractical for one man to monitor all of them, so that task was given to another device to carry out. It was the control-central unit, in substance a specialized computer to which innumerable reports were routed, and from which routine orders issued.

Calhoun did not need, for example, to read off the CO_2 content in the ship's air, the rate of air-renewal, the ionization constant, the barometric pressure and the humidity and temperature to know that the air of the ship was right. The control-central unit issued orders to keep it right, and informed him when it was, and would order a warning if it went wrong. Then he could check the different instruments and find out what was the trouble. However, the control-central made no decisions. It only observed and gave routine orders. The orders that were routine could be changed.

Somebody had changed them; very probably a new and extra control-central unit had been plugged into the ship and the original one cut off. The extra one had orders that when the ship came out of overdrive it was to present pictures of Med Service Headquarters and report other data to match. It could not question these orders. It was only a machine, and it would carry them out blindly and without evaluation.

So now Calhoun ought to be floating in emptiness, his body an unrecognizable object whose outer surface had exploded and whose inner parts were ice. The ship had carried out its orders. Now, undoubtedly, there was something scheduled to happen next. Calhoun hadn't started the signal. It would not be transmitted—it would not have been planned—unless there would be something listening for it, another ship, almost certainly.

Another item. This had been most painstakingly contrived. There must be orders to take effect if the first part did not dispose of Calhoun. The ship had been a deadfall trap, which he'd evaded. It might now be a booby trap, just in case the deadfall failed to work. Yes. A man who orders a machine to commit murder will have given it other orders in case its first attempt fails. If Calhoun went down to verify his suspicion of an extra control-central, that might be the trigger that would blast the whole ship; that in any event would try to kill him again.

Murgatroyd said, *"Chee! Chee!"* The vision screens meant to him that there must be people waiting outside to give him sweet cakes and coffee. He began to be impatient. He added in a fretful tone, *"Chee!"*

"I don't like it either, Murgatroyd," said Calhoun wryly. "Somebody's tried to kill us—at any rate me—and he must think he had some reason, but I can't guess what it is! I can't even guess how anybody could get to a Med Ship at headquarters to gimmick it if they wanted to slaughter innocent people like you and me! Somebody must have done it!"

"Chee! Chee!" said Murgatroyd, urgently.

"You may have a point there," said Calhoun slowly. "We, or at least I, should be dead. We are expected to be dead. There may be arrangements to make certain we don't disappoint somebody. Maybe we'd better play dead and find out. It's probably wiser than trying to find out and getting killed."

A man who has detected one booby trap or deadfall designed for him is likely to suspect more. Calhoun was inclined to go over his ship with a fine-toothed comb and look for them. A setter of booby traps would be likely to anticipate exactly that and prepare for it. Lethally.

Calhoun looked at the pilot's chair. It might not be wise to sit there. Anybody who received the ship's self-sent call would receive with it an image of that chair and whoever sat in it. To play dead, he shouldn't do anything a dead man couldn't do. So he shrugged. He sat down on the floor.

Murgatroyd looked at him in surprise. The signal going-out light burned steadily. That signal now filled a sphere two hundred million miles across. If there was a ship waiting to pick it up—and there'd be no reason for the call otherwise—it might be one or two or ten light-hours away. Nobody could tell within light-hours where a ship would break out of overdrive after three weeks in it.

Calhoun began to rack his brains. He couldn't guess the purpose of his intended murder, but he didn't mean to underestimate the man who intended it.

Murgatroyd went to sleep, curled up against Calhoun's body. There were the random noises a ship tape makes for human need. Absolute silence is unendurable. So there were small sounds released in the ship. Little, meaningless noises. Faint traffic. Faint conversation. Very faint music. Rain, and wind, and thunder as heard from a snug, tight house. It had no significance, so one did not listen to it, but its absence would have been unendurable.

The air apparatus came on and hummed busily, and presently shut off. The separate astrogation unit seemed to cough, somewhere. It was keeping track of the position of the ship, adding all accelerations and their durations—even in overdrive—ending with amazingly exact data on where the ship might be.

Presently Murgatroyd took a deep breath and woke up. He regarded Calhoun with a sort of jocular interest. For Calhoun to sit on the floor was unusual. Murgatroyd realized it.

It was at just this moment, but it was hours after breakout, that the space communicator speaker said metallically, *"Calling ship in distress! Calling ship in distress! What's the trouble?"*

This was not a normal reply to any normal call. A ship answering any call whatever should identify the caller and itself. This wasn't normal. Calhoun did not stir from where he sat on the floor. From there, he wouldn't be visible to whoever saw a picture of the pilot's chair. The call came again.

"Calling ship in distress! Calling ship in distress! What's your trouble? We read your call! What's the trouble?"

Murgatroyd knew that voices from the communicator

should be answered. He said, *"Chee?"* and when Calhoun did not move he spoke more urgently, *"Chee-chee-chee!"*

Calhoun lifted him to his feet and gave him a pat in the direction of the pilot's chair. Murgatroyd looked puzzled. Like all *tormals*, he liked to imitate the actions of men. He was disturbed by breaks in what he'd considered unchangeable routine. Calhoun pushed him. Murgatroyd considered the push a license. He padded to the pilot's chair and swarmed into it. He faced the communicator screen.

"Chee!" he observed. *"Chee! Chee-chee! Chee!"*

He probably considered that he was explaining that for some reason Calhoun was not taking calls today, and that he was substituting for the Med Ship man. However, it wouldn't give that impression at the other end of the communication link-up. It would be some time before his words reached whoever was calling, but Murgatroyd said zestfully, *"Chee-chee!"* and then grandly, *"Chee!"* and then in a confidential tone he added, *"Chee-chee-chee-chee!"*

Anybody who heard him would be bound to consider that he was the *tormal* member of the Med Ship's crew, that her human crew member was somehow missing, and that Murgatroyd was trying to convey that information.

There came no further calls. Murgatroyd turned disappointedly away. Calhoun nodded rather grimly to himself; somewhere there would be a ship homing on the call the Med Ship was sending without orders from him. Undoubtedly somebody in that other ship watched, and had seen Murgatroyd or would see him. It would be making a very brief overdrive hop toward the Med Ship. Then it would check the line again, and another hop. It would verify everything. The care taken in the call just made was proof that somebody was cagey. At the next call, if they saw Murgatroyd again, they would be sure that Calhoun was gone from the Med Ship. Nobody would suspect a furry small animal with long whiskers and a prehensile tail of deception.

Murgatroyd came back to Calhoun, who still sat on the floor lest any normal chair be part of a booby trap to check on the success of the air-lock device.

Time passed. Murgatroyd went back to the communicator and chattered at it. He orated in its direction. He was disappointed that there was no reply.

A long time later the communicator spoke briskly— the automatic volume control did not work, until the first syllable was halfway spoken. It had to be very neat indeed.

"Calling distressed ship! Calling distressed ship! We are close to you. Get a line on this call and give us coordinates."

The voice stopped and Calhoun grimaced. While the distress call—if it was a distress call—went out from the Med Ship there was no need for better guidance. Normally, a ship legitimately answering a call will write its own identification on the spreading waves of its communicator. However, this voice didn't name *Aesclipus Twenty*. It didn't name itself. If these messages were picked up some light-hours away on a planet of the sun Kryder, nobody could realize that a Med Ship was one of the two ships involved, or gain any idea who or what the other ship might be. It was concealment. It was trickiness. It fitted into the pattern of the false images still apparent on the Med Ship's screens and the deceptive data given by its instruments.

The voice from outside the ship boomed once more and then was silent. Murgatroyd went back to the screen. He made oratorical gestures, shrilled, *"Chee-chees,"* and then moved away as if very busy about some other matter.

Again a long, long wait before anything happened. Then there was a loud, distinct clanking against the Med Ship's hull. Calhoun moved quickly. He couldn't have been seen from the communicator before, and he'd wanted to hear anything that came to the Med Ship. Now it would probably be boarded, but he did not want to be seen until he had more information.

He went into the sleeping cabin and closed the door behind him. He stopped at a very small cupboard and put something in his pocket. He entered a tall closet where his uniforms hung stiffly. He closed that door. He waited.

More clankings. At least two spacesuited figures had landed on the Med Ship's hull-plating. They'd still have long, slender space ropes leading back to their own ship. They clanked their way along the hull to the open airlock door. Calhoun heard the changed sound of their magnetic shoe soles as they entered the air-lock. They'd loosen the space ropes now and close the door. They did. He heard the sound of the outer door sealing itself. There was the hissing of air going into the lock.

Then the inner door opened. Two figures came out. They'd be carrying blasters at the ready as they emerged. Then he heard Murgatroyd.

"Chee-chee-chee! Chee!"

He wouldn't know exactly how to act. He normally took his cue from Calhoun. He was a friendly little animal. He had never received anything but friendliness from humans, and of course he couldn't imagine anything else. So he performed the honors of the ship with a grand air. He welcomed the newcomers. He practically made a speech of cordial greeting.

Then he waited hopefully to see if they'd brought him any sweet cakes or coffee. He didn't really expect it, but a *tormal* can always dream.

They hadn't brought gifts for Murgatroyd. They

didn't even respond to his greeting. A *tormal* was standard on a Med Ship. They ignored him. Calhoun heard the clickings as spacesuit faceplates opened.

"Evidently," said a rumbling voice, "he's gone. Very neat. Nothing to clean up. Not even anything unpleasant to remember."

A second voice said curtly, "It'll be unpleasant if I don't cut off the rest of it!"

There was a snapping sound, as if a wire had forcibly been torn free from something. It was probably a cable to the control-board which, in the place of a rarely or never used switch, had connected something not originally intended, but which if the cable were broken could not act. Most likely the snapping of this wire should return the ship to a proper control-central system's guidance and operation. It did.

"Hm," said the first voice, "there's Kryder on the screens, and there's our ship. Everything's set."

"Wait!" commanded the curt voice. "I take no chances, I'm going to cut that thing off down below!"

Someone moved away. He wore a spacesuit. The faint creaking of its constant volume joints were audible. He left the control-room. His magnetic shoes clanked on uncarpeted metal steps leading down. He was evidently headed for the mechanical and electronic section of the ship. Calhoun guessed that he meant to cut completely loose the extra, gimmicked control-central unit that had operated the ship through the stages that should have led to his death. Apparently it could still destroy itself and the Med Ship.

The other man moved about the cabin. Calhoun heard Murgatroyd say, *"Chee-chee!"* in a cordial tone of voice. The man didn't answer. There are people to whom all animals, and even *tormals* are merely animate objects. There was suddenly the rustling of paper.

He'd found the data sheets Calhoun had been study-ing to the very last instant before breakout.

Clankings. The man with the curt voice came back from below.

"I fixed it," he said shortly. "It can't blow now!"

"Look here!" said the rumbling voice, amused. "He had reports about your Med Ship on Castor IV!" He quoted sardonically, "It has to be assumed that a blaster was fired inside the ship. In any event the ship's fuel stores blew and shattered it to atoms. There is no possibility for more than guesses as to the actual cause of the disaster. The Med Ship's doctor was evidently killed, and there was some panic. The destruction of a large sum in currency, which the Med Ship was to have left off at a nearby planet to secure the shipment of uncontaminated foodstuffs to Castor IV, caused some delay in the restoration of normal health and nourishment on the planet. However—" The rumbling voice chuckled. "That's Kelo! Kelo wrote this report!"

The curt voice said, "I'm going to check things."

Calhoun heard the sounds of a thorough checkover, from air apparatus to space communicator. Then the ship was swung about, interplanetary drive went on and off and somebody who knew Med Ships made sure that the *Aesclipus Twenty* responded properly to all con-trols. Then the curt voice said, "All right. You can go now."

One man went to the air-lock and entered it. The lock-pumps boomed and stopped. The outer lock door opened and closed. The man left behind evidently got out of his spacesuit. He carried it below. He left it. He returned as the rumbling voice came out of a speaker, "I'm back on our ship. You can go now."

"Thanks," said the curt voice, sarcastically.

Calhoun knew that the newcomer to the ship had

seated himself at the control-board. He heard
Murgatroyd say, almost incredulously, *"Chee? Chee?"*

"Out of my way!" snapped the curt voice.

Then the little Med Ship swung, and seemed to
teeter very delicately as it was aimed with very great
care close to the nearby yellow star. Before, the
ship's screens had untruthfully insisted that Med
Service Headquarters surrounded the ship. Now they
worked properly. There were stars by myriads of
myriads, and they looked as if they might be very
close. Yet the bright yellow sun would be the nearest, and it was light-hours away. A light-hour is the
distance a ray of light will travel, at a hundred
eighty-odd thousand miles per second, during thirty-
six hundred of them.

There was a sensation of shocking dizziness and
intolerable nausea, swiftly repeated as the Med Ship
made an overdrive hop to carry it only a few light-
hours. Then there was that appalling feeling of contracting spiral fall. Murgatroyd said protestingly,
"Chee!"

Then Calhoun moved quietly out of the closet into
the sleeping cabin, and then out of that. He was more
than halfway to the control-board before the man
seated there turned his head. Then Calhoun leaped
ferociously. He had a pocket blaster in his hand, but
he didn't want to use it if it could be helped.

It was just as effective as a set of brass knuckles
would have been, though. Before the other man
regained consciousness, Calhoun had him very tidily
bound and was looking interestedly over the contents
of his pockets. They were curious. Taken literally, they
seemed to prove that the man now lying unconscious
on the floor was a Med Ship man on professional
assignment, and that he was entitled to exercise all the
authority of the Med Service itself.

On the word of his documents, he was considerably more of a Med Ship man than Calhoun himself.

"Curiouser and curiouser!" observed Calhoun to Murgatroyd. "I'd say that this is one of those tangled webs we weave when first we practice to deceive. But what's going on?"

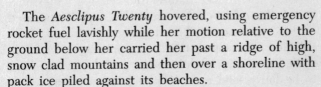

The *Aesclipus Twenty* hovered, using emergency rocket fuel lavishly while her motion relative to the ground below her carried her past a ridge of high, snow clad mountains and then over a shoreline with pack ice piled against its beaches.

This was not the planet from which a call had been sent and which Calhoun was answering. There was no sign of habitation anywhere. Cold blue sea swept past below. There were some small ice cakes here and there, but as the shore was left behind they dwindled in number and the water surface became unbroken save by waves. The mountains sank to the horizon, and then ahead—in the direction of the Med Ship's motion—an island appeared. It was small and rocky and almost entirely snow-covered. There was no vegetation. It was entirely what Calhoun had expected from his examination by electron telescope from space.

This was approximately the equator of the planet Kryder III, which was one planetary orbit farther out than the world which was Calhoun's proper destination.

This was an almost frozen planet. It would be of very little use to the inhabitants of Kryder II. There might be mineral deposits worth the working, but for colonization it would be useless.

Calhoun very painstakingly brought the little spaceship down on the nearest possible approach to bare flat stone. Ragged, precipitous peaks rose up on either hand as the ship descended. Miniature glaciers and waterfalls of ice appeared. Once there was a sudden tumult and a swarm of furry—not feathered—creatures poured out of some crevice and swarmed skyward, doubtless making a great outcry because of having been disturbed.

Then the rocket flames touched ice and stone. Steam floated in clouds about the ship. It appeared on the vision screens as an opaque whiteness. Then the Med Ship tapped stone, and tapped again, and then settled only very slightly askew on what would have to be fairly solid rock. Writhing steam tendrils blotted out parts of all the outside world for long minutes afterward. At last, though, it cleared.

Murgatroyd looked at the snowscape. He saw a place of cold and ice and desolation. He seemed to reach a conclusion.

"*Chee!*" he said with decision.

He went back to his private cubbyhole. He'd have none of such a landing place. He preferred to touch ground where there were people to stuff him with assorted edibles.

Calhoun waited alertly until it was certain that the ship's landing-fins had complete solidity under them. Then he pushed himself away from the control-board and nodded to his prisoner.

"Here we are," he observed. "This is Kryder III. You didn't intend to land here. Neither did I. We both expected to touch ground on Kryder II, which is inhabited. This world isn't. According to the Directory, the average daytime temperature here is two degrees Centigrade. We've landed on an island which is forty miles away from a continental landmass. Since you aren't inclined to be cooperative, I'm going to leave you here, with such food as I can spare and reasonable equipment for survival. If I can, I'll come back here for you. If I can't, I won't. I suggest that while I get things ready for you to go aground, that you think over your situation. If you give me information that will make it more likely I can come back, it'll be all to the good for you. Anything you hold out will lessen my chances and therefore yours. I'm not going to argue about it. I'm not threatening you. I'm simply stating the facts. Think it over."

He left the control-room to go down into the storage compartments of the ship. It was in no sense a cargo-carrier, but it had to be prepared for highly varied situations its occupant might have to meet. Calhoun began to gather divers items. To gather them he had to put carefully away two objects he'd sealed quite airtight in plastic bags. One was a duplicate of the control-central device that had tried to get him out the air-lock. It was sealed up so no trace of odor could escape, or slowly evaporating oil—such as make fingerprints—or any of those infinitesimal traces of one's identity every man leaves on anything he handles. The other was the spacesuit the prisoner had worn when he boarded the Med Ship. It was similarly sealed in. The technicians back at Headquarters could make an absolute, recorded analysis of such identifying items, and could prove who'd handled the one device or worn the other.

He came back to the control-room. He carried bundles. He adjusted the lock so both inner and outer doors could be open at the same time. A cold and daunting wind came in as the doors spread wide.

Calhoun went down to ground. His breath was like white smoke when he returned.

"Tent and sleeping bag," he commented. "It's chilly!"

He went down to the storage compartments again. He came up with another burden.

"Food and a heater, of sorts," he said.

He went out. He came back. He went below again. He was definitely generous in the food supply he piled about the first two loads of equipment. When he'd finished, he checked on his fingers. Then he shook his head and went below for cold-climate garments. He brought them up and put them with the rest.

"Anything you want to say?" he asked pleasantly when he returned. "Anything to help me survive and get back here to pick you up again?"

The bound man ground his teeth.

"You won't get away with turning up in my place!"

Calhoun raised his eyebrows.

"How bad's the plague?"

"Go to the devil!" snapped the bound man.

"You were going to land as a Med Ship man," observed Calhoun. "Judging by two previous operations like this, you were going to check the plague. You did that on Castor IV."

The bound man cursed him.

"I suspect," said Calhoun, "that since you blamed the first plague on contaminated grain, and it did stop when all the grain on the planet was burned and fresh supplies brought in from elsewhere, *and* since the same thing happened with the blame on meats on Castor IV, my guess is also contaminated food on Kryder II. Criminals rarely change their method of operation as long as it works well. But there are two things wrong with this one. One is that no bacterium or virus was ever identified as the cause of the plagues. The other is that two *tormals* died. *Tormals* don't die of plagues.

They can't catch them. It's impossible. I'm confident that I can keep Murgatroyd from dying of the plague on Kryder II."

The bound man did not speak, this time.

"And," said Calhoun thoughtfully, "there's the very curious coincident that somebody stole the money to buy uncontaminated grain, in the first plague, and the money to buy meat for Castor IV was destroyed when your Med Ship blew up in the spaceport. It was your Med Ship, wasn't it? And you were reported killed. Something had gone around—had, I said—which was about as lethal as the toxin made by *clostridium botulinum*. Only it wasn't a germ caused toxin, because there wasn't any germ, or virus either. Are you sure you don't want to talk?"

The man on the floor spat at him. Then he cursed horribly. Calhoun shrugged. He picked up his prisoner and carried him to the lock door. He took him out. He laid him on the pile of stores and survival equipment. He carefully unknotted some of the cords that bound his prisoner's hands.

"You can get loose in five minutes or so," he observed. "By the sunset line when we came in, night is due to fall before long. I'll give you until dark to improve your chances of living by improving mine, then . . ."

He went back to the Med Ship. He entered it and closed the lock doors. Murgatroyd looked inquisitively at him. He'd watched out the lock while Calhoun was aground. If he'd moved out of sight, the little *tormal* would have tried to follow him. Now he said reproachfully, *"Chee! Chee!"*

"You're probably right," said Calhoun dourly. "I couldn't get anywhere by arguing with him, and I wasn't more successful with threats. I don't think he'll talk even now. He doesn't believe I'll leave him here. But I'll have to!"

Murgatroyd said, *"Chee!"*

Calhoun did not answer. He looked at the vision screen. It was close to sunset outside. His captive writhed on top of the mass of cloth and stores. Calhoun grunted impatiently, "He's not too good at loosening knots! The sun's setting and he needs light to get the tent up and the heater going. He'd better hurry!"

He paced up and down the control-room. There were small, unobtrusive sounds within the Med Ship. They were little, meaningless noises. Remote traffic sounds. Snatches of talk, which were only murmurings. Almost infinitely faint tinklings of music not loud enough to identify. In the utter soundlessness of empty space, a ship would be maddeningly silent except for such wisps of things to hear. They kept him from feeling maddeningly alone. They kept him reminded that there were worlds on which people moved and lived. They were links to the rest of humanity and they prevented the psychosis of solitude—with, of course, the help of a companionable small animal who adored being noticed by a man.

He went back to the screens. The sun was actually setting, now, and the twilight would be brief, because despite the ice and snow about, this was the equator of this particular world. The prisoner outside still struggled to free himself. He had moved, in his writhing, until he was almost off the pile of dark stuff on the snow. Calhoun scowled. He needed information. This man, who'd shared in a trick designed to kill him, could give it to him. He'd tried to persuade the man to talk. He'd tried to trap him into it. He'd tried everything but physical torture to get a clear picture of what was going on, on Kryder II. A plague which had no bacterium or virus as its cause was unreasonable. The scheduling of a fake Med Ship man's arrival—at the cost of a very neat trick to secure the death of the real one—and the coordination of a human scheme with the progress of a pestilence, this was not reasonable either. Though Calhoun had irritated his prisoner into fury after persuasion failed, the man had given no information. He'd cursed Calhoun. He'd raged foully. But he'd given no plausible information at all.

It became dark outside. Calhoun adjusted the screens to a higher light-gain. There was only starlight and even with the screens turned up he could see only convulsive struggling movements of a dark figure upon a dark patch of equipment.

He swore.

"The clumsy idiot!" he snapped. "He ought to be able to get loose! Maybe he'll think I meant just to scare him . . ."

He took a hand lamp and opened the air-lock doors again. He cast the light ahead and down. His captive now lay face-down, struggling.

Growling, Calhoun descended to the snow, leaving the air-lock doors open. He went over to his prisoner. Innumerable stars glittered in the sky, but he was accustomed to the sight of space itself. He was unimpressed by the firmament. He bent over the squirming, panting figure of the man he'd apparently not helped enough toward freedom.

But at the last instant the hand lamp showed the former prisoner free and leaping from a crouched position with his hands plunging fiercely for Calhoun's throat. Then the two bodies came together with an audible impact. Calhoun found himself raging at his own stupidity in being fooled like this. The man now grappling him had been full party to one attempt to kill him by a trick. Now he tried less cleverly but more desperately to kill him with his bare hands.

He fought like a madman, which at that moment

he very possibly was. Calhoun had been trained in
unarmed combat, but so had his antagonist. Once
Calhoun tripped, and the two of them rolled in pow-
dery snow with uneven ice beneath it. In that wrenching struggle, Calhoun's foot hit against something solid.
It was a landing-fin of the *Aesclipus Twenty*. He kicked
violently against it, propelling himself and his antagonist
away. The jerk should have given Calhoun a momentary
advantage. It didn't. It threw the two of them suddenly
away from the ship, but onto a place where the stone
under the snow slanted down. They rolled. They slid,
and they went together over a stony ledge and fell,
still battling, down into a crevasse.

Murgatroyd peered anxiously from the air-lock door.
There was no light save what poured out from behind
him. He fairly danced in agitation, a small, spidery,
furry creature silhouetted in the air-lock door. He was
scared and solicitous. He was panicky. He made shrill
cries for Calhoun to come back. *"Chee!"* he cried
desperately. *"Chee-chee! Chee-chee-chee-chee! . . ."*

He listened. There was the keening sound of wind.
There was a vast, vast emptiness all around. This was
a world of ice and dreariness, its continents were white
and silent, and its beaches were lined with pack ice,
there was nothing to be heard anywhere except cold
and senseless sounds of desolation. Murgatroyd wailed
heartbrokenly.

But after a long, long time there were scratching
sounds. Still later, pantings. Then Calhoun's head came
up, snow-covered, over the edge of the crevasse into
which he'd tumbled. He rested, panting. Then, desperately, he managed to crawl to where snow was
waist-deep but the ground proven solid by his previous footprints. He staggered upright. He stumbled
to the ship. Very, very wearily, he climbed to the lock
door. Murgatroyd embraced his legs, making a clamor

of reproachful rejoicing that after going away he had come back.

"Quit it, Murgatroyd," said Calhoun wearily. "I'm back, and I'm all right. He's not. He was underneath when we landed, thirty feet down. I heard his skull crack when we hit. He's dead. If he hadn't been, how I'd have gotten him up again I don't know, but he was dead. No question."

Murgatroyd said agitatedly, *"Chee! Chee-chee!"*

Calhoun closed the lock doors. There was a nasty rock scrape across his forehead. He looked like a man of snow. Then he said heavily, "He could have told me what I need to know! He could have told me how they make the plagues work! He could have helped me finish the whole business in a hurry, when there are men dying of it. But he didn't believe I'd actually do anything to him. Stupid! It's insane!"

He began to brush snow off of himself, with an expression of such sickish bitterness on his face as was normal for a Med Ship man—whose business it is to keep people from dying—when he realized that he had killed a man.

Murgatroyd went padding across the control-room. He swarmed up to where Calhoun kept the crockery. He jumped down to the floor again. He pressed his private, tiny coffee cup upon Calhoun.

"Chee!" said Murgatroyd agitatedly. *"Chee-chee! Chee!"*

He seemed to feel that if Calhoun made coffee, that all matters would be returned to normal and distressing memories could be cast aside. Calhoun grimaced.

"If I died you'd have no coffee, eh? All right, as soon as we're on course for Kryder II I'll make you some. But I think I've blundered. I tried to act like a detective instead of a medical man because it should have been quicker. I'll make some coffee in a little while."

He seated himself in the pilot's chair, glanced over the instrument readings, and presently pressed a button.

The *Aesclipus Twenty* lifted from her landing place, her rockets lighting the icy stone spires of the island with an unearthly blue-white flame. The speed of her rising increased. A little later, there was only a dwindling streak of rocket fire ascending to the stars.

IV

The crescent which was the planet Kryder II enlarged gradually, with the sun many millions of miles beyond it. The *Aesclipus Twenty* swung in its course, pointing at a right angle to the line along which it had been moving. Its drive-baffles glowed faintly as the Lawlor interplanetary drive gave it a new impetus, changing its line of motion by adding velocity in a new direction to the sum of all the other velocities it had acquired. Then the ship swung back, not quite to its former bearing but along the line of its new course.

Inside the ship, Calhoun again aimed the ship. He used the sighting circle at the very center of the dead-ahead vision screen. He centered a moderately bright star in that glowing circle. The star was a certain number of seconds of arc from the planet's sunlit edge. Calhoun watched. All about, in every direction, multitudes of shining specks—actually suns—floated in space. Many or most of them warmed their families of planets with the solicitude of brooding hens. Some circled each other in stately, solemn sarabands. There were some, the Cepheids, which seemed to do neither but merely to lie in emptiness, thin and gaseous, pulsating slowly as if breathing.

Calhoun relaxed, satisfied. The guide star remained at exactly the same distance from the crescent planet, while the Med Ship hurtled toward it. This arrangement was a standard astrogational process. If the moving planet and the sighting star remained relatively motionless, the total motion of the Med Ship was exactly adjusted for approach. Of course, when close enough the relationship would change, but if the ship's original line was accurate, the process remained a sound rule-of-thumb method for approaching a planet.

The Med Ship sped on. Calhoun, watching, said over his shoulder to Murgatroyd, "We're pretty much in the dark about what's going on, Murgatroyd, not in the matter of the plague, of course. That's set up to be ended by somebody arriving in a Med Ship, as in two cases before this one. But if they can end it, they needn't have started it. I don't like the idea of anything like this being unpunished."

Murgatroyd scratched reflectively. He could see the vision screens. He could have recognized buildings as such, though probably not as individual ones. On the screens, save for the sun and one crescent planet, there were only dots of brightness of innumerable colorings. To Murgatroyd, who spent so much of his life in space travel, the stars had no meaning whatever.

"Technically," observed Calhoun, "since medicine has become a science, people no longer believe in plague-spreaders. Which makes spreading plagues a possible profession." *

---

* In June of 1630 (standard) one Guglielmo Piazza, who was commissioner of health of the city of Milan, was seen to wipe ink off his fingers against a building wall. He was

Murgatroyd began to clean his whiskers, elaborately licking first the right-hand and then the left-hand ones.

Calhoun again checked the relative position of the sighting star and Kryder II. He brought up a file on the computer. It was a resume of the history of toxicology. He hunted busily for items having to do with the simulation of bacterial toxins by inorganic compounds. He made notes, not many. He consulted another file. It dealt with antigens and antibodies. He made more notes and consulted a third file.

He worked carefully with pencil and paper and then, with his memos at hand, Calhoun set the computer to find the known compounds with such-and-such properties, a boiling point above so-and-so, with an inhibitive effect upon the formation of certain other compounds.

He went back to the pilot's chair. The crescent world was noticeably nearer and larger. Calhoun became absorbed in the delicate task of putting the Med Ship in suitable orbit around Kryder II. The ship obeyed him. It swung around to the green world's sunlit hemisphere. He addressed the communicator microphone:

"*Med Ship* Aesclipus Twenty *calling ground to report arrival and ask coordinates for landing. Our mass is*

---

immediately accused of wiping the walls with matter to produce bubonic plague. Put to the torture, he finally confessed; when pressed for confederates he despairingly named a barber named Mora. The barber, under torture, named a Don Juan de Padilla as another confederate in the dissemination of bubonic plague. They were not asked to name others, but were executed in the utterly barbarous methods of the period and a "column of infamy" erected to warn others against this crime. This is but one example. See "*Devils, Drugs and Doctors*," Haggard, Harper and Bro., N.Y., 1929.

fifty standard tons. Repeat, five-oh tons. Purpose of landing . . . response to planetary health department request for service."

Calhoun watched as more of the surface of the nearing planet came into view with the Med Ship's swing around it. There were bright green continents, showing irregular streaks of white glaciation where mountain ranges rose. There were seas and oceans and cloud masses and that filmy blue haze at the horizon which so much surprised the first explorers of space.

"Med Ship Aesclipus—" Calhoun's recorded voice repeated the call. Murgatroyd popped his head out of his personal cubbyhole. When Calhoun talked, but not to him, it meant that presently there would be other people around. And people did not long remain strangers to Murgatroyd. He made friends with ease and zest. Except for Calhoun, Murgatroyd defined friends as people who gave him sweet cakes and coffee.

The communicator speaker said, *"Calling Med Ship! Ground calling Med Ship! Coordinates are . . ."* the voice named them. It sounded warm and even rejoicing through the speaker, as if the landing-grid operator had a personal interest in the arrival of a man sent by the Interstellar Medical Service. *"We're plenty glad you've come, sir! Plenty glad! Did you get the coordinates? They're . . ."*

"Chee!" said Murgatroyd zestfully.

He clambered down to the control-room floor and looked at the screen. When Calhoun spoke again to the grid operator, Murgatroyd strutted. He would land, and he would be the center of attention everywhere so long as the Med Ship was aground. He practically crooned his delight.

"Yes, sir!" said the voice from the ground. *"Things were looking pretty bad! There's a Doctor Kelo here, sir. He was on Castor IV when they had a plague there.*

He says the Med Service man that came there got it licked right off. Excuse me, sir. I'm going to report you're coming in."

The voice stopped. Calhoun glanced at the coordinates he'd written down and made adjustment for the Med Ship's needed change of course. It was never necessary to be too precise in making a rendezvous with a landing grid. A ship had to be several planetary diameters out from ground to have even its interplanetary drive work. But a grid's force fields at so many thousands of miles distance were at first widely spread and tenuous. They reported to ground when they first touched the incoming ship. Then they gathered together and focused on the spacecraft, and then they tightened and grew strong. After that they pulled the ship down gently out of emptiness to the center of that half-mile-high circle of steel girders and copper cable which was the landing grid. It took time to pull a ship down some thousands of miles. Too violent a pull could be disastrous to the crew, but ordinarily it was marvelously effective and totally safe.

The communicator screen swirled suddenly and then presented a very clear picture of the grid-control office. It showed the operator. He gazed admiringly at Calhoun.

"I've reported, sir," he said warmly, *"and Doctor Kelo's coming right now! He was at the big hospital, where they've been working on what the plague can be. He's coming by copter . . . won't be long."*

Calhoun reflected. According to his data, Doctor Kelo had been a prominent physician on Castor IV when the Med Ship man there had presumably been killed in the detonation of the ship. Doctor Kelo had made a report on that matter. The two men who'd come to take over the Med Ship at its breakout point, not an untold number of hours ago, had read his report with seeming amusement. They'd noted Doctor Kelo's name. It was at least interesting that this same Doctor Kelo was here, where there also was a plague. However, the Med Ship man he expected wasn't Calhoun. Calhoun was supposed to be floating somewhere in emptiness, light-hours away from here.

The grid operator watched his dials. He said, pleased, *"Got it, sir! Fifty tons, you said. I'll lock on."*

Calhoun felt the curious fumbling sensation the grid's force fields produced when they touched and gathered around the ship, and then the cushiony thrustings and pushings when the fields focused and intensified. The *Aesclipus Twenty* began its descent.

"I'll bring you down now, sir," said the operator of the grid, very happily. *"I'll make it as quick as I can, but you're a long way out!"*

Landing was bound to be a lengthy process, much longer than lifting off. One could not snatch a ship from space. It had to be brought down with no more acceleration planetward than a ship's company could endure. Eventually the downward speed had to be checked so the contact with the ground would be a gentle one. A grid could smash a ship to atoms by bringing it down on the spaceport tarmac with a velocity of miles per second. This was why interplanetary wars were impossible. A landing grid could smash any ship in space if it approached a planet with hostile intentions.

"I suppose," said Calhoun, "there's a lot of concern about the—epidemic. The planetary health department asked for me."

"Yes, sir! It's real bad! Started three months ago. There were half a dozen cases of pneumonia. Nobody thought much about it. They were treated, and stopped having pneumonia, but they weren't well. They had something else, not the same thing, either. There was

typhoid and meningitis and so on. This is what the newscasts say. Then other cases turned up. A child would have measles, and it would turn to tetanus, and that to pneumonia, and that to scarlet fever. . . . It couldn't happen, the doctors said, but it was happening! The hospitals filled up. More came in all the time, and none of them could leave. They could keep most of the cases alive, but they had to cure 'em of something else all the time. They had to turn schools and churches into hospitals. One person in ten is sick already. More are taken down every minute. Presently, there won't be doctors enough to diagnose the diseases patients contract continually. They figure that a quarter of the whole population will be down inside of two weeks more, and then they'll start dying faster than they do now, because there won't be enough well people to take care of 'em. They figure there won't be anybody on his feet in a month and a half from now and that'll be the end for everybody."

Calhoun clamped his jaws together.

"They've stopped giving it out," said the grid operator. He added professionally, *"I've got you coming down at four hundred feet a second, but I'm going to pull a lot harder! You're needed down here in a hurry! I'll put on the brakes at a thousand miles, and you'll touch ground like a feather."*

Calhoun ground his teeth. Strictly speaking, he should discuss the plague only with qualified medical men. But the public attitude toward a disease has to be considered in its treatment. This, however, was plainly not a disease. A given bacterium or virus can produce one disease only. Its activity may vary in virulence, but not in kind. Viruses do not change to bacteria. Cocci do not change to spirochetes. Each pathogenic organism that exists remains itself. It may change in viciousness, but never in form. The plague as described could not be a plague! It could not be!

Immediately one ceased to think of it as a natural plague; immediately one considered it artificial, it made sense. It tended to spread toward a total, cent-percent matching of number of cases to the number of people on the planet. Normal pestilences do not. It was planned that a fake Med Ship man should arrive at a certain time and end it. This would be absurd if the plague were a natural one. It was the third of its kind, and the first two had killed *tormals*—which pestilences could not—and in each case large sums of money had disappeared.

"*Doctor Kelo, sir*," said the grid operator, *said he was sure that if a Med Ship man could get here with his—what's that little creature? A tormal? Once a Med Ship man got here with his* tormal, *the plague was as good as licked.*" He stopped and listened. "*Doctor Kelo must be here now. There's a copter landing outside.*"

Then the grid man said with a rather twisted grin, "*I tell you, everybody's glad you're here! I've got a wife and kids. They haven't got the plague yet, but . . .*"

He stood up. He said joyously, "*Doctor Kelo! Here he is! Right here on the screen! We've been talkin'. He's comin' down fast, and I'll have him aground in a hurry!*"

A voice said, "*Ah, yes! I am most pleased. Thank you for notifying me.*"

Then a new figure appeared on the vision screen. It was dignified. It was bearded. It was imposing in the manner of the most calmly confident of medical men. One could not look at Doctor Kelo without feeling confidence in him. He seemed benign. He beamed at the grid man and turned to the vision screen.

He saw Calhoun. Calhoun regarded him grimly. Doctor Kelo stared at him. Calhoun was not the man who'd been put aboard the Med Ship at first breakout point. He wasn't the man who'd handled the Castor IV epidemic, or the one before that. He wasn't the man who was supposed to have been killed when a Med Ship blew up in the Castor IV spaceport. He wasn't . . .

"How do you do?" said Calhoun evenly. "I gather we are to work together—again, Doctor Kelo."

Doctor Kelo's mouth opened, and shut. His face went gray. He made an inarticulate sound. He stared at Calhoun in absolute stupefaction. Murgatroyd squirmed past Calhoun's body to look into the communicator screen. He saw a man, and to Murgatroyd that meant that shortly he would be aground among people who admired him adoringly and would therefore stuff him with all the things he liked to eat and drink.

"*Chee!*" said Murgatroyd cordially. "*Chee-chee!*"

The stark incredulity of the bearded face changed to shock. That expression became purest desperation. One of Doctor Kelo's beautifully manicured hands disappeared. It appeared again. There was a tiny snapping sound and the grid operator became suddenly boneless. He seemed to bend limply in all his joints and almost to pour downward to the floor.

Doctor Kelo turned swiftly to the dials of the landing-grid control-board. He surveyed them, panting suddenly. Of course, a landing grid can do its work in many different fashions. It can use the processes of normal space commerce to make space war impossible. Because it can be deadly.

Doctor Kelo reached out. Calhoun could not see exactly what he did, but he could guess its purpose. Immediately he felt a surging of the Med Ship which told him exactly what had been done. It was an increased downward velocity of the ship, which had to be brought down rapidly for most of its descent, or otherwise the grid would swing around to the night side of this world where, with a planet's bulk between, it could not do anything with the Med Ship at all. However, high acceleration toward the ground could be used to a certain point only. Below a critical distance the ship couldn't be stopped. It would be bound to crash to flaming destruction against the world it had meant to land on.

The ship surged again. It plunged planetward with doubled acceleration. In the grip of the landing grid's force fields, it built up to a velocity far beyond any at which it could be slowed for a safe landing. It was building up toward the speed of shooting stars, which consume themselves when they touch atmosphere. It was still thousands of miles out in emptiness, still speeding crazily to inevitable destruction.

V

Calhoun said coldly, "I've got to learn how a murderer thinks, Murgatroyd. While I'm thinking there's a situation they have to meet, these characters work out a way to kill me, as if that was bound to settle everything. I can't anticipate the ideas they get automatically!"

He placed his hands on the control-board where he could act in an infinitesimal fraction of a second. He waited. The Med Ship was in the grip of an immaterial field of force which was capable of handling a merchant ship of space, whereas the *Aesclipus Twenty* was as small as a ship could be and still perform a Med Ship's functions.

The fact that a field of force is not a solid object has its consequences. A solid object can exert a thrust in three dimensions. If it is rigid, it can resist or impose thrusts in any direction, up or down, right or left, and away from or toward itself. However, a field of force can only act in one: toward or away from, or up or down, or left or right. It cannot push in one direction while resisting a thrust from another. So a grid field could pull a ship downward with terrific force, but it could not pull the ship sidewise at the same moment, and that happened to be what was necessary.

There is a certain principle known as the conservation of angular momentum. A ship approaching a planet has always some velocity relative to the planet's surface. Within a wide range of speeds, that angular velocity will make a ship take up an orbit at a distance appropriate to its speed. The greater the speed, the lower the orbit. It is like a weight on a string, twirled around one's finger. As the string winds up, the weight spins faster. It is like a figure skater spinning in one spot on the ice with arms outstretched, who spins more and more rapidly as he brings his arms closer to his body. The *Aesclipus Twenty* had such orbital, angular momentum. It could not descend vertically without losing its velocity. If it was to land safely, it would have to lose its velocity and at the moment it touched ground it must have exactly the motion of the ground it touched, for exactly the same reason that one stops a ground-car before stepping out of it.

But a grid field could only push or pull in one direction at a time. To land a ship it must cease to pull planetward from time to time, and push the ship sidewise to match its speed to that of the ground. If it didn't, the ship would go on beyond the horizon— or seem to.

So Calhoun waited. Grimly. The ship, plunging vertically, still retained its lateral speed. That speed drove it toward the horizon. It was necessary to pull it back to pull it down. So the bearded man, cursing as the ship swung away from the vertical, fumbled to pull it back.

An extremely skilled operator might well have done so, even against Calhoun's resistance. The shift of

directional pull—or thrust—could have been made so
swiftly that the ship would be actually free of all fields
for less than the hundredth of a second. However, such
fine work required practice.

Calhoun felt the ship shiver for the fraction of an
instant. For that minute portion of a heartbeat, the
downward pull had to be cut off so the sidewise push
could be applied. But in that instant Calhoun jammed
down the emergency rockets' control to maximum possible thrust. He was flung back into the pilot's chair. The
weight of his chest forced air explosively out of his lungs.
Murgatroyd went skittering across the floor. He caught
an anchored chair leg with a wide sweep of his spidery
arms and clung there desperately, gasping.

Three. Four. Five seconds. Calhoun swung the ship's
nose and went on. Seven. Eight. Nine. Ten.

He cut the rocket-blast at the last instant before he
would have blacked out. He panted. Murgatroyd said
indignantly, *"Chee! Chee! Chee!"*

Calhoun said with some difficulty, "Right! I did you
a dirty trick, but it had to be done! Now if we can
keep him from getting his field locked on us—
again . . ."

He sat alertly in the pilot's chair, recovering from
the strain of such violent acceleration for even so brief
a period. A long time later there was a faint, fumbling
sensation as if a force field, groping, touched the ship.
He blasted off at an angle at high acceleration again.

Then the ship was clear. It reached a spot where
the landing grid, on the curved surface of Kryder II,
was below the horizon. The Med Ship had orbital
velocity. Calhoun made certain of it when he looked
at the nearest-object indicator. He was then very close
to atmosphere but the planet now below him curved
downward and away from his line of flight. The ship
was actually rising from the planetary surface. Calhoun

had escaped a collision with Kryder II by speeding up across its face. One can sometimes avoid a collision in traffic by speeding up, but it is not the safest thing for either ground-cars or spaceships to do.

Murgatroyd made querulous noises to himself. Calhoun got out the data on the planet Kryder II. There were continents and highways and mountain ranges and cities. He studied the maps and a view of the actual surface beneath him. The communicator screen was blank, and had been since the horizon rose between the grid and the fleeing ship. He flipped it off. At the sunset line there was a city. He located himself.

Murgatroyd said *"Chee!"* in an apprehensive tone as the emergency rockets roared again.

"No," said Calhoun. "No more full-force rocketeering, Murgatroyd. And I'm not going to take the chance of being outwitted again. I've been fooled twice by not knowing how a murderer's mind works. I'm going to operate out of contact with such characters for a while. I'm going to land and do a burglary and get back out to space again."

He checked on maps. He glanced frequently at the nearest-object dial. He swung the ship and blasted his rockets again, and watched the dial, and used the rockets still again. The Med Ship was slowing. It curved downward. Presently, the needle of the nearest-object dial quivered. The Med Ship, still out of atmosphere, was passing above mountains.

"Now, if we can land beyond, here . . ." said Calhoun.

Murgatroyd was not reassured. He watched. He grew uneasy as Calhoun went through the elaborate, tricky and definitely dangerous operation of landing the Med Ship in the dark, on unknown terrain, and by instruments only except for the last few minutes.

During those last few minutes the screens showed forests below the hovering Med Ship, lighted in unearthly fashion by the rocket flames. With that improbable light he finished the landing. He remained alert until sure that the ship was steady on her landing-fins. He cut off the rockets. He listened to the outside microphones' report. There were only the night sounds of a long colonized planet, where a Terran ecological system had been established and there were birds and insects of totally familiar varieties.

He nodded to himself. He turned on the planetary communications receiver. He listened for a long time. He heard news broadcasts. There was no mention of the Med Ship reported as arriving. There was resolutely hopeful news of the plague. It had broken out in a new area, but there was great hope that it could be contained. The use of combined antibiotics seemed to promise much. The death rate was said to be down slightly. There was no mention of the fact that the real percentage of deaths might be obscured by a large increase of new patients who wouldn't normally die just yet.

Calhoun listened. At last, he stirred. His eyes fell upon the small computer which had searched in the ship's microfiles for data on compounds with boiling points below such-and-such, with absorption coefficients in certain ranges, which had an inhibitive effect upon the formation of certain other substances. It was waiting to give him the information he'd asked for. He read it. He looked pleased.

"Not bad," he told Murgatroyd. "The broadcasts say the plague is prevalent in this area, and this says we want some groceries and ditch water. I've the crudes to make up these prescriptions."

He made ready to go aground. He was armed. He took a compass. He took certain highly odorous pellets. Murgatroyd zestfully made ready to accompany him.

"No," said Calhoun. "Not this time, Murgatroyd! You have many gifts, but burglary isn't one of them. I couldn't even depend on you to be a properly suspicious lookout."

Murgatroyd could not understand. He was bewildered when Calhoun left him in the Med Ship with water and food at hand. When Calhoun closed the inner air-lock door, he could still hear Murgatroyd arguing desperately, *"Chee! Chee-chee!"*

Calhoun dropped an odorous pellet on the ground and moved away on a compass course. He had a hand lamp, which he used sparingly. There were tree trunks to run into and roots to stumble over and much brushwood to be thrust through. Ultimately he came upon a highway. He deposited a pellet. With his hand lamp off, he searched as much of the sky as he could. He concluded that there was a faint glow in the sky to southward. He set out along the highway toward it.

It was not less than four miles away, and then there was a small town, and it seemed lifeless. Street lights burned, but there were no lighted windows anywhere. There was no motion.

He moved cautiously among its streets. Here and there he saw a sign, *"Quarantine."* He nodded. Things had gotten really bad! Normal sanitary measures would prevent the spread of contagion of a normal kind. When infections led to the quarantine of every house where plague appeared, it meant that doctors were getting panicky and old-fashioned. However, the ideas of the causes of pestilences would remain modern. Nobody would suspect an epidemic of being actually a crime.

He found a merchandise center. He found a food

shop. All the night was dark and silent. He listened for a long, long time, and then committed burglary.

With his hand lamp turned down to the faintest of glimmers, he began to accumulate parcels. There was plague in this area and this town. Therefore, he painstakingly picked out parcels of every variety of foodstuff in the food shop's stock. He stuffed his loot into a bag. He carried everything, even salt and sugar and coffee, meat, bread, and vegetables in their transparent coverings. He took a sample—the smallest possible—of everything he could find.

He piously laid an interstellar currency note on the checkout desk. He left. He went back to the highway by which he'd arrived. He trudged four miles to where a pellet designed for something else made a distinctive patch of unpleasant smell. He turned and traveled by compass until he found another evil-smelling spot. Again by compass . . . and he arrived back at the Med Ship. He went in.

Murgatroyd greeted him with inarticulate cries, embracing his legs and protesting vehemently of his sufferings during Calhoun's absence. To keep from stepping on him, Calhoun tripped. The bag of his burglarized acquisitions fell. It broke. Something smashed.

"Stop it!" commanded Calhoun firmly. "I missed you too. But I've got work to do, and I didn't run across any ditch water. I've got to go out again."

He forcibly prevented Murgatroyd from going with him, and he spent an hour fumbling for a swampy spot in the dark forest. In the end he packed up damp and half-rotted woods-mold. He carried that back to the ship. Then he began to collect the grocery packages he'd dropped. A package of coffeebeans had broken.

"Damn!" said Calhoun.

He gathered up the spilled beans. Murgatroyd

assisted. Murgatroyd adored coffee. Calhoun found him popping the beans into his mouth and chewing in high delight.

He went about the essential, mundane labor he'd envisioned. He prepared what a physician of much older times would have called a decoction of rotted leaves. He examined it with a microscope. It was admirable! There were paramecia and rotifers and all sorts of agile microscopic creatures floating, swimming, squirming and darting about in the faintly brownish solution.

"Now," said Calhoun, "we will see if we see anything."

He put the fraction of a drop of a standard and extremely mild antiseptic on the microscope slide. The rotifers and the paramecia and the fauna of the ditch water died. Which, of course, was to be expected. Single-celled animals are killed by concentrations of poison which are harmless to greater animals. Antiseptics are poisons and poisons are antiseptics, but antiseptics are poisons only in massive doses. But to a rotifer or to paramecia all doses are massive.

"Therefore," explained Calhoun to a watching and inquisitive Murgatroyd, "I act more like an alchemist than a sane man. I feel apologetic, Murgatroyd. I am embarrassed to make decoctions and to mix them with synthesized ditch water. But what else can I do? I have to identify the cause of the plague here, without having contact with a single patient because Doctor Kelo . . ."

He shrugged and continued his activities. He was making solutions, decoctions, infusions of every kind of foodstuff the food shop he'd burglarized contained. The plague was not caused by an agent itself in infections. It was caused by something which allowed infections to thrive unhindered in human bodies. So Calhoun made soups of meat, all the kinds of meat, or grain and grain products, and vegetables taken from their transparent coverings. Even such items as sugar, salt, pepper and coffee were included.

Those solutions went upon microscope slides, one by one. With each, in turn, Calhoun mingled the decoction of rotting vegetation which was, apparently, as well-suited for his research as stagnant water from a scummy pond. The animalcules of the decoction appreciated their diverse food supplies. They fed. They throve. Given time, they would have multiplied prodigiously.

Eventually Calhoun came to the solution of coffee. He mixed it with his experimental microscope-animal zoo, and the paramecia died. Rotifers ceased to whirl and dart about upon their sub-miniature affairs. When an infusion of coffee from the food shop was added to the liquid environment of one-celled animals, they died.

Calhoun checked. It was so. He made an infusion of coffee from the Med Ship's stores. It was not so. Coffee from the ship was not fatal to paramecia. Coffee from the shop was. But it would not follow that coffee from the shop would be fatal to humans. The alcoholic content of beer is fatal to paramecia. Wine is a fair antiseptic. No! The food store coffee could very well be far less toxic than the wildest of mouth-washes, and still kill the contents of Calhoun's ditch-water zoo.

However, the point was that something existed which allowed infections to thrive unhindered in human bodies. Something destroyed the body's defenses against infections. Nothing more would be needed to make the appearance of a plague. Every human being carries with him the seeds of infection, from oral bacteria to intestinal flora, and even often streptococci in the hair follicles of the skin. Destroy the body's means of defense and anyone was bound to develop one of the diseases whose sample bacteria he carries about with him.

Instantly one ceased to think of the plague on Kryder II—and Castor IV before it—instantly one ceased to think of the epidemic as an infection miraculously spreading without any germ or bacterium or virus to carry it, instantly one thought of it as a toxin only, a poison only, a compound as monstrously fatal as the toxin of—say—the bacillus *clostridium botulinum*. Immediately everything fell into place. The toxin that could simulate a plague could be distributed on a food-stuff: grain or meat or neatly packaged coffee. It would be distributed in such dilution that it was harmless. It would not be detected by any culture-medium process. In such concentration as humans would receive, it would have one effect, and one effect only. It would hinder the body's formation of antibodies. It would prevent the production of those compounds which destroy infective agents to which human beings are exposed. It would simply make certain that no infection would be fought. Antibodies introduced from outside could cure a disease the body could not resist, but there would always be other diseases. . . . Yet, in a concentration greater than body fluids could contain, it killed the creatures that thrived in ditch water.

Calhoun consulted the slip of paper the computer had printed out for him. He went down to the ship's stores. A Med Ship carries an odd assortment of supplies. Here were the basic compounds from which an unlimited number of other compounds could be synthesized. With the computer-slip for a prescription form, he picked out certain ones. He went back to the ditch-water samples presently. He worked very pains-takingly. Presently, he had a whitish powder. He made a dilute—a very dilute solution of it. He added that solution to ditch water. The paramecia and rotifers and other tiny creatures swam about in bland indifference. He put in a trace of coffee decoction. Presently, he was trying to find out how small a quantity of his new solution, added to the coffee infusion, made it harmless to paramecia.

It was not an antidote to the substance the coffee contained. It did not counter the effects of that monstrously toxic substance, but it combined with that substance. It destroyed it; it was the answer to the plague on Kryder II.

It was broad daylight when he'd finished the horribly tedious detail work the problem had required. In fact, it was close to sundown. He said tiredly to Murgatroyd, "Well, we've got it!"

Murgatroyd did not answer. Calhoun did not notice for a moment or so. Then he jerked his head about.

Murgatroyd lay on the Med Ship floor, his eyes halfclosed. His breath came in quick, shallow pantings.

He'd eaten coffeebeans when they fell on the floor of the control-room. Calhoun picked him up, his lips angrily compressed. Murgatroyd neither resisted nor noticed. Calhoun examined him with a raging, painstaking care.

Murgatroyd was ill. He came of a tribe which was never sick of any infectious disease; they reacted with explosive promptness to any trace of contagion and produced antibodies which would destroy any invading pathogen. His digestive system was normally no less efficient, rejecting any substance which was unwholesome. But the toxic compound which caused the plague on Kryder II was not unwholesome in any direct sense. It did not kill anybody, by itself. It simply inhibited, it prevented, the formation of those antibodies which are a creature's defense against disease.

Murgatroyd had a fully developed case of pneumonia. It had developed faster in him than in a human being. It was horribly more severe. He'd developed it from some single *diplococcus pneumonia* upon his fur, or perhaps on Calhoun's garments, or possibly from the floor or wall of the Med Ship. Such microorganisms are everywhere. Humans and animals are normally immune to any but massive infection. But Murgatroyd was at the very point of death from a disease his tribe normally could not—could not!—contract.

Calhoun made the tests required to make him absolutely certain. Then he took his new solution and prepared to make use of it.

"Fortunately, Murgatroyd," he said grimly, "we've something to try for this situation. Hold still!"

VI

Murgatroyd sipped a cup of coffee with infinite relish. He finished it. He licked the last drop. He offered it to Calhoun and said inquiringly, *"Chee?"*

"It probably won't hurt you to have one more cup," said Calhoun. He added irrelevantly, "I'm very glad you're well, Murgatroyd!"

Murgatroyd said complacently, *"Chee-chee!"*

Then the space communicator said metallically, *"Calling Med Ship! Calling Med Ship! Calling Med Ship Aesclipus Twenty! Ground calling Aesclipus Twenty!"*

The Med Ship was then in orbit around Kryder II. It was a sound, high orbit, comfortably beyond atmosphere. Calhoun was officially waiting for word of how his communication and instruction to the authorities aground had turned out. He said, "Well?"

"I'm the Planetary Health Minister," said a voice. Somehow it sounded infinitely relieved. *"I've just had reports from six of our hospitals. They check with what you told us. The paramecia test works. There were a*

111

number of different foods—ah—contaminated at their packaging points, so that even if someone had identified one food as the cause of the plague in one place, in another area it wouldn't be true. It was clever! It was damnably clever! And of course we've synthesized your reagent and tried it on laboratory animals we were able—by your instructions—to give the plague."

"I hope," said Calhoun politely, "that the results were satisfactory."

The other man's voice broke suddenly.

"One of my children . . . he will probably recover, now. He's weak. He's terribly weak! But he'll almost certainly live, now that we can protect him from reinfection. We've started planet-wide use of your reagent."

"Correction," said Calhoun. "It's not my reagent. It is a perfectly well-known chemical compound. It's not often used, and perhaps this is its first use medically, but it's been known for half a century. You'll find it mentioned . . ."

The voice at the other end of the communication link said fiercely, *"You will excuse me if I say nonsense! I wanted to report that everything you've told us has proved true. We have very many desperately ill, but new patients have already responded to medication to counter the—contamination of food they'd taken. They've gotten thoroughly well of normal disease and haven't developed others. Our doctors are elated. They are convinced. You can't have any idea how relieved . . ."*

Calhoun glanced at Murgatroyd and said dryly, "I've reason to be pleased myself. How about Doctor Kelo and his friends?"

"We'll get him! He can't get off the planet, and we'll find him! There's only one ship aground at the spaceport; it came in two days ago. It's stayed in port under self-quarantine at our request. We've instructed it not

*to take anyone aboard. We're chartering it to go to
other planets and buy foodstuffs to replace the ones
we're testing and destroying."*

Calhoun, stroking Murgatroyd, said more dryly than
before, "I wouldn't. You'd have to send currency to
pay for the stuff you want to import. On two previous occasions very, very large sums gathered for that
purpose have disappeared. I'm no policeman but that
could be the reason for the plague. There are some
people who might start a plague for the express
purpose of being entrusted with some scores of
millions of credits . . ."

There was silence at the other end of the conversation. Then a man's voice, raging, *"If that's it!"*

Calhoun broke in.

"In my orbit I'll be below your horizon in minutes.
I'll call back. My orbit's very close to two hours
duration."

"If that's it," repeated the voice, raging, *"We'll . . ."*

There was silence. Calhoun said very cheerfully,
"Murgatroyd, I'm good at guessing the way a relatively
honest man's mind works. If I'd told them earlier that
the plague victims were murdered, they'd have dis-
counted the rest of what I had to say. But I'm learning the way a criminal's mind works too! It takes a
criminal to think of burning down a house to cover
up the fact that he robbed it. It takes a criminal to
think of killing a man for what he may carry in his
pockets. It would take a criminal to start a plague so
he can gather money to steal, under the pretense that
he's going to use it to buy unpoisoned food to replace
the food he's poisoned. I had trouble understanding
that!"

Murgatroyd said, *"Chee!"*

He got up. He walked in a rather wobbly fashion
as if testing his strength. He came back and nestled

against Calhoun. Calhoun petted him. Murgatroyd yawned. He'd been weakened by his illness. He still didn't understand it. *Tormals* are not accustomed to being ill.

"Now," said Calhoun reflectively, "I make a guess at how certain criminal minds will work if they eavesdropped just then. We've spoiled their crime on Kryder II. They'd put a lot of time and trouble into committing it. Now they've had their trouble and committed their murders for nothing. I think, I *think* they'll be angry. With me."

He settled Murgatroyd comfortably. He went about the ship stowing things away. The samples of ditch water and of foodstuffs he placed so no shock or sudden acceleration could spill them. He made sure there were no loose objects about the control-room. He went down below and made especially sure that the extra plastic-sealed control-central unit was properly stowed, and that the spacesuit worn by one of the two men to board the Med Ship at breakout was suitably held fast. They'd be turned over to the laboratories at headquarters. If carefully disassembled the control-central unit would give positive proof that a certain man in the headquarters technical staff had installed it. Suitable measures would be taken. The spacesuit would identify the man now at the bottom of a rocky crevasse on an icy, uninhabited world.

By the time Calhoun's preparations were finished, the ship had nearly completed its orbital round. Calhoun put Murgatroyd in his cubbyhole. He fastened the door so the little animal couldn't be thrown out. He went to the pilot's chair and strapped in.

Presently he called, "*Med Ship* Aesclipus Twenty *calling ground! Med Ship calling ground!*"

An enraged voice answered immediately.

"*Ground to Med Ship! You were right! The ship in*

*the spaceport lifted off on emergency rockets before we
could stop it! It must have listened in when you talked
to us before! It got below the horizon before we could
lock on!*"

"Ah!" said Calhoun comfortably. "And did Doctor
Kelo get aboard?"

"*He did!*" raged the voice. "*He did! It's inexcusable!
It's unbelievable! He did get aboard and we moved to
seize the ship and its rockets flamed and it got away!*"

"Ah!" said Calhoun, again comfortably. "Then give
me coordinates for landing."

He had them repeated. Of course, if someone were
eavesdropping . . . but he shifted the Med Ship's orbit
to bring him to rendezvous at a certain spot at a certain time, a certain very considerable distance out from
the planet.

"Now," he said to Murgatroyd, "we'll see if I
understand the psychology of the criminal classes, in
fact . . ."

Then he remembered that Murgatroyd was locked
in his cubbyhole. He shrugged. He sat very alertly in
the pilot's chair while the planet Kryder II revolved
beneath him.

There was silence except for those minute noises
a ship has to make to keep from seeming like the
inside of a tomb. Murmurings. Musical notes. The
sound of traffic. All very faint but infinitely companionable.

The needle of the nearest-object dial stirred from
where it had indicated the distance to the planet's
surface. Something else was nearer. It continued to
approach. Calhoun found it and swung the Med Ship
to face it, but he waited. Presently, he saw an infinitesimal sliver of reflected sunlight against the background of distant stars. He mentally balanced this fact
against that, this possibility against that.

He flicked on the electron telescope. Yes. There were minute objects following the other ship. More of them appeared, and still more. They were left behind by the other ship's acceleration, but they spread out like a cone of tiny, deadly, murderous missiles. They were. If any one crashed into the Med Ship it could go clear through from end to end.

This was obviously the ship that had placed a man aboard the Med Ship to impersonate Calhoun aground. It was the ship whose company was ultimately responsible for the plague on Kryder II, and before that on Castor IV, and for another before that. It had been aground to receive, at a suitable moment, very many millions of credits in currency to pay for unpoisoned foodstuffs for Kryder II. Through Calhoun, it had had all its trouble for nothing. It came to destroy the Med Ship as merited if inadequate punishment.

However, Calhoun found himself beautifully confident in his own competence. He was headed, of course, for a ship that meant to destroy him. It tossed out missiles to accomplish that purpose. Dropping behind as they did, the effect was of the other ship towing a cone-shaped net of destruction.

So Calhoun jammed down his rocket-controls to maximum acceleration and plunged toward it. It was a ship guided by criminals, with criminal psychology. They couldn't understand and at first couldn't believe that Calhoun—who should be their victim—would think of anything but attempts to escape. But presently it was borne upon them that he seemed to intend to ram them in mid-space.

The other ship swerved. Calhoun changed course to match. The other ship wavered. Its pilot couldn't understand. He'd lost the initiative. The Med Ship plunged for the very nose of the other vessel. They moved toward each other with vastly more than the speed of rifle bullets. At the last instant the other ship tried crazily to sheer off. At that precise moment Calhoun swung the Med Ship into a quarter-turn. He cut his rockets and the *Aesclipus Twenty* plunged ahead, moving sidewise, and then Calhoun cut in his rockets again. Their white-hot flames, flittering through a quarter-mile of space, splashed upon the other ship. They penetrated. They sliced the other ship into two ragged and uneven halves, and those two halves wallowed onward.

The communicator chattered, *"Calling Med Ship! Calling Med Ship! What's happened?"*

At that time Calhoun was too busy to reply. The Med Ship was gaining momentum away from the line of the other ship's course, around which very many hurtling objects also moved. They would sweep through the space in which the other ship had died. Calhoun had to get away from them.

He did. Minutes later he answered the still-chattering call from the ground.

"There was a ship," he said evenly, "some ship which tried to smash me out here. but something seems to have happened to it. It's in two parts now, and it will probably crash in two pieces somewhere aground. I don't think there will be any survivors. I think Doctor Kelo was aboard."

The voice aground conferred agitatedly with others. Then it urgently requested Calhoun to land and receive the gratitude of people already recovering from the virulent pestilence. Calhoun said politely, "My *tormal* has been ill. It's unprecedented. I need to take him back to headquarters. I think I'm through here, anyhow."

He aimed the Med Ship, while voices made urgent official noises from the planet. He aimed very carefully for the sun around which the planet which was

the Med Service Headquarters revolved. Presently he
pushed a button, and the Med Ship did something
equivalent to making a hole, crawling into it, and
pulling the hole in after itself. In fact, it went into
overdrive. It sped on toward headquarters at many
times the speed of light, nestled in that cocoon of
stressed space which was like a private sub-cosmos of
its own.

Calhoun said severely, when matters settled down,
"Three weeks of peace and quiet in overdrive,
Murgatroyd, will be much better for you than landing on Kryder II and being fed to bursting with sweet
cakes and coffee! I tell you so as your physician!"

"Chee," said Murgatroyd dolefully. *"Chee-chee-chee!"*
The Med Ship drove on.

THE MUTANT WEAPON

I

"The probability of unfavorable consequences cannot be zero in any action of common life, but the probability increases by a very high power as a series of actions is lengthened. The effect of moral considerations, in conduct, may be stated to be a mathematically verifiable reduction in the number of unfavorable possible chance happenings. Of course, whether this process is called the intelligent use of probability, or piety, makes no difference in the facts. It is the method by which unfavorable chance happenings are made least probable. Arbitrary actions such as we call criminal cannot ever be justified by mathematics. For example . . ."

Probability and Human Conduct—Fitzgerald

Calhoun lay on his bunk and read Fitzgerald on *Probability and Human Conduct* as the little Med Ship floated in overdrive. In overdrive travel there is nothing to do but pass the time away. Murgatroyd, the *tormal*, slept curled up in a ball in one corner of the small ship's cabin. His tail was meticulously curled about his nose. The ship's lights burned steadily. There were those small random noises which have to be provided to keep a man sane in the dead stillness of a ship traveling at very many times the speed of light. Calhoun turned a page and yawned.

Something stirred somewhere. There was a click, and a voice said:

"When the tone sounds, breakout will be five seconds off."

A metronomic clicking, grave and deliberate, resounded in the stillness. Calhoun heaved himself up from the bunk and marked his place in the book. He moved to and seated himself in the control chair and fastened the safety belt. He said, "Murgatroyd. Hark, hark the lark in Heaven's something-or-other doth sing. Wake up and comb your whiskers. We're getting there."

Murgatroyd opened one eye and saw Calhoun in the pilot's chair. He uncurled himself and padded to a place where there was something to grab hold of. He regarded Calhoun with bright eyes.

"Bong!" said the tape. It counted down. *"Five . . . four . . . three . . . two . . . one . . ."*

It stopped. The ship popped out of overdrive. The sensation was unmistakable. Calhoun's stomach seemed to turn over twice, and he had a sickish feeling of spiraling dizzily in what was somehow a cone. He swallowed. Murgatroyd made gulping noises. Outside, everything changed.

The sun Maris blazed silently in emptiness off to port. The Cetis star-cluster was astern, and the light by which it could be seen had traveled for many years to reach here, though Calhoun had left Med Headquarters only three weeks before. The third planet of Maris swung splendidly in its orbit. Calhoun checked, and nodded in satisfaction. He spoke over his shoulder to Murgatroyd.

"We're here, all right."

"*Chee!*" shrilled Murgatroyd.

He uncoiled his tail from about a cabinet handle and hopped up to look at the vision screen. What he saw, of course, meant nothing to him. But all *tormals* imitate the actions of human beings, as parrots imitate their speech. He blinked wisely at the screen and turned his eyes to Calhoun.

"It's Maris III," Calhoun told him, "and pretty close. It's a colony of Dettra Two. One city was reported started two Earth-years ago. It should just about be colonized now."

"*Chee-chee!*" shrilled Murgatroyd.

"So get out of the way," commanded Calhoun. "We'll make our approach and I'll tell 'em we're here."

He made a standard approach on interplanetary drive. Naturally, it was a long process. But after some hours he flipped over the call switch and made the usual identification and landing request.

"Med Ship *Aesclipus Twenty* to ground," he said into the transmitter. "Requesting coordinates for landing. Our mass is fifty tons. Repeat, five-oh tons. Purpose of landing: planetary health inspection."

He relaxed. This job ought to be pure routine. There was a landing grid in the spaceport city on Maris III. From its control room instructions should be sent, indicating a position some five planetary diameters from the surface of that world. Calhoun's little ship should repair to that spot. The giant landing grid should then reach out its specialized force field, lock onto the ship, and bring it gently but irresistibly down to ground. Then Calhoun, representing Med Service, should confer gravely with planetary authorities about public health conditions on Maris III.

It was not expected that anything important would turn up. Calhoun would deliver full details of recent advances in the science of medicine. These might already have reached Maris III in the ordinary course of commerce, but he would make sure. He might— but it was unlikely—learn of some novelty worked out here. In any case, within three days he should return to the small Med Ship, the landing grid should heave it firmly heavenward to not less than five planetary diameters distance, and there release it. And Calhoun and Murgatroyd and the Med Ship should flick into overdrive and speed back toward headquarters, from whence they had come.

Right now, Calhoun waited for an answer to his landing call. But he regarded the vast disk of the nearby planet.

"By the map," he observed to Murgatroyd, "the city ought to be on shore of that bay somewhere near the terminus. Close to the sunset line."

His call was answered. A voice said incredulously on the spacephone speaker, *"What? What's that? What's that you say?"*

"Med Ship *Aesclipus Twenty*," Calhoun repeated patiently. "Requesting coordinates for landing. Our mass is fifty tons. Repeat, five-oh tons. Purpose of landing: planetary health inspection."

The voice said more incredulously still, *"A Med Ship? Holy—"* By the change of sound, the man down on the planet had turned away from the microphone. *"Hey! Listen to this!"*

There was abrupt silence. Calhoun raised his eyebrows. He drummed on the control desk before him. There was a long pause. A very long pause. Then a new voice came on the spacephone, up from the ground, *"You up there! Identify yourself!"*

Calhoun said very politely, "This is Med Ship

Aesclipus Twenty. I would like to come to ground. Purpose of landing: health inspection."

"Wait," said the voice from the planet. It sounded strained.

A murmuring sounded, transmitted from fifty thousand miles away. Then there was a click. The transmitter down below had cut off. Calhoun raised his eyebrows again. This was not according to routine. Not at all! The Med Service was badly overworked and understaffed. The resources of interplanetary services were always apt to be stretched to their utmost, because there could be no galactic government as such. Many thousands of occupied planets, the closest of them light-years apart, couldn't hold elections or have political parties for the simple reason that travel, even in overdrive, was too slow. They could only have service organizations whose authority depended on the consent of the people served, and whose support had to be gathered when and as it was possible.

But the Med Service was admittedly important. The local Sector Headquarters was in the Cetis cluster. It was a sort of interstellar clinic, with additions. It gathered and disseminated the results of experience in health and medicine among some thousands of colony-worlds, and from time to time it made contact with other headquarters carrying on the same work elsewhere. It admittedly took fifty years for a new technique in gene selection to cross the occupied part of the galaxy, but it was a three-year voyage in overdrive to cover the same distance direct. And the Med Service was worthwhile. There was no problem of human ecological adjustment it had so far been unable to solve, and there were some dozens of planets whose human colonies owed their existence to it. There was nowhere, nowhere at all, that a Med Ship was not welcomed on its errand from headquarters.

"Aground there!" said Calhoun sharply. "What's the matter? Are you landing me or not?"

There was no answer. Then, suddenly, every sound-producing device in the ship abruptly emitted a hoarse and monstrous noise. The lights flashed up and circuit breakers cut them off. Every device within the ship designed to notify emergency clanged or shrieked or roared or screamed. There was momentary bedlam.

It lasted for part of a second only. Then everything stopped. There was no weight within the ship, and there were no lights. There was dead silence, and Murgatroyd made whimpering sounds in the darkness.

Calhoun thought absurdly to himself, *According to the book, this is an unfavorable chance consequence of something or other*. But it was more than an unfavorable chance occurrence. It was an intentional and drastic and possibly a deadly one.

"Somebody's acting up," said Calhoun measuredly, in the blackness. "What the hell's the matter with them?"

He flipped the screen switch to bring back vision of what was outside. The vision screens of a ship are very carefully fused against overload burnouts, because there is nothing in all the cosmos quite as helpless and foredoomed as a ship which is blind in the emptiness of space. But the screens did not light again. They couldn't. The cutouts hadn't worked in time.

Calhoun's scalp crawled. But as his eyes adjusted, he saw the pale fluorescent handles of switches and doors. They hadn't been made fluorescent in expectation of an emergency like this, of course, but they would help a great deal. He knew what had happened. It could only be one thing—a landing-grid field clamped on the fifty-ton Med Ship with the power needed to grasp and land a twenty-thousand-ton liner. At that strength it would paralyze every instrument and blow every cutoff. It could not be accidental. The reception of the news of his identity, the repeated request that he identify himself, and then the demand that he wait . . . This murderous performance was deliberate.

"Maybe," said Calhoun in the inky-black cabin, "as a Med Ship our arrival is an unfavorable chance consequence of something—and somebody means to keep us from happening. It looks like it."

Murgatroyd whimpered.

"And I think," added Calhoun coldly, "that somebody may need a swift kick in the negative feedback!"

He released himself from the safety belt and dived across the cabin in which there was now no weight at all. In the blackness he opened a cabinet door. What he did inside was customarily done by a man wearing thick insulated gloves, in the landing grid back at headquarters. He threw certain switches which would allow the discharge of the power-storage cells which worked the Med Ship's overdrive. Monstrous quantities of energy were required to put even a fifty-ton ship into overdrive, and monstrous amounts were returned when it came out. The power amounted to ounces of pure, raw energy, and as a safety precaution such amounts were normally put into the Duhanne cells only just before a Med Ship's launching, and drained out again on its return. But now, Calhoun threw switches which made a rather incredible amount of power available for dumping into the landing-grid field about him—if necessary.

He floated back to the control chair.

The ship lurched. Violently. It was being moved by the grid field without any gentleness at all. Calhoun's hands barely grasped the back of his pilot's chair before the jerk came, and it almost tore them free. He just missed being flung against the back of the cabin by

the applied acceleration. But he was a long way out
from the planet. He was at the end of a lever fifty
thousand miles long, and for that lever to be used to
shake him too brutally would require special adjustments. But somebody was making them. The jerk
reversed directions. He was flung savagely against the
chair to which he'd been clinging. He struggled.
Another yank, in another direction. Another one still.
It flung him violently into the chair.

Behind him, Murgatroyd squealed angrily as he went
hurtling across the cabin. He grabbed for holding
places with all four paws and his tail.

Another shake. Calhoun had barely fastened the
safety belt before a furious jolt nearly flung him out
of it again to crash against the cabin ceiling. Still
another vicious surge of acceleration, and he scrabbled
for the controls. The yanking and plunging of the ship
increased intolerably. He was nauseated. Once he was
thrust so furiously into the control chair that he was
on the verge of blacking out; and then the direction
of thrust was changed to the exact opposite so that
the blood rushing to his head seemed about to explode
it. His arms flailed out of control. He became dazed.
But when his hands were flung against the control-
board, he tried, despite their bruising, to cling to the
control-knobs, and each time he threw them over.
Practically all his circuits were blown, but there was
one—

His numbing fingers threw it. There was a roar so
fierce that it seemed to be an explosion. He'd reached
the switch which made effective the discharge circuit
of his Duhanne cells. He'd thrown it. It was designed
to let the little ship's overdrive power reserve flow into
storage at headquarters on return from duty. Now,
though, it poured into the landing field outside. It
amounted to hundreds of millions of kilowatt hours,

delivered in a fraction of a second. There was the smell of ozone. The sound was like a thunderclap.

But abruptly there was a strange and incredible peace. The lights came on waveringly as his shaking fingers restored the circuit breakers. Murgatroyd shrilled indignantly, clinging desperately to an instrument rack. But the vision screens did not light again. Calhoun swore. Swiftly, he threw more circuit restorers. The nearest-object indicator told of the presence of Maris III at forty-odd thousand miles. The hull-temperature indicator was up some fifty-six degrees. The internal-gravity field came on faintly, and then built up to normal. But the screens would not light. They were permanently dead. Calhoun raged for seconds. Then he got hold of himself.

"Chee-chee-chee!" chattered Murgatroyd desperately. *"Chee-chee!"*

"Shut up!" growled Calhoun. "Some bright lad aground thought up a new way to commit murder. Damned near got away with it, too! He figured he'd shake us to death like a dog shakes a rat, only he was using a landing-grid field to do it with. Right now, I hope I fried him!"

But it was not likely. Such quantities of power as are used to handle twenty-thousand-ton spaceliners are not controlled direct, but by relays. The power Calhoun had flung into the grid field should have blown out the grid's transformers with a spectacular display of fireworks, but it was hardly probable it had gotten back to the individual at the controls.

"But I suspect," observed Calhoun vengefully, "that he'll consider this business an unfavorable occurrence. Somebody'll twist his tail too, either for trying what he did or for not getting away with it! Only, as a matter of pure precaution—"

His expression changed suddenly. He'd been trying

not to think of the consequences of having no sight
of the cosmos outside the ship. Now he remembered
the electron telescope. It had not been in circuit, so
it could not have been burned out like his vision
screens. He switched it on. A star-field appeared over
his head.

"Chee-chee!" cried Murgatroyd hysterically.

Calhoun glanced at him. The jerking of the ship had
shifted the instruments in the rack to which
Murgatroyd clung. Clipped into place though they
were, they'd caught Murgatroyd's tail and pinched it
tightly.

"You'll have to wait," snapped Calhoun. "Right now
I've got to make us look like a successful accident.
Otherwise, whoever tried to spread us all over the
cabin walls will try something else!"

The Med Ship flung through space in whatever
direction and at whatever velocity it had possessed
when the grid field blew. Calhoun shifted the electron
telescope's field and simultaneously threw on the
emergency rocket controls. There was a growling of
the pencil-thin, high-velocity blasts. There was a surging of the ship.

"No straight-line stuff," Calhoun reminded himself.

He swung the ship into a dizzy spiral, as if innumerable things had been torn or battered loose in the
ship and its rockets had come on of themselves. Painstakingly, he jettisoned in one explosive burst all the
stored waste of his journey which could not be dis-
posed of while in overdrive. To any space-scanning
instrument on the ground, it would look like something
detonating violently inside the ship.

"Now—"

The planet Maris III swung across the electron
telescope's field. It looked hideously near, but that was
the telescope's magnification. Yet Calhoun sweated. He

looked at the nearest-object dial for reassurance. The planet was nearer by a thousand miles.

"Hah!" said Calhoun.

He changed the ship's spiral course. He changed it again. He abruptly reversed the direction of its turn. Adequate training in space combat could have helped plot an evasion course, but it might have been recognizable. Nobody could anticipate his maneuvers now, though. He adjusted the telescope next time the planet swept across its field, and flipped on the photorecorder. Then he pulled out of the spiral, whirled the ship until the city was covered by the telescope, and ran the recorder as long as he dared keep a straight course. Then he swooped toward the planet in a crazy, twisting fall with erratic intermissions, and made a final lunatic dash almost parallel to the planet's surface.

At five hundred miles he unshielded the ports, which of necessity had to be kept covered in clear space. There was a sky which was vividly bright with stars. There was a vast blackness off to starboard which was the night side of the planet.

He went down. At four hundred miles the outside-pressure indicator wavered away from its pin. He used it like a pilot-tube recording, doing sums in his head to figure the static pressure that should exist at this height, to compare with the dynamic pressure produced by his velocity through the near hard vacuum. The pressure should have been substantially zero. He swung the ship end-for-end and killed velocity to bring the pressure indication down. The ship descended. Two hundred miles. He saw the thin bright line of sunshine at the limb of the planet. Down to one hundred. He cut the rockets and let the ship fall silently, swinging its nose up.

At ten miles he listened for man-made radiation. There was nothing in the electromagnetic spectrum but the crackling of static in an electric storm which might be a thousand miles away. At five miles height the nearest-object indicator, near the bottom of its scale, wavered in a fashion to prove that he was still moving laterally across mountainous country. He swung the ship and killed that velocity too.

At two miles he used the rockets for deceleration. The pencil-thin flame reached down for an incredible distance. By naked-eye observation out a port, he tilted the fiercely roaring, swiftly falling ship until hillsides and forests underneath him ceased to move. By that time he was very low indeed.

He reached ground on a mountainside which was lighted by the blue-white flame of the rocket blast. He chose an area in which the treetops were almost flat, indicating something like a plateau underneath. Murgatroyd was practically frantic by this time because of his capture and the pinching of his tail, but Calhoun could not spare time to release him. He let the ship down gently, gently, trying to descend in an absolutely vertical line.

If he didn't do it perfectly, he came very close. The ship settled into what was practically a burned-away tunnel among monstrous trees. The slender, high-velocity flame did not splash when it reached ground. It penetrated. It burned a hole for itself through humus and clay and bedrock. When the ship touched and settled, there was boiling molten stone some sixty feet underground; but there was only a small scratching sound as it came to rest. A flame-amputated tree limb rubbed tentatively against the hull.

Calhoun turned off the rockets. The ship swayed slightly and there were crunching noises. Then it was still on its landing fins.

"Now," said Calhoun, "I can take care of you, Murgatroyd."

He flicked on the switches of the exterior microphones, which were much more sensitive than human ears. The radiation detectors were still in action. They reported only the cracklings of the distant storm.

But the microphones brought in the moaning of wind over nearby mountaintops, and the almost deafening susurrus of rustling leaves. Underneath these noises there was a bedlam of other natural sounds. There were chirpings and hootings and squeaks, and the gruntings made by native animal life. These sounds had a singularly peaceful quality. When Calhoun toned them down to be no more than background noise, they suggested the sort of concert of night creatures which to men has always seemed an indication of purest tranquility.

Presently Calhoun looked at the pictures the photorecorder had taken while the telescope's field swept over the city. It was the colony-city reported to have been begun two years before to receive colonists from Dettra Two. It was the city of the landing grid which had tried to destroy the Med Ship as a dog kills a rat, by shaking it to fragments, some forty thousand miles in space. It was the city which had made Calhoun land with his vision plates blinded; which had drained his power reserves of some hundreds of millions of kilowatt-hours of energy. It was the city which had made his return to Med Headquarters impossible.

He inspected the telescopic pictures. They were very clear. They showed the city with astonishing detail. There was a lacy pattern of highways, with their medallions of multiple-dwelling units. There were the lavish park areas between the buildings of this planetary capital. There was the landing grid itself, a half-mile high structure of steel girders, a full mile in diameter.

But there were no vehicles on the highways. There were no specks on the overpasses to indicate people on foot. There were no 'copters on the building roofs, nor were there objects in mid-air to tell of air traffic.

The city was either deserted or it had never been occupied. But it was absolutely intact. The structures were perfect. There was no indication of past panic or disaster, and even the highways had not been overgrown by vegetation. But it was empty—or else it was dead.

But somebody in it had tried very ferociously and with singular effectiveness to try to destroy the Med Ship.

Calhoun raised his eyebrows and looked at Murgatroyd.

"Why is all this?" he asked. "Have you any ideas?"

"Chee!" shrilled Murgatroyd.

■ ■

"The purpose of a contemplated human action is always the attainment of a desired subjective experience. But a subjective experience is desired both in terms of intensity and of duration. For an individual the temptingness of different degrees of intensity—of experience is readily computed. However, the temptingness of different durations is equally necessary for an estimate of the probability of a given person performing a given action. This modification depends on the individual's time sense; its acuity and its accuracy. Measurements of time sense . . ."

Probability and Human Conduct—Fitzgerald

Eventually Calhoun left the ship and found a cultivated field and a dead man and other things. But while in the Med Ship he found only bewilderment. The first morning he carefully monitored the entire communications spectrum. There were no man-made signals in the air of Maris III. That was proof the world was uninhabited. But the ship's external microphones picked up a rocket roar in mid-morning. Calhoun looked, and saw the faint white trail of the rocket against the blue of the sky. The fact that he saw it was proof that it was in atmosphere. And that was evidence that the rocket was taking photographs for signs of the crater the Med Ship should have made in a crash landing.

The fact of search was proof that the planet was inhabited, but the silence of the radio spectrum said that it wasn't. The absence of traffic in the city said that it was dead or empty, but there were people there because they'd answered Calhoun's hail, and tried to kill him when he identified himself. But nobody would want to destroy a Med Ship except to prevent a health inspection unless there was a situation aground that the Med Service ought to know about. But there should not be such a situation.

There was no logical explanation for such a series of contradictions. Civilized men acted either this way or that. There could only be civilized men here, yet they acted neither this way nor that. Therefore—and the confusion began all over again.

Calhoun dictated an account of events into the emergency responder in the ship. If a search call came from space, the responder would broadcast this data and Calhoun's intended action. He carefully shut off all other operating circuits so the ship couldn't be found by their radiation. He equipped himself for travel, and he and Murgatroyd left the ship. Obviously, he headed toward the city where whatever was wrong was centered.

Travel on foot was unaccustomed, but not difficult. The vegetation was semi-familiar. Maris III was an Earth-type planet and circled a Sol-type sun, and given similar conditions of gravity, air, sunlight, and temperature range, similar organisms should develop. There would be room, for example, for low-growing ground-cover plants, and there would also be advantages to height. There would be some equivalent of grass, and there would be the equivalent of trees, with intermediate forms having in-between habits of growth. Similar reasoning would apply to animal life. There would be parallel ecological niches for animals to fill, and animals would adapt to fill them.

Maris III was not, then, an "unearthly" environment. It was much more like an unfamiliar part of a known planet than a new world altogether. But there were some oddities. An herbivorous creature without legs which squirmed like a snake. A pigeon-sized creature whose wings were modified, gossamer-thin scales with iridescent colorings. There were creatures which seemed to live in lunatic association, and Calhoun was irritably curious to know if they were really symbiotes or only unrecognizable forms of the same organism, like the terrestrial male and female firefly-glowworm.

But he was heading for the city. He couldn't spare time to biologize. On his first day's journey he looked for food to save the rations he carried. Murgatroyd was handy here. The little *tormal* had his place in human society. He was friendly, and he was passionately imitative of human beings, and he had a definite psychology of his own. But he was useful, too. When Calhoun strode through the forests, Murgatroyd strode grandly with him, imitating his walk. From time to time he dropped to all four paws to investigate something. He invariably caught up with Calhoun within seconds.

Once Calhoun saw him interestedly bite a tiny bit out of a most unpromising-looking shrub stalk. He savored its flavor, and then swallowed it. Calhoun took note of the plant and cut off a section. He bound it to the skin of his arm up near the elbow. Hours later there was no allergic reaction, so he tasted it. It was almost familiar. It had the flavor of a bracken shoot, mingled with a fruity taste. It would be a green bulk food like spinach or asparagus, filling but without much substance.

Later, Murgatroyd carefully examined a luscious-seeming fruit which grew low enough for him to pluck. He sniffed it closely and drew back. Calhoun noted that plant, too. Murgatroyd's tribe was bred at head-quarters for some highly valuable qualities. One was a very sensitive stomach—but it was only one. Murgatroyd's metabolism was very close to man's. If he ate something and it didn't disagree with him, it was very likely safe for a man to eat it too. If he rejected something, it probably wasn't. But his real value was much more important than the tasting of questionable foods.

When Calhoun camped the first night, he made a fire of a plant shaped like a cactus barrel and permeated with oil. By heaping dirt around it, he confined its burn-ing to a round space very much like the direct-heat element of an electronic stove. It was an odd illustra-tion of the fact that human progress does not involve anything really new in kind, but only increased conve-nience and availability of highly primitive comforts. By the light of that circular bonfire, Calhoun actually read a little. But the light was inadequate. Presently he yawned. One did not get very far in the Med Service without knowing probability in human conduct. It enabled one to check on the accuracy of statements made, whether by patients or officials, to a Med Ship man. Today, though, he'd traveled a long way on foot. He glanced at Murgatroyd, who was gravely pretend-ing to read from a singularly straight-edged leaf.

"Murgatroyd," said Calhoun, "it is likely that you will interpret any strange sound as a possible undesirable subjective experience. Which is to say, as dangerous.

So if you hear anything sizable coming close during the night, I hope you'll squeal. Thank you."

Murgatroyd said, *"Chee,"* and Calhoun rolled over and went to sleep.

It was mid-morning of the next day when he came upon a cultivated field. It had been cleared and planted, of course, in preparation for the colonists who'd been expected to occupy the city. Familiar Earth plants grew in it, ten feet high and more. And Calhoun examined it carefully, in the hope of finding how long since it had received attention. In this examination, he found the dead man.

As a corpse, the man was brand new, and Calhoun very carefully put himself into a strictly medical frame of mind before he bent over for a technical estimate of what had happened, and when. The dead man seemed to have died of hunger. He was terribly emaciated, and he didn't belong in a cultivated field far from the city. By his garments he was a city dweller and a prosperous one. He wore the jewels which nowadays indicated a man's profession and status much more than the value of his possessions. There was money in his pockets, and writing materials, a wallet with pictures and identification, and the normal oddments a man would carry. He'd been a civil servant of the city. And he shouldn't have died of starvation.

He especially shouldn't have gone hungry here! The sweet maize plants were tall and green. Their ears were ripe. He hadn't gone hungry! There were the inedible remains of at least two dozen sweet maize ears. They had been eaten some time—some days—ago, and one had been left unfinished. If the dead man had eaten them but was unable to digest them, his belly should have been swollen with undigested food. It wasn't. He'd eaten and digested and still had died, at least largely of inanition.

Calhoun scowled.

"How about this corn, Murgatroyd?" he demanded.

He reached up and broke off a half-yard-long ear. He stripped away the protecting, stringy leaves. The soft grains underneath looked appetizing. They smelled like good fresh food. Calhoun offered the ear to Murgatroyd.

The little *tormal* took it in his paws and on the instant was eating it with gusto.

"If you keep it down, he didn't die of eating it," said Calhoun, frowning. "And if he ate it—which he did—he didn't die of starvation. Which he did."

He waited. Murgatroyd consumed every grain upon the oversized cob. His furry belly distended a little. Calhoun offered him a second ear. He set to work on that, too, with self-evident enjoyment.

"In all history," said Calhoun, "nobody's ever been able to poison one of you *tormals* because your digestive system has a qualitative analysis unit in it that yells bloody murder if anything's likely to disagree with you. As a probability of *tormal* reaction, you'd have been nauseated before now if that stuff wasn't good to eat."

But Murgatroyd ate until he was distinctly pot-bellied. He left a few grains on the second ear with obvious regret. He put it down carefully on the ground. He shifted his left-hand whiskers with his paw and elaborately licked them clean. He did the same to the whiskers on the right-hand side of his mouth. He said comfortably, *"Chee!"*

"Then that's that," Calhoun told him. "This man didn't die of starvation. I'm getting queasy!"

He had his lab kit in his shoulder pack, of course. It was an absurdly small outfit, with almost microscopic instruments. But in Med Ship field work the techniques of microanalysis were standard. Distastefully, Calhoun took the tiny tissue sample from which he

could gather necessary information. Standing, he ran
through the analytic process that seemed called for.
When he finished, he buried the dead man as well as
he could and started off in the direction of the city
again. He scowled as he walked.

He journeyed for nearly half an hour before he
spoke. Murgatroyd accompanied him on all fours now
because of his heavy meal. After a mile and a half,
Calhoun stopped and said grimly, "Let's check you over,
Murgatroyd."

He verified the *tormal's* pulse and respiration and
temperature. He put a tiny breath sample through the
part of the lab kit which read off a basic metabolism
process. He submitted blandly. The result of the
checkover was that Murgatroyd the *tormal* was perfectly normal.

"But," said Calhoun angrily, "that man died of starvation! There was practically no fat in the tissue sample
at all! He arrived where we found him while he was
strong enough to eat, and he stayed where there was
good food, and he ate it, and he digested it, and he
died of starvation: Why?"

Murgatroyd wriggled unhappily, because Calhoun's
tone was accusing. He said, *"Chee!"* in a subdued tone
of voice. He looked pleadingly up at Calhoun.

"I'm not angry with you," Calhoun told him, "but
dammit—"

He packed the lab kit back into his pack, which
contained food for the two of them for about a week.

"Come along!" he said bitterly. He started off. Ten
minutes later he stopped. "What I said was impossible.
But it happened, so it mustn't have been what I said.
I must have stated it wrongly. He could eat, because
he did. He did eat, because of the cobs left. He did
digest it. So why did he die of starvation? Did he stop
eating?"

"Chee!" said Murgatroyd with conviction.

Calhoun grunted and marched on once more. The man had not died of a disease, not directly. The tissue analysis gave a picture of death which denied that it came of any organ ceasing to function. Was it the failure of the organism—the man—to take the action required for living? Had he stopped eating?

Calhoun's mind skirted the notion warily. It was not plausible. The man had been able to feed himself and had done so. Anything which came upon him and made him unable to feed himself . . .

"He was a city man," growled Calhoun, "and this is a damned long way from the city. What was he doing out here, anyhow?"

He hesitated and tramped on again. A city man found starved in a remote place might have become lost, somehow or other. But if this man was lost, he was assuredly not without food.

"He belonged in the city," said Calhoun vexedly, "and he left it. The city's almost but not quite empty. Our would-be murderers are in it. This is a new colony. There was a city to be built and fields to be plowed and planted, and then a population was to come here from Dettra Two. The city's built and the fields are plowed and planted. Where's the population?"

He scowled thoughtfully at the ground before him. Murgatroyd tried to scowl too, but he wasn't very successful.

"What's the answer, Murgatroyd? Did the man come away from the city because he had a disease? Was he driven out?"

"Chee," said Murgatroyd without conviction.

"I don't know either," admitted Calhoun. "He walked out into the middle of that field and then stopped walking. He was hungry and he ate. He digested. He stayed there for days. Why? Was he waiting to die of something? Presently he stopped eating. He died. What made him leave the city? What made him stop eating? Why did he die?"

Murgatroyd investigated a small plant and decided that it was not interesting. He came back to Calhoun.

"He wasn't killed," said Calhoun, "but somebody tried to kill us—somebody who's in the city now. That man could have come out here to keep from being killed by the same people. Yet he died anyhow. Why'd they want to kill him? Why'd they want to kill us? Because we were a Med Ship? Because they didn't want Med Service to know there was a disease here? Ridiculous!"

"Chee," said Murgatroyd.

"I don't like the looks of things," said Calhoun. "For instance, in any ecological system there are always carrion eaters. At least some of them fly. There would be plain signs if the city was full of corpses. There aren't any. On the other hand, if the city was inhabited, and there was sickness, they would welcome a Med Ship with open arms. But that dead man didn't come away from the city in any ordinary course of events, and he didn't die in any conventional fashion. There's an empty city and an improbable dead man and a still more improbable attempt at murder! What gives, Murgatroyd?"

Murgatroyd took hold of Calhoun's hand and tugged at it. He was bored. Calhoun moved on slowly.

"Paradoxes don't turn up in nature," said Calhoun darkly. "Things that happen naturally never contradict each other. You only get such things when men try to do things that don't fit together—like having a plague and trying to destroy a Med Ship, if that's the case, and living in a city and not showing on its streets, if that is occurring, and dying of starvation while one's digestion is good and there's food within hand's reach.

And that did happen! There was dirty work at the spaceport, Murgatroyd. I suspect dirty work at every crossroad. Keep your eyes open."

"*Chee,*" said Murgatroyd. Calhoun was fully in motion, now, and Murgatroyd let go of his hand and went on ahead to look things over.

Calhoun crossed the top of a rounded hillcrest some three miles from the shallow grave he'd made. He began to accept the idea that the dead man had stopped eating for some reason, as the only possible explanation of his death. But that didn't make it plausible. He saw another ridge of hills ahead.

In another hour he came to the crest of that farther range. It was the worn-down remnant of a very ancient mountain chain, now eroded to a mere fifteen hundred or two thousand feet. He stopped at the very top. Here was a time and place to look and take note of what he saw. The ground stretched away in gently rolling fashion for very many miles, and there was the blue blink of sea at the horizon. A little to the left he saw shining white. He grunted.

That was the city of Maris III, which had been built to receive colonists from Dettra and relieve the population pressure there. It had been planned as the nucleus of a splendid, spacious, civilized world-nation to be added to the number of human-occupied worlds. From its beginning it should have held a population in the hundreds of thousands. It was surrounded by cultivated fields, and the air above it should have been a-shimmer with flying things belonging to its inhabitants.

Calhoun stared at it through his binoculars. They could not make an image, even so near, to compare with that which the electron telescope had made from space, but he could see much. The city was perfect. It was intact. It was new. But there was no sign of occupancy anywhere. It did not look dead, so much as frozen. There were no fliers above it. There was no motion on the highways. He saw one straight road which ran directly away along his line of sight. Had there been vehicles on it, he would have seen at least shifting patches of color as clots of traffic moved together. There were none.

He pressed his lips together and began to inspect the nearer terrain. He saw foreshortened areas where square miles of ground had been cleared and planted with Earth vegetation. This was a complicated process. First the ground had to be bulldozed clean, and then great sterilizers had to lumber back and forth, killing every native seed and root and even the native soil bacteria. Then the land had to be sprayed with cultures of the nitrogen-fixing and phosphorous-releasing microscopic organisms which normally live in symbiosis with Earth plants. These had to be tested beforehand for their ability to compete with indigenous bacterial life. And then Earth plants could be sown.

They had been. Calhoun saw that inimitable green which a man somehow always recognizes. It is the green of plants whose ancestors thrived on Earth and which have followed that old planet's children halfway across the galaxy.

"There's a look to a well-tended field," said Calhoun, after a long look through binoculars, "that shows what kind of people cultivated it. There are fields up ahead that are well laid out, but nobody's touched them for weeks. The furrows are straight and the crops healthy. But they're beginning to show neglect. If the city was finished and waiting for its population, there would be caretakers tending the fields until the people came. There's been no caretaking done here!"

Murgatroyd stared wisely about as he considered Calhoun to be doing.

"In short," said Calhoun, "something's happened that I don't like. The population must be nearly zero or the fields would have been kept right. One man can keep a hell of a lot of ground in good shape, with modern machinery. People don't plant fields with the intention to neglect them. There's been a considerable change of plans around here. Enmity to a Med Ship is something more than a random impulse." Calhoun was not pleased. With the vision screens of his ship burned out, a return to headquarters was out of the question. "Whoever was handling the landing grid doesn't want help. He doesn't even want visitors. But Med Service was notified to come and look over the new colony. Either somebody changed his views drastically, or the people in charge of the landing grid aren't the ones who asked for a public health checkup."

Murgatroyd said profoundly, *"Chee!"*

"The poor devil I buried even seems to hint at something of the sort. He could have used help! Maybe there are two kinds of people here. One kind doesn't want aid and tried to kill us because we'd offer it. The other kind needs it. If so, there might be a certain antagonism . . ."

He stared with knitted brows over the vast expanse toward the horizon. Murgatroyd, at this moment, was a little way behind Calhoun. He stood up on his hind legs and stared intently off to one side. He shaded his eyes with a forepaw in a singularly humanlike fashion and looked inquisitively at something he saw. Calhoun did not notice.

"Make a guess, Murgatroyd," he commanded. "Make a wild one. A dead man who'd no reason for dying. Live people who should have no reason for wanting to spatter us against the walls of our Med Ship. Something was fatal to that dead man. Somebody tried to be fatal to us. Is there a connection?"

Murgatroyd stared absorbedly at a patch of brush-wood some fifty yards to his left. Calhoun started down the hillside. Murgatroyd remained fixed in a pose of intensely curious attention to the patch of brush. Calhoun went on. His back was toward the brush thicket.

There was a deep-toned, musical twanging sound from the thicket. Calhoun's body jerked violently from an impact. He stumbled and went down, with the shaft of a wooden projectile sticking out of his back. He lay still.

Murgatroyd whimpered. He rushed to where Calhoun lay upon the ground. He danced in agitation, chattering shrilly. He wrung his paws in humanlike distress. He tugged at Calhoun, but Calhoun made no response.

A girl emerged from the thicket. She was gaunt and thin, yet her garments had once been of admirable quality. She carried a strange and utterly primitive weapon. She moved toward Calhoun, bent over him and laid a hand to the wooden projectile she had fired into his back.

He moved suddenly. He grappled. The girl toppled, and he swarmed upon her savagely as she struggled. But she was taken by surprise. There was the sound of panting, and Murgatroyd danced in a fever of anxiety.

Then Calhoun stood up quickly. He stared down at the emaciated girl who had tried to murder him from ambush. She was panting horribly now.

"Really," said Calhoun in a professional tone, "as a doctor I'd say that you should be in bed instead of wandering around trying to murder total strangers. When did this trouble begin? I'm going to take your temperature and your pulse. Murgatroyd and I have been hoping to find someone like you. The only other human being I've met on this planet wasn't able to talk."

He swung his shoulder pack around and impatiently jerked a sharp-pointed stick out of it. It was the missile, which had been stopped by the pack. He brought out his lab kit. With absolute absorption in the task, he prepared to make a swift check of his would-be murderer's state of health.

It was not good. There was already marked emaciation. The desperately panting girl's eyes were deep-sunk, hollow. She gasped and gasped. Still gasping, she lapsed into unconsciousness.

"Here," said Calhoun curtly, "you enter the picture, Murgatroyd. This is the sort of thing you're designed to handle."

He set to work briskly. Presently he observed, "Besides a delicate digestion and a hair-trigger antibody system, Murgatroyd, you ought to have the instincts of a watchdog. I don't like coming that close to being shot by a lady patient. See if there's anybody else around, will you?"

"Chee," said Murgatroyd shrilly. But he didn't understand. He watched as Calhoun deftly drew a small sample of blood from the unconscious girl's arm and painstakingly put half the tiny quantity into an almost microscopic ampule in the lab kit. Then he moved toward Murgatroyd. The *tormal* wriggled as Calhoun made the injection. But it did not hurt. There was an insensitive spot on his flank where the nerves had been blocked off before he was a week old.

"As one medical man to another," said Calhoun, "you've noticed that the symptoms are of anoxia—oxygen starvation. Which doesn't make sense in the open air where we're breathing comfortably. Another paradox, Murgatroyd! But there's an emergency, too. How can you relieve anoxia when you haven't any oxygen?"

He looked down at the unconscious girl. She displayed the same sort of emaciation he'd noted in the dead man in the field some miles back. Patients with a given disease often acquire a certain odd resemblance to each other. This girl seemed to be in an earlier stage of whatever had killed the civil servant in the corn field. He'd died of starvation with partly eaten food by his hand. She'd tried to murder Calhoun, just as persons unknown, in the city, had tried to kill both Calhoun and Murgatroyd in the Med Ship some forty thousand miles out in space. But her equipment for murder was not on a par with that of the operators of the landing grid. She didn't belong in their class. She might be a fugitive from them.

Calhoun put these things together. Then he swore in sudden bitter anger. He stopped abruptly, in concern lest she'd heard.

She hadn't. She was still insensible.

III

"That pattern of human conduct which is loosely called 'self-respecting' has the curious property of restricting to the individual, through his withdrawal of acts to communicate misfortune, the unfavorable chance occurrences which probability insists must take place. On the other hand, the same pattern of human conduct tends to disseminate and to share chance favorable occurrences among the group. The members of a group of persons practicing 'self-respect,' then, increase the mathematical probability of cultures in which principles leading to this type of behavior become obsolete. A decadent society brings bad luck upon itself by the operation of the laws of probability . . ."

Probability and Human Conduct—Fitzgerald

She came very slowly back to consciousness. It was almost as if she waked from utterly exhausted sleep. When she first opened her eyes, they wandered vaguely until they fell upon Calhoun. Then a bitter and contemptuous hatred filled them. Her hand fumbled

weakly to the knife at her waist. It was not a good
weapon. It had been table cutlery, and the handle was
much too slender to permit a grip by which somebody
could be killed. Calhoun bent over and took the knife
away from her. It had been ground unskillfully to a
point.

"In my capacity as your doctor," he told her, "I must
forbid you to stab me. It wouldn't be good for you."
Then he said, "Look, my name's Calhoun. I came from
Sector Med Headquarters to make a planetary health
inspection here, and some lads in the city apparently
didn't want a Med Ship aground. So they tried to kill
me by battering me all over the walls of my ship with
the landing-grid field. I made what was practically a
crash landing, and now I need to know what's up."

The burning hatred remained in her eyes, but there
was a trace of doubt.

"Here," said Calhoun, "is my identification."

He showed her the highly official documents which
gave him vast authority—where a planetary government
was willing to concede it.

"Of course," he added, "papers can be stolen. But
I have a witness that I'm what and who I say I am.
You've heard of *tormals*? Murgatroyd will vouch for
me."

He called his small and furry companion.
Murgatroyd advanced and politely offered a small,
prehensile paw. He said *"Chee"* in his shrill voice, and
then solemnly took hold of the girl's wrist in imita-
tion of Calhoun's previous action of feeling her pulse.

Calhoun watched. The girl stared at Murgatroyd.
But all the galaxy had heard of *tormals*. They'd been
found on a planet in the Deneb region, and they were
engaging pets and displayed an extraordinary immunity to the diseases men were apt to scatter in their
interstellar journeying. A forgotten Med Service

researcher made an investigation of the ability of *tormals* to live in contact with men. He came up with a discovery which made them very much too valuable to have their lives wasted in mere sociability. There were still not enough of Murgatroyd's kind to meet the need that men had of them, and laymen had to forego their distinctly charming society. So Murgatroyd was an identification.

The girl said faintly, "If you'd only come earlier . . . but it's too late now. I—I thought you came from the city."

"I was headed there," said Calhoun.

"They'll kill you."

"Yes," agreed Calhoun, "they probably will. But right now you're ill and I'm Med Service. I suspect there's been an epidemic of some disease here, and that for some reason the people in the city don't want the Med Service to know about it. You seem to have it, whatever it is. Also, that was a very curious weapon you shot me with."

The girl said drearily, "One of our group had made a hobby of such things. Ancient weapons. He had bows and arrows and—what I shot you with was a crossbow. It doesn't need power. Not even chemical explosives. So when we ran away from the city, he ventured back in and armed us as well as he could."

Calhoun nodded. A little irrelevant talk is always useful at the beginning of a patient interview. But what she said was not irrelevant. A group of people had fled the city. They'd needed arms, and one of their number had gone back into the city for them. He'd known where to find reconstructions of ancient lethal devices—a hobby collection. It sounded like people of the civil service type. Of course there were no longer social classes separated by income. Not on most worlds, anyhow. But there were social groupings based on similar tastes, which had led to similar occupations and went on to natural congeniality. Calhoun placed her now. He remembered a long-outmoded term, "upper middle class," which no longer meant anything in economics but did in medicine.

"I'd like a case history," he said conversationally. "Name?"

"Helen Jons," she said wearily.

He held the mike of his pocket recorder to pick up her answers. Occupation: statistician. She'd been a member of the office force which was needed during the building of the city. When the construction work was finished, most of the workmen returned to the mother world Dettra, but the office staff stayed on to organize things when the colonists arrived.

"Hold it," said Calhoun. "You were a member of the office staff who stayed in the city to wait for the colonists. But a moment ago you said you fled from the city. There are still some people there, at least around the landing grid. I've reason to be sure of it. Were they part of the office staff too? If not, where did they come from?"

She shook her head weakly.

"Who are they?" he repeated.

"I don't know," she said drearily. "They came after the plague."

"Oh," said Calhoun. "Go on. When did the plague turn up? And how?"

She continued in a feeble voice. The plague appeared among the last shipload of workmen waiting to be returned to the mother world. There were then about a thousand people in the city, of all classes and occupations. The disease appeared first among those who tended the vast fields of planted crops.

It was well established before its existence was suspected. There were no obvious early symptoms, but those affected felt a loss of energy and they became listless and lackadaisical. The listlessness showed first in a cessation of griping and quarreling among the workmen. Norman, healthy human beings are aggressive. They squabble with each other as a matter of course. But squabbling ceased. Men hadn't the energy for it.

Shortness of breath appeared later. It wasn't obvious, at first. Men who lacked energy to squabble wouldn't exert themselves and so get out of breath. It was one of the medical staff who drove himself impatiently in spite of what he thought was a transient weariness, and discovered himself gasping without cause. He took a metabolism test, suspicious because the symptoms were so extreme. His metabolic rate was astonishingly low.

"Hold it again," commanded Calhoun. "You're a statistician, but you're talking medical talk. How's that?"

"Kim," the girl said tiredly. "He was on the medical staff. I was—I was going to marry him."

Calhoun nodded. "Go on."

She seemed to need to gather strength even to talk. She did not go on. Shortness of breath among the plague victims was progressive. Presently they gasped horribly from the exertion of getting to their feet, even. Walking, however slowly, could be done only at the cost of panting for breath. After a certain time they simply lay still. They could not summon the energy to stir. Then they sank into unconsciousness and died.

"What did the doctors think about all this?" demanded Calhoun.

"Kim could tell you," said the girl exhaustedly. "The doctors worked frantically. They tried everything— everything! They could get the symptoms in experimental animals, but they couldn't isolate the germ or whatever it was that caused the disease. Kim said they couldn't get a pure culture. It was incredible. No technique would isolate the cause of the symptoms, and yet the plague was contagious. Terribly so!"

Calhoun scowled. A new pathogenic mechanism was always possible, but it was at least unlikely. Still, something that standard bacteriological methods couldn't track down was definitely a job for the Med Service. But there were people in the city who didn't want the Med Service to interfere. The girl had referred to them once, when she spoke of a flight from the city, and again when she said someone ventured back for weapons. And she'd used a weapon on him, thinking him from the city. The description of the plague, too, was remarkable.

It was able to hide from men, which was something no other microorganism could accomplish. It was an ability that would offer no advantage to a disease germ in a state of purely natural happenings. Disease germs do not encounter bacteriological laboratories, as a rule, often enough to need to adapt to escape them. It would not help an average germ or microbe to be invisible to an electron microscope. There would be no reason for such invisibility to be developed.

But more than that, why should anybody want to keep a Med Service man like Calhoun from investigating a plague? When infected people fled from the city to die in the wilds, why should people remaining in the city try to destroy a Med Ship which might help to end the deaths? Ordinarily, well people in the middle of an epidemic are terrified lest they catch it. They'd be as anxious for Med Service help as those already infected. What was going on here?

"You said about a thousand people were in the city," observed Calhoun. "They tended the crops and waited for the city's permanent inhabitants. What happened after the plague was recognized to be one?"

"The first shipload of emigrants came from Dettra

Two," said the girl hopelessly. "We didn't bring them
to ground with the landing grid. Instead, we described
the plague. We warned them away. We quarantined
ourselves while our doctors tried to fight the disease.
The shipload of new people went back to Dettra without landing."

Calhoun nodded. This would be normal.

"Then another ship came. There were maybe two
hundred of us left alive. More than half of us already
showed signs of the plague. This other ship came. It
landed on emergency rockets because we had nobody
left who knew how to work the grid."

Then her voice wavered a little as she told of the
landing of the strange ship in the landing grid of the
city that was dying without ever having really lived.
There was no crowd to meet the ship. Those people
who were not yet stricken had abandoned the city and
scattered themselves widely, hoping to escape contagion by isolating themselves in new and uncontaminated dwelling units. But there was no lack of
communication facilities. Nearly all the survivors
watched the ship come down through vision screens
in the control building of the then-useless grid.

The ship touched ground. Men came out. They did
not look like doctors. They did not act like them. The
vision screens in the control building were snapped
off immediately. Contact could not be restored. So the
isolated groups spoke agitatedly to each other by vision
screen. They exchanged messages of desperate hope.
Then, newly landed men appeared at an apartment
whose occupant was in the act of such a conversation
with a group in a distant building. He left the visiphone
on as he went to admit and greet the men he hoped
were researchers, at least, come to find the cause of
the plague and end it.

The viewers at the other visiphone plate gazed

eagerly into his apartment. They saw the group of newcomers enter. They saw them deliberately murder their friend and the survivors of his family.

Plague-stricken or merely terrified people—in pairs or trios widely separated through the city— communicated in swift desperation. It was possible that there had been a mistake, a blunder, and an unauthorized crime had been committed. But it was not a mistake. Unthinkable as such an idea was, there developed proof that the plague on Maris III was to be ended as if it were an epizootic among animals. Those who had it and those who had been exposed to it were to be killed to prevent its spread among the newcomers.

A conviction of such horror could not be accepted without absolute proof. But when night fell, the public power supply of the city was cut off and communications ended. The singular sunset hush of Maris III left utter stillness everywhere—except for the screams which echoed among the city's innumerable empty-eyed, unoccupied buildings.

The scant remainder of the plague survivors fled in the night. They fled singly and in groups, carrying the plague with them. Some carried members of their families who were too weak to walk. Others helped already-doomed wives or friends or husbands to the open country. Flight would not save their lives. It would only prevent their murder. But somehow that seemed a thing to be attempted.

"This," said Calhoun, "is not a history of your own case. When did you develop the disease, whatever it may be?"

"Don't you know what it is?" asked Helen hopelessly.

"Not yet," admitted Calhoun. "I've very little information. I'm trying to get more."

He did not mention the information gathered from a dead man in a corn field some miles away.

The girl told of her own case. The first symptom was listlessness. She could pull out of it by making an effort, but it progressed. Day by day more urgent, more violent effort was needed to pay attention to anything, and she noted greater weakness when she tried to act. She felt no discomfort, not even hunger or thirst. She'd had to summon increasing resolution even to become aware of the need to do anything at all.

The symptoms were singularly like those of a man too long at too high an altitude without oxygen. They were even more like those of a man in a non-pressurized flier, whose oxygen supply was cut off. Such a man would pass out without realizing that he was slipping into unconsciousness, only it would happen in minutes. Here the process was infinitely gradual. It was a matter of weeks. But it was the same thing.

"I'd been infected before we ran away," said Helen drearily. "I didn't know it then. Now I know I've a few more days of being able to think and act, if I try hard enough. But it'll be less and less each day. Then I'll stop being able to try."

Calhoun watched the tiny recorder roll its multiple-channel tape from one spool to the other as she talked.

"You had energy enough to try to kill me," he observed.

He looked at the weapon. There was an arched steel spring placed crosswise at the end of a barrel like a sporting blast-gun. Now he saw a handle and a ratchet by which the spring was brought to tension, storing up power to throw the missile. He asked, "Who wound up this crossbow?"

Helen hesitated. "Kim—Kim Walpole," she said finally.

"You're not a solitary refugee now? There are others of your group still alive?"

She hesitated again, and then said, "Some of us

came to realize that staying apart didn't matter. We couldn't hope to live anyhow. We already had the plague. Kim is one of us. He's the strongest. He wound up the crossbow for me. He had the weapons to begin with."

Calhoun asked seemingly casual questions. She told him of a group of fugitives remaining together because all were already doomed. There had been eleven of them. Two were dead now. Three others were in the last lethargy. It was impossible to feed them. They were dying. The strongest was Kim Walpole, who'd ventured back into the city to bring out weapons for the rest. He'd led them, and now was still the strongest and—so the girl considered— the wisest of them all.

They were waiting to die. But the newcomers to the planet—the invaders, they believed—were not content to let them wait. Groups of hunters came out of the city and searched for them.

"Probably," said the girl dispassionately, "to burn our bodies against contagion. They kill us so they won't have to wait. And it just seemed so horrible that we felt we ought to defend our right to die naturally. That's why I shot at you. I shouldn't have, but . . ."

She stopped helplessly. Calhoun nodded.

The fugitives now aided each other simply to avoid murder. They gathered together exhaustedly at nightfall, and those who were strongest did what they could for the others. By day, those who could walk scattered to separate hiding places, so that if one was discovered, the others might still escape the indignity of being butchered. They had no stronger motive than that. They were merely trying to die with dignity, instead of being killed as sick beasts. Which bespoke a tradition and an attitude that Calhoun approved. People like these would know something of the science of probability in human conduct. Only they would call it ethics. But the strangers—the invaders—were of another type. They probably came from another world.

"I don't like this," said Calhoun coldly. "Just a moment."

He went over to Murgatroyd. Murgatroyd seemed to droop a little. Calhoun checked his breathing and listened to his heart. Murgatroyd submitted, saying only *"Chee"* when Calhoun put him down.

"I'm going to help you to your rendezvous," said Calhoun abruptly. "Murgatroyd's got the plague now. I exposed him to it, and he's reacting fast. And I want to see the others of your group before nightfall."

The girl just managed to get to her feet. Even speaking had tired her, but she gamely though wearily moved off at a slant to the hillside's slope. Calhoun picked up the odd weapon and examined it thoughtfully. He wound it up as it was obviously meant to be. He picked up the missile it had fired, and put it in place. He went after the girl, carrying it. Murgatroyd brought up the rear.

Within a quarter of a mile the girl stopped and clung swaying to the trunk of a slender tree. It was plain that she had to rest, and dreaded getting off her feet because of the desperate effort needed to arise.

"I'm going to carry you," said Calhoun firmly. "You tell me the way."

He picked her up bodily and marched on. She was light. She was not a large girl, but she should have weighed more. Calhoun still carried the quaint antique weapon without difficulty.

Murgatroyd followed as Calhoun went up a small incline on the greater hillside and down a very narrow ravine. Through brushwood he pushed until he came to a small open space where shelters had been made for a dozen or so human beings. They were utterly primitive—merely roofs of leafy branches over framework of sticks. But of course they were not intended for permanent use. They were meant only to protect plague-stricken folk while they waited to die.

But there was disaster here. Calhoun saw it before the girl could. There were beds of leaves underneath the shelters. There were three bodies lying upon them. They would be those refugees in the terminal coma which, since the girl had described it, accounted for the dead man Calhoun had found, dead of starvation with food plants all around him. But now Calhoun saw something more. He swung the girl swiftly in his arms so that she would not see. He put her gently down and said, "Stay still. Don't move. Don't turn."

He went to make sure. A moment later he raged. It was Calhoun's profession to combat death and illness in all its forms, and he took his profession seriously. There are defeats, of course, which a medical man has to accept, though unwillingly. But nobody in the profession, and least of all a Med Ship man, could fail to be roused to fury by the sight of people who should have been his patients, lying utterly still with their throats cut.

He covered them with branches. He went back to Helen.

"This place has been found by somebody from the city," he told her harshly. "The men in coma have been murdered. I advise you not to look. At a guess, whoever did it is now trying to track down the rest of you."

He went grimly over the small open glade, searching the ground for footprints. There was ground-cover at most places, but at the edge of the clearing he found one set of heavy footprints leading away. He put his own foot beside a print and rested his weight on it. His foot made a lesser depression. The other print had been made by a man weighing more than

Calhoun. Therefore it was not one of the party of plague victims.

He found another set of such footprints, entering the glade from another spot.

"One man only," he said icily. "He won't think he has to be on guard, because a city's administrative personnel—such as was left behind for the plague to hit—doesn't usually have weapons among their possessions. And he's confident that all of you are weak enough not to be dangerous to him."

Helen did not turn pale. She was pale before. She stared numbly at Calhoun. He looked grimly at the sky.

"It'll be sunset within the hour," he said savagely. "If it's the intention of the newcomers—the invaders— to burn the bodies of all plague victims, he'll come back here to dispose of these three. He didn't do it before lest the smoke warn the rest of you. But he knows the shelters held more than three people. He'll be back!"

Murgatroyd said *"Chee!"* in a bewildered fashion. He was on all fours, and he regarded his paws as if they did not belong to him. He panted.

Calhoun checked him over. Respiration way up. Heart action like that of the girl Helen. His temperature was not up, but down. Calhoun said remorsefully, "You and I, Murgatroyd, have a bad time of it in our profession. But mine is the worse. You don't have to play dirty tricks on me, and I've had to, on you!"

Murgatroyd said *"Chee!"* and whimpered. Calhoun laid him gently on a bed of leaves which was not occupied by a murdered man.

"Lie still!" he commanded. "Exercise is bad for you."

He walked away. Murgatroyd whined faintly, but lay still as if exhausted.

"I'm going to move you," Calhoun told the girl, "so

you won't be seen if that man from the city comes back. And I've got to keep out of sight for a while or your friends will mistake me for him. I count on you to vouch for me later. Basically, I'm making an ambush." Then he explained irritably, "I daren't try to trail him because he might not backtrack to return here."

He lifted the girl and placed her where she could see the glade in its entirety, but would not be visible. He settled down himself a little distance away. He was acutely dissatisfied with the measures he was forced to take. He could not follow the murderer and leave Helen and Murgatroyd unprotected, even though the murderer might find another victim because he was not being trailed. In any case Murgatroyd's life, just now, was more important than the life of any human being on Maris III. On him depended everything.

But Calhoun was not pleased with himself at all.

There was silence except for the normal noises of living wild things. There were fluting sounds, which later Calhoun would be told came from crawling creatures not too much unlike the land turtles of Earth. There were deep-bass hummings, which came from the throats of miniature creatures which might roughly be described as birds. There were chirpings which were the cries of what might be approximately described as wild pigs, except that they weren't. But the sun Maris sank low toward the nearer hillcrests, and behind them, and there came a strange, expectant hush over all the landscape. At sundown on Maris III there is a singular period when the creatures of the day are silent and those of the night are not yet active. Nothing moved. Nothing stirred. Even the improbable foliage was still.

It was into this stillness and this half-light that small and intermittent rustling sounds entered. Presently there was a faint murmur of speech. A tall, gaunt young man came out of the brushwood, supporting a pathetically feeble old man, barely able to walk. Calhoun made a gesture of warning as the girl Helen opened her lips to speak. The slowly moving pair came into the glade, the young man moving exhaustedly, the old man staggering with weakness despite his help. The younger helped the older to sit down. He stood panting.

A woman and a man came together, assisting each other. There was barely light enough from the sun's afterglow to show their faces, emaciated and white.

A fifth feeble figure came tottering out of another opening in the brush. He was dark-bearded and broad, and he had been a powerful man. But now the plague lay heavily upon him.

They greeted each other listlessly. They had not yet discovered those of their number who had been murdered.

The gaunt young man summoned his strength and moved toward the shelter where Calhoun had covered an unseemly sight with branches.

Murgatroyd whimpered.

There came another rustling sound, but this had nothing of feebleness in it. Branches were pushed forthrightly out of the way and a man came striding confidently into the small open space. He was well-fleshed, and his color was excellent. Calhoun automatically judged him to be in superlative good health, slightly overweight, and of that physical type which suffers very few psychosomatic troubles because it lives strictly and enjoyably in the present.

Calhoun stood up. He stepped out into the fading light just as the sturdy stranger grinned at the group of plague-stricken semi-skeletons.

"Back, eh?" he said amiably. "Saved me a lot of trouble. I'll make one job of it."

With leisurely confidence he reached to the blaster at his hip.

"Drop it!" snapped Calhoun from behind him. "Drop it!"

The sturdy man whirled. He saw Calhoun with a crossbow raised to cover him. There was light enough to show that it was not a blast-rifle—in fact, that it was no weapon of any kind modern men would ordinarily use. But much more significant to the sturdy man was the fact that Calhoun wore a uniform and was in good health.

He snatched out his blast-pistol with professional alertness.

And Calhoun shot him with the crossbow. It happened that he shot him dead.

IV

> "Statistically, it must be recognized that no human action is
> without consequences to the man who acts. Again
> statistically, it must be recognized that the consequences of
> an action tend with strong probability to follow the general
> pattern of the action. A violent action, for example, has a
> strong probability of violent consequences, and since at
> least some of the consequences of an act must affect the
> person acting, a man who acts violently exposes himself to
> the probability that chance consequences which affect him,
> if unfavorable, will be violently so."
>
> *Probability and Human Conduct*—Fitzgerald

Murgatroyd had been inoculated with a blood
sample from the girl Helen some three hours or less
before sunset. But it was one of the more valuable
genetic qualities of the *tormal* race that they reacted
to bacterial infection as a human being reacts to
medication. Medicine on the skin of a human being
rarely has any systemic effect. Medication on mucous

membrane penetrates better. Ingested medication—medicine that is swallowed—has greater effectiveness still. But substances injected into tissues or the bloodstream have the most effect of all. A centigram of almost any drug administered by injection will have an effect close to that of a gram taken orally. It acts at once and there is no modification by gastric juices.

Murgatroyd had had half a cubic centimeter of the girl's blood injected into the spot on his flank where he could feel no pain. It contained the unknown cause of the plague on Maris III. Its effect as injected was incomparably greater than the same infective material smeared on his skin or swallowed. In either such case, of course, it would have had no effect at all, because *tormals* were to all intents and purposes immune to ordinary contagions. Just as they had a built-in unit in their digestive tract to cause the instant rejection of unwholesome food, their body cells had a built-in ability to produce antibodies immediately if the toxin of a pathogenic organism came into contact with them. So *tormals* were effectively safe against any disease transmitted by ordinary methods of infection. Yet if a culture of pathogenic bacteria, say, were injected into their bloodstream, their whole body was attacked, and all at once. There was practically no incubation period.

Murgatroyd, who had been given the plague in mid-afternoon, was reacting violently to its toxins by sunset. But two hours after darkness fell he arose and said shrilly, *"Chee-chee-chee!"* He'd been sunk in heavy slumber. When he woke, there was a small fire in the glade, about which the exhausted, emaciated fugitives consulted with Calhoun.

Calhoun was saying bitterly, "The whole thing is wrong! It's self-contradictory, and that means a man, or men, trying to meddle with the way the universe was made to run. Those characters in the city aren't fighting the plague—they're cooperating with it! When I came in a Med Ship, they should have welcomed my help. Instead they tried to kill me so I couldn't perform the function I was made for and trained for! They're going against the way the universe works. From what Helen tells me, they landed with the purpose of helping the plague wipe out everybody else on the planet. They began their butchery immediately. That's why you people ran away."

The weary, weakened people listened almost numbly.

"The invaders—and that's what they are," said Calhoun angrily, "have to be immune and know it, or else they wouldn't risk contagion by tracking you down to murder you. The city's infected and they're not alarmed. You're dying and they only try to hasten your death. I arrive, and I might be of use, so they try to kill me. They must know what the plague is and what it does, because their only criticism of it seems to be that it doesn't kill fast enough. And that is out of the ordinary course of nature. It's not intelligent human conduct."

Murgatroyd peered about. He'd just waked, and the look of his surroundings had changed entirely while he slept.

"A plague's not pleasant, but it's natural. This plague is neither pleasant *nor* natural. There's human interference with the normal course of events—certainly the way things are going is abnormal. I'm not too sure somebody didn't direct this from the beginning. That's why I shot that man with the crossbow instead of taking a blaster to him. I meant to wound him so I could make him answer questions, but the crossbow's not an accurate weapon and it happened that I killed him instead. There wasn't much information in the stuff in his pockets. The only significant item was a ground-car key, and that only means there's a car waiting for him to come back from hunting you."

The gaunt young man said drearily, "He didn't come from Dettra, which is our planet. Fashions are different on different worlds, and he wears a uniform we don't have. His clothing uses fasteners we don't use, too. He's from another solar system entirely."

Murgatroyd saw Calhoun and rushed to him. He embraced Calhoun's legs with enthusiasm. He chattered shrilly of his relief at finding the man he knew. The skeletonlike plague victims stared at him.

"This," said Calhoun with infinite relief, "is Murgatroyd. He's had the plague and is over it. So now we'll get you people cured. I wish I had better light!"

He counted Murgatroyd's breathing and listened to his heart. Murgatroyd was in that state of boisterous good health which is standard in any well-cared-for lower animal, but amounts to genius in a *tormal*. Calhoun regarded him with deep satisfaction.

"All right!" he said. "Come along!"

He plucked a brand of burning resinous stuff from the campfire. He handed it to the gaunt young man and led the way. Murgatroyd ambled complacently after him. Calhoun stopped under one of the unoccupied shelters and got out his lab kit. He bent over Murgatroyd. What he did, did not hurt. When he stood up, he squinted at the red fluid in the instrument he'd used.

"About twenty cc's," he observed. "This is strictly emergency stuff I'm doing now. But I'd say that there's an emergency."

The gaunt young man said, "I'd say you've doomed yourself. The incubation period seems to be about six days. It took that long to develop among the doctors we had on the office staff."

Calhoun opened a compartment of the kit, whose

miniscule test tubes and pipettes gleamed in the torch-light. He absorbedly transferred the reddish fluid to a miniature filter-barrel, piercing a self-healing plastic cover to do so. He said, "You're a pre-med of course. The way you talk—"

"I was an intern," said Kim. "Now I'm pre-corpse."

"I doubt that last," said Calhoun. "But I wish I had some distilled water . . . this is anticoagulant." He added a trace of a drop to the sealed, ruddy fluid. He shook the whole filter to agitate it. The instrument was hardly bigger than his thumb. "Now a clumper . . ." He added a minute quantity of a second substance from an almost microscopic ampule. He shook the filter again. "You can guess what I'm doing. With a decent lab I'd get the structure and formula of the antibody Murgatroyd has so obligingly turned out for us. We'd set to work synthesizing it, and in twenty hours we would have it coming out of the reaction flasks in quantity. But there is no lab."

"There's one in the city," said the gaunt young man hopelessly. "It was for the colonists who were to come. And we were staffed to give them proper medical care. When the plague came, our doctors did everything imaginable. They not only tried the usual culture tricks, but they cultured samples of every separate tissue in fatal cases. They never found a single organism, even with electron microscopes, that would produce the plague." He said with a sort of weary pride, "Those who'd been exposed worked until they had the plague, and then others took over. Every man worked as long as he could make his brain serve him."

Calhoun squinted through the glass tube of the filter at the light of the sputtering torch.

"Almost clumped," he said. Then he added, "I suspect there's been some very fine laboratory work done

somewhere to give the invaders their confidence of
immunity to this plague. They landed and instantly set
to work to mop up the city—to complete the job the
plague hadn't quite finished. I suspect there could have
been some fine lab work done to make plague mechanism undetectable. I don't like the things I'm forced
to suspect!"

He inspected the glass filter again.

"Somebody," he said coldly, "considered that my
arrival would be an unfavorable circumstance to him
and what he wanted to happen. I think it is. He tried
to kill me. He didn't. I'm afraid I consider his existence an unfavorable circumstance." He paused, and
said very measuredly, "Cooperating with a plague is
a highly technical business; it needs as much information as fighting a plague. Cooperation could no more
be done from a distance than fighting it. If the invaders
had come to fight the plague, they'd have sent their
best medical men to help. If they came to assist it,
they'd have sent butchers, but they'd also send the very
best man they had to make sure that nothing went
wrong with the plague itself. The logical man to be
field director of the extermination project would be
the man who'd worked out the plague himself." He
paused again, and said icily, "I'm no judge to pass on
anybody's guilt or innocence or fate, but as a Med
Service man I've authority to take measures against
health hazards!"

He began to press the plunger of the filter, judging by the wavering light of the torch. The piston was
itself the filter, and on one side a clear, mobile liquid began very slowly to appear.

"Just to be sure, though—you said there was a lab
in the city and the doctors found nothing."

"Nothing," agreed Kim hopelessly. "There'd been a
complete bacteriological survey of the planet. Nothing

new appeared. Everybody's oral and intestinal flora were normal. Naturally, no alien bug would be able to compete with the strains we humans have been living with for thousands of years. So there wasn't anything unknown in any culture from any patient."

"There could have been a mutation," said Calhoun. He watched the clear serum increase. "But if your doctors couldn't pass the disease—"

"They could!" said Kim bitterly. "A massive shot of assorted bugs would pass it, breathed or swallowed or smeared on the skin. Experimental animals could be given the plague. But no one organism could be traced as giving it. No pure culture would!"

Calhoun continued to watch the clear fluid develop on the delivery side of the filter piston. Presently there was better than twelve cubic centimeters of clear serum on one side, and an almost solid block of clumped blood cells on the other. He drew off the transparent fluid with a fine precision.

"We're working under far from aseptic conditions," he said wryly, "but we have to take the chances. Anyhow, I'm getting a hunch. A pathogenic mechanism that isn't a single, identifiable bug—it's not natural. It smells of the laboratory, just as uniformed murderers who are immune to a plague do. It's not too wild a guess to suspect that somebody worked out the plague as well as the immunization of the invaders. That it was especially designed to baffle the doctors who might try to fight it."

"It did," agreed Kim bitterly.

"So," said Calhoun, "maybe a pure culture wouldn't carry the plague. Maybe the disaster-producing apparatus simply isn't there when you make pure cultures. There's even a reason to suspect something specific. Murgatroyd was a very sick animal. I've only known of one previous case in which a *tormal* reacted as

violently as Murgatroyd did to an injection. That case
had us sweating."

"If I were going to live," said Kim grimly, "I might
ask what it was."

"Since you're going to," Calhoun told him, "I'll tell
you. It was a pair of organisms. Separately, they were
so near harmless as makes no difference. Together,
their toxins combined to be pure poison. It was synergy. They were a synergic pair which, together, were
like high explosive. That one was the devil to track
down!"

He went back across the glade. Murgatroyd came
skipping after him, scratching at the anesthetic patch
on his side.

"You go first," said Calhoun briefly to Helen Jons.
"This is an antibody serum. You may itch afterward,
but I doubt it. Your arm, please."

She bared her pitifully thin arm. He gave her practically a cc of fluid which—plus corpuscles and some
forty-odd other essential substances—had been circu-
lating in Murgatroyd's bloodstream not long since. The
blood corpuscles had been clumped and removed by
one compound plus the filter, and the anticoagulant
had neatly modified most of the others. In a matter
of minutes, the lab kit had prepared as usable a serum
as any animal-using technique would produce. Logically, the antibodies it contained should be isolated and
their chemical structure determined. They should be
synthesized, and the synthetic antibody-complex administered to plague victims. But Calhoun faced a group
of people doomed to die. He could only use his field
kit to product a small-scale miracle for them. He could
not do a mass-production job.

"Next!" said Calhoun. "Tell them what it's all about,
Kim."

The gaunt young man bared his own arm. "If what

he says is so, this will cure us. If it isn't so, nothing can do us any more harm."

And Calhoun briskly gave them, one after another, the shots of what ought to be a curative serum for an unidentified disease which he suspected was not caused by any single germ, but by a partnership. Synergy is an acting together. Charcoal will burn quietly. Liquid air will not burn at all. But the two together constitute a violent explosive. The ancient simple drug sulfa is not intoxicating. A glass of wine is not intoxicating. But the two together have the kick of dynamite. Synergy in medicine is a process by which, when one substance with one effect is given in combination with another substance with another effect, the two together have the consequences of a third substance intensified to fourth or fifth or tenth power.

"I think," said Calhoun when he'd finished, "that by morning you'll feel better—perhaps cured of the plague entirely and only weak from failure to force yourselves to take nourishment. If it turns out that way, then I advise you all to get as far away from the city as possible for a considerable while. I think this planet is going to be repopulated. I suspect that shiploads of colonists are on the way here now, but not from Dettra, which built the city. And I definitely guess that, sick or well, you're going to be in trouble if or when you contact the new colonists."

They looked tiredly at him. They were a singular lot of people. Each one seemed half-starved, yet their eyes had not the brightness of suffering. They looked weary beyond belief, and yet there was no self-neglect. They were of that singular human type which maintains human civilization against the inertia of the race, because it drives itself to get needed things done. It is not glamorous, this dogged part of mankind which keeps things going. It is sometimes absurd. For dying folk to wash themselves when even such exertion calls for enormous resolution is not exactly rational. To help each other to try to die with dignity was much more a matter of self-respect than of intellectual decision. But as a Med Ship man, Calhoun viewed them with some warmth. They were the type that has to be called on when an emergency occurs and the wealth-gathering type tends to flee and the low time-sense part of a population inclines to riot or loot or worse.

Now they waited listlessly for their own deaths.

"There's no exact precedent for what's happened here," explained Calhoun. "A thousand years or so ago there was a king of France—a country back on old Earth—who tried to wipe out a disease called leprosy by executing all the people who had it. But lepers were a nuisance. They couldn't work. They had to be fed by charity. They died in inconvenient places and only other lepers dared handled their bodies. They tended to throw normal human life out of kilter. That wasn't the case here. The man I killed wanted you dead for another reason. He and his friends wanted you dead right away."

The gaunt Kim Walpole said tiredly, "He wanted to dispose of our bodies in a sanitary fashion."

"Nonsense!" snapped Calhoun. "The city's infected. You lived, ate, breathed, walked in it. Nobody can dare use that city unless they know how the contagion's transmitted, and how to counteract it. Your own colonists turned back. These men wouldn't have landed if they hadn't known they were safe!"

There was silence.

"If the plague is an intended crime," added Calhoun, "you are the witnesses to it. You've got to be gotten rid of before colonists from somewhere other than Dettra arrive here."

The dark-bearded man growled, "Monstrous! Monstrous!"

"Agreed," said Calhoun. "But there's no interstellar government now, any more than there was a planetary government in the old days back on Earth. So if somebody pirates a colony ready to be occupied, there's no authority able to throw them out. The only recourse would be war. And nobody is going to start an interplanetary war—not with the bombs that can be landed! If the invaders can land a population here, they can keep the place." He paused, and said with irony, "Of course they could be persuaded that they were wrong."

But that was not even worth thinking about. In the computation of probabilities in human conduct, self-interest is a high-value factor. Children and barbarians have clear ideas of justice due *to* them, but no idea at all of justice due *from* them. And though human colonies spread toward the galaxy's rim, there was still a large part of every population which was civilized only in that it could use tools. Most people still remained comfortably barbaric or childish in their emotional lives. It was a fact that had to be considered in Calhoun's profession. It bore remarkably on matters of contagion, and health, and life itself.

"You'll have to hide. Perhaps permanently," he told them. "It depends partly on what happens to me, however. I have to go to the city. There's a very serious health problem there."

Kim said with irony, "In the city? Everybody's healthy there. They're so healthy that they come out to hunt us down for sport!"

"Considering that the city's thoroughly infected, their immunity is a health problem," said Calhoun. "But besides that, it looks like the original cause of the plague is there, too. I'd guess that the originator of this plague is technical director of the exterminating operation that's in progress on this planet. I'd guess he's in the ship that brought the butcher-invaders. I'd be willing to bet that he's got a very fine laboratory on the ship."

Kim stared at him. He clenched and unclenched his hands.

"And I'd say it ought to be quite useless to fight this plague before that man and that laboratory were taken care of," said Calhoun. "You people are probably all right. I think you'll wake up feeling better. You may be well. But if the plague is artificial, if it was developed to make a colony planet useless to the world that built it, but healthy for people who want to seize it . . ."

"What?"

"It may be the best plague that was developed for the purpose, but you can be sure it's not the only one. Dozens of strains of deadly bugs would have to be developed to be sure of getting the deadliest. Different kinds of concealment would have to be tried, in case somebody guessed the synergy trick, as I did, and could do something about the first plague used. There'd have to be a second and third and fourth plague available. You see?"

Kim nodded, speechless.

"A setup like that is a real health hazard," said Calhoun. "As a Med Service man, I have to deal with it. It's much more important than your life or mine or Murgatroyd's. So I have to go into the city to do what can be done. Meanwhile, you'd better lie down now. Give Murgatroyd's antibodies a chance to work."

Kim started to move away. Then he said, "You've been exposed. Have you protected yourself?"

"Give me a quarter-cc shot," said Calhoun. "That should do."

He handed the injector to the gaunt young man. He noted the deftness with which Kim handled it. Then he helped get the survivors of the original group—there were six of them now—to the leafy beds under the shelters. They were very quiet, even more quiet than their illness demanded. They were very polite. The old man and woman who'd struggled back to the glade together made a special effort to bid Calhoun good night with the courtesy appropriate to city folk of tradition.

Calhoun settled down to keep watch through the night. Murgatroyd snuggled confidingly close to him. There was silence.

But not complete silence. The night of Maris III was filled with tiny noises, and some not so faint. There were little squeaks which seemed to come from all directions, including overhead. There were chirpings which were definitely at ground level. There was a sound like effortful grunting in the direction of the hills. In the lowlands there was a rumbling which moved very slowly from one place to another. By its rate of motion, Calhoun guessed that a pack or herd of small animals was making a night journey and uttering deep-bass noises as it traveled.

He debated certain grim possibilities. The man he'd killed had had a ground-car key in his pocket. He'd probably come out in a powered vehicle. He might have had a companion, and the method of hunting down fugitives—successful, in his case—was probably well established. That companion might come looking for him, so watchfulness was necessary.

Meanwhile, there was the plague. The idea of synergy was still most plausible. Suppose the toxins—the poisonous metabolic products—of two separate kinds of bacteria combined to lessen the ability of the blood to carry oxygen and scavenge away carbon dioxide? It would be extremely difficult to identify the pair, and the symptoms would be accounted for. No pure culture of any organism to be found would give the plague. Each, by itself, would be harmless. Only a combination of the two would be injurious. And if so much was assumed, and the blood lost its capacity to carry oxygen, mental listlessness would be the first symptom of all. The brain requires a high oxygen level in its blood supply if it is to work properly. Let a man's brain be gradually, slowly, starved of oxygen and all the noted effects would follow. His other organs would slow down, but at a lesser rate. He would not remember to eat. His blood would still digest food and burn away its own fat—though more and more sluggishly, while his brain worked only foggily. He would become only semiconscious, and then there would come a time of coma when unconsciousness claimed him and his body lived on only as an idling machine, until it ran out of fuel and died.

Calhoun tried urgently to figure out a synergic combination which might make a man's blood cease to do its work. Perhaps only minute quantities of the dual poison might be needed. It might work as an antivitamin or an antienzyme, or—

The invaders of the city were immune, though. Quite possibly the same antibodies Murgatroyd had produced were responsible for their safety. Somewhere, somebody had very horribly used the science of medicine to commit a monstrous crime. But medicine was still a science. It was still a body of knowledge of natural law. And natural laws are consistent and work together toward that purpose for which the universe was made.

He heard a movement across the clearing. He reached for his blaster. Then he saw what the motion was. It was Kim Walpole, intolerably weary, trudging with infinite effort to where Helen Jons lay. Calhoun heard him ask heavily, "You're all right?"

"Yes, Kim," said the girl softly. "I couldn't sleep. I'm wondering if we can hope."

Kim didn't answer.

"If we live . . ." said the girl yearningly. She stopped.

Calhoun felt that he ought to put his fingers in his ears. The conversation was strictly private. But he needed to be on guard, so he coughed, to give notice that he heard. Kim called to him, "Calhoun?"

"Yes," said Calhoun. "If you two talk, I suggest that you do it in whispers. I'm going to watch in case the man I killed had a companion who might come looking for him. One question, though. If the plague is artificial, it had to be started. Did a ship land here two weeks or a month before your workmen began to be ill? It could have come from anywhere."

"There was no landing of any ship," said Kim. "No."

Calhoun frowned. His reasoning seemed airtight. The plague must have been introduced here from somewhere else!

"There had to be," he insisted. "Any kind of ship! From anywhere!"

"There wasn't," repeated Kim. "We had no off-planet communication for three months before the plague appeared. There's been no ship here at all except from Dettra, with supplies and workmen and that sort of thing."

Calhoun scowled. This was impossible. Then Helen's voice sounded very faintly. Kim made a murmurous response. Then he said, "Helen reminds me that there was a queer roll of thunder one night not long before the plague began. She's not sure it means anything, but in the middle of the night, with all the stars shining, thunder rolled back and forth across the sky above the city. This was a week or two before the plague. It waked everybody. Then it rolled away to the horizon and beyond. The weather people had no explanation for it."

Calhoun considered. Murgatroyd nestled still closer to him. He snapped his fingers suddenly.

"That was it!" he said savagely. "That's the trick! I haven't all the answers, but I know some very fine questions to ask now. And I think I know where to ask them."

He settled back. Murgatroyd slept. There was the faintest possible murmur of voices where Kim Walpole and the girl Helen talked wistfully of the possibility of hope.

Calhoun contemplated the problem before him. There were very, very few survivors of the people who belonged in the city. There was a shipload of murderers—butchers!—who had landed to see that the last of them were destroyed. Undoubtedly there was a highly trained and probably brilliant microbiologist in the invaders' expedition. One would be needed, to make sure of the success of the plague and to verify the absolute protection of the butchers, so that other colonists could come here to take over and use the planet. There could be no failure of protection for the people *not* of Dettra who expected to inhabit this world. There would have to be completely competent supervision of this almost unthinkable, this monstrous stealing of a world.

"The plague would probably be a virus pair," muttered Calhoun. "Probably introduced and scattered by a ship with wings *and* rockets. It'd have wings because it wouldn't want to land, but did want to sweep back and forth over the city. It'd drop frozen pellets of the double virus culture. They'd drop down toward the ground, melting and evaporating as they fell, and they'd flow over the city as an invisible, descending blanket of contagion coating everything. Then the ship would head away over the horizon and out to space on its rockets. Its wings wouldn't matter out of atmosphere and it'd go into overdrive and go back home to wait . . ."

He felt an icy anger, more savage than any rage could be. With this technique, a confederation of human beings utterly without pity could become parasitic on other worlds. They could take over any world by destroying its people, and no other people could make any effective protest, because the stolen world would be useless except to the murderers who had taken it over. This affair on Maris III might be merely a test of the new ruthlessness. The murderer planet could spread its ghastly culture like a cancer through the galaxy.

But there were two other things involved beside a practice of conquest through murder by artificial plagues. One was what would happen to the people—the ordinary, commonplace citizens—of a civilization which spread and subsisted by such means. It would not be good for them. In the aggregate, they'd be worse off than the people who died.

The other?

"They might make a field test of their system," said Calhoun very coldly, "without doing anything more serious to the Med Service than killing one man—me—and destroying one small Med Ship. But they couldn't adopt this system on any sort of scale without destroying the Med Service first. I'm beginning to dislike this business excessively!"

V

"Very much of physical science is merely the comprehension of long-observed facts. In human conduct there is a long tradition of observation, but a very brief record of comprehension. For example, human lives in contact with other human lives follow the rules of other ecological systems. All too often, however, a man imagines that an ecological system is composed only of things, whereas such a system operates through the actions of things. It is not possible for any part of an ecological complex to act upon the other parts without being acted upon in its turn. So that it follows that it is singularly stupid——but amazingly common——for an individual to assume human society to be passive and unreactive. He may assume that he can do what he pleases, but inevitably there is a reaction as energetic as his action, and as well-directed. Moreover, probability . . ."

Probability and Human Conduct——Fitzgerald

An hour after sunrise Calhoun's shoulder pack was empty of food. The refugees arose, and they were weak

and ravenous. Their respiration had slowed to normal.
Their pulses no longer pounded. Their eyes were no
longer dull, but very bright. But they were in advanced
states of malnutrition, and now were aware of it. Their
brains were again receiving adequate oxygen and their
metabolism was at normal level—and they knew they
were starving.

Calhoun served as cook. He trudged to the spring
that Helen described. He brought back water. While
they sucked on sweet tablets from his rations and
watched with hungry eyes, he made soup from the
dehydrated rations he'd carried for Murgatroyd and
himself. He gave it to them as the first thing their
stomachs were likely to digest.

He watched as they fed themselves. The elderly man
and woman sipped delicately, looking at each other.
The man with the broad dark beard ate with tremendous self-restraint. Helen fed the weakest, oldest man,
between spoonsful for herself, and Kim Walpole ate
slowly, brooding.

Calhoun kept them going, slowly providing them
with food, until he had no more to offer. By then they
had made highly satisfying gains in strength. But it was
then late morning.

He drew Kim aside.

"During the night," he said, "I got another lot of
serum ready. I'm leaving it with you, with an injector. You'll find other fugitives. I gave you massive doses.
You'd better be stingy. Try half-cc shots. Maybe you
can skimp that."

"What about you?" demanded Kim.

Calhoun shrugged.

"I've got an awful lot of authority, if I can make it
stick," he said dryly. "As a Med Ship man I've power
to take complete charge of any health emergency. You
people have a plague here. That's one emergency. It's

artificial. That's another. The people who've spread it here have reason, in their success to date on this planet, to think they can take over any other world they choose. And, human nature being what it is, that's the biggest health hazard in history. I've got to get to work on it."

"There's a shipload of armed murderers here," said Kim.

"I'm not much interested in them," admitted Calhoun. "I want to get at the man who's at the head of this thing. As I told you, he should have other plagues in stock. It's entirely possible that the operation here is no more than a small-scale field test of a new technique for conquest."

"If those butchers find you, you'll be killed."

"True," admitted Calhoun. "But the number of chance happenings that could favor me is much greater than the number that could favor them. I'm working with nature, and they're working against it. Anyhow, as a Med Service man, I should prevent the landing of anybody—anybody at all—on a plague-stricken planet like this. And I suspect there are plans for landings. I should set up an effective quarantine."

His tone was dry. Kim Walpole stared. "You mean you'll try to stop them?"

"I shall try," said Calhoun, "to implement the authority vested in me by the Med Service for such cases as this. The rules about quarantine are rather strict."

"You'll be killed," said Kim again.

Calhoun ignored the repeated prediction.

"That invader found you," he observed, "because he knew that you'd have to drink. So he found a brook and followed it up, looking for signs of humans drinking from it. He found footprints about the spring. I found his footprints there, too. That's the trick you'll use to find other fugitives. But pass on the word not to leave tracks hereafter. For the other advice, I advise you to get all the weapons you can. Modern ones, of course. You've got the blaster from the man I killed."

"I think," said Kim between his teeth, "that I'll get some more. If hunters from the city do track us to our drinking places, I'll know how to get more weapons!"

"Yes," agreed Calhoun. "Now. Murgatroyd made the antibodies that cured you. As a general rule, you can expect antibody production in your own bodies once an infection begins to be licked. In case of extreme emergency, each of you can probably supply antibodies for a fair number of other plague victims. You might try serum from blisters you produce on your skin. Quite often antibodies turn up there. I don't guarantee it, but sometimes it works."

He paused. Kim Walpole said harshly, "But you! Isn't there anything we can do for you?"

"I was going to ask you something," said Calhoun. He produced the telephoto films of the city as photographed from space. "There's a laboratory in the city. A biochemistry lab. Show me where to look for it."

Walpole gave explicit directions, pointing out the spot on the photo. Calhoun nodded. Then Kim said fiercely, "But tell us something we can do! We'll be strong, presently, and we'll have weapons. We'll track downstream to where hunters leave their ground-cars and be equipped with them. We can help you!"

Calhoun nodded approvingly.

"Right. If you see the smoke of a good-sized fire in the city, and if you've got a fair number of fairly strong men with you, and if you've got ground-cars, you might investigate. But be cagey about it. Very cagey!"

"If you signal we'll come," said Kim Walpole grimly, "no matter how few we are."

"Fine," said Calhoun. He had no intention of calling on these weakened, starving people for help.

He swung his depleted pack on his back again and slipped away from the glade. He made his way to the spring, which flowed up clear and cool from unseen depths. He headed down the little brook which flowed away from it. Murgatroyd raced along its banks. He hated to get his paws wet. Presently, where the underbrush grew thickly close to the water's edge, Murgatroyd wailed, *"Chee! Chee!"* Calhoun plucked him from the ground and set him on his shoulder. Murgatroyd clung blissfully there as Calhoun followed down the stream bed. He adored being carried.

Two miles down, there was another cultivated field. This one was planted with an outsized root crop, and Calhoun walked past shoulder-high bushes with four-inch blue-and-white flowers. He recognized the plant as one of the family Solanaceae—belladonna was still used in medicine—but he couldn't identify it until he dug up a root and found a tuber. But the six-pound specimen he uncovered was still too young and green to be eaten. Murgatroyd refused to touch it.

Calhoun was ruefully considering the limitations of specialized training when he came to the end of the cultivated field. There was a highway. It was new, of course. City, fields, highways, and all the physical aspects of civilized life had been built on this planet before the arrival of the colonists who were to inhabit it. It was extraordinary to see such preparations for a population not yet on hand. But Calhoun was much more interested in the ground-car he found waiting on the highway, hard by a tiny bridge under which a small brook flowed.

The key he'd taken from the dead invader fitted. He got in the car and beckoned Murgatroyd to the seat beside him.

"Characters like the man I killed, Murgatroyd," he observed, "aren't very important. They're mere butchers—killers. That sort of character likes to loot. There's nothing here for them to loot. They're bound to be bored. They're bound to be restless. We won't have much trouble with them. I'm worrying about the man who possibly designed and is certainly supervising the action of the plague. I look for trouble with him."

The ground-car was in motion then, toward the city. He drove on.

It was a good twenty miles, but he did not encounter a single other vehicle. Presently the city lay spread out before him. He surveyed it thoughtfully. It was very beautiful. Fifty generations of architects on many worlds had played with stone and steel, groping for perfection. This city was a close approach. There were towers which glittered whitely, and low buildings which seemed to nestle on the vegetation-covered ground. There were soaring bridges and gracefully curving highways, and park areas laid out and ready. There was no monotony anywhere.

The only exception to gracefulness was the massive landing grid, half a mile high and a mile across, which was a lacework of monster steel girders with spider-thin wires of copper woven about them in the complex curves its operation required. Inside it, Calhoun could see the ship of the invaders. It had landed in the grid enclosure, and later Calhoun had blown out the transformers of the grid. They were probably in process of repair now. But the ship stood sturdily on the ground inside the great structure which dwarfed it.

"The man we're after will be in that ship, Murgatroyd," said Calhoun. "He'll have inner and outer lock-doors fastened, and he'll be inside a six-inch beryllium-steel wall. Rather difficult to break in upon.

And he'll be uneasy. An intellectual type gone wrong doesn't feel at ease with the kind of butchers he has to associate with. I think the problem is to get him to invite us into his parlor. But it may not be simple."

"*Chee*," said Murgatroyd doubtfully.

"Oh, we'll manage," Calhoun assured him. "Somehow!"

He spread out his photographs. Kim Walpole had marked where he should go and a route to it. Having been in the city while it was being built, he knew even the service lanes which, being sunken, were not a part of the city's good looks.

"But the invaders," explained Calhoun, "won't deign to use grubby service lanes. They consider themselves aristocrats because they were sent to be conquerors, though the work required of them was simple butchery. I wonder what sort of swine run the world they came from!"

He put away the photos and headed for the city again. He branched off the main highway, near the city. A turn-off descended into a cut. The road in the cut was intended for loads of agricultural produce entering the city. It was strictly utilitarian. It ran below the surface of the park areas, and entered the city without pride. When among the buildings it ran between rows of undecorated gates, behind which waste matter was destined to be collected to be carted away as fertilizer for the fields. The city was very well designed.

Rolling through the echoing sunken road, Calhoun saw, just once, a ground-car in motion on a far-flung, cobwebby bridge between two tall towers. It was high overhead. Nobody in it would be watching grubby commerce roads.

The whole affair was very simple indeed. Calhoun brought the car to a stop beneath the overhang of a balconied building many stories high. He got out and opened the gate. He drove the car into the cavernous, so-far-unused lower part of the building. He closed the gate behind him. He was in the center of the city, and his presence was unknown. This was at three or later in the afternoon.

He climbed a clean new flight of steps and came to the sections the public would use. There were glassy walls which changed their look as one moved between them. There were the lifts. Calhoun did not try to use them. He led Murgatroyd up the circular ramps which led upward in case of unthinkable emergency. He and Murgatroyd plodded up and up. Calhoun kept count.

On the fifth level there were signs of use, while all the others had that dusty cleanness of a structure which has been completed but not yet occupied.

"Here we are," said Calhoun cheerfully.

But he had his blaster in his hand when he opened the door of the laboratory. It was empty. He looked approvingly about as he hunted for the storeroom. It was a perfectly equipped biological laboratory, and it had been in use. Here the few doomed physicians awaiting the city's population had worked desperately against the plague. Calhoun saw the trays of cultures they'd made, dried up and dead now. Somebody had turned over a chair. Probably when the laboratory was searched by the invaders, in case someone not of their kind still remained alive in it.

He found the storeroom. Murgatroyd watched with bright eyes as he rummaged.

"Here we have the things men use to cure each other," said Calhoun oracularly. "Practically every one a poison save for its special use! Here's an assortment of spores—pathogenic organisms, Murgatroyd. They have their uses. And here are drugs which are synthesized nowadays, but are descended from the poisons found on the spears of savages. Great helps in medicine. And here are the anesthetics—poisons too. These are what I am counting on."

He chose, very painstakingly. Dextrethyl. Polysulfate. The one marked inflammable and dangerous. The other with the maximum permissible dose on its label, and the names of counteracting substances which would neutralize it. He burdened himself. Murgatroyd reached up a paw. Since Calhoun was carrying something, he wanted to carry something, too.

They went down the circular ramp again as sunset drew near. Calhoun searched once more in the below-surface levels of the buildings. He found what he wanted—a painter's vortex-gun which would throw "smoke rings" of tiny paint droplets at a wall or object to be painted. One could vary the size of the ring at impact from a bare inch to a three-foot spread.

Calhoun cleaned the paint-gun. He was meticulous about it. He filled its tank with dextrethyl brought down from the laboratory. He piled the empty containers out of sight.

"This trick," he observed, as he picked up the paint-gun again, "was devised to be used on a poor devil of a lunatic who carried a bomb in his pocket for protection against imaginary assassins. It would have devastated a quarter-mile circle, so he had to be handled gently."

He patted his pockets. He nodded.

"Now we go hunting—with an oversized atomizer loaded with dextrethyl. I've polysulfate and an injector to secure each specimen I knock over. Not too good, eh? But if I have to use a blaster I'll have failed."

He looked out a window at the sky. It was now late dusk. He went back to the gate to the service road. He went out and carefully closed it behind him. On foot, with many references to the photomaps, he began to find his way toward the landing grid. It ought to be something like the center of the invaders' location.

It was dark when he climbed other service stairs from the cellar of another building. This was the communications building of the city. It had been the key to the mopping-up process the invaders began on landing. Its callboard would show which apartments had communicators in use. When such a call showed, a murder party could be sent to take care of the caller. Even after the first night, some individual, isolated folk might remain, unaware of what was happening. So there would be somebody on watch, just in case a dying man called for the solace of a human voice while still he lived.

There was a man on watch. Calhoun saw a lighted room. Paint-gun ready, he moved very silently toward it. Murgatroyd padded faithfully behind him.

Outside the door, Calhoun adjusted his curious weapon. He entered. The man nodded in a chair before the lifeless board. When Calhoun entered he raised his head and yawned. He turned.

Calhoun sprayed him with smoke rings—vortex rings. But the rings were spinning missiles of vaporized dextrethyl, that anesthetic developed from ethyl chloride some two hundred years before, and not yet bettered for its special uses. One of its properties was that the faintest whiff of its vapor produced a reflex to gasp. A second property was that, like the ancient ethyl chloride, it was the quickest-acting anesthetic known.

The man by the callboard saw Calhoun. His nostrils caught the odor of dextrethyl. He gasped.

He fell unconscious.

Calhoun waited patiently until the dextrethyl was out of the way. It was almost unique among vapors in that at room temperature it was lighter than air. It rose toward the ceiling. Presently Calhoun moved forward and brought out the polysulfate injector. He bent over the unconscious man. He did not touch him otherwise.

He turned and walked out of the room with Murgatroyd piously marching behind him.

Outside, Calhoun said, "As one medical man to another, perhaps I shouldn't have done that. But I'm dealing with a health hazard, a plague. Sometimes one has to use psychology to supplement standard measures. I consider that the case here. Anyhow this man should be missed sooner than most. He has a job where his failure to act should be noticed."

"*Chee?*" asked Murgatroyd zestfully.

"No," said Calhoun. "He won't die. He wouldn't be so unkind."

It was dark outdoors now. When Calhoun stepped out into the street—he'd touched nothing in the callboard office to show that he'd entered it—nightfall was complete. Stars shone brightly, but the empty, unlighted ways of the city were black. There seemed to be a formless menace in the air. When Calhoun moved down the street, Murgatroyd, who hated the dark, reached up a furry paw and held on to Calhoun's hand for reassurance.

Calhoun moved silently and Murgatroyd's footfalls were inaudible. The feel of the never-lived-in city was appalling. A sleeping city seems ghostly and strange, even with lighted streets. An abandoned city is intolerably desolate, with all its inhabitants gone or dead. But a city which has never lived, which lies lifeless under a night sky because its people never came to occupy it—that city has the worst feeling of all. It seems unnatural. It seems insane. It is like a corpse which could have lived but never acquired a soul, and now waits horribly for something demoniac to enter it and give it a seeming of life too horrifying to imagine.

The invaders unquestionably felt that creeping atmosphere of horror. Presently there was proof. Calhoun heard small, drunken noises in the street. He tracked them cautiously. He found the place—one lighted ground-floor window on a long street lined on both sides with towering structures reaching for the sky. The sheer walls were utterly dark. The narrow lane of stars that could be seen overhead seemed utterly remote. The street itself was empty and dark, and murmurous with echoes of sounds that had not ever really been made. And here there were no natural sounds at all. Building walls cut off the normal night-sounds of the open country. There was a dead and muffled and murmurous stillness fit to crack one's eardrums.

Except for the drunken singing. Men drank together in an unnecessarily small room, which they had lighted very brightly to try to make it seem alive. All about them was deadness and stillness, so they made supposedly festive noises, priming themselves to cheerfulness with many bottles. With enough to drink, perhaps the illusion could be believed in. But it was a pitifully tiny thread of sound in a dark and empty city. Outside, where Calhoun and Murgatroyd paused to listen, the noise of drunken singing had a quality of biting irony.

Calhoun grunted, and the sound echoed endlessly between the stark walls around and above.

"We could use those characters," he said coldly, "only there are too many of them."

He and Murgatroyd went on. He'd familiarized himself with the stars, earlier, and knew that he moved in the direction of the landing grid. He'd arranged for one man on duty—at the callboard—to fail to do his work. The process was carefully chosen. He'd knocked out the invader with vortex rings of dextrethyl vapor, and then had given him a shot of polysulphate. The combination was standard, like magnesium sulphate and ether, centuries before. Polysulphate was an assisting anesthetic, never used alone because a man who was knocked out by it stayed out for days. In surgery it was used in a quantity which seemed not to affect a man at all, yet the least whiff of dextrethyl would then put him under for an operation, while he could instantly be revived. It was safer and under better control than any other kind of anesthesia.

But Calhoun had reversed the process. He'd put the callboard operator under with vapor, and then given polysulphate to keep him under for sixty hours or more. And then he'd left him. When the invader was found unconscious, it would bother the other butchers very much. They'd never suspect his condition to be the result of enemy action. They'd consider him in a coma. A coma was the last effect of the plague that had presented them with a planet. They'd believe their fellow to be dying of the plague they were supposed to be immune to. They would panic, expecting immediate death for themselves. But more than one man in a comalike state would be more effective in producing complete disorganization and despair.

A door banged, back by the lighted window in the desolate black street. Someone came out. Someone else. A third man. They moved along the street, singing hoarsely and untunefully and with words as slurred and uncertain as their footsteps. Echoes resounded between the high building walls. The effect was eerie.

Calhoun moved into a doorway. He waited. When the three men were opposite him, they linked arms to steady themselves. One man roared out quite unprintable verses of a song in which another joined uncertainly from time to time. The third protested aggrievedly. He halted, and the three of them argued solemnly about something indefinable, swaying as they talked with owlish, drunken gravity.

Calhoun lifted the paint-gun. He held down the trigger. Invisible rings of dextrethyl vapor whisked toward the trio. They gasped. They collapsed. Calhoun took his measures.

Presently one man lay unconscious on the street in a coma which imitated perfectly, except for the emaciation, the terminal coma of the fugitives from the city. Some distance away Calhoun plodded on toward the landing grid with a second man, also unconscious, over his shoulder. Murgatroyd followed closely. The third man, stripped to his underwear, waited where he might be found within the next day or two.

VI

"It is improper to use the term 'gambler' of a man who uses actuarial tables or tables of probability to make wagers which ensure him a favorable percentage of returns. Still less is it proper to call a man who cheats a gambler. He eliminates chance from his operations by his cheating. He does not gamble at all.

"The only true gambler is one who takes risks without considering chance; who acts upon reason or intuition or hunch or superstition without advertising to probability. He ignores the fact that chance as well as thought has a share in determining the outcome of any action. In this sense, the criminal is the true gambler. He is always confident that probability will not interfere; that no random happening will occur. To date, however, there has been no statistical analysis of a crime which has proved it an action which a reasonably prudent man would risk. The effects of pure, random happen-chance can be so overwhelming . . ."

Probability and Human Conduct—Fitzgerald

The night noises of the planet Maris III came from all the open space beyond the city itself. From the buildings themselves, of course, there was only silence. There were park areas left between them here and there, and green spaces bordered all the highways. But only small chirping sounds came from the city. The open country sang to the stars.

Calhoun settled himself, with an unconscious burden and Murgatroyd. He could not know how long it would be before the callboard operator would be missed and checked on. He was sure, though, that the appearance of terminal coma in a man who should be immune to the plague would produce results. The callboard man would be brought to the microbiologist who must be in charge of this murder operation. There had to be such a man. He had to know all about the plague. He had to be able to meet any peculiarity that came up. At a guess, only the best qualified of all the men who'd worked to develop the plague would be trusted with its first field test. He might even be the man who himself had devised the synergic combination. He'd be on hand. He'd have every possible bit of equipment he could need, in a superlatively arranged laboratory on the ship. And the callboard man would be brought to him.

Calhoun waited. He had another man in seeming coma, ready for use when the time came. Now he rested in the deep star-shadow of one of the landing grid's massive supports. Murgatroyd stayed close to him. The *tormal* was normally active by day. Darkness daunted him. He tended to whimper if he could not be close to Calhoun.

Overhead loomed the soaring, heavy arches of the landing grid. The grid could handle twenty-thousand-ton liners, and heavier ones too. It was designed to conduct the interstellar business of a world. Beyond it, the city reared up against the stars. The control building, from which the grid was operated, sprawled over half an acre, not far from where Calhoun lay in wait. His eyes were adjusted to the darkness, and he could see faint glows as if there were lighted windows facing away from him. He was within a hundred yards of the giant, globular ship which had brought the invaders here to do their work of butchery.

There was quiet save for the chorus of myriads of small voices which serenaded the heavens. It was a remarkable total sound. Now and again Calhoun heard sustained deep-bass notes, like the lowest possible tones of a great organ. Then there were liquid trillings, which might come from any kind of bird or beast or reptile. In between came chirpings and abrupt paeans of music, like woodwinds essaying tentative melodic runs.

It was easy for Calhoun to wait. The whole affair had added itself up in his mind. He felt that he not only knew what had happened on this world, but what might happen elsewhere if this particular enterprise proved profitable. Men who could arrange this could go further. Much further. What he'd imagined was trivial compared to what could come next.

There was a light in motion in the city. Calhoun sat up, all alertness, to watch it. It was a ground-car on a highway, headlights glaring to light the way before it. It vanished behind buildings. It reappeared. It crossed a far-flung bridge and vanished again, and again reappeared. It was drawing closer, and presently its lights glared in Calhoun's eyes as it sped furiously across the landing grid's turf floor, headed for the sprawling building where the transformers and the controls for the grid were housed.

There it came to a swiftly braked stop. Its light stayed on. Men jumped from it and ran into the control building. Calhoun heard no voices. The songs of the night creatures would have blotted out human voices. In minutes, though, more men came out of the building. They clustered about the ground-car. After only seconds, the car was again in motion, jouncing and bouncing over the turf toward the grounded spaceship.

It stopped within a hundred yards of where Calhoun had concealed himself. The headlights glittered and glistened against the bulging, silvery metal of the spacecraft. A man shouted at it, "Open up! Open up! Something's happened! A man's sick! It looks like the plague!"

There was no sign. He shouted again. Another man pounded on the thick metal of the airlock's outer door.

A voice spoke suddenly out of external loudspeakers. *"What's this? What's the matter?"*

Many voices tried to babble, but a harsh voice silence them and barked statements, every one of which Calhoun could have written down in advance. There'd been a man on watch in the city's communication center. He didn't put through calls from different places in use by the invaders. Someone went to find out why. The man at the callboard was unconscious. It looked like he had the plague. It looked like the shots he'd had to make him immune didn't work.

The voice coming over the loudspeakers said, *"Nonsense! Bring him in!"*

Seconds later the airlock door cracked open and descended outward, making a ramp from the ground to the cubbyhole which was the lock as now revealed. The men on the ground hauled a limp figure out of the ground-car. They half-carried and half-dragged it up the ramp into the lock. Calhoun saw the inner door open. They dragged the figure inside.

Then nothing happened, except that one man came out almost immediately, wiping his hands on his uniform as if hysterically afraid that by touching his unconscious companion he'd infected himself with the plague.

Presently another man came out. He trembled. Then the others. The harsh voice said savagely, "So he's got to find out what's the matter. It *can't* be the plague. We had shots against it. It's bound to be all right. Maybe he fainted or something. Stop acting like you're going to die! Go back on duty! I'll order a roll call, just in case."

Calhoun listened with satisfaction. The inner airlock door closed, but the outer one remained down as a ramp. The car trundled away, stopped and discharged some passengers at the control building, and went off into the distance. It disappeared on the highway where it had first appeared.

"The man I knocked out," he said dryly, to Murgatroyd, "impresses them unfavorably. They hope he's only an accident. We'll see. But that authoritative person is going to order a roll call. He ought to find something to bother them all, when that takes place."

"*Chee*," said Murgatroyd in a subdued tone.

There was again silence and stillness save for the open country song to the stars. There seemed to be occasional drumbeats in that chorus now.

It was half an hour before light showed on the ground by the control building. It was as if invisible doors had been opened, and light streamed out of them. In minutes a traveling light appeared. It vanished and was again visible, like the lights of the first car.

"Ha!" said Calhoun, gratified. "Checking up, they found the invader we left in the street. They reported it by communicator. Maybe they reported two others missing—one of whom is beside you, Murgatroyd. They ought to feel slightly upset."

The car dashed across the landing grid's center and braked. Figures waited for it. With the briefest of pauses it came again to the ship with the opened airlock door. The harsh voice panted, "Here's another one! We're bringing him in."

The loudspeaker said, somehow vexedly, *"Very well. But the first man hasn't got the plague. His metabolic rate is normal. He has not got the plague!"*

"Here's another one, just the same!"

The figures struggled up the ramp with a second limp burden. Minutes later they emerged again.

"He didn't get that first man awake," said an uneasy voice. "That looks bad to me."

"He says it ain't the plague."

"If he says it's not," snapped the authoritative voice, "then it's not! He ought to know. He invented the plague!"

Calhoun, behind the giant support for the landing grid, said, "Ah!" very quietly to himself.

"But—look here," said a frightened voice. "There were doctors in the city when we got here. Maybe some of 'em got away. Maybe—maybe they had some kinda germ that they've turned loose to kill us . . ."

The authoritative voice snarled. All the voices broke into a squabbling babble. The invaders were worried. They were frightened. Normally it would never have occurred to them to suspect a disease deliberately introduced among them. But they were here to follow up just such a disease. They did not understand such menaces. They'd been willing enough to profit, so long as the matter was strictly one-sided. But now it looked like some disease was striking them down. It seemed very probable that it was the plague to which they had been assured that they were immune. Some of them already had the shakes.

The car went away from the grounded spaceship. It stopped for a long time before the control building. There was agitated argument there. Calhoun heard the faint squabbling sound above the voices of the night. The car went away again.

He allowed twenty minutes to pass. They seemed very long to him. Then he picked up the man he'd knocked out, outside the room with the noisy drinking party. He heaved him over his shoulder. He'd pulled the uniform of the third of his dark-street victims over his own, and that third man lay in an areaway in his underwear. He'd be found eventually.

"We'll ask for our invitation into the ship—and the laboratory, Murgatroyd. Come along!"

He moved toward the still and silent spaceship.

It swelled and loomed enormously as he approached it. The outside lock door still lay extended downward as a ramp. He tramped on the metal incline. He went into the lock. There he banged on the inner door and called, "Here's another one! Out like the others! What'll I do with him?"

A metallic voice said angrily, *"Wait!"*

Calhoun waited. Two unconscious men, brought separately by a group of men who were more frightened the second time than the first, made it extremely likely that a third unconscious man would not have a group of solicitous companions with him. One man to risk the supposed contagion was very much more likely.

He heard footsteps beyond the inner lock door. It opened. A voice rasped, "Bring him in!"

He turned his back, this man who had come down to the airlock to spring the catch of the inner door. Calhoun followed him inside the ship, with Murgatroyd trotting fearfully between his feet. The lock door clicked shut. The figure in the white lab coat went trudging on ahead. It was a small figure. It limped a little. It was not well shaped.

Calhoun, with an unconscious member of the invading party used as a drape to hide his paint-gun—

so suitable a weapon, as it had turned out up to now—followed after him. He listened grimly for any sound which would indicate any other human being inside the spaceship. Now that he had seen—even from behind—the figure of the field director of the project to exterminate the proper inhabitants of Maris III, he coldly reasoned that there would probably not be even a laboratory assistant.

The queer figure moving before him fitted in a specific niche. There are people who, because they are physically unattractive, become personalities. All too many girls—and men, too—do not bother to become anything but good to look at. Some people who are not good to look at accept the situation courageously and become people who are good to know. But others rebel bitterly.

Knowing, as he did, that this man had used brains and skill and tedious labor to devise a method of mass murder, Calhoun felt almost able to write his biography. He had been grotesque. He hated those who found him grotesque. He dreamed grandiose dreams of gaining power so that he could punish those he envied and hated. He put into his schemes for revenge against a cosmos that gave him scorn all the furious energy that could have been used in other ways. He would develop an astounding patience and an incredible venom. He would scheme and scheme and scheme . . .

Calhoun had met people who could have chosen this way. One of the great men at Sector Headquarters, whose praise was more valued than fine gold, was odd to look at when you first glimpsed him. But you never noticed it after five minutes. There was a planetary president in Cygnus, a teacher on Cetis Alpha, a musician . . . Calhoun could think of many. But the hobbling figure before him hadn't chosen to follow the natural law, which advises courage. He'd chosen hate instead, and frustration was inevitable.

Into the laboratory. Here Murgatroyd cheered. This place was brightly lighted. Gleaming instruments were familiar. Even the smells of a beautifully equipped biological laboratory were reassuring and homelike to Murgatroyd. He said happily, *"Chee-chee-chee!"*

The small figure whirled. Dark eyes widened and glared. Calhoun slipped his burden to the floor. His Med Service uniform appeared beneath the invaders' tunic as the downward-sliding body tugged at the cloth.

"I'm sorry," said Calhoun gently, "but I have to put you under arrest for violating the basic principles of public health. Contriving and spreading a lethal plague amounts to at least that."

The figure whirled. It snatched. Then it darted toward Calhoun, desperately trying to use a surgeon's scalpel, the only deadly weapon within reach.

Calhoun pressed the trigger of the vortex-ring apparatus which was designed to paint the walls of buildings. Only this one didn't have paint in it. It shot invisible vortex rings of dextrethyl vapor instead.

VII

"In one perfectly real sense, all motives and all satisfactions are subjective. After all, we do live in our own skulls. But a man can do something he wishes to do and then contemplate the consequences of his action with pleasure. This pleasure, to be sure, is subjective, but it is directly related to reality and to the objective cosmos about him. However, there is an ultrasubjective type of motivation and satisfaction which is of great importance in human conduct. Many persons find their greatest satisfaction in contemplating themselves in some particular context. Such people find apparently complete satisfaction in a dramatic gesture, in a finely stated aspiration, or simply in a mere pretense of significance or wisdom or worth. The objective results of such gestures or pretenses are rarely considered. Very often great hardship and suffering and even deaths have been brought about by some person who raptly contemplated the beautiful drama of his behavior, and did not even think of its consequences to someone else . . ."

Probability and Human Conduct—Fitzgerald

Calhoun made the small man helpless with the invader's uniform he'd pulled over his own, and now tore it into strips. He was painstaking about the job. He tied his captive in a chair, and then encased him in a veritable cocoon of cloth strips. Then he examined the laboratory.

Murgatroyd strutted as Calhoun went over the equipment. Most of it was totally familiar. There were culture trays, visual and electron microscopes, autoclaves and irradiation apparatus, pipettes and instruments for microanalysis, thermostatic cabinets capable of keeping culture material within the hundredth of a degree of desired temperature. Murgatroyd was completely at home now.

Presently Calhoun heard a gasp. He turned and nodded to his prisoner.

"How-do," he said politely. "I've been very much interested in your work. I'm Med Service, by the way. I came here to do a routine planetary health check and somebody tried to kill me when I called for landing coordinates. They'd have done better to let me land and then blast me when I came out of my ship. The other was the more dramatic gesture, of course."

Dark, beady eyes regarded him. They changed remarkably from moment to moment. At one instant they were filled with a flaming fury which was practically madness. At another they seemed to grow cunning. Yet again they showed animal-like fear.

Calhoun said detachedly, "I doubt that there's any use in talking to you now. I'll wait until you have the situation figured out. I'm in the ship. There appears to be nobody else in a condition to start any trouble. The two men your—ah—mop-up party brought here are out for some days." He added explanatorily, "Polysulphate. An overdose. It's so simple I didn't think you'd guess it. I knocked them out so you'd be ready to let me in with a third specimen."

The mummylike bound figure made inarticulate noises. There was the sound of grinding teeth. There were bubbling sounds of crazy, frustrated rage.

"You're in a state of emotional shock," said Calhoun. "I guess that part is real and part is faked. I'll leave you alone to get over it. I want some information. I think you'll want to bargain. I'll leave you alone to work it out."

He went out of the laboratory. He felt an acute distaste for the man he'd captured. It was true that he believed the small man had received an emotional shock on finding himself captured and helpless. But a part of that shock would be rage so horrible as to threaten madness. Calhoun guessed coldly that anyone who had made the decision and lived the life he ascribed to the bound man—his guess, as it happened, was remarkably exact—could literally be goaded to death or madness, now that he was bound and could be taunted at will. It happened that he did not want to taunt his prisoner.

He went over the ship. He checked its type and design, verified the spaceyard in which it had been built, made an exact list in his own mind of what would be needed to make it into an inert hulk of no use to anybody, and then went back to the laboratory.

His prisoner panted, exhausted. There were very minor stretchings of the cloth strips which held him. Calhoun matter-of-factly made them tight again. His prisoner spat unspeakable, hysterical curses at him.

"Good," said Calhoun, unmoved. "Get the madness out of your system and we'll talk."

He moved to leave the laboratory again. A voice came out a loudspeaker, and he instantly searched for and found the microphone by which it could be answered. He flicked it off as his prisoner tried to scream commands into it.

"*Haven't you found out yet?*" asked the loudspeaker apprehensively. "*Don't you know what's the matter with those men? There are two more missing on roll call. There's something like panic building up. The men are guessing that a native doctor's spreading a plague among us!*"

Calhoun shrugged. The voice came from outside. It had been an authoritative voice, not long since. Now it was a badly worried one. He did not answer its questions. It repeated them. It waited and asked again. It almost pleaded for a reply. With the microphone off, however, the authoritative voice, which must be that of the commander of the butchers, grew resentful at being ignored. It faded out, trembling, shaking a little, but whether with hatred or terror he could not be sure. It could be either.

"Your popularity's diminishing," said Calhoun. He put down the microphone, safely off. He noted a spacephone receiver alongside the speaker-amplifier. "Hm," he said. "Suspicious, eh? You didn't even trust the skipper. Had to do your own receiving. Typical!"

The trussed-up, wizened man spoke suddenly with absolute cold precision.

"What do you want?" he demanded.

"Information," said Calhoun.

"For yourself? What do you want? I can give it to you!" said the mouth beneath the half-mad dark eyes. "I can give you anything you can imagine! I can give you riches more than you can dream!"

Calhoun sat negligently on the arm of a chair.

"I'll listen," he observed. "But apparently you're only technical director of the operation here. It's not a very big operation. You had only a thousand people to kill.

You're acting under orders. How could you give me anything important?"

"This—" his prisoner cursed. "This is a test—an experiment! Let me go, let it be finished, and I can give you a world to rule. I'll make you king of a planet! You'll have millions of slaves! You'll have women by the hundreds or thousands if you choose!"

Calhoun said detachedly, "You wouldn't expect me to believe that without the details."

The dark eyes flamed. Then, with an effort of will that was as violent as his rage had been, the small bound figure brought itself to composure. It was not calmness. Fury surged up when he attempted a persuasive gesture and could not move. Frustration maddened him to panting for breath. But between such moments, he talked with a terrifying plausibility, with a precision of detail that showed a scheme worked out with infinite care. It was *his* scheme. He had convinced a planetary government to try it. He was necessary to it. He would have power to spare and he could bribe Calhoun with everything that was rich and alluring and apparently irresistible. He set persuasively to work to bribe him.

It was quite horrible.

His captive went on. His tone wheedled, and was strident, and in turn was utterly convincing and remarkably persuasive.

Once Maris III was occupied by colonists from the world that had sent the plague, nothing could be done. Dettra Two could never land its people in the city. They would die. Only the usurping population could survive there. For all time to come the world of Maris III must belong to the folk who had planted it with death. The permanent colonists here must be immunized like the members of the invading party themselves.

"Who," said Calhoun, "are not as happy as they used to be."

His captive licked his lips and went on, his eyes deadly and his tone reasonable and seductive and remarkably hypnotic.

But Maris III was only a test. Once the process was proved here, there were other worlds to be taken over. Not only new colony-worlds like this. Old and established worlds would find themselves attacked by plagues their doctors would be helpless to combat. Then there would come ships from the world that had tried out its technique on Maris III. The ships would end the plagues. They would prove it. They would offer to sell life to all the citizens of the dying worlds—at a price.

"Unprofessional," said Calhoun, "but probably profitable."

The price, in effect, would be submission. It would amount to slavery. Those who would not accept the bargain would die.

"Of course," said Calhoun, "they might try to back out of such a bargain later."

His captive smiled a thin-lipped smile, while his eyes did not change at all. He explained convincingly that if there was a revolt, it would not matter. The countermeasure to a new defiance would always be a new plague. There were many plagues ready to use. They would build an interstellar empire in which rebellion would be a form of suicide. No world once taken over could ever free itself. No world once chosen could possibly resist. There would be worlds by tens and scores and hundreds to be ruled by men like Calhoun. He would rate a planet-kingdom of his own. His Med Service training entitled him to an empire! He would be absolute ruler and absolute master of millions of abject slaves who must please his most trivial whim or die!

"An objection," said Calhoun. "You haven't mentioned the Med Service. I don't think it would take kindly to such a system of planetary conquest."

Here was the highest test of the prisoner's ability
to sway and persuade and convince and almost to
hypnotize. He had a matter of minutes to make the
Med Service ridiculous, and to point out the defenselessness of its Sector Headquarters, and then—without
arousing ancient prejudices—to make it seem natural
and inevitable and almost humorous that Med Service
Sector Headquarters would receive special precaution-
ary fusion-bomb treatment as soon as the Maris III
task was finished. Calhoun stirred. His prisoner spoke
even more urgently, more desperately. He pictured
worlds on which every living being would be Calhoun's
slave—

"That'll do," said Calhoun. "I've got the information I wanted."

"Then release me," said his prisoner eagerly. And
then his burning eyes read Calhoun's no-longer-guarded
expression.

"You accept," he cried fiercely. "You accept! You
can't refuse! *You can't!*"

"Of course I can," said Calhoun annoyedly. "You've
no idea! I wouldn't want a million slaves, or even one.
I'm reasonably sane! And such a crazy scheme couldn't
work anyhow. Sheer probability would throw in so
many unfavorable chance happenings that it would be
bound to go smash. I'm proof of it. I'm an unfavorable chance happening right here, the very first time
you tried the beastly business."

His prisoner tried to talk more persuasively still. He
tried to be more tempting still. He tried, but his throat
clicked. He struggled to be more convincing and more
alluring than it was possible to be. Suddenly he
shrieked curses at Calhoun. They were horrible to
listen to. He screamed—

Calhoun raised the paint-gun, his features twisted
and wry. He sent a single small vortex ring.

In the sudden silence that fell, a tiny, tinny voice sounded from the spacephone receiver at one side of the laboratory.

"Calling ground," said a voice faintly. *"Ship from home with passengers calling ground on Maris III. Calling ground . . ."*

Calhoun jerked his head about and listened to the reiterated call. Then he bent to the necessary next thing to be done with his prisoner.

"Calling ground," said the voice patiently. *"We do not read you. If you are answering, we do not pick up your signal. We will go in orbit and continue to call. Calling ground . . ."*

Calhoun turned it off. Murgatroyd said inquiringly, *"Chee!"*

"That's a deadline," said Calhoun grimly. "For us. It's a shipload of happy, immunized colonists, ready to land here. We blew the landing grid, Murgatroyd, when they tried to butter us over the inside of the Med Ship. Apparently we blew their spacephone at the same time. So the spacephone in this ship here is the only one working. And we have too much sense to answer that call. But it gives us a deadline, just the same. If they still don't raise their friends, the ship may stay in orbit, but somebody'll come down in a lifeboat to find out what's wrong. And that will shoot the works! We'll have a passenger ship full of enthusiasts ready to land and finish the mopping-up business—and us! There's just you and me, Murgatroyd, to take care of the situation. Let's get at it!"

But it was very close to dawn when he and Murgatroyd left the grounded ship. Calhoun grimaced when he saw the vast crimson glory of approaching sunrise in the sky to the east. He saw a ground-car before the building in which the landing grid controls were housed.

"Worked up like these characters are," said Calhoun, "and suspecting somebody of spreading plagues for them to catch, they won't be cordial to anybody who didn't come here with them. I don't like the idea of trying simply to walk away when there's all this daylight. I think we'd better try to take that car, Murgatroyd. Come along!"

He headed for the control building. Judging by the night before, the occupied rooms had no windows facing toward the landed spacecraft. But he moved cautiously from one great arch-foundation to the next. When he'd reached the last possible bit of shelter, however, the ground-car was still fifty yards away.

"We run for it," he told Murgatroyd.

He and the tiny *tormal* bolted through the rosy dawn light. They had covered thirty yards when someone came out of the control building. He moved toward the ground-car. He heard Calhoun's pelting footsteps on the turf. He turned. For one instant he stared. Calhoun was a stranger. There should be no living strangers on this planet—they should all be dead. Here was an explanation of two men found unconscious and probably dying, and two more missing. The invader roared. His blaster came out.

Calhoun fired first. The snarling rasp of a blaster is unmistakable. The invader's weapon burst thunderously.

"Run!" snapped Calhoun.

Voices. A man peered out a window. Calhoun was a stranger with a blaster in his hand. The sight of him was a challenge to murder. The man in the window yelled. As Calhoun snapped a shot at him he jerked inside and the window crackled and smoked where the blaster-charge hit.

Man and *tormal* reached the line of the ground-car and the building door. The door was open. Calhoun swung up the dextrethyl sprayer and pumped explosive dextrethyl vapor into the room in a steady stream of vortex rings. He backed toward the ground-car, with Murgatroyd dancing agitatedly about his feet.

There was a crash of glass. Somebody'd plunged out a window. There were rushing feet inside. They'd be racing toward the door, from inside. But the hallway, or whatever was immediately inside, would be filled with anesthetic gas. Men would gasp and fall.

A man did fall. Calhoun heard the crash of his body as it hit the floor. But another man came plunging around the building's corner, blaster out, searching for Calhoun. He had to sight his target though, and then aim for it. Calhoun had only to pull his trigger. He did.

More shouting inside the building. More rushing feet. More falls. Then there was the beginning of the rasping snarl of a blaster, and finally a cushioned, booming, roaring detonation which was the ignited dextrethyl vapor. The blast lifted part of the building's roof. It shattered partitions. It blew out windows.

Calhoun backed toward the ground-car. A blaster-bolt flashed past him. He deliberately traversed the building with his trigger held down. Smoke and flame leaped up. At least one more invader crumpled. Calhoun heard a voice yelling, *"We're being attacked! The natives are throwing bombs! Rally! Rally! We need help!"*

It would be a broadcast call for assistance. Wherever men idled or loafed or tried desultorily to find something to loot, they would hear it. Even the crew working to repair the landing grid—and they would be close by—would hear it and swarm to help. Hunters would come. Men in cars—

Calhoun snatched Murgatroyd to the seat beside him. He turned the ignition key and tires screamed as he shot away.

VIII

"It has to be recognized that man is a social animal in the same sense, though in a different manner, that ants and bees are social creatures. For an ant city to prosper, there have to be natural laws to protect it against unfavorable actions on the part of its members. It is not enough to speak of instincts to prevent antisocial actions. There are mutations of instinct as well as of form, in ants as in other creatures. It is not enough even to speak of social pressure, which among ants would be an impulse to destroy deviant members of the community. There are natural laws to protect an ant city against the instinct-control which would destroy it, as well as against the abandonment of instincts or actions necessary to the ant city as a whole. There are, in short, natural laws and natural forces which protect societies against their own members. In human society . . ."

Probability and Human Conduct—Fitzgerald

The highways were, of course, superb. The car raced forward, and its communicator began to chatter as somebody in the undamaged part of the grid-control building announced hysterically that a stranger had killed men and gotten away in a car. It described its course. It commanded that he be headed off. It shrilly demanded that he be killed, killed, killed!

Another voice took over. This voice was curt and coldly furious. It snapped precise instructions.

And Calhoun found himself on a gracefully curving, rising road. It soared, and he was midway between towers when another car flashed toward him. He took his blaster in his left hand. In the split second during which the cars passed each other, he blasted it. There was a monstrous surge of smoke and flame as the stricken car's Duhanne cell shorted and vaporized half the metal of the car itself.

There came other voices. Somebody had sighted the explosion. The voice in the communicator roared for silence.

"You," he rasped. *"If you got him, report yourself!"*

"Chee-chee-chee!" chattered Murgatroyd excitedly.

But Calhoun did not report.

"He got one of us," raged the icy voice. *"Get ahead of him and blast him!"*

Calhoun's car went streaking down the far side of the traffic bridge. It rounded a curve on two wheels. It flashed between two gigantic empty buildings and came to a side road, and plunged into that, and came again to a division and took the left-hand turn, and next time took the right. But the muttering voices continued in the communicator. One of the invaders was ordered to the highest possible bridge from which he could watch all lower-level roadways. Others were to post themselves here and there—and to stay still! A group of four cars was coming out of the storage building. Blast any single car in motion. Blast it! And report, report, report!

"I suspect," said Calhoun to the agitated Murgatroyd beside him, "that this is what is known as military tactics. If they ring us in . . . There aren't but so many of them, though. The trick for us is to get out of the city. We need more choices for action. So—"

The communicator panted a report of his sighting from a cobweblike bridge at the highest point of the city. He was heading—

He changed his heading. He had so far seen but one of his pursuers' cars. Now he went racing along empty, curving highways, among untenanted towers and between balconied walls with blank-eyed windows gazing at him everywhere.

It was nightmarish because of the magnificence and the emptiness of the city all about him. He plunged along graceful highways, across delicately arched bridges, through crazy ramifications of its lesser traffic arteries—and he saw no motion anywhere. The wind whistled past the car windows, and the tires sang a high-pitched whine, and the sun shone down and small clouds floated tranquilly in the sky. There were no signs of life or danger anywhere on the splendid highways or in the beautiful buildings. Only voices muttered in the communicator of the car. He'd been seen here, flashing around a steeply banked curve. He'd swerved from a waiting ambush by pure chance. He'd—

He saw green to the left. He dived down a sloping ramp toward one of the smaller park areas of the city.

And as he came from between the stone guard rails of the road, the top of the car exploded over his head. He swerved and roared into dense shrubbery, jerked Murgatroyd free despite the *tormal's* clinging fast with all four paws and his tail, and dived into the underbrush. Somehow, instinctively, he clung to the vortex-gun.

He ran, with his free hand plucking solidified droplets of hot metal from his garments and his flesh. They hurt abominably. But the man who'd fired wouldn't believe he'd missed, followed as his blasting was by the instant wrecking of the car. That man would report success before he moved in to view the corpse of his supposed victim. But there'd be other cars coming. At the moment it was necessary for Calhoun to get elsewhere, fast.

He heard the rushing sound of arriving cars while he panted and sweated through the foliage of the park. He reached the far side and a road, and on beyond there was a low stone wall. He knew instantly what it was. Service highways ran in cuts, for the most part roofed over to hide them from sight, but now and again open to the sky for ventilation. He'd entered the city by one of them. Here was another. He swung himself over the wall and dropped. Murgatroyd recklessly and excitedly followed.

It was a long drop, and he staggered when he landed. He heard a soft rushing noise above. A car raced past. Instants later, another.

Limping, Calhoun ran to the nearest service gate. He entered and closed it. Scorched and aching, he climbed to the echoing upper stories of this building. Presently he looked out. His car had been wrecked in one of the smaller park areas of the city. Now there were other cars at two-hundred-yard intervals all about it. It was believed that he was in the brushwood somewhere. Besides the cars of the cordon, there were now twenty men on foot receiving orders from an authoritative figure in their midst.

They scattered. Twenty yards apart, they began to move across the park. Other men arrived and strengthened the cordon toward which he was supposed to be driven. A fly could not have escaped.

Those who marched across the park began methodically to burn it to ashes before them with their blasters.

Calhoun watched. Then he remembered something and was appalled. Two days before while he was among the fugitives in the glade, Kim Walpole had asked hungrily if they whose lives he had saved could not do something to help him. And he'd said that if they saw the smoke of a good-sized fire in the city they might investigate. He'd had not the faintest intention of calling on them. But they might see this cloud of smoke and believe he wanted them to come and help!

"Damn!" he said wryly to Murgatroyd. "After all, there's a limit to any one series of actions with probable favorable chance consequences. I'd better start a new one. We might have whittled the invaders down and made the rest run away, but I had to start using a car! And that led to the chance making of a fire! So now we start all over with a new policy."

He explored the building quickly. He prepared his measures. He went back to the window from which he'd looked. He cracked it open.

He opened fire with his blaster. The range was long, but with the beam cut down to minimum spread he'd knocked over a satisfying number of the men below before they swarmed toward the building, sending before them a barrage of blaster-fire that shattered the windows and had the stone façade smoking furiously.

"This," said Calhoun, "is an occasion where we have to change their advantage in numbers and weapons into an unfavorable circumstance for them. They'll be brave because they're many. Let's go!"

He met four ground-car loads of refugees with his arms in the air. He did not want to be shot down by mistaken. He said hurriedly, when Kim and the other lean survivors gathered about him, "Everything's all right. We've a pack of prisoners but we won't bother to feed them intravenously for the moment. How'd you get the ground-cars?"

"Hunters," said Kim savagely. "We found them and killed them and took their cars. We found some other refugees, too, and I cured them—at least they will be cured soon. When we saw the smoke, we started for the city. Some of us still have the plague, but we've all had our serum shots. And half of us have arms now."

"All of us have arms," said Calhoun, "and to spare. The invaders are quite peacefully sleeping—just about all of them. I did knock over a few with long-range blaster-shots, and they won't wake up. Most of them, though, tried to storm a building from which I'd fired on them. I stood them off a fair length of time, and then ducked after dumping dextrethyl in the air-conditioning system. Murgatroyd and I waited a suitable time and then lengthened their slumber period with polysulphate. I doubt there'll be any more trouble with the butchers. But we've got to get to the spaceship they landed in. I fixed it so it couldn't possibly take off, but there are some calls coming in from space. The only working spacephone here is in the ship. The first load of immunized, enthusiastic colonists are in orbit now, giving the gang aground a little more time to answer. I want you people to talk to them."

"We'll bring their ship down," said the broad-bearded man hungrily, "and blast them as they come out of the port!"

Calhoun shook his head.

"To the contrary," he said mildly. "You'll put on the clothes of some of our prisoners, and you'll let yourselves be seen by the joyous newcomers in their spacephone screen. You'll pretend to be the characters we really have safely sleeping, and you'll say that the

plague worked much too well. You'll say it wiped out
the original inhabitants—that's you—and then changed
into a dozen other plagues and wiped out all the little
butcher-boys who came to mop up. You'll give details
of the other kinds of plague that the real plague turned
into. You'll be pathetic. You'll beg them to land and pick
up you four or five dying, multiply diseased, highly
contagious survivors. You'll tell them the plague has
mutated until even the native animals are dying of it.
Flying things fall dead from the air. Chirping things in
the trees and grass are wiped out. You'll picture Maris
III as a world on which no animal life can hope ever
to live again—and you'll beg them to come down and
pick you up and take you home with them."

The broad-bearded man stared. Then he said, "But
they won't land."

"No," agreed Calhoun. "They won't. They'll go
home. Unless the government has them all killed
before they can talk, they'll tell their world what
happened. They'll be half-dead with fear that the
immunizing shots they received will mutate and turn
them into the kind of plague victims you'll make
yourself look like. And just what do you think will
happen on the world they came from?"

Kim said hungrily, "They'll kill their rulers.
They'll try to do it before they die of the plagues they'll
imagine. They'll revolt! If a man has a belly-ache he'll
go crazy with terror and try to kill a government official
because his government has murdered him!"

Kim drew a deep breath. He smiled with no amusement at all.

"I like that," he said with a sort of deadly calm. "I
like that very much."

"After all," observed Calhoun, "once an empire had
been started, with the subjugated populations kept
subdued by a threat of plague, how long would it

be before the original population was enslaved by the
same threat? Go and invent some interesting plagues
and make yourselves look terrifying. Heaven knows
you're lean enough! But you can make yourselves look
worse. I said, once, that a medical man sometimes
has to use psychology in addition to the regular measures against plague. The Med Service will check on
that planet presently, but I think its ambition to be
a health hazard to the rest of the galaxy will be
ended."

"Yes," said Kim. He moved away. Then he stopped.
"What about your prisoners? They're knocked out now.
What about them?"

Calhoun shrugged.

"Oh, we'll let them sleep until we finish repairing
the landing grid. I think I can be helpful with that."

"Every one of them is a murderer," growled the
broad-bearded man.

"True," agreed Calhoun. "But lynching is bad business. It even offers the possibility of unfavorable chance
consequences. Let's take care of the shipload of colonists first."

So they did. It was odd how they could take a sort
of pleasure in the enactment of imagined disaster even
greater than they had suffered. Their eyes gleamed
happily as they went about their task.

The passenger ship went away. It did not have a
pleasant journey. When it landed, its passengers burst
tumultuously out of the spaceport to tell their story.
Their home world went into a panic which was the
more uncontrollable because the people had been very
carefully told how deadly the tamed plagues would be
to the inhabitants of worlds that they might want to
take over. But now they believed the tamed plagues
had turned upon them.

The deaths, especially among members of the ruling

class, were approximately equal in number to those a deadly pandemic would have caused.

But back on Maris III things moved smoothly. Rather more than eighty people, altogether, were found and treated and ultimately helped with the matter of the slumbering invaders. That was almost a labor of love. Certainly it gave great satisfaction. The landing grid was back in operation two days after the passenger ship left. They took the landed spaceship and smashed its drive and communicators, and they wrecked its Duhanne cells. They took out the breech-plugs of the rockets and dumped the rocket fuel, saving just enough for the little Med Ship. Naturally, they removed the lifeboats.

And then they revived the unconscious butcher-invaders and put them, one by one, into the space-craft in which they had come. That craft was now a hulk. It could not drive or use rockets or even signal. Its vision screens were blind; the Med Ship used some of them.

And then they used the landing grid—Calhoun checking the figures—and they put their prisoners up in orbit to await the arrival of proper authority. They could feed themselves, but any attempt at escape would be pure and simple suicide. They could not attempt to escape.

"And now," said Calhoun, when the planet was clean of strangers again, "now I'll bring my ship to the grid. We'll recharge my Duhanne cells and replace my vision screens. I can make it here on rockets, but it's a long way to headquarters. So I'll report, and a field team will come here and check out the planet, artificial plagues included. They'll arrange, somehow, to take care of the prisoners up in orbit. That's not my affair. Maybe Dettra Two would like to have them. In the meantime, they can search their consciences."

Kim said, frowning, "You put something over on us! You kept us so busy we forgot one man. You said there'd be a microbiologist in the invaders' party. You said he'd probably be the man who had invented the plague. And he's up there in orbit with the rest—he'll get no more than they get! You put something over on us. He deserves some special treatment!"

Calhoun said very evenly, "Revenge is always apt to have unfavorable chance consequences. Let him alone. You've no right to punish him. You've only a right to punish a child to correct it, or to punish a man to deter others from doing what he's done. Do you expect to correct the kind of man who'd invent the plague that flourished here, and meant to use it for the making of an empire of slaves? Do you think others need to be deterred from trying the same thing?"

Kim said thickly, "But he's a murderer! All the murders were his! He deserves—"

"Condign punishment?" asked Calhoun sharply. "You've no right to administer it. Anyhow, think what he's up against!"

"He's—he's . . ." Kim's face changed. "He's up there in orbit, hopeless, with his butchers all around him and blaming him for the fix they're in. They've nothing to do but hate him. Nothing . . ."

"You didn't arrange that situation," said Calhoun coldly. "He did. You simply put prisoners in a safe place because it would be impractical to guard them, otherwise. I suggest you forget him."

Kim looked sickish. He shook his head to clear it. He tried to thrust the man who'd planned pure horror out of his mind. He said slowly, "I wish we could do something for you."

"Put up a statue," said Calhoun dryly, "and in twenty years nobody will know what it was for. You and Helen are going to be married, aren't you?" When Kim nodded, Calhoun said, "In course of time, if you remember and think it worthwhile, you may inflict a child with my name. That child will wonder why, and ask, and so my memory will be kept green for a full generation."

"Longer than that," insisted Kim. "You'll never be forgotten here!"

Calhoun grinned at him.

Three days later, which was six days longer than he'd expected to be aground on Maris III, the landing grid heaved the little Med Ship out to space. The beautiful, nearly empty city dwindled as the grid field took the tiny spacecraft out to five planetary diameters and there released it. And Calhoun spun the Med Ship about and oriented it carefully for that place in the Cetis cluster where Med Service Headquarters was. He threw the overdrive switch.

The universe reeled. Calhoun's stomach seemed to turn over twice, and he had a sickish feeling of spiraling dizzily in what was somehow a cone. He swallowed. Murgatroyd made gulping noises. There was no longer a universe perceptible about the ship. There was dead silence. Then those small random noises began which have to be provided if a man is not to crack up in the dead stillness of a ship traveling at thirty times the speed of light.

Then there was nothing more to do. In overdrive travel there is never anything to do but pass the time away.

Murgatroyd took his right-hand whiskers in his right paw and licked them elaborately. He did the same to his left-hand whiskers. He contemplated the cabin, deciding upon a soft place in which to go to sleep.

"Murgatroyd," said Calhoun severely, "I have to have

an argument with you. You imitate us humans too much! Kim Walpole caught you prowling around with an injector, starting to give our prisoners another shot of polysulfate. It might have killed them! Personally, I think it would have been a good idea, but in a medical man it would have been most unethical. We professional men have to curb our impulses! Understand?"

"Chee!" said Murgatroyd. He curled up and wrapped his tail meticulously about his nose, preparing to doze.

Calhoun settled himself comfortably in his bunk. He picked up a book. It was Fitzgerald on *Probability and Human Conduct*.

He began to read as the ship went on through emptiness.

RIBBON IN THE SKY

"An error is a denial of reality, but mistakes are mere
mental malfunctionings. In an emergency, a mistake may be
made because of the need for precipitate action. There is
no time to choose the best course; something must be done
at once. Most mistakes, however, are made without any such
exterior pressure. One accepts the first-imagined solution
without examining it, either out of an urgent desire to
avoid the labor of thinking, or out of impassioned
reluctance to think about the matter at hand when prettier
or more pleasurable other things can be contemplated . . ."
The Practice of Thinking—Fitzgerald

It turned out that somebody had punched the wrong
button in a computer. It was in a matter in which
mistakes are not permissible, but just as nothing can
be manufactured without an ordinary hammer figur-
ing somewhere in the making or the making-ready-to-
make, so nothing can be done without a fallible human
operator at some stage of the proceedings. And humans

make mistakes casually, offhandedly, with impartial lack
of either malice or predictability, so . . .

Calhoun heard the speaker say, *"When the gong
sounds, breakout will follow in five seconds."* Then it
made solemn ticking noises while Calhoun yawned and
put aside the book, *The Practice of Thinking*. He'd
been studying. Study was a necessity in his profession.
Besides, it helped to pass the time in overdrive. He
went to the control-desk and strapped in. Murgatroyd
the *tormal* uncoiled his tail from about his nose and
stood up from where he was catching twenty winks.
He padded to the place under Calhoun's chair where
there were things to grab hold of, if necessary, with
one's four black paws and prehensile tail.

"Chee," said Murgatroyd conversationally, in his shrill
treble.

"I agree," Calhoun told him gravely. "Stone walls
do not a prison make, nor Med Ship hulls a cage. But
it will be good to get outside for a change."

The speaker ticked and tocked and ticked and
tocked. There was the sound of a gong. A voice said
measuredly, *"Five—four—three—two—one."*

The ship came out of overdrive. Calhoun winced
and swallowed. Nobody ever gets used to going into
overdrive or coming out of it. One is hideously dizzy
for an instant, and his stomach has a brief but violent urge to upchuck, and no matter how often one
has experienced it, it is necessary to fight a flash of
irrational panic caused by the two sensations together.

After an instant Calhoun stared about him as the
vision screens came to life. They showed the cosmos
outside the Med Ship. It was a perfectly normal
cosmos—not at all the cosmos of overdrive—but it
looked extremely wrong to Calhoun. He and
Murgatroyd and the Med Ship were in emptiness.
There were stars on every hand, and they were of every

conceivable color and degree of brightness. But every one of them was a point of light, and a point only.

This, obviously, was not what he'd expected. These days ships do not stop to view the universe from the monstrous loneliness which is between-the-stars. All ships go into overdrive as near their port of departure as they can. Usually, it is something like five or six planetary diameters out from the local spaceport. All ships come out of overdrive as near their destinations as computation makes possible. They do not stop to look at scenery on the way. It isn't good for humans to look at stars when there are only stars to see. The sight has a tendency to make them feel small—too small. Men have been known to come out of such an experience gibbering.

Calhoun scowled at the sight of between-the-stars. This was not good. But he wasn't frightened—not yet. There should have been a flaming sun somewhere nearby, and there should have been bright crescents of half-disks or mottled cloudy planets swimming within view. The sun should have been the star Merida, and Calhoun should land in commonplace fashion on Merida II and make a routine planetary health check on a settled, complacent population, and presently he should head back to Med Headquarters with a report containing absolutely nothing of importance. However, he couldn't do any of these things. He was in purely empty space. It was appalling.

Murgatroyd jumped up to the arm of the control-chair, to gaze wisely at the screens. Calhoun continued to scowl. Murgatroyd imitated him with a *tormal's* fine satisfaction in duplicating a man's actions. What he saw meant nothing to him, of course. But he was moved to comment.

"*Chee,*" he said shrilly.

"To be sure," agreed Calhoun distastefully. "That is

a very sage observation, Murgatroyd. Though I deplore the situation that calls for it. Somebody's bilged on us."

Murgatroyd liked to think that he was carrying on a conversation. He said zestfully, *"Chee-chee! Chee-chee-chee!"*

"No doubt," conceded Calhoun. "But this is a mess! Hop down and let me try to get out of it."

Murgatroyd disappointedly hopped to the floor. He watched with bright eyes as Calhoun annoyedly went to the emergency equipment locker and brought out the apparatus designed to take care of problems like this. If the situation wasn't too bad, correcting it should be simple enough. If it was too bad, it could be fatal.

The average separation of stars throughout the galaxy, of course, is something like four or five light-years. The distance between Sol-type stars is on an average very much higher, and with certain specific exceptions habitable planets are satellites of Sol-type suns. But only a fraction of the habitable planets are colonized, and when a ship has traveled blind, in overdrive, for two months or more, its pilot cannot simply look astern and recognize his point of departure. There's too much scenery in between. Further, nobody can locate himself by the use of star-maps unless he knows where something on the star-map is with reference to himself. This makes a star-map not always useful.

The present blunder might not be serious. If the Med Ship had come out into normal space no more than eight to ten light-years from Merida, Calhoun might identify that sun by producing parallax. He could detect relative distances for a much greater range. However, it was to be hoped that his present blunder was small.

He got out the camera with its six lenses for the

six vision screens which showed space in all directions. He clamped it in place and painstaking snapped a plate. In seconds he had everything above third magnitude faithfully recorded in its own color, and with relative brightnesses expressed in the size of the dots of tint. He put the plate aside and said, "Overdrive coming, Murgatroyd."

He pressed the short-hop button and there was dizziness and nausea and a flash of fear—all three sensations momentary. Murgatroyd said, *"Chee"* in a protesting tone, but Calhoun held down the button for an accurate five minutes. He and Murgatroyd gulped together when he let up the button again and all space whirled and nausea hit as before. He took another plate of all the heavens, made into one by the six-lensed camera. He swung the ship by ninety degrees and pressed the short-hop button a second time; more dizziness, panic and digestive revolt followed. In five minutes it was repeated as the ship came out to normal space yet again.

"Chee-chee!" protested Murgatroyd. His furry paws held his round little belly against further insult.

"I agree," said Calhoun. He exposed a third film. "I don't like it either. But I want to know where we are, if anywhere."

He set up the comparator and inserted the three plates. Each had images of each of the six vision screens. When the instrument whirled, each of the plates in turn was visible for part of a second. Extremely remote stars would not jiggle perceptibly— would not show parallax—but anything within twenty light-years should. The jiggling distance could be increased by taking the plates still farther apart. This time, though, there was one star which visibly wavered in the comparator. Calhoun regarded it suspiciously.

"We're Heaven knows where," he said dourly.

"Somebody really messed us up! The only star that shows parallax isn't Merida. In fact, I don't believe in it at all. Two plates show it as a Sol-class sun and the third says it's a red dwarf!"

On the face of it, such a thing was impossible. A sun cannot be one color as seen from one spot, and another color seen from another. Especially when the shift of angle is small.

Calhoun made rough computations. He hand-set the overdrive for something over an hour's run in the direction of the one star-image which wobbled and thereby beckoned. He threw the switch. He gulped, and Murgatroyd acted for a moment as if he intended to yield unreservedly to the nausea of entering overdrive, but he refrained.

There was nothing to do but kill time for an hour. There was a microreel of starplates, showing the heavens as photographed with the same galactic coordinates from every visited Sol-class star in this sector of the galaxy. Fewer than one in forty had a colonized planet, but if the nearest had been visited before, and if the heavens had been photographed there, by matching the stars to the appropriate plate he could find out where he was. Then a star-map might begin to be of some use to him. But he had still to determine whether the error was in his astrogation unit, or in the data fed to it. If the first he'd be very bad off indeed. If the second he could still be in a fix. But there was no point in worrying while in overdrive. He lay down on his bunk and tried to concentrate again on the book he'd laid aside.

"*Human error, moreover,*" he read, "*is never purely random. The mind tends to regard stored data as infallible and to disregard new data which contradicts it . . . .*" He yawned, and skipped. "*. . . So each person has a personal factor of error which is not only quantitative but qualitative . . . .*"

He read on and on, only half absorbing what he read. A man who has reached the status of a Med Ship man in the Interstellar Medical Service hasn't finished learning. He's still a way down the ladder of rank. He has plenty of studying before him before he gets very far.

The tape-speaker said, *"When the gong sounds, breakout will be five seconds off."* It began to tick-tock, slowly and deliberately. Calhoun got into the control-seat and strapped in. Murgatroyd said peevishly, *"Chee!"* and went to position underneath the chair. The voice said, *"Five—four—three—two—one."*

The little Med Ship came out of overdrive, and instantly its emergency rockets kicked violently and Murgatroyd held desperately fast. Then the rockets went off. There'd been some unguessable nearby, perhaps cometary debris at the extremist outer limit of a highly eccentric orbit. Now there was a star-field and a sun within two light-hours. If Calhoun had stared, earlier, when there was no sun in sight at all, now he gazed blankly at the spectacle before him.

There was a sun off to starboard. It was a yellow sun, a Sol-type star with a barely perceptible disk. There were planets. Calhoun saw immediately one gas-giant near enough to be more than a point, and a sliver of light which was the crescent of another more nearly in line toward the sun. But he gazed at a belt, a band, a ribbon of shining stuff which was starkly out of all reason.

It was a thin curtain of luminosity circling this yellow star. It was not a ring from the break-up of a satellite within Roche's Limit. There were two quite solid planets inside it and nearer to the sun. It was a thin, wide, luminous golden ribbon which looked like something that needed a flat iron to smooth it out. It looked somewhat like an incandescent smoke ring. It was not

smooth. It had lumps in it. There were corrugations
in it. An unimaginable rocket with a flat exhaust could
have made it while chasing its tail around the sun. But
that couldn't have happened, either.

Calhoun stared for seconds.

"Now," he said, "now I've seen everything!" Then
he grunted as realization came. "Mmmmh! We're all
right, Murgatroyd! It's not our computers that went
wrong. Somebody fed them wrong data. We arrived
where we aimed for, and there'll be a colonized planet
somewhere around."

He unlimbered the electron telescope and began a
search; he couldn't resist a closer look at the ribbon
in space. It had exactly the structure of a slightly
wobbly wrinkled belt without beginning or end. It had
to be a complex of solid particles, of course, and an
organization of solid particles cannot exist in space
without orbital motion. However, orbits would smooth
out in the course of thousands of revolutions around
a primary. This was not smoothed out. It was relatively
new.

"It's sodium dust," said Calhoun appreciatively. "Or
maybe potassium. Hung out there on purpose. Particles
small enough to have terrific surface and reflective
power, and big enough not to be pushed out of orbit
by light-pressure. Clever, Murgatroyd! At a guess it'll
have been put out to take care of the climate on a
planet just inside it. Which would be—there! Let's go
look!"

He was so absorbed in his admiration that the
almost momentary overdrive-hop needed for approach
went nearly unnoticed. He even realized—his apprecia-
tion increasing—that this cloud of tiny particles
accounted for the red dwarf appearance on one of the
plates he'd taken. Light passing through widely dis-
persed, very small particles turns red. From one

position, he'd photographed moving through this dust cloud.

The ribbon was a magnificent idea, the more magnificent because of its simplicity. It would reflect back otherwise wasted sun-heat to a too-cold planet and make it warmer. There was probably only an infinitesimal actual mass of powder in the ring, at that. Tens of scores of tons in all, hardly more.

The planet for which it had been established was the third world out. As is usual with Sol-class systems, the third planet's distance from the sun was about a hundred twenty million miles. It had ice caps covering more than two-thirds of its surface. The sprawling white fingers of glaciation marked mountain chains and highlands nearly to the equator. There was some blue sea, and there was green vegetation in a narrow belt of tropicality.

Calhoun jockeyed the Med Ship to position for a landing call. This was not Merida II; there should be a colony here! That glowing ribbon had not been hung out for nothing.

"Med Ship *Aesclipus Twenty*," he said confidently into the space-phone mike. "Calling ground. Requesting coordinates for landing. My mass is fifty tons. Repeat, five-oh tons. Purpose of landing, to find out where I am and how to get where I belong."

There was a clicking. Calhoun repeated the call. He heard murmurings which were not directed into the transmitter on the planet. They were speaking in the transmitter room aground. He heard an agitated: *"How long since a ship landed?"* Another voice was saying fiercely, *"Even if he doesn't come from Two City or Three City, who knows what sickness . . ."* There was sudden silence, as if a hand had been clapped over the microphone below. Then a long pause. Calhoun made the standard call for the third time.

"*Med Ship* Aesclipus Twenty," said the space-phone speaker grudgingly, "*you will be allowed to land. Take position.*" Calhoun blinked at the instructions he received. The coordinates were not the normal galactic ones. They gave the local time at the spaceport, and the planetary latitude. He was to place himself overhead. He could do it, of course, but the instructions were unthinkable. Galactic coordinates had been used ever since Calhoun knew anything about such matters. But he acknowledged the instructions. Then the voice from the speaker said truculently: "*Don't hurry! We might change our minds! And we have to figure settings for an only fifty-ton ship, anyhow.*"

Calhoun's mouth dropped open. A Med Ship was welcome everywhere, these days. The Interstellar Medical Service was one of those over-worked, under-staffed, kicked-around organizations that are everywhere taken for granted. Like breathable air, nobody thought to be grateful for it, but nobody was suspicious of it, either.

The suspicion and the weird coordinates and the ribbon in space combined to give Calhoun a highly improbable suspicion. He looked forward with great interest to this landing. He had not been ordered to land here, but he suspected that a Med Ship landing was a long, long time overdue.

"I forgot to take star-pictures," he told Murgatroyd, "but a ribbon like this would have been talked about if it had been reported before. I doubt star-pictures would do us any good. The odds are that our only chance to find out where we are is to ask." Then he shrugged his shoulders. "Anyhow this won't be routine!"

"*Chee!*" agreed Murgatroyd profoundly.

> "An unsolvable but urgent problem may produce in a society, as in an individual, an uncontrollable emotional tantrum, an emotional denial of the problem's existence, or purposeful research for a solution. In olden days, the first reaction produced mass-tantrums then called "wars." The second produced dogmatic ideologies. The third produced modern civilization. All three reactions still appear in individuals. If the first two should return to societies, as such . . ."
>
> *The Practice of Thinking*—Fitzgerald

The descent, at least, was not routine. It was nerve-racking. The force field from the planet's giant steel landing grid reached out into space and fumbled for the Med Ship. That was clumsily done. When it found the ship, it locked on, awkwardly. The rest was worse. Whoever handled the controls, aground, was hopelessly inept. Once the Med Ship's hull-temperature began to climb, and Calhoun had to throw on the space-phone and yelp for caution. He did not see as much of the nearing planet as he'd have liked.

At fifty miles of height, the last trace of blue sea vanished around the bulge of the world. At twenty miles, the mountain chains were clearly visible, with their tortured, winding ice rivers which were glaciers. At this height three patches of green were visible from aloft. One, directly below, was little more than a mile in diameter and the landing grid was its center and almost its circumference. Another was streaky and long, and there seemed to be heavy mist boiling about it and above it. The third was roughly triangular. They were many miles apart. Two of them vanished behind mountains as the ship descended.

There were no cities in view. There were no highways. This was an ice world with bare ground and open water at its equator only. The spaceport was placed in a snow ringed polar valley.

Near landing, Calhoun strapped in because of the awkwardness with which the ship was lowered. He took Murgatroyd on his lap. The small craft bounced and wabbled as unskilled hands let it down. Presently, Calhoun saw the angular girders of the landing grid's latticed top rise past the opened ports. Seconds later, the Med Ship bumped and slid and bounced heart-stoppingly. Then it struck ground with a violent jolt.

Calhoun got his breath back as the ship creaked and adjusted itself to rest on its landing-fins, after some months in space.

"Now," said the voice in the space-phone speaker— but it sounded as if it were trying to conceal relief— *"now stay in your ship. Our weapons are bearing on you. You may not come out until we've decided what to do about you."*

Calhoun raised his eyebrows. This was very unusual

indeed. He glanced at the external-field indicator. The landing-grid field was off. So the operator bluffed. In case of need Calhoun could blast off on emergency rockets and probably escape close-range weapons anyhow—if there were any—and he could certainly get around the bulge of the world before the amateur at the grid's controls could lock on to him again.

"Take your time," he said with irony. "I'll twiddle my fingers. I've nothing better to do!"

He freed himself from his chair and went to a port to see. He regarded the landscape about him with something like disbelief.

The landing grid itself was a full mile across and half as high. It was a vast, circular frame of steel beams reaching heavenward, with the curiously curving copper cables strung as they had to be to create the highly special force field which made space transportation practical. Normally, such gigantic structures rose in the centers of spaceport cities. They drew upon the planet's ionosphere for power to lift and land cargo ships from the stars, and between-times they supplied energy for manufactures and the operation of cities. They were built, necessarily, upon stable bed-rock formations, and for convenience were usually located where the cargoes to be shipped would require least surface transportation.

But here, there was no city. There was perhaps a thousand acres of greenness, a mere vague rim around the outside of the grid. There was a control-room building to one side, of course. It was solidly made of stone, but there had been an agglomeration of lean-tos added to it with slanting walls and roofs of thin stratified rock. There were cattle grazing on the green grass. The center of the grid was a pasture!

Save for the clutter about the grid-control building there were no structures, no dwellings, no houses or homes anywhere in view. There was no longer even a highway leading to the grid. Calhoun threw on the outside microphones and there was no sound except a thin keening of wind in the steelwork overhead. But presently one of the cattle made a mournful bellowing sound.

Calhoun whistled as he went from one port to another.

"Murgatroyd," he said meditatively on his second round, "you observe—if you observe—one of the consequences of human error. I still don't know where I am, because I doubt that starplates have ever been made from this solar system, and I didn't take one for comparison anyhow. But I can tell you that this planet formerly had a habitability rating of something like oh point oh, meaning that if somebody wanted to live here it would be possible but it wouldn't be sensible. Although people did come here, and it was a mistake."

He stared at a human figure, far away. It was a woman, dressed in shapeless, badly draping garments. She moved toward a clump of dark-coated cattle and did something in their midst.

"The mistake looks pretty evident to me," added Calhoun. "I see some possibilities I don't like at all. There is such a thing as an isolation syndrome, Murgatroyd. A syndrome is a complex of pathological symptoms which occur together as a result of some morbid condition. To us humans, isolation is morbid. You help me to endure it, Murgatroyd, but I couldn't get along with only even your society—charming as it is—for but so long. A group of people can get along longer than a single man, but there is a limit for any small-sized group."

"*Chee,*" said Murgatroyd.

"In fact," said Calhoun, frowning, "there's a specific

health problem involved, which the Med Service
recognizes. There can be partial immunity, but there
can be some tricky variations. If we're up against a
really typical case we have a job on hand. And how
did these people get that dust ring out in space? They
surely didn't hang it out themselves!"

He sat down and scowled at his thoughts. Presently,
he rose again and once more surveyed the icy landscape. The curious green pasture about the landing grid
was highly improbable. He saw glaciers overhanging
this valley. They were giant ice rivers which should
continue to flow and overwhelm this relatively sheltered spot. They didn't. Why not?

It was more than an hour before the space-phone
clattered. When Calhoun threw the switch again a new
voice came out of it. This was also a male voice, but
it was high-pitched as if from tension.

"*We've been talking about you,*" said the voice. It
quivered with agitation which was quite out of reason. "*You say you're Med Service. All right. Suppose
you prove it!*" The landed Med Ship should be proof
enough for anybody. Calhoun said politely, "I have the
regular identification. If you'll go on vision I'll show
you my credentials."

"*Our screen's broken,*" said the voice, suspiciously.
"*But we have a sick cow. It was dumped on us night
before last. Cure her and we'll accept it as identification.*"

Calhoun could hardly believe his ears. This was an
emergency situation! The curing of a sick cow was
considered more convincing than a Med Ship man's
regular credentials! Such a scale of values hinted at
more than a mere isolation syndrome. There were
thousands of inhabited worlds, now, with splendid cities
and technologies which most men accepted with the
same bland confidence with which they looked for

sunrise. The human race was civilized! Suspicion of a Med Ship was unheard of, but here was a world . . .

"Why—certainly," said Calhoun blankly. "I suppose I may go outside to—ah—visit the patient?"

"We'll drive her up to your ship," said the high, tense voice. *"And you stay close to it!"* Then it said darkly, *"Men from Two City sneaked past our sentries to dump it on us. They want to wipe out our herd! What kind of weapons have you got?"*

"This is a Med Ship!" protested Calhoun. "I've nothing more than I might need in an emergency!"

"We'll want them anyhow," said the voice. *"You said you need to find out where you are. We'll tell you, if you've got enough weapons to make it worthwhile."*

Calhoun drew a deep breath.

"We can argue that later," he said. "I'm just a trifle puzzled. But first things first. Drive your cow."

He held his head in his hands. He remembered to throw off the space-phone and said, "Murgatroyd, say something sensible! I never ran into anybody quite as close to coming apart at the seams as that! Not lately! Say something rational!"

Murgatroyd said, *"Chee?"* in an inquiring tone.

"Thanks," said Calhoun. "Thanks a lot."

He went back to the ports to watch. He saw men come out of the peculiar agglomeration of structures that had been piled around the grid's sturdy control-building. They were clothed in cloth that was heavy and very stiff, to judge by the way it shifted with its wearers' movements. Calhoun wasn't familiar with it. The men moved stolidly, on foot, across the incredible pasture which had been a landing space for ships of space at some time or other.

They reached a spot where a dark animal form rested on the ground. Calhoun hadn't noticed it particularly. Cattle, he knew, folded their legs and lay down and chewed cuds. They existed nearly everywhere that human colonies had been built. On some worlds there were other domestic animals descended from those of Earth. Of course, there were edible plants and some wholesome animals which had no connection at all with humanity's remote ancestral home, but from the beginning human beings had been adjusted to symbiosis with the organic life of Earth. Foodstuffs of non-terrestrial origin could only supplement Earth food, of course. In some cases Earth foods were the supplements and local, non-terrestrial foodstuffs the staples. However, human beings did not thrive on a wholly un-Earthly diet.

The clump of slowly moving men reached the reclining cow. They pulled up stakes which surrounded her, and coiled up wire or cordage which had made the stakes into a fence. They prodded the animal. Presently, it lurched to its feet and swung its head about foolishly. They drove it toward the Med Ship.

Fifty yards away they stopped, and the outside microphones brought the sound of their voices muttering. By then Calhoun had seen their faces. Four of the six were bearded. The other two were young men. On most worlds men prided themselves that they needed to shave, but few of them omitted the practice.

These six moved hastily away, though the two younger ones turned often to look back. The cow, deserted, stumbled to a reclining position. It lay down, staring stupidly about. It rested its head on the ground.

"I go out now, eh?" asked Calhoun mildly.

"We're watching you!" grated the space-phone speaker.

Calhoun glanced at the outside temperature indicator and added a garment. He put a blaster in his pocket. He went out the exit port.

The air was bitter cold, after two months in a heat-metered ship, but Calhoun did not feel cold. It took him seconds to understand why. It was that the ground was warm! Radiant heat kept him comfortable, though the air was icy. Heat elements underground must draw power from somewhere—the grid's tapping of the ionosphere and heating this pasture from underneath enabled forage plants to grow here. They did. The cattle fed on them. There would be hydroponic gardens somewhere else, probably underground. They would supply vegetable food in greater quantity. In the nature of things human beings had to have animal food in a cold climate.

Calhoun went across the pasture with the frowning snowy mountains all about. He regarded the reclining beast with an almost humorous attention. He did not know anything about the special diseases of domestic animals. He had only the knowledge required of a Med Ship man, but that should be adequate. The tense voice had said that this beast had been "dumped," to "wipe out" the local herd. So there "was" infection and there would be some infective agent.

He painstakingly took samples of blood and saliva. In a ruminant, certainly, any digestive-tract infection should show up in the saliva. He reflected that he did not know the normal bovine temperature, so he couldn't check it, nor the respiration. The Interstellar Medical Service was not often called on to treat ailing cows.

Back in the ship he diluted his samples and put traces in the usual nutrient solutions. He sealed up droplets in those tiny slides which let a culture be examined as it grows. His microscope, of course, allowed for inspection under light of any wave-length desired, and so yielded information by the frequency of the light which gave clearest images of different features of the microorganisms.

After five minutes of inspection he grunted and hauled out his antibiotic stores. He added infinitesimal traces of cillin to the culture media. In the microscope, he watched the active microscopic creatures die. He checked with the other samples.

He went out to the listless, enfeebled animal. He made a wry guess at its body-weight. He used the injector. He went back to the Med Ship. He called on the space-phone.

"I think," he said politely, "that your beast will be all right in thirty hours or so. Now, how about telling me the name of this sun?"

The voice said sharply, *"There's a matter of weapons, too! Wait till we see how the cow does! Sunset will come in an hour. When day comes again, if the cow is better—we'll see!"*

There was a click. The space-phone cut off.

Calhoun pulled out the log-mike. There was already an audio record of all ship operations and communications. Now he added comments: a description of the ribbon in the sky, the appearance of the planet, and such conclusions as he'd come to. He ended: "The samples from the cow were full of a single coccus, which seemed to have no resistance to standard antibiotics. I pumped the beast full of cillin and called it a day. I'm concerned, though, because of the clear signs of an isolation syndrome here. They're idiotically suspicious of me and won't even promise a bargain, as if I could somehow overreach them because I'm a stranger. They've sentries out—they said somebody sneaked past them—against what I imagine must be Two City and Three City. I've an impression that the sentries are to enforce a quarantine rather than to put up a fight. It is probable that the other communities practice the same tactics, plus biological cold war if somebody did bring a sick cow here to infect and destroy the local herd. These people may have a landing grid, but they've an isolation syndrome and I'm afraid there's a classic Crusoe health problem in being. If that's so, it's going to be nasty!"

He cut off the log. The classic Crusoe problem would be extremely awkward if he'd run into it. There was a legend about an individual back on old Earth who'd been left isolated on an island by shipwreck for half a lifetime. His name was given to the public-health difficulties which occurred when accidental isolations occurred during the chaotic first centuries of galactic migration. There was one shipwreck to which the name was first applied. The ship was missing, and the descendants of the crew and passengers were not contacted until three generations had passed. Larger-scale and worse cases occurred later, when colonies were established by entrepreneurs who grew rich in the establishment of the new settlements, and had no interest in maintaining them. Such events could hardly happen now, of course, but even a Crusoe condition was still possible in theory. It might exist here. Calhoun hoped not.

It did not occur to him that the affair was not his business because he hadn't been assigned to it. He belonged to the Med Service, and the physical well being of humans everywhere was the concern of that service. If people lived by choice in an inhospitable environment, that was not a Med man's problem, but anything which led to preventable deaths was. In a Crusoe colony there were plenty of preventable deaths!

He cooked a meal to have something to occupy his mind. Murgatroyd sat on his haunches and sniffed blissfully. Presently, Calhoun ate, and again presently darkness fell on this part of the world. There were new noises, small ones. He went to look. The pasture inside the landing grid was faintly lighted by the glowing ribbon in the sky. It looked like a many-times-brighter Milky Way. The girders of the landing grid looked very black against it.

He saw a dark figure plodding away until he vanished. Then he reappeared as a deeper black against the snow beyond the pasture. He went on and on until he disappeared again. A long time later another figure appeared where he'd gone out of sight. It plodded back toward the grid. It was a different individual. Calhoun had watched a changing of sentries. Suspicion, hostility, the least attractive qualities of the human race, were brought out by isolation.

There could not be a large population here, since such suspicions existed. It was divided into—most likely—three, again, isolated communities. This one had the landing grid, which meant power, and a spacephone but no vision screen attached to it. The fact that there were hostile separate communities made the situation much more difficult, from a medical point of view. It multiplied the possible ghastly features which could exist.

Murgatroyd ate until his furry belly was round as a ball, and settled to stuffed slumber with his tail curled around his nose. Calhoun tried to read. But he was restless. His own time-cycle on the ship did not in the least agree with the time of daylight here on this planet. He was wakeful when there was utter quiet outside. Once one of the cattle made a dismal noise. Twice or three times he heard crackling sounds, like sharp detonations, from the mountains; they would be stirrings in the glaciers.

He tried to study, but painstaking analysis of the

methods by which human brains defeated their own ends and came up with wrong answers was not appealing. He grew horribly restless.

It had been dark for hours when he heard rustling noises on the ground outside, through the microphones, of course. He turned up the amplification and made sure that it was a small party of men moving toward the Med Ship. From time to time they paused, as if in caution.

"Murgatroyd," he said dryly, "we're going to have visitors. They didn't give notice by space-phone, so they're unauthorized."

Murgatroyd blinked awake. He watched as Calhoun made sure of the blaster in his pocket and turned on the log-mike. He said, "All set, Murgatroyd?"

Murgatroyd said *"Chee"* in his small shrill voice just as a soft and urgent knock sounded on the exit-lock door. It was made with bare knuckles. Calhoun grimaced and went into the lock. He unbolted the door and began to open it, when it was whipped from his grasp and plunging figures pushed in. They swept him back into the Med Ship's cabin. He heard the lock door close softly. Then he faced five roughly, heavily clothed men who wore cloaks and mittens and hoods, with cloth stretched tightly across their faces below the eyes. He saw knives, but no blasters.

A stocky figure with cold gray eyes appeared to be spokesman.

"You're the man who got landed today," he said in a deep voice and with an effect of curtness. "My name's Hunt. Two City. You a Med Ship man?"

"That's right," said Calhoun. The eyes upon him were more scared than threatening, all but the stocky man named Hunt. "I landed to find out where I was," he added. "The data-card for my astrogator had been punched wrong—what . . ."

"You know about sickness, eh?" demanded the stocky man evenly. "How to cure it and stop it?"

"I'm a Med Ship man," admitted Calhoun. "For whatever that may mean."

"You're needed in Two City," said the deep-voiced Hunt. His manner was purest resolution. "We came to get you. Get y'medicines. Dress warm. Load us down, if you like, with what you want to take. We got a sledge waiting."

Calhoun felt a momentary relief. This might make his job vastly easier. When isolation and fear brings a freezing of the mind against any novelty—even hope—a medical man has his troubles. But if one community welcomed him . . .

"*Chee!*" said Murgatroyd indignantly from overhead. Calhoun glanced up and Murgatroyd glared from a paw-hold near the ceiling. He was a peaceable animal. When there was scuffling he got out of the way. But now he chattered angrily. The masked men looked at him fearfully. Their deep-voiced leader growled at them.

"Just an animal." He swung back to Calhoun. "We got a need for you," he repeated. "We mean all right, and anything we got you can have if you want it. But you coming with us!"

"Are your good intentions," asked Calhoun, "proved by your wearing masks?"

"They're to keep from catchin' your sickness," said the deep voice impatiently. "Point to what you want us to take!"

Calhoun's feeling of encouragement vanished. He winced a little. The isolation syndrome was fully developed. It was a matter of faith that strangers were dangerous. All men were assumed to carry contagion. Once, they'd have been believed to carry bad luck. However, a regained primitiveness would still retain

some trace of the culture from which it had fallen. If
there were three settlements as the pasture lands seen
from space suggested, they would not believe in magic,
but they would believe in contagion. They might have,
or once have had, good reason. Anyhow, they would
fanatically refrain from contact with any but their own
fellow citizens. Yet, there would always be troubles to
excite their terrors. In groups of more than a very few
there would always be an impulse against the isolation which seemed the only possible safety in a hostile world. The effectiveness of the counter-instinct
would depend in part on communications, but the urge
to exogamy can produce serious results in a small culture gone fanatic.

"I think," said Calhoun, "that I'd better come with
you. But the people here have to know I've gone. I
wouldn't like them to heave my ship out to space in
pure panic because I didn't answer from inside it!"

"Leave a writing," said Hunt's deep voice, as impatiently as before. "I'll write it. Make them boil, they
won't dare follow us!"

"No?"

"Think One City men," asked the stocky man scornfully, "think One City men will risk us toppling ava-
lanches on them?"

Calhoun saw. Amid mountain country in a polar
zone, travel would be difficult at best. These intrud-
ers had risked much to come here for him; they were
proud of their daring. They did not believe that the
folk of lesser cities—tribes—groups other than theirs
had courage like theirs. Calhoun recognized it as a part
of that complex of symptoms which can begin with an
epidemic and end with group-madness.

"I'll want this, and this, and that," said Calhoun. He
wouldn't risk his microscope. Antibiotics might be useful.
Antiseptics, definitely. His med-kit. . . . "That's all."

"Your blankets," said Hunt. "Y'want them too."

Calhoun shrugged. He clothed himself for the cold outside. He had a blaster in his pocket, but he casually and openly took down a blast-rifle. His captors offered no objection. He shrugged again and replaced it. Starting to take it was only a test. He made a guess that this stocky leader, Hunt, might have kept his community just a little more nearly sane than the group that had set him to the cure of a sick cow. He hoped so.

"Murgatroyd," he said to the *tormal* still clinging up near the control-room's top. "Murgatroyd, we have a professional call to make. You'd better come along. In fact, you must."

Murgatroyd came suspiciously down, and then leaped to Calhoun's shoulder. He clung there, gazing distrustfully about. Calhoun realized that his captors—callers—whatever they were—stayed huddled away from every object in the cabin. They fingered nothing. The scared eyes of most of them proved that it was not honesty which moved them to such meticulousness. It was fear. Of contagion.

"They're uncouth, eh?" said Calhoun sardonically. "But think, Murgatroyd, they may have hearts of gold! We physicians have to pretend to think so, in any case!"

"*Chee!*" said Murgatroyd resentfully as Calhoun moved toward the lock.

III

> "Civilization is based upon rational thought applied to thinking. But there can be a deep and fundamental error about purposes. It is simply a fact that the purposes of human beings are not merely those of rational animals. It is the profoundest of errors to believe otherwise, to consider, for example, that prosperity or pleasure or even survival cannot be priced so high that their purchase is a mistake."
>
> *The Practice of Thinking*—Fitzgerald

There was a sheet of paper fastened outside the combination lock of the Med Ship's exit port. It said that Calhoun had been taken away by men of Two City, to tend some sick person. It said that he would be returned. The latter part might not be believed, but the Med Ship might not be destroyed. The colony of the landing grid might try to break into it, but success was unlikely.

Meanwhile, it was an odd feeling to cross the grassy

pasture land with hoar-frost crunching underfoot. The grid's steel girders made harsh lace of blackness against the sky, with its shining ribbon slashing across it. Calhoun found himself reflecting that the underground heat applied to the thousand-acre pasture had been regulated with discretion. There was surely power enough available from the grid to turn the area into a place of tropic warmth, in which only lush and thick-leaved vegetation could thrive. However, a storm from the frigid mountains would destroy such plants. Hardy, low-growing, semi-arctic grass was the only suitable ground cover. The iciest of winds could not freeze it so long as the ground was warmed.

Tonight's wind was biting. Calhoun had donned a parka of synthetic fur on which frost would not congeal at any temperature, but he was forced to draw fur before his face and adjust heated goggles before his eyes would stop watering. Yet in the three-quarter-mile trudge to the edge of the snow, his feet became almost uncomfortably warm.

That, though, ended where a sledge waited at the edge of the snow. Five men had forced themselves inside the Med Ship. A sixth was on guard beside the sledge. There had been no alarm. Now the stocky man, Hunt, urged him to a seat upon the sledge.

"I'm reasonably able-bodied," said Calhoun mildly.

"You don't know where we're going, or how," growled Hunt.

Calhoun got on the sledge. The runners were extra-ordinarily long. He could not see small details, but it appeared that the sledge had been made of extreme length to bridge crevasses in a glacier. There were long thin metal tubes to help. At the same time, it looked as if it could be made flexible to twist and turn in a narrow or obstacle-strewn path.

The six clumsily clad men pushed it a long way,

while Calhoun frowned at riding. Murgatroyd shivered, and Calhoun thrust him inside the parka. There Murgatroyd wriggled until his nose went up past Calhoun's chin and he could sniff the outside air. From time to time he withdrew his nose—perhaps with frost-crystals on it. But always he poked his small black snout to sniff again. His whiskers tickled.

Two miles from the pastureland, the sledge stopped. One man fumbled somewhere behind Calhoun's seat and a roaring noise began. All six piled upon the long, slender snow-vehicle. It began to move. A man swore. Then, suddenly, the sledge darted forward and went gliding up a steep incline. It gathered speed. Twin arcs of disturbed snow rose up on either side, like bow-waves from a speeding water-skimmer. The sledge darted into a great ravine of purest white and the roaring sound was multiplied by echoes.

For better than half an hour, then, Calhoun experienced a ride which for thrills and beauty and hair-raising suspense made mere space-travel the stodgiest of transportation. Once the sledge shot out from bee-tling cliffs—all icy and glittering in the light from the sky—and hurtled down a slope of snow so swiftly that the wind literally whistled about the bodies of its occupants. Then the drive roared more loudly, and there was heavy deceleration, and abruptly the sledge barely crawled. The flexibility of the thing came into operation. Four of the crew, each controlling one segment of the vehicle, caused it to twist and writhe over the surface of a glacier, where pressure-ridges abounded and pinnacles of shattered, squeezed-up ice were not uncommon.

Once they stopped short and slender rods reached out and touched, and the sledge slid delicately over them and was itself a bridge across a crevasse in the ice that went down an unguessable distance. Then it went on and the rods were retrieved. Minutes later, the sledge-motor was roaring loudly, but it barely crawled up to what appeared to be a mountain crest—there were ranges of mountains extending beyond sight in the weird blue and golden skylight—and then there was a breathtaking dash and a plunge into what was incredibly a natural tunnel beside the course of an ice river; abruptly, there was a vast valley below.

This was their destination. Some thousands of feet down in the very valley bottom there was a strange, two-mile-long patch of darkness. The blue-gold light showed no color there, but it was actually an artificially warmed pasture land like that within and about the landing grid. From this dark patch vapors ascended, and rolled, and gathered to form a misty roof, which was swept away and torn to tatters by an unseen wind.

The sledge slowed and stopped beside a precipitous upcrop of stone while still high above the valley bottom. A voice called sharply.

"It's us," growled Hunt's deep voice. "We got him. Everything all right?"

"No!" rasped the invisible voice. "They broke out—he broke out and got her loose, and they run off again. We shoulda killed 'em and had done with it!"

Everything stopped. The man on the sledge seemed to become still in the shock of pure disaster, pure frustration. Calhoun waited. Hunt was motionless. Then one of the men on the sledge spat elaborately. Then another stirred.

"Had your work for nothing," rasped the voice from the shadow. "The trouble that's started goes for nothing, too!"

Calhoun asked crisply, "What's this? My special patients ran away?"

"That the Med man we heard about?" The invisible speaker was almost derisive with anger. "Sure! They've run off, all right . . . man and girl together. After we made trouble with Three City by not killin' 'em and with One City by sneakin' over to get you! Three City men'll come boiling over. . . ." The voice raised in pitch, expressing scorn and fury. "Because they fell in love! We shoulda killed 'em right off or let 'em die in the snow like they wanted in the first place!"

Calhoun nodded almost imperceptibly to himself. When there is a syndrome forbidding association between societies, it is a part of the society's interior struggle against morbidity that there shall be forbidden romances. The practice of exogamy is necessary for racial health, hence there is an instinct for it. The more sternly a small population restricts its human contacts to its own members, the more repressed the exogamic impulse becomes. It is never consciously recognized for what it is. But especially when repressed, other-than-customary contacts trigger it explosively. The romantic appeal of a stranger is at once a wise provision of nature and a cause of incredible furies and disasters. It is notorious that spaceship crews are inordinately popular where colonies are small and strangers infrequent. It is no less notorious that a girl may be destitute of suitors on her own world, but has nearly her choice of husbands if she merely saves the ship-fare to another.

Calhoun could have predicted defiances of tradition and law and quarantine alike, as soon as he began to learn the state of things here. The frenzied rage produced by this specific case was normal. Some young girl must have loved terribly, and some young man been no less impassioned, to accept expulsion from society on a world where there was no food except in hydroponic gardens and artificially warmed pastures. It was no less than suicide for those who loved. It was no less than a cause for battle among those who did not.

The deep-voiced Hunt said now, in leaden, heavy

tones, "Cap it. This is my doing. It was my daughter I did it for. I wanted to keep her from dying. I'll pay for trying. They'll be satisfied in Three City and in One alike if you tell 'em it's my fault and I've been drove out for troublemaking."

Calhoun said sharply, "What's that? What's going on now?"

The man in the shadows answered, by his tone as much to express disgust as to give information. "His daughter Nym was on sentry duty against Three City sneaks. They had a sentry against us. The two of 'em talked across the valley between 'em. They had walkies to report with. They used 'em to talk. Presently, she sneaked a vision screen out of store. He prob'ly did, too. So presently they figured it was worth dyin' to die together. They run off for the hotlands. No chance to make it, o'course!"

The hotlands could hardly be anything but the warm equatorial belt of the planet.

"We should've let them go on and die," said the stocky Hunt, drearily. "But I persuaded men to help me bring 'em back. We were careful against sickness! We—I—locked them separate and I—I hoped my daughter mightn't die of the Three City sickness. I even hoped that young man wouldn't die of the sickness they say we have that we don't notice and they die of. Then we heard your call to One City. We couldn't answer it, but we heard all you said, even to the bargain about the cow. And—we'd heard of Med men who cured sickness. I hoped you could save Nym from dying of the Three City sickness or passing it in our city. My friends risked much to bring you here. However my daughter and the man have fled again."

"And nobody's goin' to risk any more!" rasped the voice from the shadow of the cliff. "We held a council! It's decided! They gone and we got to burn out the

places they was in! No more! You don't head the
Council any more, either! We decided that, too. And
no Med man! The Council ruled it!"

Calhoun nodded yet again. It is a part of fear, elaborately to ignore everything that can be denied about
the thing feared. Which includes rational measures
against it. This was a symptom of the state of things
which constituted a Med Service emergency, because
it caused needless deaths.

Hunt made a gesture which was at once commanding and filled with despair.

"I'll take the Med Man back so One City can use
him if they dare and not blame you for me taking him.
I'll have to take the sledge, but he's used it so it'd have
to be burned anyhow. You men be sure to burn your
clothes. Three City'll be satisfied because I'm lost to
balance for their man lost. The Med Man will tell One
City I'm drove out. You've lost me and my daughter
too, and Three City's lost a man. One City'll growl and
threaten, but they win by this. They won't risk a show-
down."

Silence again. As if reluctantly, one man of the party
that had abducted Calhoun moved away from the
sledge and toward the abysmally deep shadow of the
cliff. Hunt said harshly, "Don't forget to burn your
clothes! You others, get off the sledge. I'm taking the
Med man back and there's no need for a war because
I made the mistake and I'm paying for it."

The remaining men of the kidnapping party stepped
off the sledge into the trampled snow, just here. One
said clumsily, "Sorry, Hunt. 'Luck!"

"What luck could I have?" asked the stocky man,
wearily.

The roaring of the sledge's drive, which had been
a mere muffled throbbing, rose to a booming bellow.
The snow-vehicle surged forward, heading downward

into the valley with the dark area below. Half a mile down, it began to sweep in a great circle to return upon its former track. Calhoun twisted in his seat and shouted above the roar. He made violent gestures. The deep-voiced Hunt, driving from a standing position behind the seat, slowed the sledge. It came nearly to a stop and hissing noises from snow passing beneath it could be heard.

"What's the matter?" His tone was lifeless. "What d'you want?"

"Two people have run away," said Calhoun vexedly, "your daughter Nym and a man from Three City, whatever that is. You're driven out to prevent fighting between the cities."

"Yes," said Hunt, without expression.

"Then let's go get the runaways," said Calhoun irritably, "before they die in the snow! After all, you got me to have me save them! And there's no need for anybody to die unless they have to!"

Hunt said without any expression at all, "They're heading for the hotlands, where they'd never get. It's my meaning to take you back to your ship, and then find them and give them the sledge so's they'll—so Nym will keep on living a while longer."

He moved to shift the controls and set the sledge again in motion. His state of mind was familiar enough to Calhoun, shock or despair so great that he could feel no other emotion. He would not react to argument. He could not weigh it. He'd made a despairing conclusion and he was lost to all thought beyond carrying it out. His intention was not simply a violent reaction to a single event, such as an elopement. He intended desperate means by which a complex situation could be kept from becoming a catastrophe to others. Three City had to be dealt with in this fashion, and One City in that, and it was requisite that he die, himself. Not only for his daughter but for his community. He had resolved to go to his death for good and sufficient reasons. To get his attention to anything else, he would have to be shocked into something other than despair.

Calhoun brought his hand out of its pocket. He held the blaster. He'd pocketed the weapon before he went to examine the cow. He'd had the power to stop his own abduction at any instant. But a medical man does not refuse a call for professional service.

Now he pointed the blaster to one side and pressed the stud. A half-acre of snow burst into steam. It bellowed upward and went writhing away in the peculiar blue-gold glow of this world at night.

"I don't want to be taken back to my ship," said Calhoun firmly. "I want to catch those runaways and do whatever's necessary so they won't die at all. The situation here has been thrown into my lap. It's a Med Service obligation to intervene in problems of public health, and there's surely a public health problem here!"

Murgatroyd wriggled vigorously under Calhoun's parka. He'd heard the spitting of the blaster and the roaring of exploded steam. He was disturbed. The stocky man stared.

"What's that?" he demanded blankly. "You pick up . . ."

"We're going to pick up your daughter and the man she's with," Calhoun told him crossly. "Dammit, there's an isolation syndrome from what looks like a Crusoe health problem here! It's got to be dealt with! As a matter of public health!"

The stocky Hunt stared at him. Calhoun's intentions were unimaginable to him. He floundered among incredible ideas.

"We medics," said Calhoun, "made it necessary for men to invent interplanetary travel because we kept people from dying and the population on old Earth got too large. Then we made interstellar travel necessary because we continued to keep people from dying and one solar system wasn't big enough. We're responsible for nine-tenths of civilization as it exists today, because we produced the conditions that make civilization necessary! And since on this planet civilization is going downhill and people are dying without necessity, I have the plain obligation to stop it! So let's go pick up your daughter Nym and this sweetheart of hers, and keep them from dying and get civilization on the up-grade again!"

The former leader of the kidnappers said hoarsely, "You mean . . ." Then he stammered, "Th-th-they're heading for the hotlands. No other way to go. Watch for their tracks!"

The drive-engine bellowed. The sledge raced ahead. And now it did not complete the circle that had been begun, to head back to the landing grid. Now it straightened and rushed in a splendid roaring fierceness down between the sides of the valley. It left behind the dark patch with its whirling mists. It flung aside bow-waves of fine snow, which made rainbows in the half-light which was darkness here. It rushed and rushed and rushed, leaving behind a depression which was a singular permanent proof of its passage.

Calhoun cringed a little against the wind. He could see little or nothing of what was ahead. The sprayed wings of upflung snow prevented it. Hunt, standing erect, could do better. Murgatroyd, inside the parka, again wriggled his nose out into the stinging wind and withdrew it precipitously.

Hunt drove as if confident of where to go. Calhoun dourly began to fit things into the standard pattern of how such things went. There were evidently three cities or colonies on this planet. They'd been named and he'd seen three patches of pasture from the stratosphere. One was plainly warmed by power applied underground, electric power from the landing grid's output. The one now falling behind was less likely to be electrically heated. Steam seemed more probable because of the vapor-veil above it. This sledge was surely fuel-powered. At a guess, a ram-jet drove it. Such motors were simple enough to make, once the principle of air inflow at low speeds was known. Two City—somewhere to the rear—might operate on a fuel technology which could be based on fossil oil or gas. The power source for Three City could not now be guessed.

Calhoun scowled as he tried to fill in the picture. His factual data was still limited. There was the misty golden ribbon in space. It was assuredly beyond the technical capacity of cities suffering from an isolation syndrome. He'd guessed at underground hydroponic gardens. There was surely no surface city near the landing grid and the city entrance they'd just left was in the face of a cliff. Such items pointed to a limited technical capacity. Both, also, suggested mining as the original purpose of the human colony or colonies here.

Only mining would make a colony self-supporting in an arctic climate. This world could have been colonized to secure rare metals from it. There could be a pipeline from an oil field or from a gas well field near a landing grid. Local technological use of gas or oil to process ores might produce ingots of rare metal worth interstellar freight charges. One could even guess that metal reduced by heat-chemistry could be transported in oil suspension over terrain and under conditions when other forms of surface transportation were impractical.

If the colony began as a unit of that sort, it would require only very occasional visits of spacecraft to carry away its products. It could be a company planet, colonized and maintained by a single interstellar corporation. It could have been established a hundred and fifty or two hundred years before, when the interstellar service organizations were in their infancy and only operated where they were asked to serve. Such a colony might not even be on record in the Medical Service files.

That would account for everything. When for some reason the mines became unprofitable, this colony would not be maintained. The people who wished to leave would be taken off, of course. However, some would elect to stay behind in the warmed, familiar cities they and their fathers had been born in. They couldn't imagine moving to a strange and unfamiliar world.

So much was normal reasoning. Now the strictly technical logic of the Med Service took over to explain the current state of things. In one century or less an isolated community could lose, absolutely, its defenses against diseases to which it was never exposed. Amerinds were without defense against smallpox, back on Earth. A brown race scattered among thousands of tiny islands was nearly wiped out by measles when it was introduced. Any contact between a long-isolated community and another—perhaps itself long isolated— would bring out violently any kind of contagion that might exist in either.

There was the mechanism of carriers. The real frequency of disease-carriers in the human race had been established less than two generations ago. But a very small, isolated population could easily contain a carrier or carriers of some infection. They could spread it so freely that every member of their group acquired immunity during infancy. A different isolated group might contain a carrier of a different infection and be immune to it but distributive of a second disease.

It was literally true that each of the three cities might have developed in their first century of isolation a separate immunity to one disease and a separate defenselessness against all others. A member of one community might be actually deadly to a member of either of the others whom he met face to face.

With icy wind blowing upon him as the sled rushed on, Calhoun wryly realized that all this was wholly familiar. It was taught, nowadays, that something of the sort had caused the ancient, primitive human belief that women were perilous to men and that a man must exercise great precaution to avoid evil *mana* emanating from his prospective bride. When wives were acquired by capture and all human communities were small and fiercely self-isolated—why each unsanitary tribal group might easily acquire a condition like that Calhoun now assumed in cities One, Two, and Three. The primitive suspicion of woman would have its basis in reality if the women of one tribe possessed immunity to some deadly microbe their skin or garments harbored, and if their successful abductors had no defense against it.

The speeding sledge swerved. It leaned inward against the turn. It swerved again, throwing monstrous sheets of snow aloft. Then the drive-jet lessened its roar. The shimmering bow-waves ceased. The sledge slowed to a mere headlong glide.

"Their trail!" Hunt cried in Calhoun's ear.

Calhoun saw depressions in the snow. There were two sets of pear-shaped dents in the otherwise virgin surface. Two human beings, wearing oblong frames on their feet, crisscrossed with cordage to support them atop the snow, had trudged ahead, here, through the gold-blue night.

Calhoun knew exactly what had happened. He could make the modifications the local situation imposed upon a standard pattern, and reconstitute a complete experience leading up to now.

A girl in heavy, clumsy garments had mounted guard in a Two City sentry post above a snow-filled mountain valley. There were long and bitter cold hours of watching, in which nothing whatever happened. Eternal snows seemed eternally the same, and there was little in life but monotony. She'd known that across the valley there was another lonely watcher from an alien city, the touch of whose hand or even whose breath would meant sickness and death. She'd have mused upon the strangeness that protected her in this loneliness, because her touch or her breath would be contagion to him, too. She'd have begun by feeling a vague dread of the other sentry. But presently, perhaps, there came a furtive call on the talkie frequency used by sentries for communication with their own cities.

Very probably she did not answer at first, but she might listen. She would hear a young man's voice, filled with curiosity about the sentry who watched as he did.

There'd come a day when she'd answer shyly. There would be relief and a certain fascination in talking to someone so much like herself but so alien and so deadly! Of course, there could be no harm in talking to someone who would flee from actual face-to-face contact as desperately as herself. They might come to joke about their mutual dangerousness. They might find it amusing that cities which dared not meet should hate. Then there'd come a vast curiosity to see each other. They'd discuss that frankly, because what possible evil could come of two persons who were deadly to each other should they actually approach?

Then there'd come a time when they looked at each other breathlessly in vision screens they'd secretly stolen from their separate cities' stores. There could be no harm. They were only curious! But she would see someone at once infinitely strange, utterly dear, and he would see someone lovely beyond the girls of his own city. Then they would regret the alienness which made them perilous to each other. Then they would resent it fiercely. They'd end by denying it.

So across the valley of eternal snow there would travel whispers of desperate rebellion, and then firmly resolute murmurings, and then what seemed the most obvious of truths, that it would be much more satisfactory to die together than to live apart. Insane plannings would follow, arrangements by which two trembling young folk would meet secretly and flee. Toward the hotlands, to be sure, but without any other belief than that the days before death, while they were together, would be more precious than the lifetimes they would give up to secure them.

Calhoun could see all this very clearly, and he assured himself that he regarded it with ironic detachment. He asserted in his own mind that it was merely the manifestation of that blind impulse to exogamy which makes spacemen romantic to girls in far spaceports. But it was something more. It was also that strange and unreasonable and solely human trait which causes one to rejoice selflessly that someone else exists, so that human life and happiness is put into its place of proper insignificance in the cosmos. It might begin in instinct, but it becomes an achievement only humans can encompass.

Hunt knew it, the stocky, deep-voiced despairing figure who looked hungrily for the daughter who had defied him and for whom he was an exile from all food and warmth.

He flung out a mittened hand.

"There!" he cried joyously. "It's them!"

There was a dark speck in the blue-gold night-glow. As the sledge crept close, there were two small figures who stood close together. They defiantly faced the approaching sledge. As its drive-motor stopped and it

merely glided on, its runners whispering on the snow,
the girl snatched away the cold-mask which all the
inhabitants of this planet wore out-of-doors. She raised
her face to the man. They kissed.

Then the young man desperately raised a knife. It
glittered in the light of the ribbon in the sky—and . . .

Calhoun's blaster made its inadequate rasping noise.
The knife-blade turned incandescent for two-thirds of
its length. The young man dropped the suddenly sear-
ing handle. The knife sank hissing into the snow.

"It's always thrilling to be dramatic," said Calhoun
severely, "but I assure you it's much more satisfying
to be sane. The young lady's name is Nym, I believe.
I do not know the gentleman. Nym's father and myself
have come to put the technical resources of two civi-
lizations at your disposal as a first step toward treatment of the pandemic isolation syndrome on this
planet, which with the complications that have developed amounts to a Crusoe health problem."

Murgatroyd tried feverishly to get his head out of
Calhoun's parka past his chin. He'd heard a blaster.
He sensed excitement. His nose emerged, whiffing
frantically. Calhoun pushed it back.

"Tell them, Hunt," he said irritably. "Tell them what
we're here for and what you've done already!"

The girl's father told her unsteadily—almost hum-
bly, for some reason—that the jet-sledge had come to
take her and her sweetheart to the hotlands where at
least they would not die of cold. Calhoun added that
he believed there would even be food there, because
of the ribbon in the sky.

Trembling and abashed, the fugitives got on the
sledge. Its motor roared. It surged toward the hotlands
under the golden glow of that ribbon, which had no
rational explanation.

IV

> "An action is normally the result of a thought. Since we cannot retract an action, we tend to feel that we cannot retract the thought which produced it. In effect, we cling desperately to our mistakes. In order to change our views we have commonly to be forced to act upon new thoughts, so urgent and so necessary that without disowning our former, mistaken ideas, we can abandon them tactfully without saying anything to anybody, even ourselves."
>
> *The Practice of Thinking*—Fitzgerald

Murgatroyd came down a tree with his cheek-pouches bulged with nuts. Calhoun inserted a finger, and Murgatroyd readily permitted him to remove and examine the results of his scramble aloft. Calhoun grunted. Murgatroyd did have other and more useful abilities in the service of public health, but right here and now his delicate digestion was extremely convenient. His stomach worked so much like a human's that anything Murgatroyd ate was safe for Calhoun to an

incredible degree of probability, and Murgatroyd ate
nothing that disagreed with him.

"Instead of 'physician, heal thyself,'" Calhoun
observed, "it's amounted to 'physician, feed thyself'
since we got past the frost line, Murgatroyd. I am gratified."

"*Chee!*" said Murgatroyd complacently.

"I expected," said Calhoun, "only to benefit by the
charm of your society in what I thought would be a
routine check-trip to Merida Two. Instead, some
unknown fumble-finger punched a wrong button and
we wound up here—not exactly here, but near enough.
I brought you from the Med Ship because there was
nobody to stay around and feed you, and now you feed
us, at least by pointing out edible things we might
otherwise miss."

"*Chee!*" said Murgatroyd. He strutted.

"I wish," protested Calhoun, annoyed, "that you
wouldn't imitate that Pat character from Three City!
As a brand-new husband he's entitled to strut a little,
but I object to your imitating him! You haven't anybody acting like Nym, gazing at you raptly as if you'd
invented not only marriage but romance itself, and all
the other desirable things back to night and morning!"

Murgatroyd said, "*Chee?*" and turned to face away
from Calhoun.

The two of them, just then, stood on a leaf-covered
patch of ground which slanted down to the singularly
smooth and reflective water of a tiny bay. Behind and
above them reared gigantic mountains. There was snow
in blinding-white sheets overhead, but the snow line
itself was safely three thousand feet above them.
Beyond the bay was a wide estuary, with more mountains behind it, with more snow fields on their flanks.
A series of leaping cascades jumped downward from
somewhere aloft where a glacier-foot melted in the

sun's heat. Everywhere that snow was not, green stuff shone in the sunlight.

Nym's father, Hunt, came hurriedly toward the pair. He'd abandoned the thick felt cloak and heavy boots of Two City. Now he was dressed nearly like a civilized man, but he carried a sharpened stick in one hand and in the other a string of authentic fish. He wore an expression of astonishment. It was becoming habitual.

"Murgatroyd," said Calhoun casually, "has found another kind of edible nut. Terrestrial, too, like half the living things we've seen. Only the stuff crowding the glaciers seems to be native. The rest originated on Earth and was brought here, some time or another."

Hunt nodded. He seemed to find some difficulty in speaking.

"I've been talking to Pat," he said at last.

"The son-in-law," observed Calhoun, "who has to thank you not only for your daughter and his life, but for your public career in Two City which qualified you to perform a marriage ceremony. I hope he was respectful."

Hunt made an impatient gesture.

"He says," he protested, "that you haven't done anything either to Nym or to him to keep them from dying."

Calhoun nodded.

"That's true."

"But—they should die! Nym should die of the Three City sickness! Three City people have always said that we had a sickness too, that did not harm us, but they died of!"

"Which," agreed Calhoun, "is undoubtedly historical fact. However, tempus fugit. Its current value is that of one factor in an isolation syndrome and consequently a complicating factor in the Crusoe health problem here. I've let Nym and Pat go untreated to prove it. I think there's only a sort of mass hypochondria based on strictly accurate tradition, which would be normal."

Hunt shook his head.

"I don't understand," he protested helplessly.

"Some day I'll draw a diagram," Calhoun told him. "It is complicated. Did you check with Pat on what Three City knows about the ribbon in the sky? I suspect it accounts for the terrestrial plants and animals here, indirectly. There wouldn't be an accidental planting of edible nuts and fish and squirrels and pigeons and rabbits and bumblebees! I suspect there was a mistake somewhere. What does Pat say?"

Hunt shrugged his shoulders.

"When I talk to him," added Calhoun, "he doesn't pay attention. He simply gazes at Nym and beams. The man's mad! But you're his father-in-law. He has to be polite to you!"

Hunt sat down abruptly. He rested his spear against a tree and looked over his string of fish. He wasn't used to the abundance of foodstuffs here, and the temperature—Calhoun estimated it at fifty degrees—seemed to him incredibly balmy. Now he thoughtfully separated one fish from the rest and with a certain new skill began to slice away two neatly boneless fillets. Calhoun had showed him the trick the day after a lesson in fish-spearing, which was two days after their arrival.

"Children in Three City," growled Hunt, "are taught the same as in Two City. Men came to this planet to work the mines. There was a Company which sent them, and every so often it sent ships to take what the mines yielded, and to bring things the people wanted. Men lived well and happily. The Company hung the ribbon in the sky so the hotlands could grow food for the men. But presently the mines could not deliver what they made to the ships when they came. The hotlands grew bigger, the glaciers flowed faster, and the pipes between the cities were broken and could not be kept repaired. So the Company said that since the mine produce could no longer be had, it could not send the ships. Those who wanted to move to other worlds would be carried there. Some men went, with their wives and children. However, the grandfathers of our fathers' grandfathers were content here. They had homes and heat and food. They would not go."

Hunt regarded the pinkish brook trout fillet he'd just separated. He bit off a mouthful and chewed, thoughtfully.

"That really tastes better cooked," said Calhoun mildly.

"But it is good this way also," said Hunt. He was grizzled and stocky and somehow possessed dignity which was not to be lost merely by eating raw fish. He waved the remainder of the fillet. "Then the ships ceased to come. Then sickness came. One City had a sickness it gave to people of Two and Three when they visited it. Two City had a sickness it gave to One and Three. Three City . . ." He grunted. "Our children in Two say only Two City people have no sickness. Three City children are taught that only Three City is clean of sickness."

Calhoun said nothing. Murgatroyd tried to gnaw open one of the nuts he'd brought down from the tree. Calhoun took it and another and struck them together. Both cracked. He gave them to Murgatroyd, who ate them with great satisfaction.

Hunt looked up suddenly.

"Pat did not give a Three City sickness to Nym," he observed, "so our thinking was wrong. And Nym has not given a Two City sickness to him. His thinking was wrong."

Calhoun said meditatively, "It's tricky. But sickness can be kept by a carrier, just as you people have believed of other cities. A carrier has a sickness but does not know it. People around the carrier have the sickness on their bodies or their clothing from the carrier. They distribute it. Soon everybody in the city where there is a carrier—" Calhoun had a moment's qualm because he used the word "city." To Hunt the idea conveyed was a bare few hundred people. "Soon everybody is used to the sickness. They are immune. They cannot know it. Somebody from another city can come, and they are not used to the sickness, and they become ill and die."

Hunt considered shrewdly.

"Because the sickness is on clothing? From the carrier?"

Calhoun nodded.

"Different carriers have different sicknesses. So one carrier in One City might have one disease, and all the people in One City became used to it while they were babies, became immune. There could be another carrier with another sickness in Two City. A third in Three City. In each city they were used to their own sickness."

"That is it," said Hunt, nodding. "But why is Pat not dying or Nym? Why do you do nothing to keep them alive?"

"Suppose," said Calhoun, "the carrier of a sickness dies. What happens?"

Hunt bit again, and chewed. Suddenly, he choked. He sputtered, "There is no sickness to spread on the clothing! The people no longer have it to give to strangers who are not used to it! The babies do not get used to it while they are little! There is no longer a One City sickness or a Two City sickness or a Three!"

"There is," said Calhoun, "only a profound belief

in them. You had it. Everybody else still has it. The cities are isolated and put out sentries because they believe in what used to be true. People like Nym and Pat run away in the snow and die of it. There is much death because of it. You would have died of it."

Hunt chewed and swallowed. Then he grinned.

"Now what?" His deep voice was quaintly respectful to Calhoun, so much younger than himself. "I like this! We were not fools to believe, because it was true. But we are fools if we still believe, because it is not true anymore. How do we make people understand, Calhoun? You tell me. I can handle people when they are not afraid. I can make them do what I think wise— when they are not afraid. But when they fear . . ."

"When they fear," said Calhoun dryly, "they want a stranger to tell them what to do. You came for me, remember? You are a stranger to One City and Three City. Pat is a stranger to Two City. If the cities become really afraid . . ."

Hunt grunted. He watched Calhoun intently, and Calhoun was peculiarly reminded of the elected president of a highly cultured planet, who had exactly that completely intent way of looking at one.

"Go on!" said Hunt. "How do we frighten them into—this?"

He waved his hand about. Calhoun, his tone very dry indeed, told him. Words would not be enough. Threats would not be enough. Promises would not be enough. Even rabbits and pigeons and squirrels and fish—fish that were frozen like other human food— and piles of edible nuts, would not be enough, by themselves, but . . .

"An isolation syndrome is a neurotic condition, and a Crusoe problem amounts to neurotic hypochondria. You can do it, you and Pat."

Hunt grimaced.

"I hate the cold, now. But I will do it. After all, if I am to have grandchildren there should be other children for them to play with! We will take you back to your ship?"

"You will," said Calhoun. "By the way, what is the name of this planet, anyhow?"

Hunt told him.

Calhoun slipped across the pasture inside the landing grid and examined the ship from the outside. There had been batterings, but the door had not been opened. In the light of the ribbon in the sky he could see, too, that the ground was trampled down but only at a respectful distance. One City was disturbed about the Med Ship, but it did not know what to do. So long as nothing happened from it . . .

He was working the combination lock door when something hopped, low-down and near him. He jumped, and Murgatroyd said, "Chee?" Then Calhoun realized what had startled him. He finished the unlocking of the port. He went in and closed the port behind him. The air inside seemed curiously dead, after so long a time outside. He flipped on the outside microphones and heard tiny patterings. He heard mildly resentful cooings. He grinned.

When morning came, the people of One City would find their pasture land inhabited by small snowshoe rabbits and small and bush-tailed squirrels and fluttering pigeons. They would react as Two City and Three City had already done—with panic. The panic would inevitably call up the notion of the most feared thing in their lives. Sickness. The most feared thing is always a rare thing, of course. One cannot fear a frequent thing, because one either dies of it or comes to take it for granted. Fear is always of the rare or nonexistent. One City would be filled with fear of sickness.

Sickness would come. Hunt would call them, presently, on a walkie-talkie communicator. He would express deep concern because—so he'd say—new domestic animals intended for Two City had been dumped on One City pasture land. He'd add that they were highly infective, and One City was already inescapably doomed to an epidemic which would begin with severe headaches, and would continue with cramps and extreme nervous agitation. He would say that Calhoun had left medicines at Two City with which that sickness and all others could be cured, and if the sickness described should appear in One City—why—its victims would be cured if they traveled to Two City.

The sickness would appear. Inevitably. There was no longer sickness in the three communities. Arctic colonies, never visited by people from reservoirs of infection, become magnificently healthy by the operation of purely natural causes, but an isolation syndrome . . .

The people of One City would presently travel, groaning, to Two City. Their suffering would be real. They would dread the breaking of their isolation. But they'd dread sickness—even sickness they only imagined—still more. When they reached Two City they would find themselves tended by Three City members, and they would be appalled and terrified. But mock medication by Hunt and Pat—and Nym for the women—would reassure them. A Crusoe condition requires heroic treatment. This was it.

Calhoun cheerfully checked over the equipment of the Med Ship. He'd have to take off on emergency rockets. He'd have to be very, very careful in setting a course back to headquarters to report before starting out again for Merida II. He didn't want to make any mistake . . . Suddenly, he began to chuckle.

"Murgatroyd," he said amiably, "it's just occurred to me that the mistakes we make, that we struggle to hard to avoid, are part of the scheme of things."

"*Chee?*" said Murgatroyd inquiringly.

"The Company that settled this planet," said Calhoun, grinning, "set up that ribbon out in space as a splendidly conservative investment to save money in freight charges. It was a mistake, because it ruined their mining business and they had to write the whole colony off. They made another mistake by not reporting to Med Service, because now they've abandoned the colony and would have to get a license to reoccupy, which they'd never be granted against the population already here. Somebody made a mistake that brought us here, and One City made a mistake by not accepting us as guests, and Two City made a mistake by sending Nym on sentry duty, and Three City made a mistake . . ."

Murgatroyd yawned.

"You," said Calhoun severely, "make a mistake in not paying attention!" He strapped himself in. He stabbed an emergency rocket control-button. The little ship shot heavenward on a pencil-thin stream of fire. Below him, people of One City would come pouring out of underground to learn what had happened, and they'd find the pasture swarming with friendly squirrels and inquisitive rabbits and cooing pigeons. They'd be scared to death. Calhoun laughed. "I'll spend part of the time in overdrive making a report on it. Since an isolation syndrome is mostly psychological, and a Crusoe condition is wholly so, I managed sound medical treatment by purely psychological means! I'll have fun with that!"

It was a mistake. He got back to headquarters, all right, but when his report was read they made him expand it into a book, with footnotes, an index, and a bibliography.

TALLIEN THREE

TALLER THREE

I

The Med Ship *Aesclipus Twenty* rode in overdrive while her ship's company drank coffee. Calhoun sipped at a full cup of strong brew, while Murgatroyd the *tormal* drank from the tiny mug suited to his small, furry paws. The astrogation-unit showed the percentage of this overdrive-hop covered up to now, and the needle was almost around to the stop-pin.

There'd been a warning gong an hour ago, notifying that the end of overdrive journeying approached. Hence the coffee. When breakout came, the overdrive field should collapse and the Duhanne cells down near the small ship's keel absorb the energy which maintained it. Then *Aesclipus Twenty* would appear in the normal universe of suns and stars with the abruptness of an explosion. She should be somewhere near the sun Tallien. She should then swim toward that Sol-type sun and approach Tallien's third planet out at the less-than-light-speed rate necessary for solar-system travel. And presently she would signal down to ground and Calhoun set about the purpose of his three-week journey in overdrive. His purpose was a routine check-up on public health on Tallien Three. Calhoun had lately completed five such planetary visits, with from one to three weeks of overdrive travel between each pair. When he left Tallien Three he'd head back to Sector Headquarters for more orders about the work of the Interstellar Medical Service.

Murgatroyd zestfully licked his empty cup to get the last least drop of coffee. He said hopefully:

"Chee?" He wanted more.

"I'm afraid," said Calhoun, "that you're a sybarite, Murgatroyd. This impassioned desire of yours for coffee disturbs me."

"Chee!" said Murgatroyd, with decision.

"It's become a habit," Calhoun told him severely. "You should taper off. Remember, when anything in your environment becomes a normal part of your environment, it becomes a necessity. Coffee should be a luxury, to be savored as such, instead of something you expect and resent being deprived of."

Murgatroyd said impatiently:

"Chee-chee!"

"All right, then," said Calhoun, "if you're going to be emotional about it! Pass your cup."

He reached out and Murgatroyd put the tiny object in his hand. He refilled it and passed it back.

"But watch yourself," he advised. "We're landing on Tallien Three. It's just been transferred to us from another sector. It's been neglected. There's been no Med Service inspection for years. There could be misunderstandings."

Murgatroyd said, *"Chee!"* and squatted down to drink.

Calhoun looked at a clock and opened his mouth to speak again, when a taped voice said abruptly:

"When the gong sounds, breakout will be five seconds off."

There was a steady, monotonous tick, tock, tick, tock, like a metronome. Calhoun got up and made a casual examination of the ship's instruments. He turned on the vision-screens. They were useless in overdrive, of course. Now they were ready to inform him about the normal cosmos as soon as the ship returned to it. He put away the coffee things. Murgatroyd was reluctant to give up his mug until the last possible lick. Then he sat back and elaborately cleaned his whiskers.

Calhoun sat down in the control-chair and waited.

"Bong!" said the loud-speaker, and Murgatroyd scuttled under a chair. He held on with all four paws and his furry tail. The speaker said, *"Breakout in five seconds . . . four . . . three . . . two . . . one . . ."*

There was a sensation as if all the universe had turned itself inside out and Calhoun's stomach tried to follow its example. He gulped, and the feeling ended, and the vision-screens came alight. Then there were ten thousand myriads of stars, and a sun flaming balefully ahead, and certain very bright objects nearby. They would be planets, and one of them showed as a crescent.

Calhoun checked the solar spectrum as a matter of course. This was the sun Tallien. He checked the brighter specks in view. Three were planets and one a remote brilliant star. The crescent was Tallien Three, third out from its sun and the Med Ship's immediate destination. It was a very good breakout; too good to be anything but luck. Calhoun swung the ship for the crescent planet. He matter-of-factly checked the usual items. He was going in at a high angle to the ecliptic, so meteors and bits of stray celestial trash weren't likely to be bothersome. He made other notes, to kill time.

He re-read the data-sheets on the planet. It had been colonized three hundred years before. There'd been trouble establishing a human-use ecological system on the planet because the native plants and animals were totally useless to humankind. Native timber could be used in building, but only after drying-out for a period of months. When growing or green it was as much water-saturated as a sponge. There had never been a forest fire here; not even caused by lightning!

There were other oddities. The aboriginal microorganisms here did not attack wastes of introduced terrestrial types. It had been necessary to introduce scavenger organisms from elsewhere. This and other difficulties made it true that only one of the world's five continents was human-occupied. Most of the landsurface was strictly as it had been before the landing of men—impenetrable jungles of sponge-like flora, dwelt in by a largely unknown because useless fauna. Calhoun read on. Population . . . government . . . health statistics . . . He went through the list.

He still had time to kill, so he re-checked his course and speed relative to the planet. He and Murgatroyd had dinner. Then he waited until the ship was near enough to report in.

"Med Ship *Aesclipus Twenty* calling ground," he said when the time came. He taped his own voice as he made the call. "Requesting coordinates for landing. Our mass is fifty tons. Repeat, five-oh tons. Purpose of landing, planetary health inspection."

He waited while his taped voice repeated and re-repeated the call. An incoming voice said sharply:

"Calling Med Ship! Cut your signal! Do not acknowledge this call! Cut your signal! Instructions will follow. But cut your signal!"

Calhoun blinked. Of all possible responses to a

landing call, orders to stop signaling would be least likely. But after an instant he reached over and stopped the transmission of his voice. It happened to end halfway through a syllable.

Silence. Not quite silence, of course, because there was the taped record of background-noise which went on all the time the Med Ship was in space. Without it, the utter absence of noise would be sepulchral.

The voice from outside said:

"You cut off. Good! Now listen! Do not—repeat, do not!—acknowledge this call or respond to any call from anyone else! There is a drastic situation aground. You must not—repeat, must not—fall into the hands of the people now occupying Government Center! Go into orbit. We will try to seize the space-port so you can be landed. But do not acknowledge this call or respond to any answer from anyone else! Don't do it! Don't do it!"

There was a click, and somehow the silence was clamorous. Calhoun rubbed his nose reflectively with his finger. Murgatroyd, bright-eyed, immediately rubbed his nose with a tiny dark digit. Like all *tormals*, he gloried in imitating human actions. But suddenly a second voice called in, with a new and strictly professional tone.

"Calling Med Ship!" said this second voice. *"Calling Med Ship! Space-port Tallien Three calling Med Ship Aesclipus Twenty! For landing repair to coordinates—"*

The voice briskly gave specific instructions. It was a strictly professional voice. It repeated the instructions with precision.

Out of sheer habit, Calhoun said, "Acknowledge." Then he added sharply: "Hold it! I've just had an emergency call—"

The first voice interrupted stridently:

"Cut your signal, you fool! I told you not to answer any other call! Cut your signal!"

The strictly professional voice said coldly:

"Emergency call, eh? That'll be paras. They're better organized than we thought, if they picked up your landing-request! There's an emergency, all right! It's the devil of an emergency—it looks like devils! But this is the space-port. Will you come in?"

"Naturally," said Calhoun. "What's the emergency?"

"You'll find out—" That was the professional voice. The other snapped angrily, *"Cut your signal!"* The professional voice again *". . . you land. It's not—" "Cut your signal, you fool! Cut it—"*

There was confusion. The two voices spoke together. Each was on a tight beam, while Calhoun's call was broadcast. The voices could not hear each other, but each could hear Calhoun.

"Don't listen to them! There's—" "to understand, but—" "Don't listen! Don't—" ". . . when you land."

Then the voice from the space-port stopped, and Calhoun cut down the volume of the other. It continued to shout, though muffled. It bellow, as if rattled. It mouthed commands as if they were arguments or reasons. Calhoun listened for fully five minutes. Then he said carefully into his microphone:

"Med Ship *Aesclipus Twenty* calling space-port. I will arrive at given coordinates at the time given. I suggest that you take precautions if necessary against interference with my landing. Message ends."

He swung the ship around and aimed for the destination with which he'd been supplied—a place in emptiness five diameters out with the center of the sun's disk bearing so-and-so and the center of the planet's disk bearing so-and-thus. He turned the communicator-volume down still lower. The miniature voice shouted and threatened in the stillness of the Med

Ship's control-room. After a time Calhoun said reflectively:

"I don't like this, Murgatroyd! An unidentified voice is telling us—and we're Med Ship personnel, Murgatroyd!—who we should speak to and what we should do. Our duty is plainly to ignore such orders. But with dignity, Murgatroyd! We must uphold the dignity of the Med Service!"

Murgatroyd said skeptically:

"*Chee?*"

"I don't like your attitude," said Calhoun, "but I'll bear in mind that you're often right."

Murgatroyd found a soft place to curl up in. He draped his tail across his nose and lay there, blinking at Calhoun above the furry half-mask.

The little ship drove on. The disk of the planet grew large. Presently it was below. It turned as the ship moved, and from a crescent it became a half-circle and then a gibbous near-oval shape. In the rest of the solar system nothing in particular happened. Small and heavy inner planets swam deliberately in their short orbits around the sun. Outer, gas-giant planets floated even more deliberately in larger paths. There were comets of telescopic size, and there were meteorites, and the sun Tallien sent up monstrous flares, and storms of improbable snow swept about in the methane atmosphere of the greater gas-giant of this particular celestial family of this sun and its satellites. But the cosmos in general paid no attention to human activities or usually undesirable intentions. Calhoun listened, frowning, to the agitated, commanding voice. He still didn't like it.

Suddenly, it cut off. The Med Ship approached the planet to which it had been ordered by Sector Headquarters now some months ago. Calhoun examined the nearing world via electron telescope. On the hemisphere rolling to a position under the Med Ship he saw a city of some size, and he could trace highways, and there were lesser human settlements here and there. At full magnification he could see where forests had been cut away in wedges and half-squares, with clear spaces between them. This indicated cultivated ground, cleared for human use in the invincibly tidy-minded manner of men. Presently he saw the landing-grid near the biggest city—the half-mile-high, cage-like wall of intricately braced steel girders. It tapped the planet's ionosphere for all the power that this world's inhabitants could use, and applied the same power to lift up and let down the ships of space by which communication with the rest of humanity was maintained. From this distance, though, even with an electron telescope, Calhoun could see no movement of any sort. There was no smoke, because electricity from the grid provided all the planet's power and heat, and there were no chimneys. The city looked like a colored map, with infinite detail but nothing which stirred.

A tiny voice spoke. It was the voice of the space-port.

"Calling Med Ship. Grid locking on. Right?"

"Go ahead," said Calhoun. He turned up the communicator.

The voice from the ground said carefully:

"Better stand by your controls. If anything happens down here you may need to take emergency action."

Calhoun raised his eyebrows. But he said:

"All set."

He felt the cushiony, fumbling motions as force-fields from the landing-grid groped for the Med Ship and centered it in their complex pattern. Then there came the sudden solid feeling when the grid locked on. The Med Ship began to settle, at first slowly but with increasing speed, toward the ground below.

It was all very familiar. The shapes of the continents

below him were strange, but such unfamiliarity was commonplace. The voice from the ground said matter-of-factly:

"We think everything's under control, but it's hard to tell with these paras. They got away with some weather-rockets last week and may have managed to mount warheads on them. They might use them on the grid, here, or try for you."

Calhoun said:

"What are paras?"

"You'll be briefed when you land," said the voice. It added, *"Everything's all right so far, though."*

The *Aesclipus Twenty* went down and down and down. The grid had locked on at forty thousand miles. It was a long time before the little ship was down to thirty thousand and another long time before it was at twenty. Then more time to reach ten, and then five, and one thousand, and five hundred. When solid ground was only a hundred miles below and the curve of the horizon had to be looked for to be seen, the voice from the ground said:

"The last hundred miles is the tricky part, and the last five will be where it's tight. If anything does happen, it'll be there."

Calhoun watched through the electron telescope. He could see individual buildings now, when he used full magnification. He saw infinitesimal motes which would be ground-cars on the highways. At seventy miles he cut down the magnification to keep his field of vision wide. He cut the magnification again at fifty and at thirty and at ten.

Then he saw the first sign of motion. It was an extending thread of white which could only be smoke. It began well outside the city and leaped up and curved, evidently aiming at the descending Med Ship. Calhoun said curtly:

"There's a rocket coming up. Aiming at me."

The voice from the ground said:

"It's spotted. I'm giving you free motion if you want to use it."

The feel of the ship changed. It no longer descended. The landing-grid operator was holding it aloft, but Calhoun could move it in evasive action if he wished. He approved the liberty given him. He could use his emergency-rockets for evasion. A second thread of smoke came streaking upward.

Then other threads of white began just outside the landing-grid. They rushed after the first. The original rockets seemed to dodge. Others came up. There was an intricate pattern formed by the smoke-trails of rockets rising and other rockets following, and some trails swerving dodging and others closing in. Calhoun carefully reminded himself that it was not likely that there'd be atomic war-heads. The last planetary wars had been fought with fusion weapons, and only the crews of single ships survived. The planetary populations didn't. But atomic energy wasn't much used aground, these days. Power for planetary use could be had more easily from the upper, ionized limits of atmospheres.

A pursuing rocket closed in. There was a huge ball of smoke and a flash of light, but it was not brighter than the sun. It wasn't atomic flame. Calhoun relaxed. He watched as every one of the first-ascended rockets was tracked down and destroyed by another. The last, at that, was three-quarters of the way up.

The Med Ship quivered a little as the force-fields tightened again. It descended swiftly. It came to ground. Figures came to meet Calhoun as, with Murgatroyd, he went out of the airlock. Some were uniformed. All wore the grim expressions and harried looks of men under long-continued stress.

The landing-grid operator shook hands first.

"Nice going! It could be lucky that you arrived. We normals need some luck!"

He introduced a man in civilian clothes as the planetary Minister for Health. A man in uniform was head of the planetary police. Another—

"We worked fast after your call came!" said the grid operators. "Things are lined up for you, but they're bad!"

"I've been wondering," admitted Calhoun dryly, "if all incoming ships are greeted with rockets."

"That's the paras," said the police head, grimly. "They'd rather not have a Med Service man here."

A ground-car sped across the space-port. It came at a headlong pace toward the group just outside the Med Ship. There was the sudden howl of a siren by the space-port gate. A second car leaped as if to intercept the first. Its siren screamed again. Then bright sparks appeared near the first car's windows. Blasters rasped. Incredulously, Calhoun saw the blue-white of blaster-bolts darting toward him. The men about him clawed for weapons. The grid operator said sharply:

"Get in your ship! We'll take care of this! It's paras!"

But Calhoun stood still. It was instinct not to show alarm. Actually, he didn't feel it. This was too preposterous! He tried to grasp the situation and fearfulness does not help at such a time.

A bolt crackled against the Med Ship's hull just behind him. Blasters rasped from beside him. A bolt exploded almost at Calhoun's feet. There were two men in the first-moving ground-car, and now that another car moved to head them off, one fired desperately and the other tried to steer and fire at the same time. The siren-sounding car sent a stream of bolts at them. But both cars jounced and bounced. There could be no marksmanship under such conditions.

But a bolt did hit. The two-man car dipped suddenly to one side. Its fore-part touched ground. It slued around, and its rear part lifted. It flung out its two passengers and with an effect of great deliberation it rolled over end for end and came to a stop upside down. Of its passengers, one lay still. The other struggled to his feet and began to run. Toward Calhoun. He fired desperately, again and again—

Bolts from the pursuing car struck all around him. Then one struck him. He collapsed.

Calhoun's hands clenched. Automatically, he moved toward the other still figure, to act as a medical man does when somebody is hurt. The grid operator seized his arm. As Calhoun jerked to get free, that second man stirred. His blaster lifted and rasped. The little pellet of ball-lightning grazed Calhoun's side, burning away his uniform down to the skin, just as there was a grating roar of blaster-fire. The second man died.

"Are you crazy?" demanded the grid operator angrily. "He was a para! He was here to try to kill you!"

The police head snapped:

"Get that car sprayed! See if it had equipment to spread contagion! Spray everything it went near! And hurry!"

There was silence as men came from the space-port building. They pushed a tank on wheels before them. It had a hose and a nozzle attached to it. They began to use the hose to make a thick, fog-like, heavy mist which clung to the ground and lingered there. The spray had the biting smell of phenol.

"What's going on here?" demanded Calhoun angrily. "Damnation! What's going on here?"

The Minister for Health said unhappily:

"Why—we've a public-health situation we haven't been able to meet. It appears to be an epidemic of—of—we're not sure what, but it looks like demoniac possession."

"I'd like," said Calhoun, "a definition. Just what do you mean by a para?"

Murgatroyd echoed his tone in an indignant, *"Chee-chee!"*

This was twenty minutes later. Calhoun had gone back into the Med Ship and treated the blaster-burn on his side. He'd changed his clothing from the scorched uniform to civilian clothing. It would not look eccentric here. Men's ordinary garments were extremely similar all over the galaxy. Women's clothes were something else.

Now he and Murgatroyd rode in a ground-car with four armed men of the planetary police, plus the civilian who'd been introduced as the Minister for Health for the planet. The car sped briskly toward the space-port gate. Masses of thick gray fog still clung to the ground where the would-be assassins' car lay on its back and where the bodies of the two dead men remained. The mist was being spread everywhere—everywhere the men had touched ground or where their car had run.

Calhoun had some experience with epidemics and emergency measures for destroying contagion. He had more confidence in the primitive sanitary value of fire. It worked, no matter how ancient the process of burning things might be. But very many human beings, these days, never saw a naked flame unless in a science class at school, where it might be shown as a spectacularly rapid reaction of oxidation. People used electricity for heat and light and power. Mankind had moved out of the age of fire. So here on Tallien it seemed inevitable that infective material should be sprayed with antiseptics instead of simply set ablaze.

"What," repeated Calhoun doggedly, "is a para?"

The Health Minister said unhappily:

"Paras are—beings that once were sane men. They aren't sane any longer. Perhaps they aren't men any longer. Something has happened to them. If you'd landed a day or two later, you couldn't have landed at all. We normals had planned to blow up the landing-grid so no other ship could land and be lifted off again to spread the—contagion to other worlds. If it is a contagion."

"Smashing the landing-grid," said Calhoun practically, "may be all right as a last resort. But surely there are other things to be tried first!"

Then he stopped. The ground-car in which he rode had reached the space-port gate. Three other ground-cars waited there. One swung into motion ahead of them. The other two took up positions behind. A caravan of four cars, each bristling with blast-weapons, swept along the wide highway which began here at the space-port and stretched straight across level ground toward the city whose towers showed on the horizon. The other cars formed a guard for Calhoun. He'd needed protection before, and he might need it again.

"Medically," he said to the Minister for Health, "I take it that a para is the human victim of some condition which makes him act insanely. That is pretty vague. You say it hasn't been controlled. That leaves everything very vague indeed. How widely spread is it? Geographically, I mean."

"Paras have appeared," said the Minister for Health, "at every place on Tallien Three where there are men."

"It's epidemic, then," said Calhoun professionally. "You might call it pandemic. How many cases?"

"We guess at thirty percent of the population—so far," said the Minister for Health, hopelessly. "But every day the total goes up." He added, "Doctor Lett has some hope for a vaccine, but it will be too late for most."

Calhoun frowned. With reasonably modern medical techniques, almost any sort of infection should be stopped long before there were as many cases as that!

"When did it start? How long has it been running?"

"The first paras were examined six months ago," said the Health Minister. "It was thought to be a disease. Our best physicians examined them. They couldn't agree on a cause, they couldn't find a germ or virus . . ."

"Symptoms?" asked Calhoun crisply.

"Doctor Lett phrased them in medical terms," said the Minister for Health. "The condition begins with a period of great irritability or depression. The depression is so great that suicide is not infrequent. If that doesn't happen, there's a period of suspiciousness and secretiveness—strongly suggestive of paranoia. Then there's a craving for—unusual food. When it becomes uncontrollable, the patient is mad!"

The ground-cars sped toward the city. A second group of vehicles appeared, waiting. As the four-car caravan swept up to them, one swung in front of the car in which Calhoun and Murgatroyd rode. The others fell into line to the rear. It began to look like a respectable fighting force.

"And after madness?" asked Calhoun.

"Then they're paras!" said the Health Minister. "They crave the incredible. They feed on the abominable. And they hate us normals as—devils out of hell would hate us!"

"And after that again?" said Calhoun. "I mean, what's the prognosis? Do they die or recover? If they recover, in how long? If they die, how soon?"

"They're paras," said the Health Minister querulously. "I'm no physician—I'm an administrator. But I don't think any recover. Certainly none die of it! They stay—what they've become."

"My experience," said Calhoun, "has mostly been with diseases that one either recovers from or dies of. A disease whose victims organize to steal weather rockets and to use them to destroy a ship—only they failed—and who carry on with an assassination-attempt, that doesn't sound like a disease. A disease had no purpose of its own. They had a purpose—as if they obeyed one of their number."

The Minister for Health said uneasily:

"It's been suggested—that something out of the jungle causes what's happened. On other planets there are creatures which drink blood without waking their victims. There are reptiles who sting men. There are even insects which sting men and inject diseases. Something like that seems to have come out of the jungle. While men sleep—something happens to them! They turn into paras. Something native to this world must be responsible. The planet did not welcome us. There's not a native plant or beast that is useful to us. We have to culture soil-bacteria so Earth-type plants can grow here. We don't begin to know all the creatures of the jungle. If something comes out and makes men paras without their knowledge—"

Calhoun said mildly:

"It would seem that such things could be discovered."

The Health Minister said bitterly:

"Not this thing. It is intelligent. It hides! It acts as if on a plan to destroy us! Why—there was a young doctor who said he'd cured a para. But we found him and the former para dead when we went to check his claim. Things from the jungle had killed them! They think! They know! They understand! They're rational, and like devils—"

A third group of ground-cars appeared ahead, waiting. Like the others, they were filled with men holding blast-rifles. They joined the procession; the rushing, never-pausing group of cars from the space-port. The highway had obviously been patrolled against a possible ambush or road-block. The augmented combat group went on.

"As a medical man," said Calhoun carefully, "I question the existence of a local, non-human rational creature. Creatures develop or adapt to fit their environment. They change or develop to fit into some niche, some special place in the ecological system which is their environment. If there is no niche, no room for a specific creature in an environment, there is no such creature there. And there cannot be a place in any environment for a creature which will change it. It would be a contradiction in terms! We rational humans change the worlds we occupy. Any rational creature will. So a rational animal is as nearly impossible as any creature can be. It's true that we've happened, but—another rational race? Oh, no!"

Murgatroyd said:

"Chee!"

The city's towers loomed higher and taller above the horizon. Then, abruptly, the fast-moving cavalcade came to the edge of the city and plunged into it.

It was not a normal city. The buildings were not eccentric. All planets but very new ones show local architectural peculiarities, so it was not odd to see all windows topped by triple arches, or quite useless pilasters in the brick walls of apartment-buildings. These would have made the city seem only individual. But it was not normal. The streets were not clean. Two windows in three had been smashed. In places Calhoun saw doors that had been broken in and splintered, and never repaired. That implied violence unrestrained. The streets were almost empty. Occasional figures might be seen on the sidewalks before the speeding ground-cars, but the vehicles never passed them. Pedestrians turned corners or dodged into doorways before the cavalcade could overtake them.

The buildings grew taller. The street-level remained empty of humans, but now and again, many storeys up, heads peered out of windows. Then high-pitched yellings came from aloft. It was not possible to tell whether they were yells of defiance or derision or despair, but they were directed at the racing cars.

Calhoun looked quickly at the faces of the men around him. The Minister for Health looked at once heart-broken and embittered. The head of the planetary police stared grimly ahead. Screechings and howlings echoed and reechoed between the building-walls. Objects began to fall from the windows. Bottles. Pots and pans. Chairs and stools twirled and spun, hurtling downward. Everything that was loose and could be thrown from a window came down, flung by the occupants of those high dwellings. With them came outcries which were assuredly cursings.

It occurred to Calhoun that there had been a period in history when mob-action invariably meant flames. Men burned what they hated and what they feared. They also burned religious offerings to divers blood-thirsty deities. It was fortunate, he reflected wryly, that fires were no longer a matter of common experience, or burning oil and flaming missiles would have been flung down on the ground-cars.

"Is this unpopularity yours?" he asked. "Or do I have a share in it? Am I unwelcome to some parts of the population?"

"You're unwelcome to paras," said the police head coldly. "Paras don't want you here. Whatever drives them is afraid the Med Service might make them no longer paras. And they want to stay the way they are." His lips twisted. "They aren't making this uproar, though. We gathered everybody we were sure wasn't—infected into Government Center. These people were left out. We weren't sure about them. So they consider we've left them to become paras and they don't like it!"

Calhoun frowned again. This confused everything. There was talk of infection, and talk of unseen creatures come out of the jungle, making men paras and then controlling them as if by demoniac possession. There were few human vagaries, though, that were not recorded in the Med Service files. Calhoun remembered something, and wanted to be sick. It was like an infection, and like possession by devils too. There would be creatures not much removed from fiends involved, anyhow.

"I think," he said, "that I need to talk to your counter-para researchers. You have men working on the problem?"

"We did," said the police head, grimly. "But most of them turned para. We thought they'd be more

dangerous than other paras, so we shot them. But it
did no good. Paras still turn up, in Government Center
too. Now we only send paras out the south gate. They
doubtless make out—as paras."

For a time there was silence in the rushing cars,
though a bedlam of howls and curses came from aloft.
Then a sudden shrieking of foreseen triumph came
from overhead. A huge piece of furniture, a couch,
seemed certain to crash into the car in which Calhoun
rode. But it swerved sharply, ran upon the sidewalk,
and the couch dashed itself to splinters where the car
should have been. The car went down on the pavement once more and rushed on.

The street ended. A high barrier of masonry rose
up at a cross-street. It closed the highway and connected the walls of apartment-buildings on either hand.
There was a gate in it, and the leading cars drew off
to one side and the car carrying Calhoun and
Murgatroyd ran through, and there was a second
barrier ahead, but this was closed. The other cars filed
in after it, Calhoun saw that windows in these
apartment-buildings had all been bricked up. They
made a many-storeyed wall shutting off all that was
beyond them.

Men from the barrier went from car to car of the
escort, checking the men who had been the escort for
Calhoun. The Minister for Health said jerkily:

"Everybody in Government Center is examined at
least once each day to see if they're turning para or
not. Those showing symptoms are turned out the south
gate. Everybody, myself included, has to have a fresh
certificate every twenty-four hours."

The inner gate swung wide. The car carrying
Calhoun went through. The buildings about them
ended. They were in a huge open space that must once
have been a park in the center of the city. There were

structures which could not possibly be other than
government buildings. But the population of this world
was small. They were not grandiose. There were walk-
ways and some temporary buildings obviously thrown
hastily together to house a sudden influx of people.

And here there were many people. There was bright
sunshine, and children played and women watched
them. There were some—not many—men in sight, but
most of them were elderly. All the young ones were
uniformed and hastily going here or there. And though
the children played gaily, there were few smiles to be
seen on adult faces.

The ground-car braked before one of those square,
unornamented buildings which are laboratories everywhere in the galaxy. The Minister for Health got out.
Calhoun followed him, Murgatroyd riding on his shoulder. The ground-car went away and Calhoun followed
into the building.

There was a sentry by the door, and an officer of
the police. He examined the Minister's one-day certificate of health. After various vision-phone calls, he
passed Calhoun and Murgatroyd. They went a short
distance and another sentry stopped them. A little
further, and another sentry.

"Tight security," said Calhoun.

"They know me," said the Minister heavily, "but they
are checking my certificate that as of this morning I
wasn't a para."

"I've seen quarantines before," said Calhoun, "but
never one like this! Not against disease!"

"It isn't against disease," said the Minister, thinly.
"It's against Something intelligent—from the jungles—
who chooses victims by reason for its own purposes."

Calhoun said very carefully:

"I won't deny more than the jungle."

Here the Minister for Health rapped on a door and

ushered Calhoun through it. They entered a huge room filled with the complex of desks, cameras, and observing and recording instruments that the study of a living organism requires. The set-up for study of dead things is quite different. Here, halfway down the room's length, there was a massive sheet of glass that divided the apartment into two. On the far side of the glass there was, obviously, an aseptic-environment room now being used as an isolation-chamber.

A man paced up and down beyond the glass. Calhoun knew he must be a para because he was cut off in idea and in fact from normal humanity. The air supplied to him could be heated almost white-hot and then chilled before being introduced into the aseptic-chamber for him to breathe, if such a thing was desired. Or the air removed could be made incandescent hot so no possible germ or its spores could get out. Wastes removed would be destroyed by passage through a carbon arc after innumerable previous sterilizing processes. In such rooms, centuries before, plants had been grown from antiseptic-soaked seeds, and chicks hatched from germ-free eggs, and even small animals delivered by aseptic Caesarian section to live in an environment in which there was no living microorganism. From rooms like this men had first learned that some types of bacteria outside the human body were essential to human health. But this man was not a volunteer for such research.

He paced up and down, his hands clenching and unclenching. When Calhoun and the Minister for Health entered the outer room, he glared at them. He cursed them, though inaudibly because of the plate of glass. He hated them hideously because they were not as he was; because they were not imprisoned behind thick glass walls through which every action and almost every thought could be watched. But there was more to his hatred than that. In the midst of fury so great that his face seemed almost purple, he suddenly yawned uncontrollably.

Calhoun blinked and stared. The man behind the glass wall yawned again and again. He was helpless to stop it. If such a thing could be, he was in a paroxysm of yawning, though his eyes glared and he beat his fists together. The muscles controlling the act of yawning worked independently of the rage that should have made yawning impossible. And he was ashamed, and he was infuriated, and he yawned more violently than seemed possible.

"A man's been known to dislocate his jaw, yawning like that," said Calhoun detachedly.

A bland voice spoke behind him.

"But if this man's jaw is dislocated, no one can help him. He is a para. We cannot join him."

Calhoun turned. He found himself regarded with unctuous condescension by a man wearing glittering thick eyeglasses—and a man's eyes have to be very bad if he can't wear contacts—and a uniform with a caduceus at his collar. He was plump. He was beaming. He was the only man Calhoun had so far seen on this planet whose expression was neither despair nor baffled hate and fury.

"You are Med Service," the beaming man observed zestfully. "Of the Interstellar Medical Service, to which all problems of public health may be referred! But here we have a real problem for you! A contagious madness! A transmissible delusion! An epidemic of insanity! A plague of the unspeakable!"

The Minister for Health said uneasily:

"This is Doctor Lett. He was the greatest of our physicians. Now he is nearly the last."

"Agreed," said the bland man, as zestfully as before. "But now the Interstellar Medical Services sends someone before whom I should bow! Someone whose knowledge and experience and training is so infinitely greater than mine that I become abashed! I am timid! I am hesitant to offer an opinion before a Med Service man!"

It was not unprecedented for an eminent doctor to resent the implied existence of greater skill or knowledge than his own. But this man was not only resentful. He was derisive.

"I came here," said Calhoun politely, "on what I expected to be a strictly routine visit. But I'm told there's a very grave public health situation here. I'd like to offer any help I can give."

"Grave!" Doctor Lett laughed scornfully. "It is hopeless, for poor planetary doctors like myself! But not, of course, for a Med Ship man!"

Calhoun shook his head. This man would not be easy to deal with. Tact was called for—but the situation was appalling.

"I have a question," said Calhoun ruefully. "I'm told that paras are madmen, and there's been mention of suspicion and secretiveness which suggests schizoparanoia and—so I have guessed—the term para for those affected in this way."

"It is not any form of paranoia," said the planetary doctor, contemptuously. "Paranoia involves suspicion of everyone. Paras despise and suspect only normals. Paranoia involves a sensation of grandeur, not to be shared. Paras are friends and companions to each other. They cooperate delightedly in attempting to make normals like themselves. A paranoiac would not want anyone to share his greatness!"

Calhoun considered, and then agreed.

"Since you've said it, I see that it must be so. But my question remains. Madness involves delusions. But paras organize themselves. They make plans and take

different parts in them. They act rationally for purposes
they agree on—such as assassinating me. But how can
they act rationally if they have delusions? What sort
of delusions do they have?"

The Minister for Health said thinly:

"Only what horrors out of the jungle might suggest!
I—I cannot listen, Doctor Lett. I cannot watch, if you
intend to demonstrate!"

The man with thick glasses waved an arm. The
Minister for Health went hastily out. Doctor Lett made
a mirthless sound.

"He would not make a medical man! Here is a para
in this aseptic room. He is an unusually good specimen for study. He was my assistant and I knew him
when he was sane. Now I know him as a para. I will
show you his delusion."

He went to a small culture-oven and opened the
door. He busied himself with something inside. Over
his shoulder he said with unction:

"The first settlers here had much trouble establishing a human-use ecology on this world. The native
plants and animals were useless. They had to be
replaced with things compatible with humans. Then
there was more trouble. There were no useful scavengers—and scavengers are essential! The rat is
usually dependable, but rats do not thrive on Tallien.
Vultures—no. Of course not. Carrion beetles . . .
Scarabeus beetles . . . the flies that produce maggots
to do such good work in refuse disposal. . . . None
thrive on Tallien Three! And scavengers are usually
specialists, too. But the colony could not continue
without scavengers. So our ancestors searched on
other worlds, and presently they found a creature
which would multiply enormously and with a fine
versatility upon the wastes of our human cities. True,
it smelled like an ancient Earth-animal called skunk—

butyl mercaptan. It was not pretty—to most eyes it is revolting. But it was a scavenger and there was no waste product it would not devour."

Doctor Lett turned from the culture-oven. He had a plastic container in his hand. A faint, disgusting odor spread from it.

"You ask what the delusions of paras may be?" He grinned derisively. He held out the container. "It is the delusion that this scavenger, this eater of unclean things; this unspeakable bit of slimy squirming flesh—paras have the delusion that it is the most delectable of foodstuffs!"

He thrust the plastic container under Calhoun's nose. Calhoun did not draw breath while it remained there. Doctor Lett said in mocking admiration:

"Ah! You have the strong stomach a medical man should have! The delusion of the para is that these squirming, writhing objects are delightful. Paras develop an irresistible craving for them. It is as if men on a more nearly Earthlike world developed an uncontrollable hunger for vultures and rats and—even less tolerable things. These scavengers—paras eat them! So normal men would rather die than become paras."

Calhoun gagged in purely instinctive revulsion. The things in the plastic container were gray and small. Had they been still, they might have been no worse to look at than raw oysters in a cocktail. But they squirmed. They writhed.

"I will show you," said Doctor Lett amiably.

He turned to the glass plate which divided the room into halves. The man beyond the thick glass now pressed eagerly against it. He looked at the container with a horrible, lustful desire. The thick-eyeglassed man clucked at him, as if at a caged animal one wishes to soothe. The man beyond the glass yawned hysterically.

He seemed to whimper. He could not take his eyes from the container in the doctor's hands.

"So!" said Doctor Lett.

He pressed a button. A lock-door opened. He put the container inside it. The door closed. It could be sterilized before the door on the other side would open, but now it was arranged to sterilize itself to prevent contagion from coming out.

The man behind the glass uttered inaudible cries. He was filled with beastly, uncontrollable impatience. He cried out at the mechanism of the contagion-lock as a beast might bellow at the opening through which food was dropped into its cage.

That lock opened, inside the glass-walled room. The plastic container appeared. The man leaped upon it. He gobbled its contents, and Calhoun was nauseated. But as the para gobbled, he glared at the two who—with Murgatroyd—watched him. He hated them with a ferocity which made veins stand out upon his temples and fury empurple his skin.

Calhoun felt that he'd gone white. He turned his eyes away and said squeamishly:

"I have never seen such a thing before."

"It is new, eh?" said Doctor Lett in a strange sort of pride. "It is new! I—even I!—have discovered something that the Med Service does not know."

"I wouldn't say the Service doesn't know about similar things," said Calhoun slowly. "There are—sometimes—on a very small scale—dozens or perhaps hundreds of victims—there are sometimes similar irrational appetites. But on a planetary scale—no. There has never been a—an epidemic of this size."

He still looked sick and stricken. But he asked:

"What's the result of this—appetite? What does it do to a para? What change in—say—his health takes place in a man after he becomes a para?"

"There is no change," said Doctor Lett blandly. "They are not sick and they do not die because they are paras. The condition itself is no more abnormal than—than diabetes. Diabetics require insulin. Paras require—something else. But there is prejudice against what paras need. It is as if some men would rather die than use insulin and those who did use it became outcastes. I do not say what causes this condition. I do not object if the Minister for Health believes that jungle-creatures creep out and—make paras of men." He watched Calhoun's expression. "Does your Med Service information agree with that?"

"No-o-o," said Calhoun. "I'm afraid it inclines to the idea of a monstrous cause, and it isn't much like diabetes."

"But it is!" insisted Lett. "Everything digestible, no matter how unappetizing to a modern man, has been a part of the regular diet of some tribe of human savages. Even prehistoric Romans ate dormice cooked in honey. Why should the fact that a needed substance happens to be found in a scavenger—"

"The Romans didn't crave dormice," said Calhoun. "They could eat them or leave them alone."

The man behind the thick glass glared at the two in the outer room. He hated them intolerably. He cried out at them. Blood-vessels in his temples throbbed with his hatred. He cursed them—

"I point out one thing more," said Doctor Lett. "I would like to have the cooperation of the Interstellar Medical Service. I am a citizen of this planet, and not without influence. But I would like to have my work approved by the Med Service. I submit that in some areas on ancient Earth, iodine was put into the public water-supply systems to prevent goiters and cretinism. Fluorine was put into drinking-water to prevent caries. On Tralee the public water-supply has traces of zinc and cobalt added. These are necessary trace elements. Why should you not concede that here there are trace elements or trace compounds needed—"

"You want me to report that," said Calhoun, flatly. "I couldn't do it without explaining—a number of things. Paras are madmen, but they organize. A symptom of privation is violent yawning. This—condition appeared only six months ago. This planet has been colonized for three hundred years. It could not be a naturally needed trace compound."

Doctor Lett shrugged, eloquently and contemptuously.

"Then you will not report what all this planet will certify," he said curtly. "My vaccine—"

"You would not call it a vaccine if you thought it supplied a deficiency—a special need of the people of Tallien."

Doctor Lett grinned again, derisively.

"Might I not supply the deficiency and call it a vaccine? But it is not a true vaccine. It is not yet efficient. It has to be taken regularly or it does not protect."

Calhoun felt as if he had gone a little pale.

"Would you give me a small sample of your vaccine?"

"No," said Doctor Lett blandly. "The little that is available is needed for high officials who must be protected from the para condition at all costs. I am making ready to turn it out in large quantities to supply all the population. Then I will give you—suitable dosage. You will be glad to have it."

Calhoun shook his head.

"Don't you see why Med Service considers that this sort of thing has a monstrous cause? Are you the monster, Doctor Lett?" Then he said sharply, "How long have you been a para? Six months?"

Murgatroyd said, *"Chee! Chee! Chee!"* in great agitation, because Doctor Lett seized a dissecting scalpel from a table-top and crouched to spring upon Calhoun. Calhoun said:

"Easy, Murgatroyd! He won't do anything regrettable!"

He had a blaster in his hand, bearing directly on the greatest and most skillful physician of Tallien Three. And Doctor Lett did not do anything. But his eyes showed the fury of a madman.

III

Five minutes later, or possibly less, Calhoun went out to where the Minister for Health paced miserably up and down the corridor outside the laboratory. The Minister looked white and sick, as if despite himself he'd been picturing the demonstration Lett would have given Calhoun. He did not meet Calhoun's eyes. He said uneasily:

"I'll take you to the Planetary President, now."

"No," said Calhoun. "I got some very promising information from Dr. Lett. I want to go back to my ship first."

"But the President wants to see you!" protested the Minister for Health. "There's something he wants to discuss!"

"I want," said Calhoun, "to ɩave something to discuss with him. There is intelligence back of this para business. I'd almost call it a demoniac intelligence. I want to get back to my ship and check on what I got from Doctor Lett."

The Minister for Health hesitated, and then said urgently:

"But the President is extremely anxious—"

"Will you," asked Calhoun politely, "arrange for me to be taken back to my ship?"

The Minister for Health opened his mouth and closed it. Then he said apologetically and—it seemed to Calhoun—fearfully:

"Doctor Lett has been our only hope of conquering this—this epidemic. The President and the Cabinet felt that they had to—give him full authority. There was no other hope! We didn't know you'd come. So— Doctor Lett wished you to see the President when you left him. It won't take long!"

Calhoun said grimly:

"And he already has you scared. I begin to suspect I haven't even time to argue with you."

"I'll get you a car and driver as soon as you've seen the President. It's only a little way!"

Calhoun growled and moved toward the exit from the laboratory. Past the sentries. Out to the open air. Here was the wide clear space which once had been a park for the city and the site of the government buildings of Tallien Three. A little distance away, children played gaily. But there were women who watched them with deep anxiety. This particular space contained all the people considered certainly free of the para syndrome. Tall buildings surrounded the area which once had been tranquil and open to all the citizens of the planet. But now those buildings were converted into walls to shut out all but the chosen— and the chosen were no better off for having been someone's choice.

"The capitol building's only yonder," said the Minister, at once urgently and affrightedly and persuasively. "It's only a very short walk. Just yonder!"

"I still," said Calhoun, "don't want to go there." He showed the Minister for Health the blaster he'd aimed at Doctor Lett only minutes ago. "This is a blaster," he said gently. "It's adjusted for low power so that is doesn't necessarily burn or kill. It's the adjustment used by police in case of riot. With luck, it only stuns. I used it on Doctor Lett," he added unemotionally. "He's a para. Did you know? The vaccine he's been giving to certain high officials to protect them against becoming paras—it satisfies the monstrous appetite of paras without requiring them to eat scavengers. But it also produces that appetite. In fact, it's one of the ways by which paras are made."

The Minister for Health stared at Calhoun. His face went literally gray. He tried to speak, and could not.

Calhoun added again, as unemotionally as before:

"I left Doctor Lett unconscious in his laboratory, knocked out by a low-power blaster-bolt. He knows he's a para. The President is a para, but with a supply of 'vaccine' he can deny it to himself. By the look on your face you've just found out you can't deny it to yourself any longer. You're a para, too."

The Minister for Health made an inarticulate sound. He literally wrung his hands.

"So," said Calhoun, "I want to get back to my ship and see what I can do with the 'vaccine' I took from Doctor Lett. Do you help me or don't you?"

The Minister for Health seemed to have shriveled inside his garments. He wrung his hands again. Then a ground-car braked to a stop five yards away. Two uniformed men jumped out. The first of them jerked at his blaster in its holster on his hip.

"That's the *tormal*!" he snapped. "This's the man, all right!"

Calhoun pulled the trigger of his blaster three times. It whined instead of rasping, because of its low-power setting. The Minister for Health collapsed. Before he touched ground the nearer of the two uniformed men seemed to stumble with his blaster halfway drawn. The third man toppled.

"Murgatroyd!" said Calhoun sharply.

"*Chee!*" shrilled Murgatroyd. He leaped into the ground-car beside Calhoun.

The motor squealed because of the violence with which Calhoun applied the power. It went shrilly away with three limp figures left behind upon the ground. But there wouldn't be instant investigation. The atmosphere in Government Center was not exactly normal. People looked apprehensively at them. But Calhoun was out of sight before the first of them stirred.

"It's the devil," said Calhoun as he swung to the right at a roadway-curve. "It's the devil to have scruples! If I'd killed Lett in cold blood, I'd have been the only hope these people could have. Maybe they'd have let me help them!"

He made another turn. There were buildings here and there, and he was often out of sight from where he'd dropped three men. But it was astonishing that action had been taken so quickly after Lett regained consciousness. Calhoun had certainly left him not more than a quarter of an hour before. The low-power blaster must have kept him stunned for minutes. Immediately he'd recovered he'd issued orders for the capture or the killing of a man with a small animal with him, a *tormal*. And the order would have been carried out if Calhoun hadn't happened to have his own blaster actually in his hand.

But the appalling thing was the over-all situation as now revealed. The people of Government Center were turning para and Doctor Lett had all the authority of the government behind him. He was the government for the duration of the emergency. But he'd stay the government because all the men in high office were paras who could conceal their condition only so long as Doctor Lett permitted it. Calhoun could picture the social organization to be expected. There'd be the tyrant; the absolute monarch at its head. Absolutely submissive citizens would receive their dosage of vaccine to keep them "normals" so long as it pleased their master. Anyone who defied him or even tried to flee would become something both mad and repulsive, because subject to monstrous and irresistible appetites. And the tyrant could prevent even their satisfaction! So the citizens of Tallien Three were faced with an ultimate choice of slavery or madness for themselves and their families.

Calhoun swerved behind a government building and out of the parking area beyond. Obviously, he couldn't leave Government Center by the way he'd entered it. If Lett hadn't ordered him stopped, he'd be ordering it now. And Murgatroyd was an absolute identification.

Again he turned a corner, thrusting Murgatroyd down out of sight. He turned again, and again. . . . Then he began concentratedly to remember where the sunset-line had been upon the planet when he was waiting to be landed by the grid. He could guess at an hour and a half, perhaps two, since he touched ground. On the combined data, he made a guess at the local time. It would be mid-afternoon. So shadows would lie to the north-east of the objects casting. Then—

He did not remain on any straight roadway for more than seconds. But now when he had a choice of turnings, he had a reason for each choice. He twisted and dodged about—once he almost ran into children playing a ritual game—but the sum total of his movements was steadily southward. Paras were turned out of the south gate. That gate, alone, would be the one where someone could go out with a chance of being unchallenged.

He found the gate. The usual tall buildings bordered it to left and right. The actual exit was bare concrete walls slanting together to an exit to the outer world no more than a house-door wide. Well back from the gate, there were four high-sided trucks with armed police in the truck-bodies. They were there to make sure that paras, turned out, or who went out of their own accord when they knew their state, would not come back.

He stopped the ground-car and tucked Murgatroyd under his coat. He walked grimly toward the narrow exit. It was the most desperate of gambles, but it was the only one he could make. He could be killed, of course, but nobody would suspect him of attempting exit at any gate. He should be too desperate to take a chance like this.

So he got out, unchallenged. The concrete walls rose higher and higher as he walked away from the trucks and the police who would surely have blasted him had they guessed. The way he could walk became narrower. It became a roofed-over passageway, with a turn in it so it could not be looked through end to end. Then— he reached open air once more.

Nothing could be less dramatic than his actual escape. He simply walked out. Nothing could be less remarkable than his arrival in the city outside of Government Center. He found himself in a city street, rather narrow, with buildings as usual all about him, whose windows were either bricked shut or smashed. There were benches against the base of one of those buildings, and four or five men, quite unarmed, lounged upon them. When Calhoun appeared one of them looked up and then arose. A second man turned to busy himself with something behind him. They were not grim. They showed no sign of being mad. But Calhoun had already realized that the appetite which was madness came only occasionally. Only at intervals which could probably be known in advance. Between one monstrous hunger-spell and another, a para might look and act and actually be as sane as anybody else. Certainly Doctor Lett and the President and the Cabinet-members who were paras acted convincingly as if they were not.

One of the men on the benches beckoned.

"This way," he said casually.

Murgatroyd poked his head out of Calhoun's jacket. He regarded these roughly dressed men with suspicion.

"What's that?" asked one of the five.

"A pet," said Calhoun briefly.

The statement went unchallenged. A man got up, lifting a small tank with a hose. There was a hissing sound. The spray made a fine, fog-like mist. Calhoun smelled a conventional organic solvent, well-known enough.

"This's antiseptic," said the man with the spray. "In case you got some disease inside there."

The statement was plainly standard, and once it had been exquisite irony. But it had been repeated until it had no meaning any more, except to Calhoun. His clothing glittered momentarily where the spray stood on its fibers. Then it dried. There was the faintest possible residue, like a coating of impalpable dust. Calhoun guessed its significance and the knowledge was intolerable. But he said between clenched teeth:

"Where do I go now?"

"Anywheres," said the first man. "Nobody'll bother you. Some normals try to keep you from getting near 'em, but you can do as you please." He added disinterestedly. "To them, too. No police out here!"

He went back to the bench and sat down. Calhoun moved on.

His inward sensations were unbearable, but he had to continue. It was not likely that instructions would have reached the para organization yet. There was one. There must be one! But eventually he would be hunted for even on the unlikely supposition that he'd gotten out of Government Center. Not yet, but presently.

He went down the street. He came to a corner and turned it. There were again a few moving figures in sight. There might be one pedestrian in a city block. This was the way they'd looked in the other part of the city, seen from a ground-car. On foot, they looked the same. Windows, too, were broken. Doors smashed in. Trash on the streets . . .

None of the humans in view paid any attention to him at all, but he kept Murgatroyd out of sight regardless. Walking men who came toward him never quite arrived. They turned off on other streets or into doorways. Those who moved in the same direction never happened to be overtaken. They also turned corners or slipped into doors. They would be, Calhoun realized dispassionately, people who still considered themselves normals, out upon desperate errands for food and trying hopelessly not to take contagion back to those they got the food for. And Calhoun was shaken with a horrible rage that such things could happen. He, himself, had been sprayed with something. . . . And Doctor Lett had held out a plastic container for him to smell. . . . He'd held his breath then, but he could not keep from breathing now. He had a certain period of time, and that period only, before—

He forced his thoughts back to the Med Ship when it was twenty miles high, and ten, and five. He'd watched the ground through the electron telescope and he had a mental picture of the city from the sky. It was as clear to him as a map. He could orient himself. He could tell where he was.

A ground-car came to a stop some distance ahead. A man got out, his arms full of bundles of food. Calhoun broke into a run. The man tried to get inside the doorway before Calhoun could arrive. But he would not leave any of the food.

Calhoun showed his blaster.

"I'm a para," he said quietly, "and I want this car. Give me the keys and you can keep the food."

The man groaned. Then he dropped the keys on the ground. He fled into the house.

"Thanks," said Calhoun politely to the emptiness.

He took his place in the car. He thrust Murgatroyd again out of sight.

"It's not," he told the *tormal* with a sort of despairing humor, "It's not that I'm ashamed of you, Murgatroyd, but I'm afraid I may become ashamed of myself. Keep low!"

He started the car and drove away.

He passed through a business district, with many smashed windows. He passed through canyons formed by office buildings. He crossed a manufacturing area, in which there were many ungainly factories but no sign of any work going on. In any epidemic many men stay home from work to avoid contagion. On Tallien Three nobody would be willing to risk employment, for fear of losing much more than his life.

Then there was a wide straight highway leading away from the city but not toward the space-port. Calhoun drove his stolen car along it. He saw the strange steel embroidery of the landing-grid rising to the height of a minor mountain against the sky. He drove furiously. Beyond it. He had seen the highway system from twenty miles height, and ten, and five. From somewhere near here stolen weather-rockets had gone bellowing skyward with explosive war-heads to shatter *Aesclipus Twenty*.

They'd failed. Now Calhoun went past the place from which they had been launched, and did not notice. Once he could look across flat fields and see the space-port highway. It was empty. Then there was sunset. He saw the topmost silvery beams and girders of the landing-grid still glowing in sunshine which no longer reached down to the planet's solid ground.

He drove. And drove. In Government Center nobody would suspect him long gone from the Center and driving swiftly away from the city. They might put a road-block to the space-port, just in case. But they'd really believe him still hiding somewhere in Government Center with no hope of—actually—accomplishing anything but his own destruction.

After sunset he was miles beyond the space-port. When twilight was done, he'd crossed to another surface-road and was headed back toward the city. But this time he would pass close to the space-port. And two hours after sundown he turned the car's running-lights off and drove a dark and nearly noiseless vehicle through deep-fallen night. Even so, he left the ground-car a mile from the tall and looming lace-work of steel. He listened with straining ears for a long time.

Presently he and Murgatroyd approached the space-port, on foot, from a rather improbable direction. The gigantic, unsubstantial tower rose incredibly far toward the sky. As he drew near it he crouched lower and lower so he was almost crawling to keep from being silhouetted against the stars. He saw lights in the windows of the grid's control-building. As he looked, a lighted window darkened from someone moving past it inside. There was an enormous stillness, broken only by faint, faint noises of the wind in the metal skeleton.

He saw no ground-cars to indicate men brought

here and waiting for him. He went very cautiously forward. Once he stopped and distastefully restored his blaster to lethal-charge intensity. If he had to use it, he couldn't hope to shoot accurately enough to stun an antagonist. He'd have to fight for his life—or rather, for the chance to live as a normal man, and to restore that possibility to the people in the ghastly-quiet city at the horizon and the other lesser cities elsewhere on this world.

He took infinite precautions. He saw the Med Ship standing valiantly upright on its landing-fins. It was a relief to see it. The grid operator could have been ordered to lift it out to space—thrown away to nowhere, or put in orbit until it was wanted again, or—

That was still a possibility. Calhoun's expression turned wry. He'd have to do something about the grid. He must be able to take off on the ship's emergency rockets without the risk of being caught by the tremendously powerful force-fields by which ships were launched and landed.

He crept close to the control-building. No voices, but there was movement inside. Presently he peered in a window.

The grid operator who'd been the first man to greet him on his landing, now moved about the interior of the building. He pushed a tank on wheels. With a hose attached to it, he sprayed. Mist poured out and splashed away from the side-walls. It hung in the air and settled on the desks, the chairs, and on the control-board with its dials and switches. Calhoun had seen the mist before. It had been used to spray instead of burning the bodies of the two men who'd tried to murder him, and their wrecked ground-car, and everywhere that the car was known to have run. It was a decontaminant spray; credited with the ability to destroy the contagion that made paras out of men.

Calhoun saw the grid operator's face. It was resolute beyond expression, but it was very, very bitter.

Calhoun went confidently to the door and knocked
on it. A savage voice inside said:

"Go away! I just found out I'm a para!"

Calhoun opened the door and walked inside.
Murgatroyd followed. He sneezed as the mist reached
his nostrils.

"I've been treated," said Calhoun, "so I'll be a para
right along with you, after whatever the development
period is. Question: can you fix the controls so nobody
else can use the grid?"

The grid operator stared at him numbly. He was
deathly pale. He did not seem able to grasp what
Calhoun had said.

"I've got to do some work on the para condition,"
Calhoun told him. "I need to be undisturbed in the
ship, and I need a patient further along toward being
a para than I am. It'll save time. If you'll help, we may
be able to beat the thing. If not, I've still got to disable the grid."

The grid operator said in a savage, unhuman voice:

"I'm a para. I'm trying to spray everything I've
touched. Then I'm going to go off somewhere and kill
myself—"

Calhoun drew his blaster. He adjusted it again to
non-lethal intensity.

"Good man!" he said approvingly. "I'll have a similar
job to do if I'm not a better medical man than Lett!
Will you help me?"

Murgatroyd sneezed again. He said plaintively:
"*Chee!*"

The grid operator looked down at him, obviously
in a state of shock. No ordinary sight or sound could
have gotten through to his consciousness. But
Murgatroyd was a small, furry animal with long

whiskers and a hirsute tail and a habit of imitating the actions of humans. He sneezed yet again and looked up. There was a handkerchief in Calhoun's pocket. Murgatroyd dragged it out and held it to his face. He sneezed once more and said, *"Chee!"* and returned the handkerchief to its place. He regarded the grid operator disapprovingly. The operator was shocked out of his despair. He said shakenly:

"What the devil—" Then he stared at Calhoun. "Help you? How can I help anybody? I'm a para!"

"Which," said Calhoun, "is just what I need. I'm Med Service, man! I've got a job to do with what they call an epidemic. I need a para who's willing to be cured. That's you! Let's get this grid fixed so it can't work and—"

There was a succession of loud clicks from a speaker-unit on the wall. It was an emergency-wave, unlocking the speaker from its off position. Then a voice:

"All citizens attention! The Planetary President is about to give you good news about the end of the para epidemic!"

A pause. Then a grave and trembling voice came out of the speaker:

"My fellow-citizens, I have the happiness to report that a vaccine completely protecting normals against the para condition, and curing those already paras, has been developed. Doctor Lett, of the planetary health service, has produced the vaccine which is already in small-scale production and will shortly be available in large quantities, enough for everyone! The epidemic which has threatened every person on Tallien Three is about to end! And to hasten the time when every person on the planet will have the vaccine in the required dosage and at the required intervals, Doctor Lett has been given complete emergency authority. He

*is empowered to call upon every citizen for any labor,
any sum, any sacrifice that will restore our afflicted
fellow-citizens to normality, and to protect the rest
against falling a victim to this intolerable disease. I
repeat: a vaccine has been found which absolutely
prevents anyone from becoming a para, and which
cures those who are paras now. And Doctor Lett has
absolute authority to issue any orders he feels necessary to hasten the end of the epidemic and to prevent
its return. But the end is sure!"*

The speaker clicked off. Calhoun said wryly:

"Unfortunately, I know what that means. The President has announced the government's abdication in
favor of Doctor Lett, and that the punishment for
disobeying Lett is—madness."

He drew a deep breath and shrugged his shoulders.

"Come along! Let's get to work!"

IV

As it happened, the timing was critical, though Calhoun hadn't realized it. There were moving lights on the highway to the city at the moment Calhoun and the grid operator went into the Med Ship and closed the airlock door behind them. The lights drew nearer. They raced. Then ground-cars came rushing through the gate of the space-port and flung themselves toward the wholly peaceful little Med Ship where it stood seeming to yearn toward the sky. In seconds they had it ringed about, and armed men were trying to get inside. But Med Ships land on very many planets, with very many degrees of respect for the Interstellar Medical Service. On some worlds there is great integrity displayed by space-port personnel and visitors. On others there is pilfering, or worse. So Med Ships are not easily broken into.

They spent long minutes fumbling unskillfully at the outer airlock door. Then they gave it up. Two car-loads of men went over to the control-building, which now was dark and silent. Its door was not locked. They went in.

There was consternation. The interior of the control-building reeked of antiseptic spray—the spray used when a para was discovered. In some cases, the spray a para used when he discovered himself. But it was not reassuring to the men just arrived from Government Center. Instead of certifying to their safety, it told of horrifying danger. Because despite a broadcast by the planetary president, terror of paras was too well-established to be cured by an official statement.

The men who'd entered the building stumbled out and stammered of what they'd smelled inside the building. Their companions drew back, frightened by even so indirect a contact with supposed contagion. They stayed outside, while a man who hadn't entered used the police-car's communicator to report to the headquarters of the planetary police.

The attempt to enter the ship was known inside, of course. But Calhoun paid no attention. He emptied the pockets of the garments he'd worn into the city. There were the usual trivia a man carries with him. But there was also a blaster—set for low-power bolts—and a small thick-glass phial of a singular grayish fluid, and a plastic container.

He was changing to other clothing when he heard the muttering report, picked up by a ship-receiver turned to planetary police wave-length. It reported affrightedly that the Med Ship could not be entered, and the grid's control-building was dark and empty and sprayed as if to destroy contagion. The operator was gone.

Another voice snapped orders in reply. The highest authority had given instructions that the Med Ship man now somewhere in the capitol city must be captured, and his escape from the planet must be prevented at all costs. So if the ship itself could not be entered and disabled, get the grid working and throw it away. Throw it out to space! Whether there was contagion in the control-building or not, the ship must be made unusable to the Med Ship man!

"They think well of me," said Calhoun. "I hope I'm as dangerous as Doctor Lett now believes." Then he said crisply, "You say you're a para. I want the symptoms; how you feel and where. Then I want to know your last contact with scavengers."

The intentions of the police outside could be ignored. It wouldn't matter if the Med Ship were heaved out to space and abandoned. Calhoun was in it. But it couldn't happen. The grid operator had brought away certain essential small parts of the grid control-system. Of course the ship could be blown up. But he'd have warning of that. He was safe except for one thing. He'd been exposed to whatever it was that made a man a para. The condition would develop. But he did have a thick-glass container of grayish fluid, and he had a plastic biological-specimen container. One came from Doctor Lett's safest pocket. It would be vaccine. The other came from the culture-oven in the Doctor's laboratory.

The thick-glass phial was simply that. Calhoun removed the cover from the other. It contained small and horrible squirming organisms, writhing in what was probably a nutrient fluid to which they could reduce human refuse. They swam jerkily in it so that the liquid seemed to seethe. It smelled. Like skunk.

The grid operator clenched his hands.

"Put it away!" he commanded fiercely. "Out of sight! Away!"

Calhoun nodded. He locked it in a small chest. As he put down the cover he said in an indescribable tone:

"It doesn't smell as bad to me as it did."

But his hands were steady as he drew a sample of

a few drops from the vaccine-bottle. He lowered a wall-panel and behind it there was a minute but astonishingly complete biological laboratory. It was designed for micro-analysis—the quantitative and qualitative analysis of tiny quantities of matter. He swung out a miniaturized Challis fractionator. He inserted half a droplet of the supposed vaccine and plugged in the fractionator's power cable. It began to hum.

The grid operator ground his teeth.

"This is a fractionator," said Calhoun. "It spins a biological sample through a chromatograph gel."

The small device hummed more shrilly. The sound rose in pitch until it was a whine, and then a whistle, and then went up above the highest pitch to which human ears are sensitive. Murgatroyd scratched at his ears and complained:

"*Chee! Chee! Chee!*"

"It won't be long," Calhoun assured him. He looked once at the grid operator and then looked away. There was sweat on the man's forehead. Calhoun said casually, "The substance that makes the vaccine do what it does do is in the vaccine, obviously. So the fractionator is separating the different substances that are mixed together." He added, "It doesn't look much like chromatography, but the principle's the same. It's an old, old trick!"

It was, of course. That different dissolved substances can be separated by their different rates of diffusion through wetted powders and gels had been known since the early twentieth century, but was largely forgotten because not often needed. But the Med Service did not abandon processes solely because they were not new.

Calhoun took another droplet of the vaccine and put it between two plates of glass, to spread out. He separated them and put them in a vacuum-drier.

"I'm not going to try an analysis," he observed. "It would be silly to try to do anything so complicated if I only need to identify something. Which I hope is all I do need!"

He brought out an extremely small vacuum device. He cleaned the garments he'd just removed, drawing every particle of dust from them. The dust appeared in a transparent tube which was part of the machine.

"I was sprayed with something I suspect the worst of," he added. "The spray left dust behind. I *think* it made sure that anybody who left Government Center would surely be a para. It's another reason for haste."

The grid operator ground his teeth again. He did not really hear Calhoun. He was deep in a private hell of shame and horror.

The inside of the ship was quiet, but it was not tranquil. Calhoun worked calmly enough, but there were times when his inwards seemed to knot and cramp him, which was not the result of any infection or contagion or demoniac possession, but was reaction to thoughts of the imprisoned para in the laboratory. That man had gobbled the unspeakable because he could not help himself, but he was mad with rage and shame over what he had become. Calhoun could become like that—

The loud-speaker turned to outside frequencies muttered again. Calhoun turned up its volume.

"Calling headquarters!" panted a voice. *"There's a mob of paras forming in the streets in the Mooreton quarter! They're raging! They heard the President's speech and they swear they'll kill him! They won't stand for a cure! Everybody's got to turn para! They won't have normals on the planet! Everybody's got to turn para or be killed!"*

The grid operator looked up at the speaker. The ultimate of bitterness appeared on his face. He saw Calhoun's eyes on him and said savagely:

"That's where I belong!"

Murgatroyd went to his cubbyhole and crawled into it.

Calhoun got out a microscope. He examined the dried glass plates from the vacuum-drier. The fractionator turned itself off and he focused on and studied the slide it yielded. He inspected a sample of the dust he'd gotten from the garments that had been sprayed at the south gate. The dust contained common dust-particles and pollen-particles and thread-particles and all sorts of microscopic debris. But throughout all the sample he saw certain infinitely tiny crystals. They were too small to be seen separately by the naked eye, but they had a definite crystalline form. And the kind of crystals a substance makes are not too specific about what the substance is, but they tell a great deal about what it cannot be. In the fractionator-slide he could get more information—the rate-of-diffusion of a substance in solution ruled out all but a certain number of compounds that it could be. The two items together gave a definite clue.

Another voice from the speaker:

"Headquarters! Paras are massing by the north gate! They act ugly! They're trying to force their way into Government Center! We'll have to start shooting if we're to stop them! What are our orders?"

The grid operator said dully:

"They'll wreck everything. I don't want to live because I'm a para, but I haven't acted like one yet. Not yet! But they have! So they don't want to be cured! They'd never forget what they've done ... They'd be ashamed!"

Calhoun punched keys on a very small computer.

He'd gotten an index-of-refraction reading on crystals too small to be seen except through a microscope. That information, plus specific gravity, plus crystalline form, plus rate of diffusion in a fractionator, went to the stores of information packed in the computer's memory-banks somewhere between the ship's living-quarters and its outer skin.

A voice boomed from another speaker, tuned to public-broadcast frequency:

"My fellow-citizens, I appeal to you to be calm! I beg you to be patient! Practice the self-control that citizens owe to themselves and their world! I appeal to you—"

Outside in the starlight the Med Ship rested peacefully on the ground. Around and above it the grid rose like geometric fantasy to veil most of the starry sky. Here in the starlight the ground-car communicators gave out the same voice. The same message. The President of Tallien Three made a speech. Earlier, he'd made another. Earlier still he'd taken orders from the man who was already absolute master of the population of this planet.

Police stood uneasy guard about the Med Ship because they could not enter it. Some of their number who had entered the control-building now stood shivering outside it, unable to force themselves inside again. There was a vast, detached stillness about the space-port. It seemed the more unearthly because of the thin music of wind in the landing-grid's upper levels.

At the horizon there was a faint glow. Street-lights still burned in the planet's capitol city, but though buildings rose against the sky no lights burned in them. It was not wise for anybody to burn lights that could be seen outside their dwellings. There were police, to be sure. But they were all in Government Center, marshaled there to try to hold a perimeter formed by bricked-up apartment buildings. But much the most of the city was dark and terribly empty save for mobs of all sizes but all raging. Nine-tenths of the city was at the mercy of the paras. Families darkened their homes and terrifiedly hid in corners and in closets, listening for outcries or the thunderous tramping of madmen at their doors.

In the Med Ship the loudspeaker went on.

"—*I have told you*," said the rounded tones of the planetary president—but his voice shook—"*I have told you that Doctor Lett has perfected and is making a vaccine which will protect every citizen and cure every para. You must believe me, my fellow-citizens. You must believe me! To paras, I promise that their fellows who were not afflicted with the same condition—I promise that they will forget! I promise that no one will remember what—what has been done in delirium! What has taken place—and there have been tragedies—will be blotted out. Only be patient now! Only—*"

Calhoun went over his glass slides again while the computer stood motionless, apparently without life. But he had called for it to find, in its memory-banks, an organic compound of such-and-such a crystalline form, such-and-such a diffusion rate, such-and-such a specific gravity, and such-and-such a refractive index. Men no longer considered that there was any effective limit to the number of organic compounds that were possible. The old guess at half a million different substances was long exceeded. It took time even for a computer to search all its microfilmed memories for a compound such as Calhoun had described.

"It's standard practice," said Calhoun restlessly, "to consider that everything that can happen, does. Specifically, that any compound that can possibly exist, sooner or later must be formed in nature. We're looking for a particular one. It must have been formed naturally at some time or another, but never before has it appeared in quantity enough to threaten a civilization. Why?"

Murgatroyd licked his right-hand whiskers. He whimpered a little—and Murgatroyd was a very cheerful small animal, possessed of exuberant good health and a fine zest in simply being alive. Now, though, he did not seem happy at all.

"It's been known for a long time," said Calhoun impatiently, "that no life-form exists alone. Every living creature exists in an environment in association with all the other living creatures around it. But this is true of compounds, too! Anything that is part of an environment is essential to that environment. So even organic compounds are as much parts of a planetary life-system as—say—rabbits on a Terran-type world. If there are no predators, rabbits will multiply until they starve."

Murgatroyd said, *"Chee!"* as if complaining to himself.

"Rats," said Calhoun, somehow angrily, "rats have been known to do that on a derelict ship. There was a man named Malthus who said we humans would some day do the same thing. But we haven't. We've taken over a galaxy. If we ever crowd this, there are more galaxies for us to colonize, forever! But there have been cases of rats and rabbits multiplying past endurance. Here we've got an organic molecule that has multiplied out of all reason! It's normal for it to exist, but in a normal environment it's held in check by other molecules which in some sense feed on it; which control the—population of that kind of molecule as rabbits or rats are controlled in a larger environment. But the check on this molecule isn't working, here!"

The booming voice of the planetary president went on and on and on. Memoranda of events taking place were handed to him, and he read them and argued with the paras who had tried to rush the north gate of Government Center, to makes its inhabitants paras like themselves. But the planetary president tried to make oratory a weapon against madness.

Calhoun grimaced at the voice. He said fretfully:

"There's a molecule which has to exist because it can. It's a part of a normal environment, but it doesn't normally produce paras. Now it does! Why? What is the compound or the condition that controls its abundance? Why is it missing here? What is lacking? What?"

The police-frequency speaker suddenly rattled, as if someone shouted into a microphone.

"All police cars! Paras have broken through a building-wall on the west side! They're pouring into the Center! All cars rush! Set blasters at full power and use them! Drive them back or kill them!"

The grid operator turned angry, bitter eyes upon Calhoun.

"The paras—we paras!—don't want to be cured!" he said fiercely. "Who'd want to be normal again and remember when he ate scavengers? I haven't yet, but— Who'd be able to talk to a man he knew had devoured—devoured—" The grid operator swallowed. "We paras want everybody to be like us, so we can endure being what we are. We can't take it any other way—except by dying!"

He stood up. He reached for the blaster Calhoun had put aside when he changed from the clothes he'd worn in the city.

"—And I'll take it that way!"

Calhoun whirled. His fist snapped out. The grid operator reeled back. The blaster dropped from his hand. Murgatroyd cried out shrilly, from his cubbyhole. He hated violence, did Murgatroyd.

Calhoun stood over the operator, raging:

"It's not that bad yet—you haven't yawned once! You can stand the need for monstrousness for a long while yet. And I need you!"

He turned away. The President's voice boomed— It cut off abruptly. Another voice took its place. And this was the bland and unctuous voice of Doctor Lett.

"My friends! I am Doctor Lett. I have been entrusted with all the powers of the government because I, and I alone, have all power over the cause of the para condition. From this moment I am the government. To paras—you need not be cured unless you choose. There will be places and free supplies for you to enjoy the deep satisfactions known only to you. To non-paras— you will be protected from becoming paras except by your own choice. In return, you will obey! The price of protection is obedience. The penalty for disobedi- ence will be a loss of protection. But those from whom protection is withdrawn will not be supplied with their necessities. Paras, you will remember this! Non-paras, do not forget it! . . ." His voice changed. *"Now I give an order. To the police and to non-paras. You will no longer resist paras. To paras: you will enter Govern- ment Center quietly and peacefully. You will not molest the non-paras you come upon. I begin at once the organization of a new social system in which paras and non-paras must cooperate. There must be obedience to the utmost—"*

The grid operator cursed as he rose from the floor. Calhoun did not notice. The computer had finally delivered the answer he had demanded. And it was of no use. Calhoun said tonelessly:

"Turn that off, will you?"

While the grid operator obeyed, Calhoun read and

re-read the answer. He had lacked something of good color before, but as he re-read, he grew paler and paler. Murgatroyd got down restlessly from his cubbyhole. He sniffed. He went toward the small locked chest in which Calhoun had put away the plastic container of living scavengers. He put his nose to the crack of that chest's cover.

"*Chee!*" he said confidently. He looked at Calhoun. Calhoun did not notice.

"This," said Calhoun, completely white. "This is bad! It's—it's an answer, but it would take time to work it out, and we haven't got the time! And to make it and to distribute it—"

The grid operator growled. Doctor Lett's broadcast had verified everything Calhoun said. Doctor Lett was now the government of Tallien Three. There was nobody who could dare to oppose him. He could make anybody into a para, and then deny that para his unspeakable necessities. He could turn anybody on the planet into a madman with ferocious and intolerable appetites, and then deny their satisfaction. The people of Tallien Three were the slaves of Doctor Lett. The grid operator said in a deadly voice:

"Maybe I can get to him and kill him before—"

Calhoun shook his head. Then he saw Murgatroyd sniffing at the chest now holding the container of live scavengers. Open, it had a faint but utterly disgusting odor. Locked up, Calhoun could not smell it. But Murgatroyd could. He sniffed. He said impatiently to Calhoun:

"*Chee! Chee-chee!*"

Calhoun stared. His lips tightened. He'd thought of Murgatroyd as immune to everything, because he could react more swiftly and produce antibodies to toxins more rapidly than microorganisms could multiply. But he was immune only to toxins. He was not immune to an appetite-causing molecule which demanded more of itself on penalty of madness. In fact—it affected him faster than it would a man.

"*Chee-chee!*" he chattered urgently. "*Chee-chee-chee!*"

"It's got him," said Calhoun. He felt sickened. "It'll have me. Because I can't synthesize anything as complex as the computer says is needed, to control—" His tone was despairing irony—"to control the molecular population that makes paras!"

Murgatroyd chattered again. He was indignant. He wanted something and Calhoun didn't give it to him. He could not understand so preposterous a happening. He reached up and tugged at Calhoun's trouser-leg. Calhoun picked him up and tossed him the width of the control-room. He'd done it often before, in play, but this was somehow different. Murgatroyd stared incredulously at Calhoun. "To break it down," said Calhoun bitterly, "I need aromatic olefines and some acetone, and acetic-acid radicals and methyl sub-molecular groups. To destroy it absolutely I need available unsaturated hydrocarbons—they'll be gases! And it has to be kept from re-forming as it's broken up, and I may need twenty different organic radicals available at the same time! It's a month's work for a dozen competent men just to find out how to make it, and I'd have to make it in quantity for millions of people and persuade them of its necessity against all the authority of the government and the hatred of the paras, and then distribute it—"

Murgatroyd was upset. He wanted something that Calhoun wouldn't give him. Calhoun had shown impatience—almost an unheard-of thing! Murgatroyd squirmed unhappily. He still wanted the thing in the chest. But if he did something ingratiating . . .

He saw the blaster, lying on the floor. Calhoun often

petted him when, imitating, he picked up something
that had been dropped. Murgatroyd went over to the
blaster. He looked back at Calhoun. Calhoun paced
irritably up and down. The grid operator stood with
clenched hands, contemplating the intolerable and the
monstrous.

Murgatroyd picked up the blaster. He trotted over
to Calhoun. He plucked at the man's trouser-leg again.
He held the blaster in the only way his tiny paws could
manage it. A dark, sharp-nailed finger rested on the
trigger.

"Chee-chee!" said Murgatroyd.

He offered the blaster. Calhoun jumped when he
saw it in Murgatroyd's paw. The blaster jerked, and
Murgatroyd's paw tightened to hold it. He pulled the
trigger. A blaster-bolt crashed out of the barrel. It was
a miniature bolt of ball-lightning. It went into the floor,
vaporizing the surface and carbonizing the multi-ply
wood layer beneath it. The Med Ship suddenly reeked
of wood-smoke and surfacer. Murgatroyd fled in panic
to his cubbyhole and cowered in its farthest corner.

But there was a singular silence in the Med Ship.
Calhoun's expression was startled; amazed. He was
speechless for long seconds. Then he said blankly:

"Damnation! How much of a fool can a man make
of himself when he works at it? Do you smell that?"
He shot the question at the grid operator. "Do you
smell that? It's wood-smoke! Did you know it?"

Murgatroyd listened fearfully, blinking.

"Wood-smoke!" said Calhoun between his teeth.
"And I didn't see it! Men have had fires for two million years and electricity for half a thousand. For two
million years there was no man or woman or child who
went a full day without breathing in some wood-smoke!
And I didn't realize that it was so normal a part of
human environment that it was a necessary one!"

There was a crash. Calhoun had smashed a chair.
It was an oddity because it was made of wood. Calhoun
had owned it because it was odd. Now he smashed
it to splinters and piled them up and flung blaster-bolt
after blaster-bolt into the heap. The air inside the Med
Ship grew pungent; stinging; strangling. Murgatroyd
sneezed. Calhoun coughed. The grid operator seemed
about to choke. But in the white fog Calhoun cried
exultantly:

"Aromatic olefines! Acetone! Acetic-acid radicals and
methyl sub-molecular groups! And smoke has unsaturated hydrocarbon gases . . . This is the stuff our
ancestors have breathed in tiny quantities for a hundred thousand generations! Of course it was essential
to them! And to us! It was a part of their environment,
so they had to have a use for it! And it controlled the
population of certain molecules . . ."

The air-system gradually cleared away the smoke,
but the Med Ship still reeked of wood-smoke smells.

"Let's check on this thing!" snapped Calhoun.
"Murgatroyd!"

Murgatroyd came timidly to the door of his cubbyhole. He blinked imploringly at Calhoun. At a
repeated command he came unhappily to his master.
Calhoun petted him. Then he opened the chest in
which a container held living scavengers which writhed
and swam and seemed to seethe. He took out that container. He took off the lid.

Murgatroyd backed away. His expression was ludi-
crous. There was no question but that his nose was
grievously offended. Calhoun turned to the grid operator. He extended the sample of scavengers. The grid
man clenched his teeth and took it. Then his face
worked. He thrust it back into Calhoun's hand.

"It's—horrible!" he said thickly. "Horrible!" Then his
jaw dropped. "I'm not a para! Not—a para—" Then

he said fiercely, "We've got to get this thing started! We've got to start curing paras—"

"Who," said Calhoun, "will be ashamed of what they remember. We can't get cooperation from them. And we can't get cooperation from the government. The men who were the government are paras and they've given their authority to Doctor Lett. You don't think he'll abdicate, do you? Especially when it's realized that he was the man who developed the strain of scavengers that secrete this modified butyl mercaptan that turns men into paras!"

Calhoun grinned almost hysterically.

"Maybe it was an accident. Maybe he found himself the first para and was completely astonished. But he couldn't be alone in what he knew he was— degradation. He wanted others with him in that ghastly state. He got them. Then he didn't want anybody not to be like himself. . . . We can't get help from him!"

Exultantly, he flipped switches to show on vision-screens what went on in the world outside the ship. He turned on all the receivers that could pick up sounds and broadcasts. Voices came in:

"There's fighting everywhere! Normals won't accept paras among them! Paras won't leave normals alone . . . They touch them; breathe on them—and laugh! There's fighting—" The notion that the para state was contagious was still cherished by paras. It was to be preferred to the notion that they were possessed by devils. But there were some who gloried in the more dramatic opinion. There were screamings on the air, suddenly, and a man's voice panting, *"Send police here fast! The paras have gone wild. They're—"*

Calhoun seated himself at the control-desk. He threw switches there. He momentarily touched a button. There was a slight shock and the beginning of a roar outside. It cut off. Calhoun looked at the vision-plates showing outside. There was swirling smoke and steam. There were men running in headlong flight, leaving their ground-cars behind them.

"A slight touch of emergency-rocket," said Calhoun. "They've run away. Now we end the plague on Tallien Three."

The grid operator was still dazed by the continued absence of any indication that he might ever become a para. He said unsteadily:

"Sure! Sure! But how?"

"Wood-smoke," said Calhoun. "Emergency-rockets. Roofs! There's been no wood-smoke in the air on this planet because there are no forest fires and people don't burn fuel. They use electricity. So we start the largest production of wood-smoke that we find convenient, and the population of a certain modified butyl mercaptan molecule will be reduced. Down to a normal level. Immediately!"

The emergency-rocket bellowed thunderously, and the little Med Ship rose.

There have been, of course, emergency measures against contagion all through human history. There was a king of France, on Earth, who had all the lepers in his kingdom killed. There have been ships and houses burned to drive out plague, and quarantines which simply interfered with human beings were countless. Calhoun's measure on Tallien was somewhat more drastic than most, but it had good justification.

He set fire to the planet's capital city. The little Med Ship swept over the darkened buildings. Her emergency-rockets made thin pencils of flame two hundred feet long. She touched off roofs to the east, and Calhoun rose to see which way the wind blew. He descended and touched here and there . . .

Thick, seemingly suffocating masses of wood-smoke flowed over the city. They were not actually strangling, but they created panic. There was fighting in Government Center, but it stopped when the mysterious stuff—not one man in a hundred had ever seen burning wood or smelled its smoke—the fighting stopped and all men fled when a choking, reeking blanket rolled over the city and lay there.

It wasn't a great fire, considering everything. Less than ten percent of the city burned, but ninety-odd percent of the paras in it ceased to be paras. More, they had suddenly regained an invisible aversion to the smell of butyl mercaptan—even a modified butyl mercaptan—and it was promptly discovered that no normal who had smelled wood-smoke became a para. So all the towns and even individual farm-houses would hereafter make sure that there was pungent wood-smoke to be smelled from time to time by everybody.

But Calhoun did not wait for such pleasant news. He could not look for gratitude. He'd burned part of a city. He'd forced paras to stop being paras and become ashamed. And those who hadn't become paras wanted desperately to forget the whole matter as soon as possible. They couldn't, but gratitude to Calhoun would remind them. He took appropriate action.

With the grid operator landed again, and after the grid was operable once more and had sent the Med Ship a good five planetary diameters into space—some few hours after the ship was in overdrive again, Calhoun and Murgatroyd had coffee together. Murgatroyd zestfully licked his emptied tiny mug, to get the last least taste of the beverage. He said happily, *"Chee!"* He wanted more.

"Coffee," said Calhoun severely, "has become a habit with you, Murgatroyd! If this abnormal appetite develops too far, you might start yawning at me, which would imply that your desire for it was uncontrollable. A yawn caused by what is called a yen has been known to make a man dislocate his jaw. You might do that. You wouldn't like it!"

Murgatroyd said, *"Chee!"*

"You don't believe it, eh?" said Calhoun. Then he said, "Murgatroyd, I'm going to spend odd moments all the rest of my life wondering about what happens to Doctor Lett. They'll kill him, somehow. But I suspect they'll be quite gentle with him. There's no way to imagine a punishment that would really fit! Isn't that more interesting than coffee?"

"Chee! Chee! Chee!" said Murgatroyd insistently.

"It wasn't wise to stay and try to make an ordinary public-health inspection. We'll send somebody else when things are back to normal."

"Chee!!!" said Murgatroyd loudly.

"Oh, all right!" said Calhoun. "If you're going to be emotional about it, pass your cup."

He reached out his hand, Murgatroyd put his tiny mug in it. Calhoun refilled it. Murgatroyd sipped zestfully.

The Med Ship *Aesclipus Twenty* went on in overdrive, back toward sector headquarters of the Interstellar Medical Service.

QUARANTINE WORLD

I

There wasn't a thing he could put his finger on, but from the beginning Calhoun didn't feel comfortable about the public health situation on Lanke. There wasn't anything really wrong about it, not anything. Calhoun felt that it was just a little bit too good to be true. He and Murgatroyd the *tormal* had arrived in the little Med Ship *Aesclipus Twenty*. They'd been greeted with effusive cordiality. Health Department officials opened everything to Calhoun's examination, with a smoothness and speed that almost looked like the planetary authorities were anxious for him to finish his job and get away from there. The Health Minister practically jumped through hoops to provide all the information he could ask for. The communicable diseases appeared to be well in hand. The average age-at-death rate for the planet was the fraction of a decimal-point low, but it was accounted for by a microscopic rise in the accidental-death reports. Calhoun couldn't find a thing to justify the feeling that a cover-up job was being done. If it was, it was being done perfectly. He was a little bit irritated by his own suspicions.

Still, he went through the routine for three sunny days and evenings. He had some new developments in the art of medicine that Med Service Headquarters wanted to have spread about. He explained them to attentive listeners. In turn, he listened interestedly to what he was told, and the night before he was to lift off for his return to headquarters he attended a top-drawer medical society meeting in a high ceilinged lecture hall in the Health Department building.

The Health Minister introduced him in a typical speech in which he expressed the value of modern medical science in strictly businessman terms. He mentioned that absenteeism due to sickness was at the lowest figure ever known in the industries of Lanke. The extension of hormone-balance checkups, with other preventive practices, had reduced the overall incidence of sickness requiring hospitalization to the point where in the past ten years or so many thousands of hospital beds had ceased to be required. Which added so many millions of credits every year to the prosperity of Lanke.

There was another item which nobody thought about, but was perhaps the most valuable of all the achievements of medical science. He referred to the fact that epidemics were now substantially impossible. It was not necessary to calculate what an actual epidemic might cost. One could think simply of what the danger might be to see what medical science added to the planetary wealth. In interstellar trade alone, the simple threat of a dangerous plague on Lanke would mean the quarantining of the planet, and that would mean a financial panic, the closing of factories whose products could not be sold, widespread unemployment, appalling drops in the values of securities, and it could mean runs on banks, the abandonment of construction projects and even curtailment of agricultural production. The wealth that modern medical science contributed to the economy was the true great achievement of the medical profession! Much of this achievement was due to Lanke physicians alone, but the Interstellar Medical Service had made its contributions too, and he was happy to present to them Doctor Calhoun of that Service, whom many of them had met and talked to in the past few days.

Calhoun's speech, of course, was anticlimactic. He said the normal thing for such occasions. It amounted to polite congratulations to the doctors of Lanke for doing what doctors were supposed to do. He did feel, definitely, that something was being hidden from him, but he hadn't the evidence to justify him in saying so. So he made a speech in no wise remarkable and sat down to wait for the end of the meeting.

He'd much rather have been aboard the Med Ship. Murgatroyd was much better company than the Health Minister beside him. Murgatroyd didn't think of every possible human activity in terms of the money it made or saved. Murgatroyd had enjoyed his stay on Lanke. Calhoun hadn't.

Murgatroyd didn't have to pretend interest while people made dull speeches. Murgatroyd was a small, furry, cordial animal who liked humans and was liked by them. Aground, in human society, he made friends and charmed people and managed to get much petting and quantities of the sweet cakes and coffee he adored. Murgatroyd had fun. There'd been no call for use of the special talent that only *tormals* in all the galaxy possess, and he'd had a happy time. Calhoun looked forward to the restfulness of being back in the Med Ship with him, unbothered by the conviction that something was being put over that he couldn't put a finger on.

Then, suddenly, there were shoutings in another part of the building. A blaster rasped savagely. More shouts, more blasters went off in a storm of fire. Then there was dead silence.

In the lecture hall there was absolute stillness, as startled men listened for more of those decidedly unusual sounds.

They didn't come, but a man in police uniform did enter the back of the hall. He wore a look of most unofficial terror on his face. He spoke to the first doctor he came to inside that door. The doctor's face went gray. He went unsteadily out. Someone asked a question of the policeman. He answered and went out also, as if reluctantly. Others at the meeting moved to ask what had happened and what the policeman said.

The news—whatever it was—went about the hall with extraordinary dispatch. As each man heard, he paled. Some seemed near to fainting. There began, immediately, a universal attempt to leave the lecture hall without attracting attention.

"Dear me!" said the Health Minister, sitting on the speakers' platform beside Calhoun. "What can be the matter? Wait here and I'll find out."

He moved away. He stopped someone and asked a question. He was startled. He asked more questions. He came back to Calhoun in something like panic.

"What was it?" asked Calhoun.

"A—a burglar," said the Health Minister. His teeth seemed to be trying to chatter. "Just a burglar. There've been—robberies. We try to keep crime down, you know. It's an economic waste—terrible! But this man was trying to commit a burglary in—this building. He was discovered and he—jumped or fell from a window." The Health Minister wiped beads of sweat from his forehead. "He's dead. A—a shocking thing, of course. But not important. Not important at all. Not worth mentioning . . ."

Calhoun didn't believe him. The Health Minister was scared. There was no danger here! He was afraid of something a politician might be afraid of. It was that sort of terror. It wasn't too likely, but it might be linked to whatever had been covered up so Calhoun wouldn't discover it. The policeman who'd come in had been frightened too. Why? Then Calhoun looked at the medical society members in the lecture hall. The meeting had been ended by whatever word passed from man to man. The members of the society were leaving. They tried to be dignified, but also they tried to hurry. There was something puzzlingly wrong, and the Health Minister had lied about it. Obviously, more questions would only produce more lies. So Calhoun shrugged.

"Anyhow," he observed, "the meeting's over. It's breaking up. I'll get back to the spaceport."

His actual intentions were somewhat different.

"Yes. Yes. Of course," said the Health Minister, shivering. He didn't seem to think of escorting Calhoun out.

Calhoun joined those leaving the hall and the building. They crowded down the stairs, not waiting for a slower lift. Very many of them looked white and sick. Calhoun reached the outer air. Only yards from the exit there was a half-circle of burning flares, stuck in the ground. They bathed the ground and the side of the Health Department building with a pitiless glare.

There was a dead man on the ground. He'd obviously fallen from a height. None of the eminent physicians streaming out of the building so much as glanced at him. They hastened away in the darkness. Only Calhoun approached the flares. A policeman on watch—badly frightened—warned him back. Calhoun considered coldly. Then he stepped into the light past the protesting officer.

The dead man's mouth was open in a gruesome fashion. While the policeman continued to protest, Calhoun made a brisk, superficial examination. The dead man had lost teeth by dental caries, which was remarkable. He had other cavities filled with metal, a process abandoned for centuries. His garments were not made of normal materials, but of some fiber Calhoun did not recognize. There was a scar on his cheek. Calhoun, bending over, saw that tissues on either side of his nose were swollen and pigmented. The appearance was abnormal.

He picked up a bit of cloth, torn in the dead man's fall down the side of the building. As he examined it, a voice gasped, "Calhoun! What are you doing?" It was the Health Minister, leaving the building of his cabinet department. He trembled uncontrollably. "Stop it! Drop it!"

"I was looking at this man," said Calhoun. "It's queer . . ."

"Come away!" cried the Health Minister hysterically. "You don't know what you're—do . . ." He stopped. He mopped his face, shaking. Then he said, desperately attempting a normal tone, "I'm sorry. It would be a good idea for you to get back to your ship. This man was a criminal. There may be others of his confederates about. The police are going to make a thorough search. We—we civilians should get out of the way."

"But I'd like to look him over!" protested Calhoun. "There's scar tissue on his face! See it? Since when have doctors allowed scar tissue to form in healing wounds? He's lost some teeth and there's a cavity in one of his incisors! How often have you seen dental caries? They simply don't happen anymore!"

The Health Minister swallowed audibly.

"Yes. Yes . . . now that you point it out, I see what you mean. We'll have to do an autopsy. Yes. We'll do an autopsy in the morning. But right now, to cooperate with the police—"

Calhoun looked again at the limp, crumpled figure on the ground. Then he turned away. The last of the medical society members came out of the building. They melted away into the night. Calhoun could almost smell panic in the air.

The Health Minister vanished. Calhoun hailed a skimmer-cab and got into it. On the way to the spaceport he considered darkly. He'd evidently seen something he wasn't supposed to see. It might well be connected with what he hadn't been able to put a finger on. He'd told the Health Minister that he was going back to the spaceport, but that hadn't been his intention then. He'd meant to find a tavern and buy drinks for its habitues until somebody's tongue got loosened. News of a man killed by the police would set tongues wagging in certain kinds of society on any planet.

However, he'd changed his intention. He had a scrap of cloth in his pocket from the dead man's clothing. There was a bit of blood on it. It was extraordinary. The dead man was extraordinary. He'd frightened everybody who seemed to know something Calhoun was not supposed to discover. Considering all he did know, he planned to find out a few things more from that cloth sample.

The skimmer-cab reached the spaceport gate. The guards waved it on. It reached the Med Ship and settled to a stop. Calhoun paid the driver and went into the Med Ship, to be greeted with extravagant enthusiasm by Murgatroyd, who explained with many shrill *"Chee-chees"* that he did not like to be left alone when Calhoun went elsewhere. Calhoun said, "Hold it, Murgatroyd! Don't touch me!"

He put the sample of cloth with its few specks of blood into a sterile bottle. He snapped the elastic cover in place. Murgatroyd said, *"Chee?"*

"I've just seen a pack of thoroughly scared men," said Calhoun dryly, "and I've got to see if they were right to be scared."

He washed his hands with some care, and then extended his precautions—he felt absurd about it— to an entire change of clothing. The terror of the dead man puzzled and bothered him.

"Chee-chee-chee!" said Murgatroyd reproachfully.

"I know!" said Calhoun. "You want coffee. I'll make it. But I'm worried!"

Murgatroyd frisked. It was Calhoun's habit to talk to him as if he were a human being. He'd mentioned coffee, and Murgatroyd could recognize that word. He waited for the drink to be made and served. Frowning, Calhoun made it, thinking hard the while. Presently, he passed over the little cup that fitted Murgatroyd's tiny paws.

"There you are. Now listen!" Calhoun spoke vexedly. "I've felt all along that there was something wrong here, and tonight something happened. It could be told in a dozen words. It was, but not to me. A man died and it terrified two policemen, an entire medical society and the Health Minister of the planet. It wasn't the death of a man which did all this. It was something his death or his presence meant. But I wasn't told. I was lied to. Lied to! What did they want me to keep on not knowing?"

Murgatroyd sipped at his cup. He said profoundly, *"Chee?"*

"I suspect the same thing," said Calhoun, again with vexation. "Generally speaking, facts are hidden only from people whose job it would be to act on them. Facts have been hidden from me. What sort of facts is it my job to act on, Murgatroyd?"

Murgatroyd seemed to consider. He sipped again, reflectively. Then he said with decision, *"Chee-chee!"*

"I'm very much afraid you're right," Calhoun told him. "The local medical profession has repressed it . . . The Health Minister has a very vivid picture in his mind of what could happen to the economy and the prosperity of Lanke if even the suspicion of an epidemic went about. In short, Murgatroyd, it looks like a thing has been covered up so carefully that it shows. When as much terror as I saw just tonight is felt by everybody—I'd better get to work!"

He put part of the cloth sample—including the small bloodstains—in a culture medium. A fiber or two, though, he examined under a microscope. He shook his head.

"Odd! It's a natural fiber, Murgatroyd. It wasn't made. It grew. They certainly don't grow fibers on Lanke! This man isn't a native son of this planet. Quaint, eh?"

It was quaint. Synthetic fibers were better than natural ones. Nobody used natural fibers anymore. Nobody!

He waited impatiently on the culture from the cloth. While it was still too early to expect any specific results, his impatience got the best of him. He filled a vivo-slide for the culture microscope which would let him watch the behavior of living microorganisms as they grew. He was startled, when he looked at the microscope-screen. There were perfectly commonplace microbes in the culture broth even so early. However, there was one variety that was astonishing. A curious, dancing, spherical, pigmented organism leaped and darted madly. It visibly multiplied at a prodigious rate.

When Calhoun added the Daflos reagent to the contents of the slide, certain highly specific color effects appeared. The Daflos pathogenicity test was not infallible, but it wasn't meaningless, either. It said that the dancing, spherical microbes should be highly toxic. They produced a toxin the reagent reacted to. The rate of reproduction was astounding. It should, then, be highly infectious and probably lethal.

Calhoun frowned over the facts. The implications were matters a businessman on Lanke would want hidden, suppressed. A businessman would lie about them, desperately, until the last possible instant. A businessman's government might very well demand of the medical profession that it take precautions without causing undue alarm, and . . . Calhoun knew why the medical men at the meeting looked scared and sick. From the clothing and the blood of a dead man Calhoun had extracted a microbe which was probably that of a deadly plague—so said the Daflor reagents—of enormous infectivity which the clothing, teeth, and scar tissue suggested had come from some other world. This was enough to worry anybody. On Lanke, any physician who caused the danger to be realized, the facts to be known, and a planetary quarantine slapped on Lanke, such a physician would instantly be discredited and subjected to merciless hostility by his government. He'd be ruined professionally, financially and socially, and his family would share in his disgrace and ruin. The terror of the doctors had reason. Until the dead man was found, they'd had no reason for unease. When he was found, they knew instantly what the culture microscope had just told Calhoun. The doctors of Lanke were in a very bad fix. The government would not—would definitely not—permit a planetary quarantine if they could help it. It would not be anything but the automatic assumption that a financial panic and an industrial collapse must be avoided, whatever else had to be allowed. It would be very bad!

Calhoun began to see this with a bitter clarity. A curious flicker of light behind him made him turn. The outside-field detector-light was glowing on the control-board. Normally it lighted only to report that the force fields of a landing grid touched the Med Ship when the ship was to be brought to ground, or else when it was to be lifted off to a distance at which a Lawlor drive could be used. There was no reason for it to come on now.

Then the G.C.—general communication—speaker said:

"*Calling Med Ship Aesclipus Twenty! Calling Med Ship Aesclipus Twenty! Spaceport control office calling Med Ship Aesclipus Twenty!*"

Calhoun threw the answer switch.

"*Aesclipus Twenty* here," he said shortly. "What's the matter?"

"*Checking, sir,*" said the voice detachedly. "*Are you sealed up?*"

Calhoun glanced at the air-lock. Aground, of course, it could be opened like the two sets of doors of a vestibule, with direct communication between the inside of the ship and the outside air. However, without thinking particularly about it, Calhoun had left the Med Ship with its own air-renewal system operating.

"Yes," said Calhoun. "I'm sealed up. Why?"

"*Message for you, sir,*" said the voice.

There was immediately the voice of the Health Minister, racked and upset, coming out of the speaker.

"*You are requested to leave Lanke at once,*" it said agitatedly. "*Complaint will be made to the Med Service that you attempted to interfere with police measures against crime. Your ship will be lifted off as of now, and you are forbidden to return.*"

Calhoun said angrily, "The devil you say! I declare a quarantine—"

The communicator clicked. The Health Minister had cut off. The detached control-office voice said woodenly, *"I'm lifting you off, sir, as ordered. Lift-off coming . . ."*

Calhoun's mouth opened, to swear. Instantly he saw very many more things it had not been the intention of the Health Minister to tell him. He clenched his hands. This wasn't good!

Then the Med Ship stirred, and instantly thereafter seemed to fall toward the sky. Calhoun angrily flipped on the outside vision-plates and his sensations and the statements of the control-office voice agreed. The Med Ship was being lifted off. Below it, the lights of the spaceport receded. Then the street lights of Lanke's capital city were coming into view from behind tall buildings. They winked into sight from farther toward the dark horizon. The small spaceship went up and up.

The smaller, fainter lights of another city appeared. A little while later, the lights of still another. The capital city's pattern of streets grew ever smaller. More other city-glows appeared and seemed at once to dwindle and to drift toward and under the rising Med Ship. There was nothing to be seen anywhere except those minute, diminishing speckles of light.

Presently, the ship went into cloud cover and for seconds the vision screens were blank. Then it reached clear air again and then there was nothing but the starlit cloud cover below, and ten thousand million stars above.

The Med Ship was being lifted by the spaceport's landing grid. Eventually, the stars crept downward, and seemed to draw together, and the world of Lanke became only a diminishing circular patch of darkness against the galaxy's all-surrounding suns. Then the communicator speaker spoke woodenly again.

"*Calling Med Ship* Aesclipus Twenty! *Calling* Aesclip . . ."

"*Aesclipus* here," said Calhoun coldly.

"*You are now five diameters out,*" said the unemotional voice, "*And I am about to release you. Check?*"

"Check," said Calhoun sardonically.

He flipped off the G.C. transmitter. He felt the new freedom of the Med Ship. He spoke in an even more sardonic tone to Murgatroyd. "This is a first, Murgatroyd! It's the first time a Med Ship man has ever been thrown off a planet because he found out too much!" Then he added with a definite grimness, "It happens that throwing us off the planet verifies what I was only partly guessing and requires what I was hesitating to do."

His tone disturbed Murgatroyd, who of course could not understand what had happened. But he was upset because Calhoun was. Murgatroyd said shrilly, "*Cheechee!*"

"We're going back to headquarters," said Calhoun sourly. "We can take our news there quicker than we can send it. Anyhow they'll need more than you and me on Lanke to handle a plague—especially if it's a bad one. But I don't like it!"

He was angry. But it wasn't unprecedented for planetary governments to try to cover up things that would be bad for business. There'd been attempts before now to conceal outbreaks of disease. Some had probably succeeded. Those that failed turned out very badly indeed. Minor epidemics had become major plagues when a prompt call for Med Service help would have kept them minor and wiped them out. The Med Service had big ships, half a mile long and longer, with laboratories and equipment and personnel that could

handle emergencies of planetary size. But very, very
many lives had been lost because of governments
subordinating everything but business to business.
They'd tried to prevent business crises and financial
panics and industrial collapse. They'd only delayed
them—at incalculable costs in lives.

There was another factor, too. If a planetary government once concealed an emergency of this sort, it
would never dare admit it later. A certain world in
Cygnus had concealed a serious epidemic in order to
protect its interstellar trade. Later the fact was learned
by Med Service. It made a check of the public health
status of that reckless world, in view of its just-learned
medical history. It discovered and announced an imminent second epidemic—a perfectly accurate statement
of fact. The first epidemic had not been cleaned up
properly by the local physicians. The epidemic was
cyclic—with a normal period of high incidence after
every so many years. So the Med Service quarantined
that world—justly—and took stringent measures—
wisely—and there was consequently no second plague.
But there were many hard-boiled businessmen who
fumed that the Med Service had no reason for its
action; that it had been punishing the Cygnus world
for violating a primary rule for galactic public health.
The planet had concealed a disease that might but
hadn't been passed on to its customers. Businessmen
believed the quarantine a penalty.

So Calhoun knew grimly that if there'd been a
hidden plague on Lanke in the past, it would never
be admitted now. Never! And any doctor who revealed
the historical fact . . . The reason for the silence of
Lanke's doctors was abundantly clear.

But this situation wasn't as simple as the Cygnus
affair. The dead man Calhoun had partly examined
wasn't a native of Lanke. Yet the doctors of Lanke

knew all about him and the plague of which he was
dying when blaster bolts drove him to a quicker death.
He didn't belong on Lanke. Worse, he didn't belong
anywhere else. His state of civilization wasn't appropriate anywhere in the galaxy. But he was positively
a man. Calhoun had seen drama tapes about lost
colonies and villages of castaways, and even elaborate
hiding places for refugees from the laws of planets.
But he didn't believe them.

"Still," he said irritably, "where did he come from?"

He felt that there were too many questions already.
But there was something definite to do. Several things.
For the first of them he swung the Med Ship about
and aimed it at the small, remote star cluster where
Sector Headquarters was established. He punched the
computer keys. He said, "Overdrive coming,
Murgatroyd! Five . . . four . . . three . . . two . . . one . . ."

There was a sudden intolerable giddiness and an
instant's insupportable nausea, and the sensation of a
spiral fall to nowhere. Then, abruptly, everything was
quite all right. The Med Ship was in overdrive, surrounded by a cocoon of stressed space which changed
its own position many times faster than the speed of
light, and carried the little Med Ship with it.

Calhoun paced up and down the control-room,
scowling. "That man," he said abruptly, "wasn't a normal inhabitant of Lanke, Murgatroyd! He didn't grow
up on it. He carried microscopic flora and fauna with
him—as don't we all?—but they were very probably
as alien to Lanke as the man himself. The doctors
knew about it, and they were afraid. Afraid! But where
did he come from?"

Murgatroyd had retreated to his little cubbyhole in
the control-room. He was curled up there with his
furry tail draped across his nose. He blinked at
Calhoun. When Calhoun talked conversationally,

Murgatroyd adored pretending that he discussed abstruse subjects with him. But now Calhoun really talked to himself. Murgatroyd realized it. He said, *"Chee!"* and prepared to take a nap.

Presently, Calhoun began an angry, systematic search through the Med Ship's library. It was a remarkable storage system for facts. The *Aesclipus Twenty* was able to carry more reference material for a Med Service man's needs than most national libraries contained. The data-retrieval system was one of the great technical achievements of the previous century. Calhoun had at his fingertips more information on medical subjects than earlier times could have imagined.

The library had nothing to say about a plague which produced—doubtless among other symptoms—enlarged and stiffened, pigmented tissues on either side of a man's nose. Nor did it have any record of a microorganism exactly matching the one he'd gotten from the cloth of the dead man's garments—or the specks of blood included—and suspected of the water he'd washed in.

The really basic question remained, too. Where had the inexplicable man come from?

Calhoun checked the progress of his cultures. All thrived.

Calhoun set up an imaginary globe in space, with Lanke as its center. He set the data-retrieval unit to find a habitable world, not known to be colonized, in that volume of emptiness. An abortive attempt at colonization might have left some castaways behind. That would raise almost as many questions as it answered, but it seemed the most likely approach to the problem.

There was no habitable world in the Stellar Directory portion of the ship's records. He tried a larger volume of space. Then a still larger one. Nothing.

He tried for less than a habitability-one world. Individual survival might be possible where a colony could not live. He set the search-unit to work again. It found a world which was airless, a gas-giant world with intolerable gravity, another which had an equatorial temperature of minus sixty degrees at noon. Another . . .

Ultimately, one turned up which looked plausible. It was the third-orbit planet of a Type G sun. It was not unduly remote from Lanke. It was listed under the name Delhi. Shallow, marshy seas. A single continent. Temperature, not unbearable. Life-types not unduly dangerous. Atmosphere typical of third-orbit planets but with .04% of a complex methane-derivative gas, apparently harmless. This data had been sent up from an exploring spaceboat, later lost. There were what was believed to be the ruins of a human settlement, photographed from space. Classed as habitability zero because no ship had ever returned to its home spaceport after landing on it. The inimical factor was assumed to exist in the atmosphere, but was not known.

Here was material for guesses, but nothing more. It threw no light on where the dead man with bad teeth had come from. Calhoun went over all the other reports. No other was even as promising as this.

He had been seven hours in overdrive when the projected letters separated into twins. Every letter doubled. The reading-matter became unreadable. With one eye covered, reading was just barely possible, but he could see nothing with real clarity.

He took his temperature. He felt perfectly well, but he had a high fever and his eyes grew progressively worse. He said grimly to Murgatroyd, "I begin to see some excuse for the doctors on Lanke. Whatever they were afraid of getting, I've got. It's highly infectious, all right!"

Ten hours out from Lanke, his vision cleared again. He could fuse the images from both eyes. He continued to feel perfectly well, but his temperature was half a degree higher than three hours earlier.

"This," he told Murgatroyd, "is not according to the rules! I may have to call on you as a member of the medical profession!"

He gave himself as thorough a physical examination as one can give himself. He used the amplifier-microscope on his saliva, his blood, on every body fluid. Each of them showed a minute, perfectly spherical pigmented microorganism in appalling numbers. As he regarded them on the screen of the amplifier-microscope they broke into halves, became small spheres, grew swiftly and prepared to divide again. Meanwhile, they danced and darted and whirled frantically. The reaction to the Daflos reagents indicated the presence of a deadly toxin.

"And I took precautions!" Calhoun said rather dizzily. "I washed and showered. I could almost have operated with no more attempt at a sterile environment!" He shook his head. "I think I can go a little longer. That dead man was farther along than this. I've time enough to call on you, Murgatroyd."

He looked at himself in the mirror. The curious enlargement of the flesh beside his nose had appeared. He began to get out his equipment. Something occurred to him.

"The Health Minister," he said sardonically, "didn't quarantine me. He sent me off. He had no fear of my reporting anything to headquarters! I should be dead before breakout, and you couldn't run the ship to headquarters and it would never be found." Then he said, "Let's prevent such an unpleasant fate, Murgatroyd!"

He drew a small sample of blood from his arm. He

injected it into Murgatroyd where a small patch of skin on the *tormal's* flank had been desensitized almost as soon as he was born. Murgatroyd made no objection.

Now Murgatroyd went back to his cubbyhole, yawning. He crawled in to doze. Calhoun made a mental note to check his pulse and breathing in half an hour. He himself, felt feverish. His head seemed to rock a little. His eyes went bad again. He saw double. Murgatroyd dozed peacefully. Calhoun doggedly waited for him to react to the microscopic spheres. His heartbeat should go up four or five counts a minute. He might run a degree of fever. He would be sleepy for two hours, or three, or even four. Then he'd wake up and his blood would contain antibodies against the material with which he'd been inoculated. He'd be back in robust health, and able to share it with Calhoun.

It didn't work out that way. When Calhoun went to check his pulse-rate in half an hour, Murgatroyd came wide awake. He said, *"Chee!"* in an inquiring tone. He scrambled out of his nest, filled with vim and zest for whatever the hour might bright forth. His pulse was normal. His temperature was equally correct.

Calhoun stared at him. Murgatroyd couldn't have looked healthier. He showed no sign of having needed to produce antibodies.

He hadn't. There are some diseases, contagious among animals, to which human beings are immune. There are some from which humans suffer, to which animals are not subject. More than once medical research has been halted while a hunt was made for an experimental animal in which a particular strain of microbes or viruses could live.

The plague of which Lanke was terrified and Calhoun a victim happened to be a plague to which Murgatroyd did not need to form antibodies. He was immune to it by the simple normal chemistry of his body, and there was nothing that Calhoun could do about it. He considered that he would unquestionably die within a certain short number of days or hours. The Med Ship would drive on, to breakout somewhere within a light-year more or less of its destination. From there, it should make a shorter overdrive-hop to a matter or no more than a million miles or two, and then it should use Lawlor Drive within the solar system, on whose planet the Interstellar Medical Service had its headquarters.

But if Calhoun was dead nothing of the sort would happen. The Med Ship would breakout. Murgatroyd might still be alive, but he could do nothing. Eventually he would die, bewildered. The Med Ship would never, never be found so long as time ran on, and Lanke . . .

"Murgatroyd," said Calhoun, "this is a bad business! And you're right in it! I know what I'm up against, but what am I going to do for you?"

Murgatroyd said confidently, *"Chee-chee-chee!"*

"I'm seeing better," said Calhoun suddenly. "It seems to come in waves of better and worse. Intermittent."

He put his hand to his face to feel the now-marked unresilient stiffened flesh beside his nose. Murgatroyd looked hopefully at the coffee pot. He said, *"Chee?"* There was nothing to indicate the possibility of anything, not anticipated. There was no reason for anything to happen.

Then, abruptly, everything changed. The *Aesclipus Twenty* was in overdrive and there was only one thing which even in theory could affect her from outside. It was said that if a ship were in overdrive and all the cosmos exploded, and everything in all the galaxies ceased to be, including the galaxies themselves, that people in a ship in overdrive would not know of the disaster and would not hear the last trumpet until breakout-time came.

But now, here at this moment, Calhoun felt a familiar and monstrous dizziness, and an equally familiar and intolerable nausea, and then all the sensations of a whirling, spinning fall toward nothingness. Simultaneously the little ship's vision screens lighted, the *Aesclipus Twenty* broke out of overdrive and lay floating in space surrounded by a myriad of stars, and a small but bright red light flashed luridly on the control-board.

■

Murgatroyd made the first comment. It was an indignant, protesting, *"Chee-chee! Chee-chee!"*

He was accustomed to the sensations of going into overdrive and out of it again. He didn't like them. Nobody did. Murgatroyd endured them for the sake of being where Calhoun was, being petted by Calhoun, drinking coffee with Calhoun, and on occasion engaging in long, leisurely discussion to which Murgatroyd contributed his shrill voice and stubborn conviction that he was actually conversing. Now, though, he protested. Before breakout there was normally an hour-off warning, then a five-minute warning, and then a solemn tick-tock-tick-tock until a gong sounded and then a voice counted down to zero. Murgatroyd had learned that this was the routine for breakout; but just now the extremely unpleasant sensations had happened with no warning whatever. It was upsetting. It was a violation of the accepted order of things. He said, *"Chee-chee! Chee-chee!"* even more indignantly.

Calhoun stared at the star-speckled screens. He was entirely incredulous. The red light on the control-board was notice of something solid nearby in space. But that was impossible! The Med Ship was in between-the-stars, light-years from Lanke. In between-the-stars there is nothing more solid than starlight. Solidity in this emptiness would be even more unlikely than a ship breaking out of overdrive strictly on its own decision. However, the limit of improbability was reached when not only a ship broke out of itself, but the near-object warning flashed simultaneously.

Calhoun stared at the screens. It didn't make sense, unless a highly theoretic happening had occurred. In theory, two overdrive fields might affect each other. Nothing else could. For extremely abstract reasons, it had been determined that *if* two ships passed close to each other, and *if* they were of nearly the same size, and *if* both overdrive-fields units were nearly of the same strength, either or both fields could blow out. For this reason a circuit-breaker was included in all overdrive designs. The odds against such a thing were ten plus a handful of zeros to one. It had never before been known to happen. Now it had.

Calhoun slipped into the pilot's chair. He threw switches. Overdrive off. It had gone off by itself. Circuit-checker on. A special instrument verified all contacts and connections. This instrument stuttered for an instant and then flashed the signal, *"Go."* A circuit-breaker had operated, but it was now reset. It was the one in the overdrive circuit. Calhoun barely noticed that the G.C. speaker had come on also and now relayed the crackling and hissing noises that would-be poets call, "the small-talk of the stars." Calhoun found himself gazing unbelievingly at the screens.

A second-magnitude star winked out and back to brightness. A less brilliant nearby star followed.

Calhoun swung the radar and looked incredulously at what it reported. There was something in between-the-stars no more than four hundred miles away. With hundreds of thousands of cubic light-years of space to move about in, something in overdrive had passed within four hundreds miles of *Aesclipus Twenty*. Two circuit-breakers had operated, and—there they were! The radar blip said the other object was a trifle smaller than the Med Ship, and it appeared to be practically motionless, moving only enough to occult two nearby stars within a few seconds.

Murgatroyd said yet again, and even more indignantly, *"Chee!! Chee!!!"*

"I didn't do it, Murgatroyd," said Calhoun abstractly. "Quiet for a minute!"

He threw another switch and the electron-telescope came on. He searched with it. He made fine adjustments for focus. Then his face expressed blank unbelief.

The telescope screen showed another ship floating in the starlight. It was not much like any other ship Calhoun had ever seen. At first it seemed a freak; not alien but eccentric, not of a non-human design, but like something made by men who'd never seen a real spaceship. There was a pipelike object sticking out of its bow.

He pressed the G.C. call-button; but first he cut off the lens that would transmit a picture of himself. He called.

"General Call!" he snapped. "General Call! Med Ship *Aesclipus Twenty* making general call! What ship's that?"

There was no answer. He frowned. Only minutes since he'd discovered himself very definitely condemned to death by an unfamiliar plague germ. A little earlier he'd been thrown off the planet Lanke for discovering too much. Before that he'd seen a dead man who couldn't come from anywhere. This extremely unusual ship couldn't come from anywhere, either.

He suddenly heard murmuring voices. There seemed to be several persons speaking in low tones near an open microphone. They were in disagreement. One voice raised itself above the others but the words were still indistinct.

"Hello!" said Calhoun sharply. "I hear your voices! Who the devil are you and what's going on?"

It occurred to him as odd that, with a plague on him and the end of all his responsibilities drawing near, he still spoke authoritatively as a Med Service man and a citizen of the galaxy to persons whose actions required to be explained. He repeated sternly, "What's going on?"

The other ship was incredible. It was patched with patches on top of patches. It was preposterous. The electron telescope could not give the finer details in mere starlight, but it was rusty and misshapen and no spaceport would ever lift it off the ground! Yet here it was.

A voice rasped from the G.C. speaker overhead, "*Look! What do you think you're doing?*" As Calhoun blinked, it said pugnaciously, "*What d'you think you're doing to us? You . . . know what I mean!*"

Calhoun said coldly, "This is Med Ship *Aesclipus Twenty*. Who are you?"

"*Med Ship?*" snapped the angry voice, "*wha—*"

The voice stopped abruptly, as if a hand had been clapped over someone's mouth. There were more murmurings.

Calhoun grimaced. He didn't understand this other ship. He'd cut off his own vision lens because he didn't want anybody to see him with the marks of the plague on him. Whoever spoke from the patched-up other spacecraft didn't want to be seen, either. The murmurings came to an end. The harsh voice snapped, *"Never mind that! What'd you do to us? We were going about our business when—whango! Something hit us. And we're here instead of where we were going! What'd you do?"*

Calhoun saw a stirring of the radar blip. The other craft was moving toward the Med Ship. Then he felt the edges of everything becoming twinned. His eyes were going bad again. No, he didn't want to mention his own situation. Nothing could be done for him, and dying is a strictly private matter. He felt concern for Murgatroyd, but he was a Med Ship man and there was a certain way he should act. He was impatient. Whoever was piloting the other ship knew nothing about his work. Calhoun felt the indignation of a professional with an inept amateur.

The rasping voice said truculently, *"I'm asking what you did!"*

"We did something to each other," said Calhoun coldly. "We came too close to each other. Our overdrive units got overloaded. Our circuit-breakers cut them off. Do you want more information than that?"

"What other information have you got?" demanded the voice.

Calhoun felt feverish. The symptoms of this plague were evidently intermittent. They came and they went. They'd probably grow more and more severe until he died of them—but . . .

"I take it," he said coldly, "that you don't know what you're doing or why, because you don't know what's happened. Do you know where you are, or how to get to where you want to go? In other words, do you want help?"

"What kind of help?" The question was asked with suspicion.

"First off," said Calhoun, "you broke out of over-drive. Have you checked your circuit-breaker?"

"We don't call it that," said the voice. *"What is it?"*

Calhoun could have sworn. Instead, he closed his eyes. He felt a diminishing of his sense of balance. He was annoyed at the prospective loss of dignity, but he said, "A circuit-breaker . . ." Then with his eyes closed he told what a circuit-breaker was, and where it would be in a power line. There should be an indicator saying, *"Off."* There had to be a circuit-breaker or the other ship would be full of smoke from burned-out insulation.

It occurred to him how the other ship came to be what it was. It was a salvage job. It had been found somewhere and cobbled back to precarious operation by men who had to guess at the functions of what they repaired. They'd lifted off to space with it, probably by rocket. It was hair-raising to think of!

All he could do was give them advice and possibly a course in drive-time so they wouldn't over-shoot, for now . . .

"When you find the circuit-breaker, turn off the overdrive switch in the control-board," he said. "Then—not before!—throw the circuit-breaker back on. Then you can go into overdrive again. How about your fuel? This is a repaired spaceboat, isn't it?"

A strained silence, and then a suspicious assent.

Calhoun had them report on the fuel, the air-pressure and the air-renewal apparatus. His sense of balance began to come back. He called for more and more instrument readings.

"You haven't too much fuel," he said briefly, "but you can get to a nearby spaceport. That's all! Where do you want to go?"

"That's our business!"

"You've only so many possible destinations," Calhoun told them. "Wait a minute."

He worked the computer and the data-retrieval device. He got courses from here to the nearest inhabited planets. There were four that they could reach handily. Calhoun named them and the time in overdrive required to get reasonably close to them— to a distance the Lawlor drive could traverse in a practicable interval. . . . One of the four was Lanke, and Calhoun frankly advised against taking the agglomeration of patches that was a ship to Lanke. His reason was the considerable likelihood that there was plague on Lanke now.

"I've written down the courses and drive-times," he observed. "Write them down as I dictate."

He dictated them. Murmurings. Discussion in the background of the other spacecraft. The harsh voice said, *"Those drive-times are pretty long. There's a yellow sun that looks close."*

"It's Delhi," said Calhoun, from memory. "It has an Earth-type planet and there may have been a colony on it once. But there's nothing there now! There's something wrong with it and no ship is known to have gotten back to its home spaceport after landing on it." He added conscientiously, "It's near enough. The drive-time's only—" He gave the drive-time and the course. "But I advise you to go to one of the other nearby worlds, go into orbit around it, and call down. They'll land you somewhere. And when they get you down to ground, stay there!"

His eyes were better. He looked at the screens. The freakish, patched-up boat was very, very close, not more than a score or two of miles away. He opened his mouth to protest indignantly. He was practically a dead man. At the moment, to be sure, he felt only feverish. Otherwise, nothing serious seemed to be wrong. However, he knew that a mirror would show his own self with the plague marks he'd seen on a dead man back on Lanke.

"Meanwhile," he added, "you'd better not come closer to me."

There was no answer. There were, though, murmurings near the microphone in the other ship. Someone protested against something. The rasping voice growled. There was a click, and the murmuring stopped. The other microphone had been cut off.

Calhoun's eyes improved still more. He looked at the electron telescope image of the other ship. It was turning to face him directly, the pipe at its bow bore exactly.

Suddenly, there was a mad, violent swirling of vapor or gases from the tube at the other ship's bow. Emptiness snatched at it, grasped it, separated it to atoms and threw them away.

The Med Ship was alone. Something minute remained where the preposterous other spacecraft had been. It was very, very small. It was only a moving speck of reflected starlight. Then the electron telescope screen showed it clearly. It was bright metal, it was torpedo-shaped, and it moved with a certain high, fixed velocity toward the *Aesclipus Twenty*.

Calhoun stared at it. He knew at once what it was, of course, but his reaction was modified by the situation he found himself in. Normally, he'd have been angered by the sending of a missile, probably charged with chemical explosive, to destroy the Med Ship after the attacking vessel had vanished in overdrive. He was acutely aware that he happened to be in one of the remission-periods of the plague which undoubtedly would kill him. If he'd thought of the future as one usually does, he'd have been angry that somebody had tried to destroy him. Now he had no future to be robbed of. If this shell shattered the Med Ship, it wouldn't be doing very much. It would deprive him of one—two—maybe three days of vanishing satisfactions, in which he could accomplish nothing whatever.

It didn't seem to matter. He found himself smiling wryly at the thing that came swiftly to destroy him. Suddenly, he changed his mind. He threw the Lawlor-drive switch and the Med Ship moved. When the explosive missile passed through the spot the ship had occupied, and went sturdily on and on to nowhere, he grimaced a little.

"I dodged that on your account," he told Murgatroyd. "But for you, I'd have no reason to bother. I can't live to reach headquarters, though with warning they could receive me without danger and soothe my final hours. I can't land on a nearer, colonized planet without introducing a plague and being a murderer. So I'll compromise and put you down where you just barely may have a sporting chance of surviving—where if you die, it won't be by starving in this ship. I'll do whatever futile things my condition permits."

He began to set up a course and drive-time on the ship's automatic pilot. A little later he said, "Overdrive coming, Murgatroyd!"

There came the intolerable accompaniments of going into overdrive. Vertigo and nausea and all the sensations of an unconscionable, spinning plunge toward oblivion. Calhoun endured them doggedly. He was convinced that presently his eyes wouldn't work again and he'd probably have to crawl to move about on the ship. Anticipation of such undignified behavior was much more annoying than a mere attempt to kill him. He didn't bother to be angry about the missile.

While he felt relatively himself, he readied a meal for Murgatroyd and ate what he could, himself. He viewed with a certain detached amusement the idea that since he couldn't live to reach headquarters, and couldn't land anywhere else without introducing the plague, he was using all the splendid technical equipment of a Med Ship, representing tens of millions of credits and the life achievements of many scientists and inventors, to put a small furry creature aground on an uninhabited world rather than leave him alone in an undirected spaceship.

"This," he told Murgatroyd while the little *tormal* zestfully ate the food he'd set out, "this is ridiculous! You'll be left alone anyhow and I've no idea how you'll make out—but . . ."

He shrugged. It would be absurd to make a dramatic production out of the business of dying.

"I'm going to put you aground and you'll have to fend for yourself. You'll probably think I'm unkind. You can't imagine my being unable to take care of you. But that's the fact. It's typical. I haven't done anything in particular."

Murgatroyd said cheerfully, *"Chee-chee!"* and finished his plate.

The *Aesclipus Twenty* drove on. Presently, Calhoun's eyes went bad again. Later, he lost all ability to distinguish up from down, or sidewise from either. He sat grimly in the pilot's chair, with a cord knotted to keep him from falling out, which for some reason he considered necessary.

He probably slept. He waked, and he was horribly thirsty. He loosened the cord and let himself fall to the floor. With all his senses assuring him that the ship revolved, he made his way on all-fours—with several falls—to where there was drinking water. He drew a glass, and then solemnly poured it out on the way to his lips, which were responsive to the feeling that he had to turn the glass to prevent it from spilling as the Med Ship turned; but the ship didn't turn and the water was wasted.

Finally, he wedged himself against the wall and

refused to believe anything but his eyes. He watched the surface of the water and denied all other evidence. He drank. He drank again and again and again.

Abruptly, he slept. Then he awoke, and acute nausea was just past, but dizziness had not woken him, and the feeling of spinning fall was only slightly different from the feelings he had all along. Now, Murgatroyd was plucking at him and chattering agitatedly, *"Chee! Chee-chee! Chee!"*

Then he knew that breakout had come, and the vision screens were lighted, and he looked and saw a blazing yellow sun and innumerable stars. The ceiling speaker crackled and whispered as in normal space. The Med Ship had arrived at the solar system of Delhi.

When he was back in the pilot's chair, Calhoun realized how weak he'd become; obviously, the effect of the plague nearing its terminal stage. He heard somebody talking. It was himself, and he paid no attention. He searched for the planet, the planet that was of no use to anybody, from which no ship returned. He found it. It was astonishingly near. One part of his brain labored gravely with the computer and inexpertly made observations while another part talked nonsense, which he resented.

There followed a period of very great confusion. There seemed to be two of him, as there appeared to be two Murgatroyds and two electron telescope screens and two control-boards. One part of his mind considered this improper, but another part gleefully took note that he had two right hands and two lefts, and watched with charmed attention as those hands simultaneously operated twin controls, and something gigantic grew more immense as the *Aesclipus Twenty* approached it. He was absurdly surprised when it became a monstrous black hole in the universe of stars. The Med Ship had swung around to its night-side in an orbit Calhoun's then-disregarded sane brain-fraction had contrived. He seemed to sleep, and to wake again, and he was extremely thirsty. Suddenly, the sane part of his mind declared loudly, that there was a settlement! It showed on the electron telescope screen! Then the part of his brain that was angry with the fevered part forcibly took charge.

The confusion he experienced did not lessen, to be sure. The part of a man which is his total consciousness, the part that uses brain-cells to store memories and present data for judgment, the part that uses brain-cells to control his body, the part which recognizes the phenomena of consciousness, that part, still functioned. One's brain can become an unreliable instrument, from fever or alcohol, but there is an ego, an id, a something, which struggles to make sane use of it. There were moments when he knew that he was singing and that his body was behaving in a fashion totally irrelevant to his situation and his purpose. There were other moments when he seemed to control his body which was astonishingly feeble, and he was clearly aware that he had turned on the Med Ship's emergency rockets and that it was balancing on a pencil-thin, blue-white flame in midair.

Confusion came again. He was lecturing Murgatroyd on medical ethics. While he lectured, the Med Ship and all its contents turned somersaults, as did the planet outside. Calhoun knew that proper planets do not turn somersaults in their own skies, so he treated this behavior with the dignified contempt it deserved.

More chaotic sensations, so bewildering that they ceased to be impressions. Suddenly, there was a distinct thump, and he was shocked into rationality. He realized that the Med Ship had touched ground. He had cut off the rockets. He stared at the scene the vision screen showed.

The *Aesclipus Twenty* had landed in a swampy valley bottom among low mountains; there was vegetation outside which swayed gently in a strong breeze. On higher ground he saw white, man-made walls with empty window openings and tree tops showing where there should have been roofs. Close to the Med Ship there was swamp, marsh, stagnant puddles, and indigenous growing things.

Murgatroyd said, *"Chee-chee!"* in an anxious tone. Calhoun was weary beyond belief, but he roused.

"All right, Murgatroyd," he said dizzily, "I've done a very silly thing, and maybe I've done you no good at all, but if you'll follow me I'll finish it."

With an overwhelming lassitude, making his arms and legs seem to weigh tons, he left the chair by the control-board. He stayed on his feet almost half the way to the air-lock, by leaning heavily against the wall. Then his knees buckled under him and the rest of the way he crawled. At the inner air-lock door he reached up and by pure habit pushed the succession of buttons which opened both the inner and the outer doors. They rumbled wide, unsealing themselves. Air came in. There was the smell of mud and vegetation and unfamiliar life. There was also one particular odor which should have been unpleasing, but that it was so faint it seemed only strange.

"There!" said Calhoun. He waved his hand feebly. "There you are, Murgatroyd! There's a world for you. You'll be lonely, and maybe you'll die or be killed by some local predator, and maybe I'm doing you a dirty trick. But my intentions are of the best. Shoo! Get out so I can close the ports again."

Murgatroyd said, *"Chee!"* in a bewildered tone. It was not customary for Calhoun to crawl on his hands and knees and urge him out the air-lock. Calhoun was behaving strangely. Murgatroyd looked at him apprehensively.

"*Chee!*" he said. "*Chee-chee!*"

Calhoun did not answer. He felt himself slipping down to the Med Ship's floor. He was intolerably weary and weak. He was wholly confused. The sane part of his consciousness relaxed. He'd finished the task he'd set himself. If he rested, maybe he'd get back enough strength to close the air-lock door. It didn't really matter. It was annoying that he hadn't been able to get word of the Lanke situation to headquarters, but the plague had been on Lanke before. The doctors knew it. They were terrified by it, but maybe . . . maybe . . .

Wryly, at the moment he believed his moment of death, Calhoun conceded to himself that he'd done the best he could. It wasn't good enough.

■■■

When Calhoun awoke, or at any rate regained consciousness, Murgatroyd was saying, *"Chee-chee! Chee-chee!"* in his high-pitched voice. He sounded unhappy. There were smells in the air. Calhoun was not on the floor, but in his bunk. He heard footsteps and the sound of wind blowing. There were cracklings which were the sounds of the G.C. speaker reporting normal shortwave broadcasts from a nearby sun. There were other and unidentifiable sounds.

Calhoun opened his eyes. This instant, instinctive effort to sit up achieved nothing whatever. He was almost wholly without strength. He did manage to make a croaking sound, and someone came to the door of his sleeping cabin. He didn't even see clearly, just now, but he said in a fretful tone and with extreme exertion, "This is the devil! I've got a plague of some kind, and it's horribly infectious. You've got to set up some sort of quarantine around me. Get a doctor to the air-lock—don't let him come in!—I'll tell him about it."

A voice—a girl's voice—said evenly, "That's all right.

386

We know about the plague. This is Delhi. We should know, shouldn't we?"

Murgatroyd hopped up on the bunk on which Calhoun inexplicably lay. He said agitatedly, "*Chee! Chee-chee!*"

Calhoun found his voice improved. He said as fretfully as before, "No doubt. No doubt. But—this is the devil!"

A surpassing bitterness filled him. There were people here where he'd landed. Inhabitants. He was a Med Ship man and he'd brought plague here! Quite automatically, he assumed that in some moment of unrealized confusion he must have set up the wrong course and drive-time in the Med Ship's automatic-pilot. He'd had four courses and timings at hand to give to the other ship encountered in space. He must blindly have used the wrong one when setting course for Delhi . . .

The girl's voice had said this was Delhi. But it couldn't be! No ship had ever gotten home from Delhi. It couldn't be colonized. It had been tried, and there were ruins to prove it, but there was something wrong with it, something yet unknown but utterly fatal. No ship had ever returned . . .

He couldn't stop to think of such things now. He'd brought plague here!

"Get a doctor to the air-lock door," he commanded as fiercely as his weakness would allow. "Quick! I've got to tell him . . ."

"We haven't any doctors," said the girl's voice, as evenly as before, "and you don't need one. This is Delhi. There's no use in having doctors on Delhi. Not for the plague. You're all right!"

He saw, with clearing eyes, that a figure bent over him. It was a girl with dark brown eyes. She lifted his head and gave him a drink from a cup.

"We heard your rockets, Rob and I," she said in a tone from which all warmth had been removed. "We could tell you were landing. We hurried, and we got here before anybody else. We found you halfway out of the air-lock with a tame little animal crying to you to wake up. So we brought you inside and Rob's watching now to see if anybody else heard you land. You can hope nobody did."

Calhoun decided that he was delirious again. He struggled to clear his brain. Murgatroyd said anxiously, *"Chee-chee?"*

"I suppose so," said Calhoun drearily. Then he said more loudly, "There has to be a quarantine! I'm carrying contagion . . ."

The girl did not answer. Murgatroyd chattered at him. It sounded as if, relieved now, he were scolding Calhoun for not having paid attention to him before.

Calhoun fell, tumbled, dropped, back into slumber.

It was a very deep sleep. A dreamless sleep. He came out of it an indefinite time later, when he could not tell whether it was day or night. There was silence, now, except for the tiny background noises from the tape. The air-lock door was evidently closed. Murgatroyd was a warm spot touching Calhoun's leg through the bed covering. Calhoun noted that his brain was clear. His fever was gone. Which could mean either that it was burned out, or that he was. In the latter case, he was experiencing that clear-headedness sometimes granted to people just about to die.

He heard a peculiar small sound. Someone—a girl— was weeping while trying not to make a noise. Calhoun blinked. He must have moved in some other fashion too, because Murgatroyd waked instantly and asked, *"Chee-chee? Chee-chee-chee?"*

There was a stirring in the control-room. The girl who'd given him a drink came in. She looked as if she'd been crying; Calhoun said, "I feel very much better. Thanks. Can you tell me where I am and what's happened?"

The girl tried to smile, not very successfully. She said, "You're on Delhi, to stay. We've locked the air-lock doors and nobody can get in. They've only banged and called, so far. Rob's looking over the ship now, trying to find out how to smash it so it can't possibly be repaired. He says you can't lift anyhow. The ground here is swamp. Your landing-feet have sunk in the mud and you can't possibly get clear. So that's all right for the time being."

Calhoun stared at her. He ignored the statement that the Med Ship was permanently aground.

"Delhi—locked doors—" He said incredulously, "Look! Delhi's not inhabited. Its air's wrong, or something. No ship that's ever landed on Delhi has ever gotten home again. Delhi doesn't have people . . ."

"There are a good two thousand of them outside just now," said the girl as detachedly as before. "And every one of them will tear this ship apart with his bare hands rather than let you leave without taking them. But the swamp has taken care of that." Then she said abruptly, "I'll get you something to eat."

She went out and Calhoun groped for meaning in this addition to the improbabilities that had started on Lanke. They'd begun with a dead man who apparently came from nowhere, and the terror he evoked in the medical profession of Lanke. There'd been the plague Calhoun contracted from the most cursory examinations of that dead man, and the patched-up life-boat quite impossibly encountered in space. It also couldn't have come from anywhere. Above all there was the plague, which on Lanke was horribly dreaded, but which this girl disregarded. Now there were two thousand inhabitants on the uninhabited planet Delhi who wouldn't let the ship leave without them, and there was somebody—his name was Rob?—who intended to wreck the Med Ship so it couldn't leave at all.

The sum of all this was bewilderment. For example, the plague. He didn't have it anymore. It was a spontaneous recovery. If its victims recovered, why the terror on Lanke? Also, why were there two thousand people who wanted to leave Delhi, and somebody named Rob who didn't want anybody to leave—not even Calhoun?

He puzzled furiously while he waited for the girl to return. He heard movements. Somebody came up into the control-room from the storage decks below. He heard voices. If that was Rob, he'd reason to be uneasy. He called. A tall, broad young man of about his own age looked in the door.

"You're Rob," said Calhoun politely. His voice was stronger than he'd expected. "Would you mind telling me why you want to wreck my ship? I'm told that it's hopelessly bogged down in marshy ground now. Why add to the disaster by wrecking it?"

"Enough men," said the young man, with some grimness, "could dig it out. And then it could go away. That has to be made impossible!"

"But this is a Med Ship!" protested Calhoun. "It has a special status!"

"And this is Delhi," said Rob sternly. "There's a plague that's native to this planet. We who live here don't have it. If someone comes here with it, he recovers. But if we leave, we develop it, and if anyone from here landed on another world, he'd die of it with the people he took it to. So nobody must leave!"

Calhoun considered for a moment.

"But somebody has, not long ago. In fact, I caught the plague from him."

He couldn't have proved the connection of the dead

man on Lanke with the freakish spaceship and that with Delhi, but he believed the connection was there. The man named Rob proved it by grinding his teeth.

"A crime!" he said fiercely. "And maybe we'll be bombed for it! It's another reason this ship has to be wrecked. We're quarantined. We have to be! The quarantine mustn't be broken!"

Calhoun considered again. There were people on Delhi, not less than two thousand of them, who would seize this ship if they could, take aboard as many as could crowd into it, and go on to other worlds where—obviously—they did not believe the plague would appear. On the other hand, there were people who knew that they'd die of the plague if they ever landed on any other world, and the plague would spread from them. The two views were contradictory, and Calhoun was for the moment in between them. He was sure the plague could be spread, though. He'd caught it. Those who wanted to risk everything to leave Delhi and escape whatever they hated here, they wouldn't listen to argument or listen to evidence. Such states of mind are standard with a certain proportion of any population.

Calhoun rubbed his nose reflectively. "This plague and this quarantine hasn't been reported to the Med Service," he observed. "When did it start, and why?"

"Delhi's been quarantined since the first ship landed," said Rob, grimly. "A ship came by and sent a lifeboat down to explore. It reported valuable minerals. The ship went back to Lanke—it hadn't landed—for equipment and supplies while the spaceboat explored further. They didn't know about the plague."

"It hadn't appeared?"

"No. The ship went back to Delhi and landed with machinery and supplies. They opened one mine. They built a settlement. They loaded the ship with ore. It went back to Lanke."

He paused dramatically. Calhoun said, "And . . ."

"It never got there! It simply never arrived. Months later an automatic distress-call was picked up from far out beyond the Lanke solar system. A ship went out to investigate. It was the ship from Delhi, floating where it had broken out of overdrive. There was no living creature aboard. Everybody was dead. It was the plague, but they didn't understand. They towed the ship to port and unloaded it; plague spread over the whole planet. They had to burn down cities to get rid of it! Delhi has been quarantined ever since, more than a hundred years."

"The Med Service should have been told," said Calhoun, annoyed. "Something would have been done about it!"

There was a sudden metallic clanging. It was a blow of something heavy against the Med Ship's exterior airlock door. There was another blow, and another, and another. Rob listened for a moment and shrugged.

"Sometimes," he said, "there's somebody dropped to us by parachute. They have the plague. They recover. They tell us what other worlds are like, now. They don't often get reconciled to staying here."

The clanging continued. The girl came in from the control-room. She said in the same detached voice, "They're trying to break in with sledge-hammers. But some of them are cutting down trees and trimming them." She looked at Calhoun. "We can help you into the other room if you want to see."

Calhoun found himself struggling to rise. The tall man helped him. The girl said, "Rob has one thing wrong. Not all the people who're parachuted down to us have the plague!"

Rob made a deprecating sound. Calhoun began to move toward the cabin door. He was stronger than he'd thought. Once he was up, with the help of Rob on one side and the wall on the other, he made his way into the control-room. Rob helped him into the pilot's chair at the control-board.

He stared at the vision screens. The *Aesclipus Twenty* had landed in a marshy, meadowlike level space with mountains all around it. He could see the white walls of what had been a settlement on a mountain side, but it was plainly abandoned. There were only walls. Trees grew all the way down into the valley bottom, and men swung axes among them. As he looked, a tree toppled. Others had already been felled. He swung an outside pick-up to look down the Med Ship's side. A brawny, red-headed man was swinging a sledge-hammer against the sealing strip of the door. The impacts rang through the ship. Calhoun could see, too, where the flat parts of the landing-fins had pressed into the soggy soil. They'd sunk a good two yards below the surface and mud had flowed in over them. They were well buried.

"I'd guess," said Calhoun, "that they're cutting down the trees to make shears from which they can swing a battering ram. I doubt that a sledge-hammer can break the air-lock door. But a heavy enough log, swung hard enough, might do it. There are a lot of people here!"

The valley floor was black with human figures. There were at least two thousand of them, staring at the Med Ship, moving about restlessly, or standing in groups on the ground that might support a man, but not a spacecraft standing upright and heavy. Still others labored at the cutting and trimming of trees. There was somehow an air of tenseness, of impassioned feeling among the figures. Calhoun flipped on the outside microphones and the noise they made became audible. There was a growling, hurried murmur of voices. Sometimes, there were shouts. It was not a group of curiosity seekers, here to look at a spaceship come to ground where spaceships never came. It was a mob. It made the sound of a mob.

"Don't they know there's somebody alive in here?" asked Calhoun.

Rob said hesitantly, "I wanted to disable the ship. I thought it might take some time. So when we found they were coming we closed the air-lock and didn't answer the calls or their bangings on the hull. I think they've decided that somebody landed the ship and then died."

The girl said detachedly, "Not long ago they finishing mending a lifeboat that was wrecked here generations ago. They went to Lanke, and they came back. One man didn't return . . . They'd hidden their ship under water. Maybe he couldn't find it after he found what he was looking for. They may think that maybe he managed to steal this ship from the spaceport and has just gotten here. It could have been. He could have been wounded. He could have landed the ship and died."

"Only he didn't," said Calhoun with some dryness. "He didn't get at the spaceport. He developed the plague instead. He gave it to me. And I met the lifeboat, too. I think I was of some service to them."

He didn't mention that for payment the freak spaceboat had fired a missile at the Med Ship. Even that was reasonable as things became clearer. If Delhi was a quarantined world, with not enough of a population to maintain a modern civilization, it would have to go back toward the primitive and the savage. The desperation of its inhabitants would be absolute. It they could manage to cobble a long-wrecked spaceboat so it could take to space, and if because of the plague all nearby planets were its enemies, astronauts from Delhi would feel justified in destroying the Med Ship to keep their secret from becoming known. They'd do it in the hope of going on to a successful breaking of the quarantine that held them on this intolerable world. Yet the plague made that quarantine necessary.

"It must smell pretty bad out there, with all those people moving about," said the girl abruptly.

Calhoun turned his head.

"Why?"

"It's marsh," said the girl. "It smells when it's stirred up. It's strong! They say that on other worlds it isn't bad. Here it is. When new people are parachuted down to us, they hate it. We're used to the regular smell of things, I suppose. We don't notice. But we don't like to stir things up. Then we notice!"

Calhoun said, "Marsh . . . how about water?"

"At worst we boil it," she said evenly. "It isn't as bad, then, as un-boiled. Sometimes we filter it through fresh charcoal. That's better. There's a dam with electric generators that were installed for the mine. Some of us run that to electrolyze water into gases that we burn back together again. The flame destroys the cause of the smell, and then we condense the steam the flame combines to. That's the best, but it's a luxury and we can't afford luxuries." She looked at the vision screen. "There are charcoal breathing-masks for working when you have to stir things up. But making charcoal isn't fun, and it has to be fresh or it doesn't work. There aren't many masks out there. It must be pretty bad."

Calhoun looked at her for long seconds.

"Have you tried my drinking water?"

She shook her head. He made a gesture. She drew water from the spigot by the food-readier. Her expression changed.

"Water tastes like this? All the time?"

She pressed a glass on Rob. He tasted it and handed back the glass.

"That," she said fiercely, "is enough to want to leave Delhi forever! I'll never taste water again without thinking of this!"

Calhoun said suddenly, "You speak of new people parachuted down. Why are they sent here?"

Her lips compressed.

"Some have the plague, not many. A case turns up now and then, they say, leftover infection, maybe, from the plague they had on Lanke . . . from the other planets . . ."

"Yes," said Calhoun. "The other planets! Which ones?"

She named three, besides Lanke. They were the three whose names and courses he'd offered to the cobbled spaceboat he'd encountered in space. They were the three colonized worlds closest to Lanke. If they sent unwilling colonists to Delhi, which they could not ever hope to leave, it was simple enough to understand that the men in the freakish ship wouldn't accept Calhoun's suggestion of them for destinations.

"How'd they get into the picture? It was Lanke that had the plague, wasn't it—and hid it?"

The girl shrugged.

"People were sent here later, from the other planets; they say that the government of Lanke got frightened, years and years ago, that another nearby planet might try to colonize Delhi as they'd tried to do. And it might get the plague, and it might re-infect Lanke. So as a state secret, it told the nearest planets why they mustn't explore Delhi. They checked on it. One of them sent a research team to try to make Delhi usable, because there are minerals here. But they couldn't do anything, and they couldn't go home. So for a while supplies were dropped to them. They lived all right, but they couldn't leave. Presently, it occurred to somebody that Delhi would be a good place to send

life prisoners, criminals. So they did. Then they sent
political offenders, it was very discreetly done—
now . . ."

"Now what?"

"It's said that the crime rate on the four planets is
very low," she told him bitterly, "because professional
criminals—disappear. It saves the cost of some pris-
ons and guards and the expense of a free criminal class
to the others. So we're the sweepings of the four
planets. Some of us were accused of having the plague
when—we didn't. Naturally, it's all very secret!"

She looked at him defiantly. Calhoun nodded.

"That's quite possible," he admitted. "In any case
it would be told, and the people who told it would
believe it."

The girl looked at him with angry eyes and compressed lips.

"Some of us," said Rob severely, "accept the facts.
We aren't all wrapped up in our own tragedies. Some
of us think of our inevitable obligation to humanity
at large. So we won't try to leave, and spread the
plague!"

Rob frowned portentously. There was friction
between these two. The girl clenched her hands. The
sledge-hammer struck again, and again, and again.
There was likely to be a quarrel between the man and
the girl who between them had quite probably saved
Calhoun's life. So he said dryly, "Swinging that sledge
must be fatiguing. In fact the whole situation outside
seems unfortunate. I'll change it."

He moved certain switches. He adjusted a dial. He
pressed a button.

A pencil-thin flame shot down from between the Med
Ship's landing-fins. It was pure, blue-white incandescence. It was the ship's emergency rocket, on which
it had landed and by which it would have to take off

again. For an instant the flame splashed out between the fins, and it was so bright that the daylight nearby seemed darkened by contrast. Then the flame bored down. In solid stone the *Aesclipus Twenty* could melt and boil away bed-rock to a depth of eighty feet. Here, in saturated meadow soil, enormous clouds of steam and smoke arose. Steam-loosened mud flew about. It looked as if the Med Ship squatted on a monstrous arc-flame which was blasting away the marsh on which it rested.

The flame cut off. It had burned for ten seconds or less, developing—under control from the pilot's chair—something less than one-eighth of its maximum power. The ship hadn't stirred.

"I suspect," said Calhoun, "that they think I tried to lift off then and couldn't.. But maybe they'll think I could make a battering-ram crew very uncomfortable, close to the ship as they'd have to work."

He watched the running figures below. There was no longer a crowd gathered about the Med Ship. Those nearest were in headlong flight. The red-headed man who'd been swinging the sledge crashed a way through those fleeing ahead of him. The roar of the rockets had stopped. Some fleeing men began to glance around them as they ran.

Then the mob ceased to flee. It formed a circle three hundred yards across, two thousand human beings facing inward. Some of them shook clenched fists. The outside microphones brought in a babbling, yapping noise that was not great in volume but appalling in the fury it expressed.

"They're not thinking straight," said Calhoun. "There are two thousand of them. Even if they could land somewhere and not die of the plague or carry it, even if they could, how many would this ship carry? How many could its air-renewer supply?" Then he said in a different tone to the girl, "You said that not everybody who's parachuted down to Delhi has the plague. Why else should they be dropped here?"

She said fiercely, "It's a way to get rid of people! It's politics! It's crooked! Anybody can be accused of having the plague. Sometimes they do have it. But sometimes they haven't. My father didn't have it, and he was sent here. Rob's grandfather didn't, and he was too. There are others!"

Calhoun nodded. He said thoughtfully, "That may be true, because there was opportunity for it. But, true or not, people would believe it. And I guess, too, that you tell each other that the plague's worn itself out. Nobody has it here. Nobody who's landed here ever gets it. If they have it when they come, they're cured immediately. I was! So how could they give it to anybody else?"

"Yes!" said the girl passionately. "That's it! How could we? Rob says we have to stay here! Here where the food has no taste, and the water . . . Where we're made nauseated when we plow the ground to grow food! Where . . . Rob says we shouldn't marry and shouldn't have children because they'd be doomed in advance to become savages! He says . . ."

Rob said unhappily, "I think that's true, Elna."

"How could it be true? How could a disease that nobody can have be carried by anybody?"

Calhoun stirred in the pilot's chair.

"I think," he said apologetically, "that I have to get back to my cabin. The plague I had has made me ridiculously weak. But I have to admit, Elna, that I caught the plague from a man who left Delhi and went to Lanke and immediately developed the plague. Rob is right. Nobody must leave Delhi, but me. I have to get some help from Med Service Headquarters. Nobody else must leave. Nobody!"

Rob helped him into his cabin again. He sank gratefully down on his bunk. The girl Elna came in minutes later with another bowl of broth. Her expression was equal parts rebellion and despair. Calhoun was suddenly so sleepy that the spoon fell from his fingers. Rob supported him while Elna fed him, spoonful by spoonful. He was totally asleep the instant she'd finished.

Elna waked him by shaking his shoulder, he didn't know how long afterward. Murgatroyd made shrill protests. Calhoun waked easily and completely, and on the instant he knew that a surprising amount of strength had come back to him. With less than a desperate effort he actually sat up. He swung his feet over the side of the bunk. He became confident that he could walk, if in a wobbly fashion. However, he still wasn't up to rough-and-tumble exercise.

"Rob's gone down," said Elna desperately, "to start smashing up the ship's drive so it can't possibly be repaired!"

"Go tell him," said Calhoun, "that the drive-units from the lifeboat just back from Lanke can be used in this ship. They'll smash the quarantine. Wrecking my drive won't stop them. Anyhow the crowd outside will tear us all to small bits—including you and including Rob—if they break in and find the ship's been smashed after landing. Tell him to come up and I'll give him better instructions."

She searched his face briefly and hurried away. He heard her footsteps clattering down the metal stair to the lower parts of the Med Ship. Murgatroyd said, "*Chee?*"

"Of course not!" said Calhoun severely. "We are members of the Interstellar Medical Service. We can't let a situation like this keep on! I should be able to stand up, now, and do something about it. Let's try!"

He found a handhold, and with arms and legs working together he got to a standing position. He was still uncertain in his steps, and his expression went wry. Finally, he got across the cabin. He opened a closet and found a robe. He put it on. He made his way unsteadily into the control-room. He opened another cupboard and brought out a blaster, almost a miniature, for the pocket. He adjusted the strength of its bolt and put it out of sight under his robe. He went dizzily to the pilot's seat at the control-board. He threw the G.C. switch.

"General call!" he said into the transmitter. "General call! Med Ship *Aesclipus Twenty* calling repaired spaceboat or any other ship. General call!"

He waited, blinking at the vision screens. There were still very many people outside. A good proportion seemed to be laboring where the trees of the nearby mountainside ceased to grow because the ground was too marshy for their kind. He saw a disturbance. A chopped through tree trunk fell.

"General call," he repeated patiently. "General call. Med Ship *Aesclipus Twenty* calling repaired . . ."

A rasping voice interrupted. It was a familiar voice to Calhoun. He'd heard it during that improbable encounter of two ships in between-the-stars. Now it said unpleasantly, *"You followed us, eh? What for?"*

"Clinical information," said Calhoun. "One man of your crew didn't come back to Delhi with you. He had the plague. In fact, I got it from him. He's dead now, by the way. Why didn't the rest of you get it?"

The voice growled, *"What're you asking me for?"*

"I'm landed on Delhi, in a swamp," said Calhoun. "It looks like I can't lift off, because I'm mired here. There's a crowd—a mob—outside, trying to contrive a way to break into my ship so they can take it over, dig it out, and lift off for somewhere else. After they break in I'm not likely to get much information. Information like the information that tells me you hid your boat underwater while somebody went to figure out the chances of seizing a ship there by surprise and getting aloft on emergency rockets. That was the idea, wasn't it?"

The harsh voice was very harsh when it demanded, *"Who told you that?"*

"Never mind," said Calhoun. "But you didn't send only one man. How many?"

A pause. The other voice said cagily, *"There were two. But one began to see double and came back."*

"Which," Calhoun observed, "was proof that when people from Delhi land on another planet they develop the plague. You'd stopped believing in that. But it was so. It pretty well killed the idea of seizing a ship without warning, picking up a crew on Delhi and moving on to seize yet other ships and break the quarantine to small and quivering bits. Right?"

The voice grated, *"What are you driving at?"*

"I'd like some cooperation," said Calhoun. "You know you can't work that scheme now! You've promised to break the quarantine by force. Now you're afraid to admit it can't be done. Right?"

"What—are—you—driving—at?" rasped the voice.

"I'm Med Service," said Calhoun. "Tell me what you know about the plague, tell your followers to leave my ship alone and to gather information and biological specimens I ask for. Then we'll have the Med Service taking over as it should have done a hundred years ago. Shortly, there'll be no more plague and no more quarantine."

Silence. What Calhoun proposed was sound sense, but it was not the sort of sound sense that people would accept. The Med Service was not a reality to the people of Delhi, and the quarantine was, and was moreover the deliberate act of the nearby occupied worlds. They were imprisoned on a world which stank, and when its surface was disturbed it reeked, and even drinking water had to be boiled before it could endurably be drank. They could have no modern tools, lest they contrive some way to damage its enemies. They could have no science, because they had to be kept imprisoned. Men will not endure such conditions, necessary or not.

Calhoun said evenly, "I know I'm asking a lot. There's a mob outside my ship now, contriving some way to break into it and seize it, so they can raid a spaceport somewhere and seize other ships to repeat and spread their revolt, and the plague. But you know it won't work. You can leave Delhi a thousand times over, but if you take the plague with you . . . it's no good!"

Silence. Calhoun, waiting, shook his head to himself. Delhi had had a century of isolation and hopelessness, and the arrival of other hopeless prisoners only reminded them of the intolerable nature of the lives they lived. Under such conditions men forget what they don't want to remember, and somehow come to believe everything they wish to be true. They'd developed a blind irrational belief that their imprisonment was unnecessary. They'd developed an unreasoned, impassioned faith in possible escape. They'd rebuilt a shattered spaceboat, learning the functions of the apparatus they rebuilt as they rebuilt it. They'd set out to accomplish the impossible.

Calhoun was asking them to abandon all efforts to help themselves, and depend on a Med Service of which most of them had not even ever heard. They couldn't do it. Especially not with the *Aesclipus Twenty* aground and needing only to be overwhelmed and then extracted from the marsh for their most desperate needs to be fulfilled. They'd only been told of the plague. They didn't have it. They didn't see it, and they were imprisoned because of it. Few of them really believed in it, as Rob did.

So Calhoun was not surprised when the rasping voice cursed him horribly and cut off communication without bothering to reply. It was a refusal.

His expression was wry as he said to Murgatroyd, "He's a disappointed man, Murgatroyd. That's why he's suspicious and angry. But I'm disappointed too. I think he could have found out things for me that I'll have trouble learning myself."

Extra movement in a vision screen drew his eyes to it. A felled and trimmed tree trunk moved from its place toward the Med Ship. It was carried by not less than fifty men, holding to short ropes passed under it. The people of Delhi had no wheeled vehicles to carry so great a load. If they'd owned them, the marsh would have made them useless. However, they did have arms and muscles. By pure brute strength, sweating in their toil, they brought the log slowly down into the valley. Calhoun had never seen the physical strength of fifty men applied to a single effort. Men used engines or machines for such work. This was like those legendary achievements of barbaric kings and pharaohs. Had they been moving stone, had there been whips cracking to urge them on, he'd have felt that he saw the process of the building of the pyramids on Earth, which were still mentioned in primary grade school texts all over the galaxy.

Then he heard the girl Elna and the man Rob coming up from below. Rob said in icy fury, "You're a woman and I'd have had to hurt you to keep you from interfering. It's because you've been listening to him! He persuaded you, but millions would die if this ship lifted off and went to another world! So I'm going to stop his persuading! Sick or well, if I have to hurt him . . ."

"But, Rob!" protested the girl. "Think, if it's true! Think! If there's a Med Service and if it can end the plague for always, think of us! You wouldn't feel that we mustn't marry. You wouldn't think there should be no children to become savages! And we could be so happy . . ."

Calhoun raised his eyebrows. Murgatroyd said, *"Chee!"* in what happened to seem a very cynical tone. The heads of the man and girl appeared at the top of the stairwell. Rob's eyes were hot and accusing.

"You!" he cried furiously at sight of Calhoun. "This ship in the hands of the fools outside could mean all the human race wiped out! Don't you see it? Nobody must leave Delhi! Nobody! And as a beginning . . ."

They reached the floor of the control-room. Rob's hands clenched and unclenched. He moved slowly toward Calhoun, glaring in a very dramatic fashion.

"You display a very noble character, Rob," said Calhoun with some irony. "Self-sacrificing, too! It must be very satisfying to feel that way! But I almost agree with you. It's true that nobody must leave Delhi. Nobody but me. If you can't agree to that, we'll have to settle it right now!"

He drew the pocket-blaster from under his robe.

IV

The settlement was necessarily on Calhoun's terms. Calhoun had a weapon. Rob didn't. Calhoun wanted to do something. Rob wanted to keep something from being done. Calhoun was an essentially simple person, inclined to think of objective results in completely matter-of-fact terms. Rob reasoned emotionally, with much attention to noble ideals he was unable to compare with reality. Calhoun considered that he had a job to do. So the matter had to be settled as he decided. Rob had a very fine stock of invective and a splendid equipment of scorn. He made use of both in what he obviously considered an especially fine opportunity for stinging speech. But it was only speech. Calhoun listened unmoved.

"All right," he said presently, with some grimness. "That'll be enough. You've got it off your chest. What do you do now? Play along or sulk over it? I have to leave this place, for Med Headquarters. I need, right now, some mud from the swamp outside for what should be obvious reasons. You can get it. Will you?"

Rob ground his teeth. He refused, eloquently. Calhoun shrugged. Elna said, "I'll get it."

She did, while Rob glowered. It was only a matter of cracking the air-lock door and reaching down with a long ladle, while Calhoun watched the vision screens for signs of mob action. He literally wasn't up to the physical effort of getting a mud sample. There were infuriated shoutings from the mob outside. Men hunted for stones to throw. There weren't any, on the surface of a semi-swamp. Elna brought up a ladleful of black stuff with evil-smelling water on top of it. She silently gave it to Calhoun. He put the mud into a centrifuge to separate the solid matter from the water that saturated it. He sat down, to rest while the centrifuge ran. Rob glared at him in the extremely unhappy state of a man with impassioned convictions he couldn't act on. He was doubtless quite capable of dying for the sake of an abstract humanity. The high drama of such an action would certainly help him do it.

The centrifuge delivered pellets of damp soil and a considerable amount of browning, malodorous water. It had been stirred and—as Elna had mentioned—it smelled very badly. The air in the ship was Delhi air, now, and doubtless it reeked also, but not so strongly that one couldn't get used to it. However, getting used to the smell of stirred swamp water was another matter.

Calhoun roused himself. He filled a culture slide almost full of the unpleasant stuff. He put it in the culture microscope which would let him watch living microbes living. A six-inch screen beside it showed the magnified image. He watched.

Without electronic amplification of the image, it was not possible to watch living microscopic creatures at high magnification. For genuinely high optical power, much light would be required on the slide. Beyond a certain point, that light would be lethal to microbes.

But electronic amplification made a sharp, clear image of everything in the culture slide. He saw the equivalent of an amoeba. He noted that it seemed furry. He saw the equivalent of rotifers. They spun madly for a certain time, and then stopped and spun as madly in an opposite direction.

Then he saw the spherical, pigmented microscopic spheres he was looking for.

But these microbes did not dance. They did not fission feverishly. They moved, but very slowly. Doubtless, they did multiply, but Calhoun saw no example of it. Save for lack of activity, though, they were twins of the plague organism.

"Ever hear of ecology, Elna?" asked Calhoun. "I think I'm observing a micro-ecological system at work."

The girl shook her head. She looked at Rob. He sat with his arms grandly folded. Calhoun didn't notice. He said, pleased, "Microbes adjust to their environment, like larger things. And like larger things, their numbers in nature depend on very complicated processes. Small animals multiply fast, because they're eaten by larger things. Larger things multiply slowly, because if they multiply too fast they wipe out their food supply and starve. There are some very curious causes for the limitation of animal populations so they won't all starve to death. *If* this bug I'm looking at is what I think it may be, it's a most interesting example."

The girl did not seem to hear him. She looked at Rob. He ignored her, with conscious tragic dignity. She'd helped Calhoun.

"Here," said Calhoun, "are what look like plague microbes in their normal Delhian environment. They're sluggish and practically comatose. Phagocytes could take care of an invasion of them into a human body. But here—' He touched a culture bottle in which he had thriving plague microbes growing, cultured from a scrap of a dead man's clothing. "Here I have what may be the same bug in a Lanke environment. The bug is wildly active. It could cause the devil of a plague, on Lanke. I'm going to see what it would do on Delhi."

He looked up for an expression of interest. The girl looked unhappily at Rob. Calhoun stared, and frowned, and shrugged. He took up a pipette which might have been made for the smallest of dolls to use. He introduced dancing, swarming, preposterously proliferating microbes from the Lanke culture into the slide of Delhi swamp water.

Rob said harshly, "They're bringing a log to be a battering ram, since the sledge-hammer didn't work."

Calhoun looked at the outside vision screen. The log was moving slowly across the marshy ground on fifty pairs of feet. It looked like a monstrous creeping insect.

"They're stumbling," said Calhoun. "They can't batter while they're stumbling."

He turned back to the culture microscope. The half-drop of liquid from the pipette had contained thousands and thousands of the dark round microscopic spheres. They showed on the screen now: dancing, swarming, dividing into half-globes and growing back to full spheres again. Their activity was more than feverish. It was frantic.

In minutes it diminished. The dancings and dartings slowed. The infinitesimal objects ceased their headlong multiplication. They became languid. Gradually, they seemed to sleep. Now and again they made trivial, stagnant motions. They were not dead. They were not spores, they were no longer active. Calhoun regarded them with satisfaction. He said, "Ah-h-h!"

It was a most gratifying development. It couldn't have been observed on Lanke, because there was no

Delhian material to show it. It couldn't have been seen on Delhi. There were no super-active specimens on Delhi. Only a Med Ship man could have made the observation, with Med Ship equipment. Calhoun looked triumphantly about. Elna still looked unhappily at Rob, and Rob still wore an air compounded equally of fury and of martyrdom.

"Murgatroyd," said Calhoun, "at least you'll be interested! Things are looking up!"

"Chee?" said Murgatroyd.

He padded across the floor and swung up to the lab table unfolded from the wall. Murgatroyd peered at the microscope screen as if it meant something to him. He said, *"Chee-chee! Chee-chee!"*

"Exactly!" said Calhoun. "This bug is comatose on Delhi, where there is no plague. It's wildly active on Lanke, where there has been, can be, and probably already is plague. We'll return these bugs to a Lanke environment."

He made it, distilled water and a nutrient substance for them to feed on. It was practically the environment of Lanke. He returned the just-made-comatose microbes to the sort of environment in which plague germs throve. These microbes regained all the enthusiasm of multiplication and dancing and—doubtless—the production of deadly toxins they'd shown before.

"Something on Delhi," said Calhoun, "slows down their activity and reduces their breeding rate as something on other worlds keeps the bigger predators from getting too numerous. Something here keeps their numbers down, and that something doesn't, on Lanke. What would you guess, Murgatroyd?"

Murgatroyd said, *"Chee!"* He moved about the lab table, with a very fine air of someone checking the various bits of equipment there. He picked up a culture slide. He sniffed at it and said, *"Chee-chee!"* in a very disapproving manner. He dropped it, and swamp water spilled. The odor was actively unpleasant. Murgatroyd sneezed, and retreated from it. He said, *"Chee!"* and rubbed his nose vigorously.

Calhoun shrugged. He mopped up the spilled half-spoonful. He had visions of living on a world where soil and swamp water stank when disturbed, and where even sea water might do the same. Where one boiled water before drinking it, not to make it germ-free but to drive out most of the taste. Elna had tasted normal water and had told Rob bitterly that she'd never taste water again without remembering how that pure water tasted.

He looked at the vision screens. There were fluffy white clouds in the bluest of blue skies. All oxygen atmosphere planets have blue skies, and those with habitability-one temperatures have winds and jetstreams and storm patterns of strictly standard types. On all the worlds with vegetation there were the equivalents of trees and brushwood and grass. The look of Delhi was not repellent, if one could only get used to the smell of the atmosphere, and not of the soil— if the reek of the swamp was simply an exaggeration of what everything smelled like and one could never fail to notice it . . . the passionate desire of its people to leave it could be understood.

The first log was almost at the Med Ship. A second was on the way. Smaller groups were bringing shorter logs. There were men coming with coils of rope.

Calhoun regarded them detachedly. He saw a man stumble and fall, and get up and be sick because of the stench of the mud he'd disturbed.

Calhoun went back to his work. He set out minute samples of swamp water, and added infinitesimal dosages of reagents to each, and then still more minute quantities of the Lanke environment, frantically active culture. Then a check to see what substance—or what substances made up a group—removed by a reagent would allow the spheres to thrive in swamp water.

It could almost have been predicted that the elaborate setup for research would be useless, and something insanely simple would give the answer. A strip of filter paper, wetted with the active culture and in a stoppered bottle with a trace of swamp fluid, that showed the active culture stopped dead. It did not touch swamp water. It was exposed only to the reek, the stench, the effluvium of the swamp. Calhoun said, "The devil!" Painstakingly, he repeated the test. He wanted to talk about it, to explain it for his own hearing so that he'd know if his reasoning made sense. He said, "Murgatroyd!"

Murgatroyd said with an air of charmed interest, *"Chee?"*

"I've got it," said Calhoun. "There is something in the swamp water that slows up the plague germs in multiplying and producing toxin to kill us humans. It's an inhibitive factor like the factors that on different worlds make large carnivores breed slowly, because if they bred fast they'd wipe out their own food supply and die of starvation. In the micro-ecology of germs in Delhi, there's something that holds down plague germs so nobody can get the plague. But on Lanke that inhibitive factor's missing."

Murgatroyd said, *"Chee!"* and, beady-eyed, watched Calhoun's face.

"I'll bet you a hogshead of coffee to a cookie," said Calhoun exuberantly, "that it's nothing but the smell, the reek, the stink of that—Ha!" He referred to the Stellar Directory. He found Delhi. "Here it is! There's a methane derivative to point oh four percent in the planet's air, about the same as carbon dioxide. Maybe

there's a bug in the ocean that produces it. Maybe—
oh, anything! There are microbes that can't live where
there's oxygen and others that can't live where it isn't.
This is a microbe that can just barely live where there's
point oh four percent of this stinking stuff. But it goes
wild where there's . . . now! You see, Murgatroyd? A
ship from here, with Delhi air, could go to Lanke and
nobody'd have the plague. But a man from it would
develop the plague when he got out into Lanke air
which hasn't the methane that holds the plague-germ
back. A ship from Lanke that left Delhi without Delhi
air in its reserve tanks . . . everybody aboard would die
of the plague on the way home. You see?"

Murgatroyd said, *"Chee!"*

The girl Elna said uneasily, "They're setting up some
sort of—thing made out of the logs."

Calhoun looked. There was no battering ram support being erected. There were two short logs upright,
and heavy logs crosswise, and a very long log with
numerous cross-pieces fastened to it lying in the disturbed ground. Men were working with ropes. It
couldn't make an effective battering ram. However,
Calhoun was much too elated to give thought to the
engineering feat in progress outside. He wanted to
verify what was at once plausible and lacking proof.
Proof would be finding a highly volatile liquid or a
condensable gas in solution in the swamp water. He
most definitely had the equipment for seeking it. He
used his swamp-water sample recklessly. He did a
reduced-pressure fractionating still-run, which could
take a full tablespoon full of swamp water and by
precise control of the temperature and pressure draw
off dissolved air, dissolved carbon dioxide, dissolved . . .

He got enough of a condensable vapor to be visible under the microscope. With the beautifully exact
temperature control he had, he found its boiling point

by watching that infinitesimal droplet disappear as vapor, and recondense as a fluid as he sent the temperature up and down, watching through a microscope.

Elna said uneasily, "They're getting ready to do something . . .

Calhoun looked at the screen. Men swarmed about an area twenty or thirty feet from the Med Ship's outer plating. They had ropes fastened here and there. They were arranging themselves in long rows about the ropes. There were hundreds of them preparing to do something with the logs. Away over at the edge of the slanting ground, there was much smoke. Men worked at something involving fire. Men shook their fists at the Med Ship, ready to grasp and haul on the ropes they'd brought and placed.

Calhoun blinked. Then he said, "Clever! That's really a beautiful trick! They're sure we can't lift off, so they're going to take the ship with the minimum of damage . . . That's really brilliant!"

Rob said fiercely, "When are you going to start smashing the ship?"

"I've much more important things to do," said Calhoun. "Much more important!"

Almost hilariously, he threw the G.C. switch and began to call: "General call! General call! To repaired lifeboat. Med Ship *Aesclipus Twenty* calling repaired lifeboat! Top emergency! Come in, repaired lifeboat!"

As he called, he regarded the work outside, which now approached a climax of activity. Men were making sure that ropes lying on the marshy ground were exactly laid to be pulled on. Other men were lining up to haul on those ropes. Leaders arranged them exactly to get the maximum of traction in exactly the proper directions-of-pull. A group of men were bringing something which gave off a thick white smoke. They kept out of the smoke.

"Calling repaired lifeboat! This is urgent! I've found out how the plague works! Calling repaired lifeboat . . ."

A voice said in icy rage, *"Well?"*

"The plague," said Calhoun, "is a spherical microbe which can't be anything but sluggish in Delhian air, sea, ground, or swamp land, because there's some sort of methane derived compound which inhibits its growth. The compound that makes soil reek when it's disturbed, that you drive out partly when you boil water, that's the stuff that keeps the plague germ inactive. It was in the air you breathed when you kept your boat hidden underwater while two men tried to make it to the spaceport. Do you understand?"

The rasping voice said suspiciously, *"What're you telling me for?"*

"Because when your two men tried to make it to the spaceport on Lanke, they were breathing air that didn't smell, and didn't hold back the plague germs from multiplying. One man went back when he saw double. Back in your ship the air stopped the germs from multiplying and he got over the plague. When I breathed Delhi air, I got over it. But one man panicked when he found he had the plague. He went to the Health Department and tried to give himself up as a plague victim. He hoped to be carried back to Delhi and to life. But they killed him."

There was a growling sound from the G.C. speaker. Calhoun said, "The Med Service can handle this, but I've got to get to headquarters! There's a mob outside my ship, getting ready to break in. I'll be wrecked! I need somebody to stop the mob from breaking in and wrecking this ship, which is needed to take these facts to Med Service Headquarters. As a matter of common sense, you'd better come here and stop them."

A pause. Then a growled, *"We'll be there!"*

Calhoun grinned. Murgatroyd said shrilly, *"Chee-chee-chee!"*

Ordinarily, when Calhoun held conversations over the general communicator phone, it meant that the Med Ship would shortly go aground and people would pet Murgatroyd and feed him sweet cakes and coffee until he almost burst. His small brain made that association again. He began to lick his whiskers and otherwise make himself tidy and irresistible.

Rob said contemptuously, "Are you fool enough to expect him to protect this ship and let you go away in it? He'll never do that! Never!"

"I don't expect him to," said Calhoun mildly. "But he really shouldn't make trips like those to Lanke. It's dangerous! There may be plague on Lanke now, because of it. I expect him to try to get the ship for his own ideas."

"But he's coming . . ."

"Yes," said Calhoun.

He turned to the vision plates again. There were at least eight hundred men lined up beside ropes. There were shoutings and orders and cursings. Under exact instructions, the rope tightened. Men heaved at the ends of the short logs. They rose. They stood up at an angle of forty-five degrees. More shoutings. Enormous, straining efforts . . .

The long log, the heaviest log, the one with the cross-pieces fastened to it, stirred. The shorter logs transferred the flat drag of the ropes to a slanting downward cable, so that the long log went wavering up from the ground. Men with ropes spreading out in every direction balanced it to a sharply vertical position. It stood on end, nearly forty feet long, with cross-pieces by which it could be climbed to its very top.

Now Calhoun observed the spike at its end. It was inches thick and six feet long. It pointed toward the Med Ship. The men with the smoking stuff were halfway across the marsh, now. They kept carefully out of the white vapor the thing they were carrying gave off.

Shoutings, making sure that everything was right.

"What . . ." That was Elna. Rob scowled, but he did not grasp the picture even yet.

The tall pole with the horizontal spike at its end wavered a little, back and forth. A bellowing voice roared . . .

Half the men at the ropes—those that kept the spiked log from falling toward the ship—let go. The other half dragged frantically at the ropes to make it fall on the Med Ship.

It was very well handled. The log crashed into the small ship's plating. The spike went through, as no battering ram could possibly do. Then there were men swarming up the cross-pieces. Those who'd been bringing the smoking stuff ran desperately to arrive at the earliest possible instant. Containers of the strangling white smoke went up.

"Clever!" said Calhoun.

He sniffed. There was an uproar of triumph outside. The citizens of Delhi howled in triumph, and in their movements they stirred up the swampy pools and many were nauseated.

Calhoun sniffed again, and nodded.

"Sulfur," he commented. "They're blowing sulfur smoke in the hole they punched in our hull. In theory, we'll have to open the air-lock doors to get out or strangle. And when we go out they'll come in. Clever!"

The smell of burning sulfur became distinct. It grew

strong. Calhoun adjusted a control governing the barometric pressure inside the ship. If by a rise in temperature or for other reasons the pressure in the ship
went up, a pump would relieve the extra pressure by
compressing it into one of the large air-tanks which
carried fourteen times the volume of the Med Ship.
Calhoun and Murgatroyd could live for a long time
on stored air if the air-renewal system failed.

Now Calhoun had raised the pressure-control. The
control called for a pressure of twenty pounds to the
square inch instead of fourteen point seven. The tanks
poured out vast volumes of air from the reserve-tanks.
The pressure inside the ship went up. The sulfur
smoke being pumped in the ship turned cold. An icy
blast poured out on the sweating men atop the log.
The burning sulfur itself was blown about . . .

The men on the log went down. The tumult of
outcries outside the Med Ship was a frenzied rage.

Calhoun restored the pressure-control to normal.
Elna shivered. The air in the ship was cold.

"What—what happens now?" she asked forlornly. "If
you can't lift off . . ."

"I'm waiting for the spaceboat that went to Lanke,"
said Calhoun. "He's going to come here. Object, to take
over the Med Ship."

The ceiling G.C. speaker rasped: *"Med Ship! You
think you're smart, eh? Come out of that ship and leave
the air-lock open or we'll kill you!"*

Calhoun said politely, "Hadn't we better talk it over?
I really should get to Med Headquarters . . ."

"We've a cannon," said the harsh voice. *"If we have
to use it—we can rebuild what it breaks. Come out!"*

Calhoun did not reply. Instead, he carefully
inspected the dials and the switches of the control-
board. Rob said savagely, "Here comes the boat! If they
fire an explosive shell into us, it'll destroy us!"

"And the Med Ship too," said Calhoun encouragingly. "Which is what you want. But they're not used to gunnery near a planet, which makes straight-line trajectories into parabolas."

He saw the lifeboat, patches on patches, dents and lumps in its hull, the very picture of makeshifts piled on each other to the point of lunacy. It landed, on what must have been a flat place on a mountain-flank. The voice came again, "Come out, leaving the air-lock open, or we kill you!"

Rob said as if reluctantly, "You should let Elna go out before they kill us."

Calhoun said, "I was just waiting for that ship. It really shouldn't go traveling about. Nobody should leave Delhi but me."

"But you're mired! You're stuck here. Your rockets can't lift you."

"I'm not counting on rocket thrust," said Calhoun cheerfully. "I'm going to use steam."

He pressed a button. As had happened once before in this place, a slender blue-white flame appeared under the stern-most part of the Med Ship's hull. It was the emergency rocket, by which the ship had landed. Now the ship was held fast by mud. It would have required a pull or push of many times the Med Ship's weight to break the suction of the mud. The rockets, as rockets, could not conceivably have pushed the spacecraft clear.

But the rocket flame bored deep down into the ground. It vaporized the water beneath it. It volatilized the ground. For eight feet down in the valley bottom's water-saturated soil, the flame bored its way. Steam pressure developed. Steam bubbles of enormous size came up. Steam broke surfaces, heaving up masses of semi-solid valley bottom and escaping at the jagged edges of the cracks between masses. The Med Ship ceased to rest upon an adhesive mass of muck, packed over the feet at the bottom of the landing-fins. The Med Ship actually floated on a mixture of solidities and semi-solidities and steam. It wasn't using the propulsive power of its rockets, at all. It used their steam-generating capacity.

She shot upward before the spaceboat could fire a shell at her. She went up three thousand feet before Calhoun cut down on the rocket power. Then he peered carefully, tilted the ship and let it drop. The valley bottom seemed to leap up. The spaceboat spouted rocket flame. Calhoun dashed at it, seeming to intend a crashing collision in mid-air. He missed it by feet. He swooped and circled and dashed in at it again. The spaceboat dodged frantically.

"I'm doing this in atmosphere," said Calhoun, with an air of apology, "because they made a leak in the hull. I have to take care of the spaceboat. It shouldn't leave Delhi."

The spaceboat fired a cannon-shell. It went completely wild. Calhoun swept in, flipped the Med Ship end for end, and his rocket flame would have cut the spaceboat in two had he swung one of his controls the quarter of an inch. He didn't. Instead he flung the Med Ship about until it was borne in upon the crew of the spaceboat. They had run up against a professional in spacecraft handling. He literally drove the spaceboat down and down and down—and he could have destroyed it a dozen times over—until at the last it made a panicky landing and figures leaped out of it and fled away.

Calhoun made the Med Ship hover above it, fifty feet high, with that deadly star-temperature flame of the rockets drilling through the hull, through the patches, and into the interior.

It was only when flames burst out of cracks and

crevices all over the grounded freakish spacecraft that he lifted the Med Ship and headed away over the horizon.

He landed once more on Delhi, some hundreds of miles away on the single continent this planet owned. He was very tired, then. He ordered Rob and Elna out of his ship.

"Nobody should leave Delhi but me," he repeated politely. "So you get out. There'll be a hospital ship here within a week, two at the outside. Are you two going to be married?"

Rob said with dignity, "Not unless the plague is defeated and we can go where we please, not if our children would have to stay on Delhi and gradually become savages."

"I'll send you a wedding present by the hospital ship," promised Calhoun. "You did me a great favor. Thanks."

He closed the air-lock. He looked at a dial. The reserve-tanks of the Med Ship had been emptied, in blowing sulfur smoke out of the single puncture in its hull. He had been pumping them up to normal reserve pressure again, and this was Delhi air. Anybody who got the plague had only to stay in Delhi air and he would be cured. However, there was work for the Med Service to do to arrange that he not relapse when he went out of Delhi air again, nor give the plague to anybody else. There'd be no difficulty about that. The Med Service had solved much more difficult problems.

Calhoun sealed the hull-puncture with a quick-setting plastic. He sealed off the compartment whose wall had been pierced. He went down to the control-room. He blinked as he set the rockets to roaring again and the Med Ship climbed for the sky.

An hour later he was intolerably tired. He aimed

the Med Ship for that far-off small star-cluster which was its home. With extra care, because of his weariness, he verified what he'd done. Then he said, "Overdrive coming, Murgatroyd. Five—four—three—two—one."

There was a revolting dizziness and an appalling nausea and then the feeling of a spinning drop to nowhere. Then the Med Ship was in overdrive. It felt solid as a rock. There was no sound but the background tape producing almost inaudible noises of traffic, and rain, and surf, and music, and human voices. There was even faint laughter.

Calhoun yawned.

"Murgatroyd?"

"*Chee-chee!*" said Murgatroyd shrilly. "*Chee?*"

"Take over the ship," commanded Calhoun. "If any emergencies turn up, you take care of them. I'm going to bed!"

And he did.

THE GRANDFATHERS' WAR

> " . . . No man can be fully efficient if he expects praise or appreciation for what he does. The uncertainty of this reward, as experienced, leads to modification of one's actions to increase its probability . . . If a man permits himself the purpose of securing admiration, he tends to make that purpose primary and the doing of his proper work secondary. This costs human lives . . ."
>
> *Manual, Interstellar Medical Service.* Pp. 17–18

The little Med Ship seemed absolutely motionless when the hour-off warning whirred. Then it continued to seem motionless. The background-noise tapes went on, making the small, unrelated sounds that exist unnoticed in all the places where human beings dwell, but which have to be provided in a ship in overdrive so a man doesn't go ship-happy from the dead stillness. The hour-off warning was notice of a change in the shape of things.

Calhoun put aside his book—the manual of the Med

Service—and yawned. He got up from his bunk to tidy ship. Murgatroyd, the *tormal*, opened his eyes and regarded him drowsily, without uncoiling his furry tail from about his nose.

"I wish," said Calhoun critically, "that I could act with your realistic appraisal of facts, Murgatroyd. This is a case of no importance whatever, and you treat it as such, while I fume whenever I think of its futility. We are a token mission, Murgatroyd—a politeness of the Med Service, which has to respond to hysterical summonses as well as sensible ones. Our time is thrown away!"

Murgatroyd blinked somnolently. Calhoun grinned wryly at him. The Med Ship was a fifty-ton space-vessel—very small indeed, in these days—with a crew consisting exclusively of Calhoun and Murgatroyd the *tormal*. It was one of those little ships the Med Service tries to have call at every colonized planet at least once in four or five years. The idea is to make sure that all new developments in public health and individual medicine will spread as widely and as fast as can be managed. There were larger Med craft to handle dangerous situations and emergencies of novel form. But all Med Ships were expected to handle everything possible, if only because space travel consumed such quantities of time.

This particular journey, for example: An emergency message had come to Sector Headquarters from the planetary government of Phaedra II. Carried on a commercial vessel in overdrive at many times the speed of light, it had taken three months to reach Headquarters. And the emergency in which it asked aid was absurd. There was, said the message, a state of war between Phaedra II and Canis III. Military action against Canis III would begin very shortly. Med Service aid for injured and ill would be needed. It was therefore requested at once.

The bare idea of war, naturally, was ridiculous. There could not be war between planets. Worlds communicated with each other by spaceships, to be sure, but the Lawlor interplanetary drive would not work save in unstressed space, and of course overdrive was equally inoperable in a planet's gravitational field. So a ship setting out for the stars had to be lifted not less than five planetary diameters from the ground before it could turn on any drive of its own. Similarly, it had to be lowered an equal distance to a landing after its drive became unusable. Space travel was practical only because there were landing grids—those huge structures of steel which used the power of a planet's ionosphere to generate the force-fields for the docking and launching of ships of space. Hence landing grids were necessary for landings. And no world would land a hostile ship upon its surface. But a landing grid could launch bombs or missiles as well as ships, and hence could defend its planet, absolutely. So there could be no attacks and there could be defense, so wars could not be fought.

"The whole thing's nonsense," said Calhoun. "We'll get there, and we've been three months on the way and the situation is six months old and either it's all been compromised or it's long forgotten and nobody will like being reminded of it. And we've wasted our time and talents on a thankless job that doesn't exist, and couldn't. The universe has fallen on evil days, Murgatroyd! And we are the victims!"

Murgatroyd leisurely uncurled his tail from about his nose. When Calhoun talked at such length, it meant sociability. Murgatroyd got up, and stretched, and said, "*Chee!*" He waited. If Calhoun really meant to go in for conversation, Murgatroyd would join in. Murgatroyd frisked a little, to show his readiness for talk.

"*Chee-chee-chee!*" he said conversationally.

"I notice that we agree," said Calhoun. "Let's clean up."

He began those small items of housekeeping which one neglects when nothing can happen for a long time ahead. Books back in place. Files restored to order. The special-data reels Calhoun had been required to study. Calhoun made all neat and orderly against landing and possible visitors.

Presently the breakout clock indicated twenty-five minutes more in overdrive. Calhoun yawned again. As an interstellar service organization, the Med Service sometimes had to do rather foolish things. Governments run by politicians required them. Yet Med Service representatives always had to be well-informed on problems which appeared. During this journey Calhoun had been ordered to read up on the ancient insanity once called the art of war. He didn't like what he'd learned about the doings of his ancestors. He reflected that it was lucky that such things couldn't happen anymore. He yawned again.

He was strapped in the control-chair a good ten minutes before the ship was due to return to a normal state of things. He allowed himself the luxury of still another yawn. He waited.

The warning tape whirred a second time. A voice said, *"When the gong sounds, breakout will be five seconds off."* There was a heavy, rhythmic tick-tocking. It went on and on. Then the gong and a voice said: *"Five—four—three—t—"*

It did not complete the count. There was a tearing, rending noise and the spitting of an arc. There was the smell of ozone. The Med Ship bucked like a plunging horse. It came out of overdrive two seconds ahead of time. The automatic, emergency-rockets roared and it plunged this way and changed course violently and plunged that, and seemed to fight desperately against something that frustrated every maneuver it tried. Calhoun's hair stood on end until he realized that the external-field indicator showed a terrific artificial force-field gripping the ship. He cut off the rockets as their jerkings tried to tear him out of his chair.

There was stillness. Calhoun rasped into the spacephone:

"What's going on? This is Med Ship *Aesclipus Twenty*! This is a neutral vessel!" The term "neutral vessel" was new in Calhoun's vocabulary. He'd learned it while studying the manners and customs of war in overdrive. "Cut off those force-fields!"

Murgatroyd shrilled indignantly. Some erratic movement of the ship had flung him into Calhoun's bunk, where he'd held fast to a blanket with all four paws. Then another wild jerking threw him and the blanket together into a corner, where he fought to get clear, chattering bitterly the while.

"We're noncombatants!" snapped Calhoun—another new term.

A voice growled out of the spacephone speaker.

"Set up for light-beam communication," it said heavily. *"In the meantime keep silence."*

Calhoun snorted. But a Med Ship was not an armed vessel. There were no armed vessels nowadays. Not in the normal course of events. But vessels of some sort had been on the watch for a ship coming to this particular place.

He thought of the word "blockade"—another part of his education in the outmoded art of war. Canis III was blockaded.

He searched for the ship that had him fast. Nothing. He stepped up the magnification of his visionscreens. Again nothing. The sun Canis flamed ahead and below, and there were suspiciously bright stars which by their coloring were probably planets. But the Med Ship was still well beyond the habitable part of a Sol-class sun's solar system.

Calhoun pulled a photocell out of its socket and waited. A new and very bright light winked into being. It wavered. He stuck the photocell to the screen, covering the brightness. He plugged its cord to an audio amplifier. A dull humming sounded. Not quite as clearly as a spacephone voice, but clear enough, a voice said:

"*If you are Med Ship* Aesclipus Twenty, *answer by light beam, quoting your orders.*"

Calhoun was already stabbing another button, and somewhere a signal-lamp was extruding itself from its recess in the hull. He said irritably:

"I'll show my orders, but I do not put on performances of dramatic readings! This is the devil of a business! I came here on request, to be a ministering angel or a lady with a lamp, or something equally improbable. I did not come to be snatched out of overdrive, even if you have a war on. This is a Med Ship!"

The slightly blurred voice said as heavily as before:

"*This is a war, yes. We expected you. We wish you to take our final warning to Canis III. Follow us to our base and you will be briefed.*"

Calhoun said tartly:

"Suppose you tow me! When you dragged me out of overdrive you played the devil with my power!"

Murgatroyd said, "*Chee?*" and tried to stand on his hind legs to look at the screen. Calhoun brushed him away. When acknowledgment came from the unseen other ship, and the curious cushiony drag of the towing began to be felt, he cut off the microphone to the lightbeam. Then he said severely to Murgatroyd:

"What I said was not quite true, Murgatroyd. But there is a war on. To be a neutral I have to appear impressively helpless. That is what neutrality means."

But he was far from easy in his mind. Wars between worlds were flatly impossible. The facts of space travel made them unthinkable.

Yet there seemed to be a war. Something was happening, anyhow, which was contrary to all the facts of life in modern times. And Calhoun was involved in it. It demanded that he immediately change all his opinions and all his ideas of what he might have to do. The Med Service could not take sides in a war, of course. It had no right to help one side or the other. Its unalterable function was to prevent the needless death of human beings. So it could not help one combatant to victory. On the other hand it could not merely stand by, tending the wounded, and by alleviating individual catastrophes allow their numbers to mount.

"This," said Calhoun, "is the devil!"

"*Chee!*" said Murgatroyd.

The Med Ship was being towed. Calhoun had asked for it and it was being done. There should have been no way to tow him short of a physical linkage between ships. There were force-fields which could perform that function—landing grids used them constantly—but ships did not mount them—not ordinary ships, anyhow. That fact bothered Calhoun.

"Somebody's gone to a lot of trouble," he said, scowling, "as if wars were going back into fashion and somebody was getting set to fight them. Who's got us, anyhow?"

The request for Med Service aid had come from Phaedra II. But the military action—if any—had been stated to be due on Canis III. The flaming nearby sun and its family of planets was the Canis solar system. The odds were, therefore, that he'd been snatched out of overdrive by the Phaedrian fleet. He'd been expected. They'd ordered him not to use the spacephone. The local forces wouldn't care if the planet overheard. The invaders might. Unless there were two space fleets in emptiness, jockeying for position for a battle in the void. But that was preposterous. There could be no battles in unstressed space where any ship could flick into overdrive flight in the fraction of a second!

"Murgatroyd," said Calhoun querulously, "this is all wrong! I can't make head or tail or anything! And I've got a feeling that there is something considerably more wrong than I can figure out. At a guess, it's probably a Phaedrian vessel that's hooked on to us. They didn't seem surprised when I said who I was. But—"

He checked his instrument board. He examined the screens. There were planets of the yellow sun, which now was nearly dead ahead. Calhoun saw an almost infinitely thin crescent, and knew that it was the sunward world toward which he was being towed. Actually, he didn't need a tow. He'd asked for it for no particular reason except to put whoever had stopped him in the wrong. To injure a Med Ship would be improper even in war—especially in war.

His eyes went back to the external-field dial. There was a force-field gripping the ship. It was of the type used by landing grids—a type impractical for use on shipboard. A grid to generate such a force-field had to have one foot of diameter for roughly every ten miles of range. A ship to have the range of his captor would have to be as big as a planetary landing grid. And no planetary landing grid could handle it.

Then Calhoun's eyes popped open and his jaw dropped.

"Murgatroyd!" he said, appalled. "Confound them, it's true! They've found a way to fight!"

Wars had not been fought for many hundreds of years, and there was no need for them now. Calhoun had only lately been studying the records of warfare in all its aspects and consequences, and as a medical man he felt outraged. Organized slaughter did not seem a sane process for arriving at political conclusions. The whole galactic culture was based upon the happy conviction that wars could never happen again. If it was possible, they probably would. Calhoun knew humanity well enough to be sure of that.

"*Chee?*" said Murgatroyd inquiringly.

"You're lucky to be a *tormal!*" Calhoun told him. "You never have to feel ashamed of your kind."

The background information he had about warfare in general made him feel skeptical in advance about the information he would presently be given. It would be what used to be called propaganda, given him under the name of briefing. It would agree with him that wars in general were horrible, but it would most plausibly point out—with deep regret—that this particular war, fought by this particular side, was both admirable and justified.

"Which," said Calhoun darkly, "I wouldn't believe even if it were true!"

> "Information secured from others is invariably inaccurate in some fashion. A complete and reasoned statement of a series of events is almost necessarily trimmed and distorted and edited, or it would not appear reasonable and complete. Truly factual accounts of any series of happenings will, if honest, contain inconsistent or irrational elements. Reality is far too complex to be reduced to simple statements without much suppression of fact . . ."
>
> *Manual, Interstellar Medical Service.* P. 25.

He was able to verify his guess about the means by which interstellar war had become practical, when the Med Ship was landed. Normally, a landing grid was a gigantic, squat structure of steel girders, half a mile high and a full mile in diameter. It rested upon bedrock, was cemented into unbreakable union with the substance of its planet, and tapped the ionosphere for power. When the Med Ship reached the abysmal darkness of the nearest planet's shadow, there were long,

long pauses in which it hung apparently motionless in space. There were occasional vast swingings, as if something reached out and made sure where it was. And Calhoun made use of his nearest-object indicator and observed that something very huge fumbled about and presently became stationary in emptiness, and then moved swiftly and assuredly down into the blackness which was the planet's night-side. When it and the planetary surface were one, the Med Ship began its swift descent in the grip of landing grid-type force-fields.

It landed in the center of a grid—but not a typical grid. This was more monstrous in size than any spaceport boasted. It was not squat, either, but as tall as it was wide. As the ship descended, he saw lights in a control-system cell, midway to the ground. It was amazing but obvious. The Med Ship's captors had built a landing grid which was itself a spaceship. It was a grid which could cross the void between stars. It could wage offensive war.

"It's infernally simple," Calhoun told Murgatroyd, distastefully. "The regular landing grid hooks onto something in space and pulls it to the ground. This thing hooks onto something on the ground and pushes itself out into space. It'll travel by Lawlor or overdrive, and when it gets somewhere it can lock onto any part of another world and pull itself down to that and stay anchored to it. Then it can land the fleet that traveled with it. It's partly a floating dry dock and partly a landing craft, and actually it's both. It's a ready-made spaceport anywhere it chooses to land. Which means that it's the deadliest weapon in the past thousand years!"

Murgatroyd climbed on his lap and blinked wisely at the screens. They showed the surroundings of the now-grounded Med Ship, standing on its tail. There were innumerable stars overhead. All about, there was the whiteness of snow. But there were lights. Ships at rest lay upon the icy ground.

"I suspect," growled Calhoun, "that I could make a dash on emergency rockets and get behind the horizon before they could catch me. But this is just a regular military base!"

He considered his recent studies of historic wars, of battles and massacres and looting and rapine. Even modern, civilized men would revert very swiftly to savagery once they had fought a battle. Enormities unthinkable at other times would occur promptly if men went back to barbarity. Such things might already be present in the minds of the crews of these spaceships.

"You and I, Murgatroyd," said Calhoun, "may be the only wholly rational men on this planet. And you aren't a man."

"*Chee!*" shrilled Murgatroyd. He seemed glad of it.

"But we have to survey the situation before we attempt anything noble and useless," Calhoun observed. "But still—what's that?"

He stared at a screen which showed lights on the ground moving toward the Med Ship. They were carried by men on foot, walking on the snow. As they grew nearer it appeared that there were also weapons in the group. They were curious, ugly instruments—like sporting rifles save that their bores were impossibly large. They would be— Calhoun searched his new store of information. They would be launchers of miniature rockets, capable of firing small missiles with shaped charges which could wreck the Med Ship easily.

Thirty yards off, they separated to surround the ship. A single man advanced.

"I'm going to let him in, Murgatroyd," observed Calhoun. "In war time, a man is expected to be polite to anybody with a weapon capable of blowing him up. It's one of the laws of war."

He opened both the inner and outer lock doors. The glow from inside the ship shone out on white, untrodden snow. Calhoun stood in the opening, observing that as his breath went out of the outer opening it turned to white mist.

"My name is Calhoun," he said curtly to the single dark figure still approaching. "Interstellar Medical Service. A neutral, a noncombatant, and at the moment very much annoyed by what has happened!"

A gray-bearded man with grim eyes advanced into the light from the opened port. He nodded.

"My name is Walker," he said, as curtly. "I suppose I'm the leader of this military expedition. At least, my son is the leader of the . . . ah . . . the enemy, which makes me the logical man to direct the attack upon them."

Calhoun did not quite believe his ears, but he pricked them up. A father and son on opposite sides would hardly have been trusted by either faction, as warfare used to be conducted. And certainly their relationship would hardly be a special qualification for leadership at any time.

He made a gesture of invitation, and the gray-bearded man climbed the ladder to the port. Somehow he did not lose the least trace of dignity in climbing. He stepped solidly into the air lock and on into the cabin of the ship.

"If I may, I'll close the lock-doors," said Calhoun, "if your men won't misinterpret the action. It's cold outside."

The sturdy, bearded man shrugged his cape-clad shoulders.

"They'll blast your ship if you try to take off," he said. "They're in the mood to blast something!"

With the same air of massive confidence, he moved to a seat. Murgatroyd regarded him suspiciously. He ignored the little animal.

"Well?" he said impatiently.

"I'm Med Service," said Calhoun. "I can prove it. I should be neutral in whatever is happening. But I was asked for by the planetary government of Phaedra. I think it likely that your ships come from Phaedra. Your grid ship, in particular, wouldn't be needed by the local citizens. How does the war go?"

The stocky man's eyes burned.

"Are you laughing at me?" he demanded.

"I've been three months in overdrive," Calhoun reminded him. "I haven't heard anything to laugh at in longer than that. No."

"The . . . our enemy," said Walker bitterly, "consider that they have won the war. But you may be able to make them realize that they have not, and they cannot. We have been foolishly patient, but we can't risk forbearance any longer. We mean to carry through to victory even if we arrive at cutting our own throats for a victory celebration. And that is not unlikely!"

Calhoun raised his eyebrows. But he nodded. His studies had told him that a war psychology was a highly emotional one.

"Our home planet Phaedra has to be evacuated," said Walker, very grimly indeed. "There are signs of instability in our sun. Five years since, we sent our older children to Canis III to build a world for all of us to move to. Our sun could burst at any time. It is certain to flare up some time—and soon! We sent our children because the place of danger was at home. We urged them to work feverishly. We sent the young women as well as the men at the beginning, so that if our planet did crisp and melt when our sun went off there would still be children of our children to live on. When we dared—when they could feed and shelter them—we sent younger boys and girls to safety, over-burdening the new colony with mouths to feed, but at the least staying ourselves where the danger was! Later we sent even the small children, as the signs of an imminent cataclysm became more threatening."

Calhoun nodded again. There were not many novas in the galaxy in any one year, even among the millions of billions of stars it held. But there had been at least one colony which had had to be shifted because of evidence of solar instability. The job in that case was not complete when the flareup came. The evacuation of a world, though, would never be an easy task. The population had to be moved light-years of distance. Space-travel takes time, even at thirty times the speed of light. Where the time of disaster—the deadline for removal—could not be known exactly, the course adopted by Phaedra was logical. Young men and women were best sent off first. They could make new homes for themselves and for others to follow them. They could work harder and longer for the purpose than any other age-group—and they would best assure the permanent survival of somebody. The new colony would have to be a place of frantic, unresting labor, of feverish round-the-clock endeavor, because the time-scale for working was necessarily unknown but was extremely unlikely to be enough. When they could be burdened further, younger boys and girls would be shipped—old enough to help but not to pioneer. They could be sent to safety in a partly-built colony. Later smaller children could be sent, needing care from their older contemporaries. Only at long last would the adults leave their world for the new. They would stay where the danger was until all the younger ones were secure.

"But now," said Walker thickly, "our children have

made their world and now they refuse to receive their parents and grandparents! They have a world of young people only, under no authority but their own. They say that we lied to them about the coming flare of Phaedra's sun: that we enslaved them and made them use their youth to build a new world we now demand to take over. They are willing for Phaedra's sun to burst and kill the rest of us, so they can live as they please without a care for us!"

Calhoun said nothing. It is a part of medical training to recognize that information obtained from others is never wholly accurate. Conceding the facts, he would still be getting from Walker only one interpretation of them. There is an instinct in the young to become independent of adults, and an instinct in adults to be protective past all reason. There is, in one sense, always a war between the generations on all planets, not only Phaedra and Canis III. It is a conflict between instincts which themselves are necessary—and perhaps the conflict as such is necessary for some purpose of the race.

"They grew tired of the effort building the colony required," said Walker, his eyes burning as before. "So they decided to doubt its need. They sent some of their number back to Phaedra to verify our observations of the sun's behavior. Our observations! It happened that they came at a time when the disturbances in the sun were temporarily quiet. So our children decided that we were overtimid; that there was no danger to us; that we demanded too much. They refused to build more shelters and to clear and plant more land. They even refused to land more ships from Phaedra, lest we burden them with more mouths to feed. They declared for rest; for ease. They declared themselves independent of us! They disowned us! Sharper than a serpent's tooth . . ."

" . . . Is an ungrateful child," said Calhoun. "So I've heard. So you declared war."

"We did!" raged Walker. "We are men! Haven't we wives to protect? We'll fight even our children for the safety of their mothers! And we have grandchildren— on Canis III! What's happened and is happening there . . . what they're doing—" He seemed to strangle on his fury. "Our children are lost to us. They've disowned us. They'd destroy us and our wives, and they destroy themselves, and they will destroy our grandchildren—We fight!"

Murgatroyd climbed into Calhoun's lap and cuddled close against him. *Tormals* are peaceful little animals. The fury and the bitterness in Walker's tone upset Murgatroyd. He took refuge from anger in closeness to Calhoun.

"So the war's between you and your children and grandchildren," observed Calhoun. "As a Med Ship man—what's happened to date? How has the fighting gone? What's the state of things right now?"

"We've accomplished nothing," rasped Walker. "We've been too softhearted! We don't want to kill them—not even after what they've done. But they are willing to kill us! Only a week ago we sent a cruiser in to broadcast propaganda. We considered that there must be some decency left even in our children. No ship can use any drive close to a planet, of course. We sent the cruiser in on a course to form a parabolic semiorbit, riding momentum down close to atmosphere above Canopolis, where it would broadcast on standard communication frequencies and go on out to clear space again. But they used the landing grid to strew its path with rocks and boulders. It smashed into them. Its hull was punctured in fifty places! Every man died!"

Calhoun did not change expression. This was an interview to learn the facts of a situation in which the

Med Service had been asked to act. It was not an occasion in which to be horrified. He said:

"What did you expect of the Med Service when you asked for its help?"

"We thought," said Walker, very bitterly indeed, "that we would have prisoners. We prepared hospital ships to tend our children who might be hurt. We wanted every possible aid in that. No matter what our children have done—"

"Yet you have no prisoners?" asked Calhoun.

He didn't grasp this affair yet. It was too far out of the ordinary for quick judgment. Any war, in modern times, would have seemed strange enough. But a full-scale war between parents and children on a planetary scale was a little too much to grasp in all its implications in a hurry.

"We've one prisoner," said Walker scornfully. "We caught him because we hoped to do something with him. We failed. You'll take him back. We don't want him! Before you go, you will be told our plans for fighting; for the destruction, if we must, of our own children. But it is better for us to destroy them than to let them destroy our grandchildren as they are doing."

This accusation about grandchildren did not seem conceivably true. Calhoun, however, did not question it. He said reflectively:

"You're going about this affair in a queer fashion, whether as a war or an exercise in parental discipline. Sending word of your plans to one's supposed enemy, for instance—"

Walker stood up. His cheek twitched.

"At any instant now, Phaedra's sun may go! It may have done so since we heard. And our wives—our children's mothers—are on Phaedra. If our children have murdered them by refusing them refuge, then we will have nothing left but the right—"

There was a pounding on the airlock door.

"I'm through," rasped Walker. He went to the lock and opened the doors. "This Med man," he said to those outside, "will come and see what we've made ready. Then he'll take our prisoner back to Canis. He'll report what he knows. It may do some good."

He stepped out of the airlock, flinging a command to Calhoun to follow.

Calhoun grunted to himself. He opened a cabinet and donned heavy winter garments. Murgatroyd said "*Chee!*" in alarm when it appeared that Calhoun was going to leave him. Calhoun snapped his fingers and Murgatroyd leaped up into his arms. Calhoun tucked him under his coat and followed Walker down into the snow.

This, undoubtedly, was the next planet out from the colonized Canis III. It would be Canis IV, and a very small excess of carbon dioxide in its atmosphere would keep it warmer—by the greenhouse effect—than its distance from the local sun would otherwise imply. The snow was winter snow only. This was not too cold a base for military operations against the planet next inward toward the sun.

Walker strode ahead toward the rows of spaceship hulls about the singularly spidery grip ship. It occurred to Calhoun that astrogating such a ship would be very much like handling an oversized, open-ended wastebasket. A monstrous overdrive field would be needed, and keeping its metal above brittle-point on any really long space voyage would be difficult indeed. But it was here. It had undoubtedly lifted itself from Phaedra. It had landed itself here, and should be able to land on Canis and then let down after itself the war fleet now clustered about its base. But Calhoun tried to take comfort in the difficulty of traveling really long distances, up in the tens or twenties of light-years, with such a creation. Possibly, just possibly, warfare would still be limited to relatively nearby worlds—

"We thought," rumbled Walker, "that we might excavate shelters here, so we could bring the rest of Phaedra's population here to wait out the war—so they'd be safe if Phaedra's sun blew. But we couldn't feed them all. So we have to blast a reception for ourselves on the world our children have made!"

They came to a ship which was larger than any except the grid ship. Nearby half its hull had been opened and a gigantic tent set up against it. It was a huge machine shop. A spaceship inside was evidently the cruiser of which Walker had spoken. Calhoun could see where ragged old holes had been made in its hull. Men of middle age or older worked upon it with a somehow dogged air. But Walker pointed to another object, almost half the size of the Med Ship. Men worked on that, too. It was a missile, not man-carrying, with relatively enormous fuel capacity for drive-rockets.

"Look that over," commanded Walker. "That's a rocket-missile, a robot fighting machine that we'll start from space with plenty of rocket-fuel for maneuvering. It will fight and dodge its way down into the middle of the grid at Canopolis—which our children refuse to use to land their parents. In three days from now we use this to blast that grid and as much of Canopolis as may go with it from the blast of a megaton bomb. Then our grid ship will land and our fleet will follow it down, and we'll be aground on Canis with blast-rifles and flame and more bombs, to fight for our rightful foothold on our children's world!

"When our fighting men are landed, our ships will begin to bring in our wives from Phaedra—if they are still alive—while we fight to make them safe. We'll

fight our children as if they were wild beasts—the way
they've treated us! We begin this fight in just three
days, when that missile is ready and tested. If they kill
us—so much the better! But we'll make them do their
murder with their hands, with their guns, with the
weapons they'd doubtless made. But they shall not
murder us by disowning us! And if we have to kill
them to save our grandchildren—we begin to do so
in just three days. Take them that message!"

Calhoun said:

"I'm afraid they won't believe me."

"They'll learn they must," growled Walker. Then he
said abruptly: "What repairs does your ship need? We'll
bring it here and repair it, and then you'll take our
prisoner and carry him and your message back to his
own kind—our children!"

The irony and the fury and the frustration in his
tone as he said, "children," made Murgatroyd wriggle,
underneath Calhoun's coat.

"I find," said Calhoun, "that all I need is power. You
drained my overdrive charge when you snatched my
ship out of overdrive. I've extra Duhanne cells, but
one overdrive charge is a lot of power to lose."

"You'll get it back," growled Walker. "Then take the
prisoner and our warning to Canis. Get them to surrender if you can."

Calhoun considered. Under his coat, Murgatroyd
said "Chee! Chee!" in a tone of some indignation.

"Thinking of the way of my own father with me,"
said Calhoun wryly, "and accepting your story itself as
quite true—how the devil can I make your children
believe that this time you aren't bluffing? Haven't you
bluffed before?"

"We've threatened," said Walker, his eyes blazing.
"Yes. And we were too soft-hearted to carry out our
threats. We've tried everything short of force. But the

time has come when we have to be ruthless! We have our wives to consider."

"Whom," observed Calhoun, "I suspect you didn't dare have with you because they wouldn't let you actually fight, no matter what your sons and daughters did."

"But they're not here now!" raged Walker. "And nothing will stop us!"

Calhoun nodded. In view of the situation as a whole, he almost believed it of the fathers of the colonists on Canis III. But he wouldn't have believed it of his own father, regardless, and he did not think the young people of Canis would believe it of theirs. Yet there was nothing else for them to do.

It looked like he'd traveled three months in overdrive and painstakingly studied much distressing information about the ancestors of modern men, only to arrive at and witness the most heart-rending conflict in human history.

"The fact that one statement agrees with another statement does not mean that both must be true. Too close an agreement may be proof that both statements are false. Conversely, conflicting statements may tend to prove each other's verity, if the conflict is in their interpretations of the facts they narrate . . ."

Manual, Interstellar Medical Service. P. 43

They brought the prisoner a bare hour later. Sturdy, grizzled men had strung a line to the Med Ship's power bank, and there was that small humming sound which nobody quite understands as power flowed into the Duhanne cells. The power men regarded the inside of the ship without curiosity, as if too much absorbed in private bitterness to be interested in anything else. When they had gone, a small guard brought the prisoner. Calhoun noted the expression on the faces of these men, too. They hated their prisoner. But their faces showed the deep and wrenching bitterness a man does feel when his children have abandoned him for companions he considers worthless or worse. A man hates those companions corrosively, and these men hated their prisoner. But they could not help knowing that he, also, had abandoned some other father whose feelings were like their own. So there was frustration even in their fury.

The prisoner came lightly up the ladder into the Med Ship. He was a very young man, with a singularly fair complexion and a carriage at once challengingly jaunty and defiant. Calhoun estimated his age as seven years less than his own, and immediately considered him irritatingly callow and immature because of it.

"You're my jailer, eh?" said the prisoner brightly, as he entered the Med Ship's cabin. "Or is this some new trick? They say they're sending me back. I doubt it!"

"It's true enough," said Calhoun. "Will you dog the airlock door, please? Do that and we'll take off."

The young man looked at him brightly. He grinned.

"No," he said happily. "I won't."

Calhoun felt ignoble rage. There had been no great purpose in his request. There could be none in the refusal. So he took the prisoner by the collar and walked him into the airlock.

"We are going to be lifted soon," he said gently. "If the outer door isn't dogged, the air will escape from the lock. When it does, you will die. I can't save you, because if the outer door isn't dogged, all the air in the ship will go if I should try to help you. Therefore I advise you to dog the door."

He closed the inner door. He looked sick. Murgatroyd looked alarmedly at him.

"If I have to deal with that kind," Calhoun told the *tormal*, "I have to have some evidence that I mean what I say. If I don't, they'll be classing me with their fathers!"

The Med Ship stirred. Calhoun glanced at the external-field dial. The mobile landing grid was locking its force-field on. The little ship lifted. It went up and up and up. Calhoun looked sicker. The air in the lock was thinning swiftly. Two miles high. Three—

There were frantic metallic clankings. The indicator said that the outer door was dogged tight. Calhoun opened the inner door. The young man stumbled in, shockingly white and gasping for breath.

"Thanks," said Calhoun curtly.

He strapped himself in the control-chair. The vision-screens showed half the universe pure darkness and the rest a blaze of many-colored specks of light. They showed new stars appearing at the edge of the monstrous blackness. The Med Ship was rising ever more swiftly. Presently the black area was not half the universe. It was a third. Then a fifth. A tenth. It was a dark of pure darkness in a glory of a myriad distant sun.

The external-field indicator dropped abruptly to zero. The Med Ship was afloat in clear space. Calhoun tried the Lawlor drive, tentatively. It worked. The Med Ship swung in a vast curved course out of the dark planet's shadow. There was the sun Canis, flaming in space. Calhoun made brisk observations, set a new course, and the ship sped on with an unfelt acceleration. This was, of course, the Lawlor propulsion system, used for distances which were mere millions of miles.

When the ship was entirely on automatic control, Calhoun swung around to his unwilling companion.

"My name's Calhoun," Calhoun told him. "I'm Med Service. That's Murgatroyd. He's a *tormal*. Who are you and how did you get captured?"

The prisoner went instantly into a pose of jaunty defiance.

"My name is Fredericks," he said blandly. "What happens next?"

"I'm headed for Canis III," said Calhoun. "In part to land you. In part to try to do something about this war. How'd you get captured?"

"They made a raid," said young Fredericks scornfully. "They landed a rocket out in open country. We thought it was another propaganda bomb, like they've landed before—telling us we were scoundrels and such bilge. I went to see if there was anything in it good for a laugh. But it was bigger than usual. I didn't know, but men had landed in it. They jumped me. Two of them. Piled me in the rocket and it took off. Then we were picked up and brought where you landed. They tried to mind-launder me!" He laughed derisively. "Showing me science stuff proving Phaedra's sun was going to blow and cook the old home planet. Lecturing me that we were all fools on Canis, undutiful sons and so on. Saying that to kill our parents wouldn't pay."

"Would it?" asked Calhoun. "Pay, that is?"

Fredericks grinned in a superior manner.

"You're pulling more of it, huh? I don't know science, but I know they've been lying to us. Look! They sent the first gang to Canis five years ago. Didn't send equipment with them, no more than they had to. Packed the ships full of people. They were twenty years old and so on. They had to sweat! Had to sweat out ores and make equipment and try to build shelters and plant food. There were more of them arriving all the time—shipped away from Phaedra with starvation rations so more of them could be shipped. All young people, remember! They had to sweat to keep from starving, with all the new ones coming all the time. Everybody had to pitch in the minute they got there. You never heard that, did you?"

"Yes," said Calhoun.

"They worked plenty!" said Fredericks scornfully. "Good little boys and girls! When they got nearly caught up, and figured that maybe in another month they could breathe easy, why then the old folks on Phaedra began to ship younger kids. Me among 'em! I was fifteen, and we hit Canis like a flood. There wasn't shelter, or food, or clothes to spare, but they had to feed us. So we had to help by working. And I worked! I built houses and graded streets and wrestled pipe for plumbing and sewage—the older boys were making it—and I planted ground and I chopped trees. No loafing! No fun! They piled us on Canis so fast it was root hog or die. And we rooted! Then just when we began to think that we could begin to take a breather they started dumping little kids on us! Ten-year-olds and nine-year-olds to be fed and watched. Seven-year-olds to have their noses wiped! No fun, no rest—"

He made an angry, spitting noise.

"Did they tell you that?" he demanded.

"Yes," agreed Calhoun. "I heard that and more."

"All the time," raged Fredericks sullenly, "they were yelling at us that the sun back home was swelling. It was wobbling. It was throbbing like it was going to burst any minute! They kept us scared that any second the ships'd stop coming because there wasn't any more Phaedra. And we were good little boys and girls and we worked like hell. We tried to build what the kids they sent us needed, and they kept sending younger and younger kids. We got to the crack-up point. We couldn't keep it up! Night, day, every day, no fun, no loafing, nothing to do but work till you dropped, and then get up and work till you dropped again."

He stopped. Calhoun said:

"So you stopped believing it could be that urgent.

You sent some messengers back to check and see. And Phaedra's sun looked perfectly normal, to them. There was no visible danger. The older people showed their scientific records, and your messengers didn't believe them. They decided they were faked. They were tired. All of you were tired. Young people need fun. You weren't having it. So when your messengers came back and said the emergency was a lie—you believed them. You believed the older people were simply dumping all their burdens on you, by lies."

"We knew it!" rasped Fredericks. "So we quit! We'd done our stuff! We were going to take time out and do some living! We were away back on having fun! We were away back on rest! We were away back just on shooting the breeze! We were behind on everything! We'd been slaves, following blueprints, digging holes and filling them up again." He stopped. "When they said all the old folks were going to move in on us, that was the finish! We're human! We've got a right to live like humans! When it came to building more houses and planting more land so more people—and old people at that—could move in to take over bossing us some more, we'd had it! We hadn't gotten anything out of the job for ourselves. If the old folks moved in, we never would! They didn't mind working us to death! To hell with them!"

"The reaction," said Calhoun, "was normal. But if one assumption was mistaken, it could still be wrong."

"What could be wrong?" demanded Fredericks angrily.

"The assumption that they lied," said Calhoun. "Maybe Phaedra's sun is getting ready to flare. Maybe your messengers were mistaken. Maybe you were told the truth."

Fredericks spat. Calhoun said:

"Will you clean that up, please?"

Fredericks gaped at him.

"Mop," said Calhoun. He gestured.

Fredericks sneered. Calhoun waited. Murgatroyd said agitatedly:

"*Chee! Chee! Chee!*"

Calhoun did not move. After a long time, Fredericks took the mop and pushed it negligently over the place he'd spat on.

"Thanks," said Calhoun.

He turned back to the control board. He checked his course and referred to the half-century-old Survey report on the Canis solar system. He scowled. Presently he said over his shoulder:

"How has the resting worked? Does everybody feel better?"

"Enough better," said Fredericks ominously, "so we're going to keep things the way they are. The old folks sent in a ship for a landing and we took the landing grid and dumped rocks where it'd run into them. We're going to set up little grids all over, so we can fling bombs up—we make good bombs—if they try to land anywhere besides Canopolis. And if they do make a landing, they'll wish they hadn't. All they've dared so far is drop printed stuff calling us names and saying we've got to do what they say."

Calhoun had the inner planet, Canis III, firmly in the center of his forward screen. He said negligently:

"How about the little kids? Most of you have quit work, you say—"

"There's not much work," bragged Fredericks. "We had to make stuff automatic as we built it, so we could all keep on making more things and not lose hands tending stuff we'd made. We got the designs from home. We do all right without working much!"

Calhoun reflected. If it were possible for any society to exist without private property, it would be this society, composed exclusively of the young. They do not want money as such. They want what it buys— now. There would be no capitalists in a world populated only by the younger generation from Phaedra. It would be an interesting sort of society, but thought for the future would be markedly lacking.

"But," said Calhoun, "what about the small children? The ones who need to be taken care of? You haven't got anything automatic to take care of them?"

"Pretty near!" Fredericks boasted. "Some of the girls like tending kids. Homely girls, mostly. But there's too many little ones. So we hooked up a psych circuit with multiple outlets for them. Some of the girls play with a couple of the kids, and that keeps the others satisfied. There was somebody studying pre-psych on Phaedra, and he was sent off with the rest to dig holes and build houses. He fixed up that trick so the girl he liked would be willing to take time off from tending kids. There's plenty of good technicians on Canis III! We can make out!"

There were evidently some very good technicians. But Calhoun began to feel sick. A psych circuit, of course, was not in itself a harmful device. It was a part of individual psychiatric equipment—not Med Service work—and its value was proved. In clinical use it permitted a psychiatrist to share the consciousness of his patient during interviews. He no longer had painfully to interpret his patient's thought-processes by what he said. He could observe the thought-processes themselves. He could trace the blocks, the mental sore spots, the ugly, not-human urges which can become obsessions.

Yes. A psych circuit was an admirable device in itself. But it was not a good thing to use for babytending.

There would be a great room in which hundreds of

small children would sit raptly with psych-circuit receptors on their heads. They would sit quietly—very quietly—giggling to themselves, or murmuring. They would be having a very wonderful time. Nearby there would be a smaller room in which one or two other children played. There would be older girls to help these few children actually play. With what they considered adult attention every second, and with deep affection for their self-appointed nurses—why the children who actually played would have the very perfection of childhood pleasure. And their experience would be shared by—would simultaneously be known and felt by—would be the conscious and complete experience of each of the hundreds of other children tuned in on it by psych circuit. Each would feel every thrill and sensation of those who truly thrilled and experienced.

But the children so kept happy would not be kept exercised, nor stimulated to act, or think, or react for themselves. The effect of psych-circuit child-care would be that of drugs for keeping children from needing attention. The merely receiving children would lose all initiative, all purpose, all energy. They would come to wait for somebody else to play for them. And the death rate among them would be high and the health rate among those who lived would be low, and the injury to their personalities would be permanent if they played by proxy long enough.

And there was another uglier thought. In a society such as must exist on Canis III, there would be adolescents and post-adolescents who could secure incredible, fascinating pleasures for themselves—once they realized what could be done with a psych circuit.

Calhoun said evenly:

"In thirty minutes or so you can call Canopolis on space phone. I'd like you to call ahead. Will there be anybody on duty at the grid?"

Fredericks said negligently:

"There's usually somebody hanging out there. It makes a good club. But they're always hoping the old folks will try something. If they do—there's the grid to take care of them!"

"We're landing with or without help," said Calhoun. "But if you don't call ahead and convince somebody that one of their own is returning from the wars, they might take care of us with the landing grid."

Fredericks kept his jaunty air.

"What'll I say about you?"

"This is a Med Ship," said Calhoun with precision. "According to the Interstellar Treaty Organization agreement every planet's population can determine its government. Every planet is necessarily independent. I have nothing to do with who runs things, or who they trade or communicate with. I have nothing to do with anything but public health. But they'll have heard about Med Ships. You had, hadn't you?"

"Y—yes," agreed Fredericks. "When I went to school. Before I was shipped off to here."

"Right," said Calhoun. "So you can figure out what to say."

He turned back to the control board, watching the steadily swelling gibbous disk of the planet as the Med Ship drew near. Presently he reached out and cut the drive. He switched on the spacephone.

"Go ahead," he said dryly. "Talk us down or into trouble, just as you please."

IV

"Experience directs that any assurance, at any time, that there is nothing wrong or that everything is all right, be regarded with suspicion. Certainly doctors often encounter patients who are ignorant of the nature of their trouble and its cause, and in addition have had their symptoms appear so slowly and so gradually that they were never noticed and still are not realized . . ."

Manual, Interstellar Medical Service. P. 68.

It was a very singular society on Canis III. After long and markedly irrelevant argument by spacephone, the Med Ship went down to ground in the grip of the Canopolis landing grid. This was managed with a deftness amounting to artistry. Whoever handled the controls did so with that impassioned perfection with which a young man can handle a mechanism he understands and worships. But it did not follow that so accomplished an operator would think beyond the perfection of performance. He came out and grinned

proudly at the Med Ship when it rested, light as a
feather, on the clear, grassy space in the center of the
city's landing grid. He was a gangling seventeen or
eighteen.

A gang—not a guard—of similar age came swaggering
to interview the two in the landed spacecraft. Fredericks
named where he'd been working and what he'd been
doing and how he'd been taken prisoner. Nobody bothered to check his statements. But his age was almost a
guarantee that he belonged on Canis. When he began
his experiences as a prisoner among their enemies, all
pretense of suspicion dropped away. The gang at the
spaceport interjected questions, and whooped at some
of his answers, and slapped each other and themselves
ecstatically when he related some of the things he'd said
and done in enemy hands, and talked loudly and boastfully of what they would do if the old folks tried to carry
out their threats. But Calhoun observed no real preparations beyond the perfect working condition of the grid
itself. Still, that ought to defend the planet adequately—
except against such a mobile spaceport as he'd been
captured by, himself.

When they turned to him for added reasons to
despise the older generation, Calhoun said coldly:

"If you ask me, they can take over any time they're
willing to kill a few of you to clear the way. Certainly
if the way you're running this particular job is a
sample!"

They bristled. And Calhoun marveled at the tribal
organization which had sprung up among them. What
Fredericks had said in the ship began to fit neatly into
place with what once had been pure anthropological
theory. He'd had to learn it because a medical man
must know more than diseases. He must also know the
humans who have them. Oddments of culture-instinct
theory popped into his memory and applied exactly to

what he was discovering. The theory says that the tribal cultures from which even the most civilized social organisms stem—were not human inventions. The fundamental facts of human society exist because human instinct directs them, in exact parallel to the basic design of the social lives of ants and bees. It seemed to Calhoun that he was seeing, direct, the operation of pure instinct in the divisions of function in the society he had encountered.

Here, where a guard must be mounted against enemies, he found young warriors. They took the task because it was their instinct. It was an hereditary impulse for young men of their age to act as youthful warriors at a post of danger. There was nothing more important to them than prestige among their fellows. They did not want wisdom, or security, or families, or possessions. The instinct of their age-group directed them as specifically as successive generations of social insects are directed. They moved about in gangs. They boasted vaingloriously. They loafed conspicuously and they would take lunatic risks for no reason whatsoever.

But they would never build cities of themselves. The was the impulse of older men. In particular, the warrior age-group would be capable of immense and admirable skill in handling anything which interested them, but they would never devise automatic devices to keep a city going with next to no attention. They simply would not think so far ahead. They would fight and they would quarrel and they would brag. But if this eccentric world had survived so far, it must have additional tribal structure—it must have some more dedicated leadership than these flamboyant young men who guarded inadequately and operated perfectly the mechanism of a spaceport facility they would never have built.

"I've got to talk to somebody higher up," said Calhoun irritably. "A chief, really—a boss. Your war with your parents isn't my affair. I'm here on Med Service business. I'm supposed to check the public health situation with the local authorities and exchange information with them. So far as I'm concerned, this is a routine job."

The statement was not altogether truthful. In a sense, preventing unnecessary deaths was routine, and in that meaning Calhoun had exactly the same purpose on Canis III as on any other planet to which he might be sent. But the health hazards here were not routine. A society is an organism. It is a whole. Instinct-theory says that it can only survive as a whole, which must be composed of such-and-such parts. This society had suffered trauma, from the predicted dissolution of Phaedra's sun. Very many lives would be lost, unnecessarily, unless the results of that traumatic experience could be healed. But Calhoun's obligation was not to be stated in such terms to these young men.

"Who is running things?" demanded Calhoun. "A man named Walker said his son was bossing things here. He was pretty bitter about it, too! Who's looking after the distribution of food, and who's assigning who to raise more, and who's seeing that the small children get fed and cared for?"

The spaceport gang looked blank. Then someone said negligently:

"We take turns getting stuff to eat, for ourselves. The ones who landed here first, mostly, go around yelling at everybody. Sometimes the things they want get done. But they're mostly married now. They live in a center over yonder."

He gestured. Calhoun accepted it as a directive.

"Can somebody take me there?" he asked.

Fredericks said grandly:

"I'll do it. Going that way, anyhow. Who's got a ground-car I can use? My girl'll be worrying about me. Been worrying because she didn't know the old folks took me prisoner."

His proposal to acquire a ground-car was greeted with derision. There were ground-cars, but those that did not need repairs were jealously reserved by individuals for themselves and their closest friends. There was squabbling. Presently a scowling young man agreed to deliver Calhoun to the general area in which the first-landed of the colonists—now grown grim and authoritative—made their homes. It was annoying to wait while so simple a matter was discussed so vociferously. By the time it was settled, Fredericks had gone off in disgust.

The scowling youth produced his ground-car. Calhoun got in. Murgatroyd, of course, was not left behind. And the car was magnificent in polish and performance. Lavish effort and real ability had gone into its grooming and adjustment. With a spinning of wheels, it shot into immediate high speed. The dark-browed youngling drove with hair-raising recklessness and expertness. He traversed the city in minutes, and at a speed which allowed Calhoun only glimpses. But he could see that it was almost unoccupied.

Canopolis had been built by the youth of Phaedra to the designs of their elders for the reception of immigrants from the mother planet. It had been put up in frantic haste and used only as a receiving-depot. It had needed impassioned and dedicated labor, and sustained and exhausting concentration to get it and the rest of the colonial facilities built against a deadline of doom. But now its builders were fed up with it. It was practically empty. The last arrivals had scattered to places where food supplies were nearer and a more satisfactory way of life was possible. There were broken windows and spattered walls. There was untidiness everywhere. But there had been great pains taken in the building. Some partly-completed enterprises showed highly competent workmanship.

Then the city ended and was a giant pile of structures which fell swiftly behind. The highways were improvised. They could be made more perfect later. Across the horizon there were jerry-built villages—temporary by design, because there had been such desperate need for so many of them so soon.

The ground-car came to a stop with a screaming of brakes at the edge of such a jerry-built group of small houses. A woman ran to hiding. A man ran into view. Another, and another, and another. They came ominously toward the car.

"Hop out," said the scowling driver. He grinned faintly. "They don't want me here. But I stirred 'em up, eh?"

Calhoun stepped out of the ground-car. It whirled on one pair of wheels and sped back to the city, its driver turning to make a derisive gesture at the men who had appeared. They were still quite young men—younger than Calhoun. They looked at him steadily.

He growled to himself. Then he called:

"I'm looking for somebody named Walker. He's supposed to be top man here."

A tense young man said sardonically:

"I'm Walker. But I'm not tops. Where'd you come from? With a Med Service uniform and a *tormal* on your shoulder you're not one of us! Have you come to argue that we ought to give in to Phaedra?"

Calhoun snorted.

"I've a message that an attack from space is due in three days, but that's all from Phaedra. I'm a Med

Service man. How's the health situation? How are you equipped for doctors and such? How about hospitals? How's the death rate?"

The younger Walker grinned savagely.

"This is a new colony. I doubt there are a hundred people on the planet over twenty-five. How many doctors would there be in a population like ours? I don't think there is a death rate. Do you know how we came to be here?"

"Your father told me," said Calhoun, "at the military base on the next planet out. They're getting ready for an attack—and they asked me to warn you about it. Three days from now."

Young Walker ground his teeth.

"They won't dare attack. We'll smash them if they do. They lied to us! Worked us to death—"

"And no death rate?" asked Calhoun.

The younger man knitted his brows.

"There's no use your arguing with us. This is our world! We made it and we're keeping it. They made fools of us long enough."

"And you've no health problems at all?"

The sardonic young man hesitated. One of the others said coldly:

"Make him happy. Let him talk to the women. They're worried about some of the kids."

Calhoun breathed a private sigh of relief. These relatively mature young men were the first-landed colonists. They'd had the hardest of all the tasks put upon the younger generation by the adults of Phaedra. They'd had the most back-breaking labor and the most urgent responsibilities. They'd been worked and stressed to the breaking-point. They'd finally arrived at a decision of desperation.

But apparently things could be worse. It is the custom, everywhere, for women to make themselves into whatever is most attractive to men. Young girls, in particular, will adopt any tradition which is approved of by their prospective husbands. And in a society to be formed brand-new, appalling new traditions could be started. But they hadn't. Deep-rooted instincts still worked. Women—young women—and girls appeared still to feel concern for young children which were not even their own. And Fredericks' story—

"By all means," agreed Calhoun. "If there's something wrong with the health of the children—"

Young Walker gestured and turned back toward the houses. He scowled as he walked. Presently he said defensively:

"You probably noticed there aren't many people in the city."

"Yes," said Calhoun. "I noticed."

"We're not fully organized yet," said Walker, more defensively still. "We weren't doing anything but building. We've got to get organized before we'll have a regular economic system. Some of the later-comers don't know anything but building. When they're ready for it, the city will be occupied. We'll have as sound a system for production and distribution of goods as anywhere else. But we've just finished a revolution. In a sense we're still in it. But presently this world will be pretty much like any other—only better."

"I see," said Calhoun.

"Most people live in the little settlements, like this—close to the crops we grow. People raise their own food, and so on. In a way you may think we're primitive, but we've got some good technicians! When they get over not having to work for the old folks and finish making things just for themselves—we'll do all right. After all, we weren't trained to make a complete world, just to make a world for the older people on Phaedra to take over. But we've taken it over for ourselves!"

"Yes," agreed Calhoun politely.

"We'll work out the other things," said young Walker truculently. "We'll have money, and credit, and hiring each other and so on. Right now defending ourselves is the top thing in everybody's mind."

"Yes," agreed Calhoun again. He was regarded as not quite an enemy, but he was not accepted as wholly neutral.

"The older ones of us are married," Walker said firmly, "and we feel responsibility, and we're keeping things pretty well in line. We were lied to, though, and we resent it. And we aren't letting in the old people to try to run us, when we've proved we can make and run a world ourselves!"

Calhoun said nothing. They reached a house. Walker turned to enter it, with a gesture for Calhoun to accompany him. Calhoun halted.

"Just a moment. The person who drove me here— when he turned up, at least one woman ran away and you men came out . . . well . . . pretty pugnaciously."

Walker flushed angrily.

"I said we had technicians. Some of them made a gadget to help take care of the children. That's harmless. But they want to use it to . . . to spy on older people with it. On us! Invasion of privacy. We don't like . . . well . . . they try to set up psych circuits near our homes. They . . . think it's fun to . . . know what people say and do—"

"Psych circuits can be useful," observed Calhoun, "or they can be pretty monstrous. On the other hand—"

"No decent man would do it!" snapped young Walker. "And no girl would have anything to do with anybody— But there are some crazy fools—"

"You have described," said Calhoun dryly, "a criminal class. Only instead of stealing other people's possessions they want to steal their sensations. Peeping-Tom stuff, eavesdropping on what other people feel about those they care for, as well as what they do and say. In a way it's a delinquency problem, isn't it?"

"There can't be a civilization without problems," said Walker. "But we're going to—" He opened a door. "My wife works with the kids the old people dumped on us. This way."

He motioned Calhoun inside the house. It was one of the shelters built during the frenzied building program designed to make an emergency refuge for the population of a planet. It was the roughest of machine-tool constructions. The floors were not finished. The walls were not smooth. The equipment showed. But there had been attempts to do something about the crudity. Colors had been used to try to make it home-like.

When a girl came in from the next room, Calhoun understood completely. She was a little younger than her husband, but not much. She regarded Calhoun with that anxiety with which a housekeeper always regards an unexpected visitor, hoping he will not notice defects.

"This is a Med Service man," said Walker briefly, indicating Calhoun. "I told him there was a health problem about some of the children." To Calhoun he said curtly: "This is my wife Elsa."

Murgatroyd said *"Chee!"* from where he clung to Calhoun's neck. He was suddenly reassured. He scrambled down to the floor. Elsa smiled at him.

"He's tame!" she said delightedly. "Maybe—"

Calhoun extended his hand. She took it. Murgatroyd, swaggering, extended his own black paw. Instead of conflict and hatred, here, Murgatroyd seemed to sense an amiable sociability such as he was used to. He felt more at home. He began zestfully to act like the human being he liked to pretend he was.

"He's delightful!" said the girl. "May I show him to Jak?"

Young Walker said:

"Elsa's been helping with the smaller kids. She says there's something the matter that she doesn't understand. She has one of the kids here. Bring him, Elsa."

She vanished. A moment later she brought in a small boy. He was probably six or seven. She carried him. He was thin. His eyes were bright, but he was completely passive in her arms. She put him down in a chair and he looked about alertly enough, but he simply did not move. He saw Murgatroyd, and beamed. Murgatroyd went over to the human who was near his own size. Swaggering, he offered his paw once more. The boy giggled, but his hand lay in his lap.

"He doesn't do anything!" said Elsa distressedly. "His muscles work, but he doesn't work them. He just sits and waits for things to be done for him. He acts as if he'd lost the idea of moving, or doing anything at all. And—it's beginning to show up among the other children. They just sit. They're bright enough . . . they see and understand—but they just sit!"

Calhoun examined the boy. His expression grew carefully impassive. But he winced as he touched the pipe-stem arms and legs. What muscles were there were almost like dough.

When he straightened up, despite himself his mouth was awry. Young Walker's wife said anxiously:

"Do you know what's the matter with him?"

"Basically," said Calhoun with a sort of desperate irony, "he's in revolt. As the rest of you are in revolt against Phaedra, he's in revolt against you. You needed rest you didn't get and recreation you couldn't have and something besides back-breaking labor under a load that grew heavier minute by minute for years. You revolted, and you've a fine justification for the war in which you're engaged. But he has needed something he hasn't had, too. So he's revolting against his lack— as you did—and he's dying as you will presently do from exactly the same final cause."

Walker frowned ominously.

"I don't understand what you're saying!" he said harshly.

Calhoun moistened his lips.

"I spoke unprofessionally. The real cause of his present troubles and your future ones is that a social system has been shattered. The pieces can't live by themselves. And I don't know what medical measures can be taken to cure an injured civilization. As a medical man, I may be whipped. But I'd better check—Did I say, by the way, that the war fleet from Phaedra is going to attack in just three days?"

V

" . . . Truth is the accord of an idea with a thing. Very often an individual fails to discover the truth about some matter because he neglects to become informed about something. But even more often, the truth is never found out because somebody refuses to entertain an idea . . ."

Manual, Interstellar Medical Service. Pp. 101–2.

On the first day, Calhoun went grimly to the *crèches* that had been set up by the first-arrived young colonists when ships began to discharge really young children at the landing grid in Canopolis. The *crèches* were not too much like orphanages, of course, but the younger generation of Phaedra had been put in a very rough situation by the adults. If the time of the imminent solar explosion had been known, the matter could have been better handled. Actually, the explosion had been delayed—to date—for nearly five years from the discovery that it must occur. If that much leeway could have been predicted, older men and many machines

would have been sent at first. But the bursting could
not be computed. It was a matter of probability. Such-
and-such unrhythmic variables must inevitably coincide
sooner or later. When they did—final and ultimate
catastrophe. The sun would flare terribly and destroy
all life in its solar system. It could be calculated that
the odds were even that the explosion would happen
within one year, two to one within two, and five to
one within three. The odds were enormous against
Phaedra surviving as long as it had. The people of the
mother-world had had a highly improbable break.

But in cold common sense they'd done the sensible
thing. They'd tried to save those of their children who
could take care of themselves first, and added others
as they dared. But the burden on the young colonists
had been monstrous. Even adults would have tended
to grow warped with such pressure to mine, build,
plough, and sow, as was put upon the youngsters.
There had never been more than barely enough of
food—and more mouths were always on the way. There
had never been extra shelter, and younger and ever
younger cargoes were constantly arriving, each needing more of shelter and of care than the ones before.
And there was the world of adults still to be provided
for.

Calhoun met the girls who had devoted themselves
to the quasi-orphaned children. They bore themselves
with rather touching airs of authority among the
smaller children. But they were capable of ferocity, on
occasion. They had the need, sometimes, not to defend
their charges but themselves against the clumsily
romantic advances of loutish teen-agers who considered themselves fascinating.

They had done very well.

The small children were exactly what Calhoun had
anticipated—in every way. The small boy Calhoun had

seen first was an extreme case, but the results of play by proxy were visible everywhere. Calhoun constrainedly inspected one after another of the children's shelters. He was anxiously watched by the sober young faces of the nurses. But they giggled when Murgatroyd tried to go through Calhoun's actions of taki ʾg temperatures and the like. He had to be stopped when he attempted to take a throat-swabbing which Calhoun had said was pure routine.

After the fourth such inspection he said to Elsa:

"I don't need to see any more. What's happened to the boys the same age as these girl nurses—the thirteen and fourteen and fifteen-year-olds?"

Elsa said uncomfortably:

"They're mostly off in the wilds. They hunt and fish and pioneer. They don't care about girls. Some of them grow things . . . I don't think there'd be enough food if they didn't, even though we're not getting anybody new to feed."

Calhoun nodded. In all the cities of the galaxy, small children of both sexes were to be seen everywhere, and girls of the early teen-ages, and adults. But the boys' age-group he'd mentioned always made itself invisible. It congregated in groups away from the public eye, and engaged in adventurous games and quite futile explorations. It was socially quite self-sufficient everywhere.

"Your husband," said Calhoun, carefully impassive, "had better try to gather in some of them. As I remember it, they're capable of a rather admirable romantic idea of duty—for a while. We're going to need some romanticists presently."

Elsa had faith in Calhoun now, because he seemed concerned about the children. She said unhappily:

"Do you really think the . . . old people will attack? I've grown older since I've been here. Those of us who came first are almost like the people on Phaedra—some ways. The younger people are inclined to be suspicious of us because we . . . try to guide them."

"If you're confiding that you think there may be two sides to this war," Calhoun told her, "you are quite right. But see what your husband can do about gathering some of the hunting-and-fishing members of the community. I've got to get back to my ship."

He got himself driven back to the landing grid. Walker did not drive him, but another of the now-suspect men of twenty-five or so, from the shelter village of the first-landed colonists. He was one of those who'd worked with Walker from the beginning and with him had been most embittered. Now he found himself almost a member of an older generation. He was still bitter against the people of Phaedra, but—

"This whole business is a mess," he said darkly as he drove through the nearly deserted city toward the landing grid. "We've got to figure out a way to organize things that'll be better than the old way. But no organization at all is no good, either! We've got some tough young characters who like it this way, but they've got to be tamed down."

Calhoun had his own unsettling suspicions. There have always been splendid ideas of social systems which will make earthly paradises for their inhabitants. Here, by happenchance, there had come to be a world inhabited only by the young. He tried to put aside, for the moment, what he was unhappily sure he'd find out back at the ship. He tried to think about this seemingly perfect opportunity for a new and better organization of human lives.

But he couldn't believe in it. Culture-instinct theory is pretty well worked out. The Med Service considered it proven that the basic pattern of human societies is instinctual rather than evolved by trial and error. The individual human being passes through a series of instinct-patterns which fit him at different times to perform different functions in a social organization which can vary but never change its kind. It has to make use of the successive functions its members are driven by instinct to perform. If it does not use its members, or give scope to their instincts, it cannot survive. The more lethal attempts at novel societies tried not only to make all their members alike, but tried to make them all alike at all ages. Which could not work.

Calhoun thought unhappily of the tests he meant to make in the Med Ship. As the ground-car swerved into the great open center of the grid, he said:

"My job is doing Med Service. I can't advise you how to plan a new world. If I could, I wouldn't. But whoever does have authority here had better think about some very immediate troubles."

"We'll fight if Phaedra attacks," said the driver darkly. "They'll never get to ground alive, and if they do—they'll wish they hadn't!"

"I wasn't thinking of Phaedra," said Calhoun.

The car stopped close by the Med Ship. He got out. There had been attempts to enter the ship in his absence. The gang which occupied the control building and in theory protected Canis III against attack from the sky had tried to satisfy their curiosity about the little ship. They'd even used torches on the metal. But they hadn't gotten in.

Calhoun did. Murgatroyd chattered shrilly when he was put down. He scampered relievedly about the cabin, plainly rejoicing at being once more in familiar surroundings. Calhoun paid no attention. He closed and dogged the air-lock door. He switched on the spacephone and said shortly:

"Med Ship *Aesclipus Twenty* calling Phaedrian fleet. Med Ship *Aesclipus Twenty* calling—"

The loud-speaker fairly deafened him as somebody yelled into another spacephone mike in the grid-control building.

"*Hey! You in the ship! Stop that! No talking with the enemy!*"

Calhoun turned down the incoming volume and said patiently:

"Med Ship *Aesclipus Twenty* calling fleet from Phaedra. Come in, fleet from Phaedra! Med Ship *Aesclipus Twenty* calling—"

There was a chorus of yelling from the nearby building. The motley, swaggering, self-appointed landing-grid guard had tried to break into the ship out of curiosity, but they were vastly indignant when Calhoun did something of which they disapproved. They made it impossible for him to have heard a reply from the space fleet presumably overhead. But after a moment someone in the control house evidently elbowed the others aside and shouted:

"*You! Keep that up and we'll smash you! We've got the grid to do it with, too!*"

Calhoun said curtly:

"Med Ship to Control. I've something to tell you. Suppose you listen. But not on spacephone. Have your best grid technician come outside and then I shall tell him by speaker."

He snapped off the spacephone and watched. The control building fairly erupted indignant youths. After a moment he saw the gangling one who'd grinned so proudly when the Med Ship was landed with absolute perfection. The others shouted and scowled at the ship.

Calhoun threw on the outside speaker—normally used for communication with a ground crew before lifting.

"I'm set," said Calhoun coldly, "for overdrive travel. My Duhanne cells are charged to the limit. If you try to form a force-field around this ship, I'll dump half a dozen overdrive charges into it in one jolt that will blow every coil you've got! And then how'll you fight the ships from Phaedra? I'm going to talk to them on spacephone. Listen in if you like. Monitor it. But don't try to bother me!"

He threw on the spacephone again and patiently resumed his calling:

"Med Ship *Aesclipus Twenty* calling fleet from Phaedra! Med Ship calling fleet from Phaedra—"

He saw violent argument outside the grid's control building. Some of the young figures raged. But the youth who'd handled the grid so professionally raged at them. Calhoun hadn't made an idle threat. A grid-field could be blown out. A grid could be made useless by one of the ships it handled. When a ship like Calhoun's went into overdrive, it put out something like four ounces of pure energy to form a field in which it could travel past the speed of light. In terms of horsepower or kilowatt hours, so much force would be meaningless. It was too big. It was a quantity of energy whose mass was close to four ounces. When the ship broke out of overdrive, that power was largely returned to storage. The loss was negligible, compared to the total. But, turned loose into a grid's force-field, even three or four such charges would work havoc with the grid's equipment.

Calhoun got an answer from emptiness just as the members of the group by the control building shouted each other down and went inside to listen with bitter unease and suspicion to his talk with the enemy.

"*Phaedra fleet calling,*" said a growling voice in the spacephone speaker. "*What do you want?*"

"To exercise my authority as a Med Service officer," said Calhoun heavily. "I warn you that I now declare this planet under quarantine. All contact with it from space is forbidden until health hazards here are under control. You will inform all other spacecraft and any other spaceport you may contact of this quarantine. Message ends."

Silence. A long silence. The growling voice rasped: *"What's that? Repeat it!"*

Calhoun repeated it. He switched off the phone and unpacked the throat-swabbings he'd made at the four children's shelters in turn. He opened up his laboratory equipment. He put a dilution of one throat-swabbing into a culture slide that allowed living organisms to be examined as they multiplied. He began to check his highly specific suspicions. Presently he was testing them with minute traces of various antibodies. He made rough but reasonably certain identifications. His expression grew very, very sober. He took another swab sample and put it through the same process. A third, and fourth, and fifth, and tenth. He looked very grim.

It was sunset outside when there was a hammering on the ship's hull. He switched on a microphone and speaker.

"What do you want?" he asked flatly.

The angry voice of young Walker came from the gathering darkness. The screens showed a dozen or more inhabitants of Canis III milling angrily about him. Some were of the young-warrior age. They engaged in bitter argument. But the younger Walker, and four or five with him, faced the ship with ominous quietness.

"What's this nonsense about quarantine?" demanded Walker harshly, from outside. *"Not that we've space-commerce to lose, but what does it mean?"*

"It means," Calhoun told him, "that your brave new world rates as a slum. You've kept kids quiet with psych circuits, and they haven't eaten properly and haven't exercised at all. They're weak from malnutrition and feeble from not doing their own playing. They're like slum children used to be in past ages. Here on Canis you're about ready to wipe yourselves out. You may have done it."

"*You're crazy!*" snapped Walker. But he was upset.

"In the four shelters I visited," Calhoun said drearily, "I spotted four cases of early diphtheria, two of typhoid, three of scarlet fever and measles, and samples of nearly any other disease you care to name. The kids have been developing those diseases out of weakness and from the reservoir of infections we humans always carry with us. They'd reached the contagious stage before I saw them—but all the kids are kept so quiet that nobody noticed that they were sick. They've certainly spread to each other and their nurses, and therefore out into your general population, all the infections needed for a first-rate multiple epidemic. And you've no doctors, no antibiotics—not even injectors to administer shots if you had them."

"*You're crazy!*" cried the young Walker. "*Crazy! Isn't this a Phaedra trick to make us give in?*"

"Phaedra's trick," said Calhoun more drearily than before, "is an atom bomb they're going to drop into this landing grid—I suspect quarantine or no quarantine—in just two days more. Considering the total situation, I don't think that matters."

VI

" . . . The most difficult of enterprises is to secure the co-operation of others in enterprises those others did not think of first . . ."

Manual, Interstellar Medical Service. P. 189.

Calhoun worked all night, tending and inspecting the culture incubators which were part of the Med Ship's technical equipment. In the children's shelters, he'd swabbed throats. In the ship, he'd diluted the swabbings and examined them microscopically. He'd been depressingly assured of his very worst fears as a medical man—all of which could have been worked out in detail from the psych circuit system of child care boastfully described by Fredericks. He could have written out his present results in advance from a glance at the child Jak shown him by the younger Walker's wife. But he hated to find that objective information agreed with what he would have predicted by theory.

In every human body there are always germs. The

process of good health is in part a continual combat with slight and unnoticed infections. Because of victories over small invasions, a human body acquires defenses against larger invasions of contagion. Without such constant small victories, a body ceases to keep its defenses strong against beachheads of infection. Yet malnutrition or even exhaustion can weaken a body once admirably equipped for this sort of guerilla warfare.

If an undernourished child fails to win one skirmish, he can become overwhelmed by a contagion the same child would never have known about had he only been a little stronger. But, overwhelmed, he is a sporadic case of disease—a case not traceable to another clinical case. And then he is the origin of an epidemic. In slum conditions a disease not known in years can arise and spread like wildfire. With the best of intentions and great technical ingenuity, the younger-generation colonists of Canis III had made that process inevitable among the younger children who were their last-imposed burden. The children were under-exercised, under-stimulated, and hence under par in appetite and nutrition. And it is an axiom of the Med Service that a single underfed child can endanger an entire planet.

Calhoun proved the fact with appalling certainty. His cultures astounded even him. But by dawn he had applied Murgatroyd's special genetic abilities to them. Murgatroyd said *"Chee!"* in a protesting tone when Calhoun did what was necessary at that small patch on his flank which was quite insensitive. But then Murgatroyd shook himself and admiringly scowled back at Calhoun, imitating the intent and worried air that Calhoun wore. Then he followed Calhoun about in high good spirits, strutting on his hind legs, man-fashion, and pretending to set out imaginary apparatus as Calhoun did, long ahead of time for what he hoped would occur.

Presently Murgatroyd tired—a little quicker than usual—and went to sleep. Calhoun bent over him and counted his respiration and heart beat. Murgatroyd slept on. Calhoun gnawed his fingers in anxious expectation.

He'd come on this assignment with some resentment because he thought it foolish. He'd carried on with increasing dismay as he found it not absurd. Now he watched over Murgatroyd with the emotional concern a medical man feels when lives depend upon his professional efficiency, but that efficiency depends on something beyond his control. Murgatroyd was that something this time—but there was one other.

The *tormal* was a pleasant little animal, and Calhoun liked him very much. But *tormals* were crew-members of one-man Med Ships because their metabolism was very similar to that of humans, but no *tormal* had ever been known to die of an infectious disease. They could play host to human infections, but only once and only lightly. It appeared that the furry little creatures had a hair-trigger sensitivity to bacterial toxins. The presence of infective material in their blood streams produced instant and violent reaction—and the production of antibodies in large quantity. Theorists said that *tormals* had dynamic immunity-systems instead of passive ones, like humans. Their body-chemistry seemed to look truculently for microscopic enemies to destroy, rather than to wait for something to develop before they fought it.

If he reacted normally, now, in a matter of hours his blood stream would be saturated with antibodies— or an antibody—lethal to the cultures Calhoun had injected. There was, however, one unfortunate fact. Murgatroyd weighed perhaps twenty pounds. There was most of a planetary population needing antibodies only he could produce.

He slept from breakfast-time to lunch. He breathed slightly faster than he should. His heart beat was troubled.

Calhoun swore a little when noon came. He looked at the equipment all laid out for biological microanalysis—tiny test tubes holding half a drop, reagent flasks dispensing fractions of milliliters, tools and scales much tinier than doll-size. If he could determine the structure and formula of an antibody—or antibodies—that Murgatroyd's tiny body formed—why synthesis in quantity should be possible. Only the Med Ship had not materials for so great an amount of product.

There was only one chance. Calhoun threw the spacephone switch. Instantly a voice came from the speaker.

" . . . *calling Med Ship* Aesclipus Twenty! *Phaedra fleet calling Med Ship* Aesclipus Twenty! *Calling*—" It went on interminably. It was a very long way off, if it took so long for Calhoun's answer to be heard. But the call-formula broke off. "*Med Ship! Our doctors want to know the trouble on Canis! Can we help? We've hospital ships equipped and ready!*"

"The question," said Calhoun steadily, "is whether I can make a formula-and-structure identification, and whether you can synthesize what I identify. How's your lab? How are you supplied with biological crudes?"

He waited. By the interval between his answer and a reply to it, the ship he'd communicated with was some five million miles or more away. But it was still not as far as the next outward planet where the Phaedrian fleet was based.

While he waited for his answer, Calhoun heard murmurings. They would come from the control building at the side of the grid. The loutish, suspicious gang there was listening. Calhoun had threatened to wreck the grid if they tried anything on the Med Ship—but he could do nothing unless they tried to use a force-field. They listened in, muttering among themselves.

A long time later the voice from space came back. The fleet of the older generation of Phaedra was grounded, save for observation ships like the one speaking. The fleet had full biological equipment for any emergency. It could synthesize any desired compound up to— The degree of complexity and the classification was satisfactory.

"Day before yesterday," said Calhoun, "when you had me aground on Canis IV, your leader Walker said your children on this planet were destroying your grandchildren. He didn't say how. But the process is well under way—only the whole population will probably go with them. Most of the population, anyhow. I'm going to need those hospital ships and your best biological chemists—I hope! Get them started this way—fast! I'll try to make a deal for at least the hospital ships to be allowed to land. Over."

He did not flick off the spacephone. He listened. And a bitter, envenomed voice came from nearby:

"Sure! Sure! We'll let 'em land ships they say are hospital ships, loaded down with men and guns! We'll land 'em ourselves, we will!"

There was a click. The spacephone in the control building was turned off.

Calhoun turned back to the sleeping Murgatroyd. There was a movement about the grid-control building. Sleek, glistening ground-cars hurtled away—two of them. Calhoun turned then to the planetary communicator. It could break in on any wave-length used for radio communication under a planet's Heaviside roof. He had to get in touch with Walker or some other of the first-landed colonists. They were still embittered against their home world, but they must be beginning to realize that Calhoun had told the truth about the youngest children. They'd find sickness if they looked for it.

But the planetary communicator picked up nothing. No radiation wave-length was in use. There was no organized news service. The young people on Canis III were too self-centered to care about news. There were no entertainment programs. Only show-offs would want to broadcast, and show-offs would not make the apparatus.

So Calhoun could not communicate save by spacephone, with a range of millions of miles, and the ship's exterior loud-speakers, with a range of hundreds of feet. If he left the Med Ship, he wasn't likely to be able to fight his way back in. He couldn't find the younger Walker on foot, in any case, and he did not know anyone else to seek.

Besides, there was work to be done in the ship.

Before Murgatroyd waked, the two ground-cars had returned. At intervals, nearly a dozen other cars followed to the control building, hurtling across the grid's clear center with magnificent clouds of dust following them. They braked violently when they arrived. Youths piled out. Some of them yelled at the Med Ship and made threatening gestures. They swarmed into the building.

Murgatroyd said tentatively, *"Chee?"*

He was awake. Calhoun could have embraced him.

"Now we see what we see," he said grimly. "I hope you've done your stuff, Murgatroyd!"

Murgatroyd came obligingly to him, and Calhoun lifted him to the table he had ready. Calhoun extracted a quantity of what he hoped was a highly concentrated bacterial antagonist. He took thirty CCs in all. He clumped the red cells. He separated the serum. He diluted an infinitesimal bit of it and with a steady hand added it to a slide of the same cultures—living—on which Murgatroyd's dynamic immunity system had worked.

The cultures died immediately.

Calhoun had an antibody sample which could end the intolerable now-spreading disaster on the world of young people—*if* he could analyze it swiftly and accurately, and *if* the hospital ships from Phaedra could be landed, and *if* they could synthesize some highly complex antibody compounds, and *if* the inhabitants of Canis III would lay aside their hatred—

He heard a tapping sound on the Med Ship's hull. He looked at a screen. Two youths stood in the doorway of the control building, leisurely shooting at the Med Ship with sporting weapons.

Calhoun set to work. Sporting rifles were not apt to do much damage.

For an hour, while there was the occasional clanking of a missile against the ship's outer planking, he worked at the infinitely delicate job of separating serum from its antibody content. For another hour he tried to separate the antibody into fractions. Incredibly, it would not separate. It was one substance only.

There was a crackling sound and the whole ship shivered. The screen showed a cloud of smoke drifting away. The members of the grid-guard had detonated some explosive—intended for mining, most likely—against one of the landing-fins.

Calhoun swore. His call to the Phaedrian fleet was the cause. The grid-guard meant to allow no landing. He'd threatened to blow out their controls if they tried to use the grid on the Med Ship, but they wanted it ready for use as a weapon against the space fleet. They couldn't use it against him. He couldn't damage it unless they tried. They wanted him away.

He went back to his work. From time to time,

annoyedly, he looked up at the outside. Presently a
young-warrior group moved toward the ship, carrying
something very heavy. A larger charge of explosive,
perhaps.

He waited until they were within yards of the ship.
He stabbed the emergency-rocket button. A thin,
pencil-like rod of flame shot downward between the
landing-fins. It was blue-white—the white of a sun's
surface. For one instant it splashed out hungrily before
it bored and melted a hole into the ground itself into
which to flow. But in that instant it had ignited the
covering of the burden the youths carried. They
dropped it and fled. The pencil flame bored deeper
and deeper into the ground. Clouds of smoke and
steam arose.

There was a lurid flash. The burden that the young
warriors had abandoned vanished in a flare that looked
like a lightning bolt. The ship quivered from the detonation. A crater appeared where the explosive had
been.

Calhoun cut off the emergency rocket, which had
burned for ten seconds at one-quarter thrust.

Sunset came and night fell for the second time. He
noticed, abruptly, that some of the ground-cars from
about the control building went racing away. But they
did not pass close to the Med Ship in their departure.
He labored on. He'd spent nearly thirty hours making cultures from the specimens swabbed from
children's throats, and injecting Murgatroyd, and waiting for his reaction, and then separating a tiny quantity of antibody—which would not total more than the
dust from a butterfly's wing—from the serum he
obtained.

Now he worked on, through the night. Far away—
some tens or scores of millions of miles—the hospital

ships of the Phaedrian fleet took off from the next outward planet. They would be coming at full speed toward Canis III. They would need the results of the work Calhoun was doing, if they were to prevent an appalling multiple plague which could wipe out all the sacrifice the building of the colony had entailed. But his work had to be exact.

It was tedious. It was exacting. It was exhaustingly time-consuming. He did have the help of previous experience, and the knowledge that the most probable molecular design would include this group of radicals and probably that, and side-chains like this might be looked for, and co-polymers might— But he was bleary-eyed and worn out before dawn came again. His eyes felt as if there were grains of sand beneath their lids. His brain felt dry—felt fibrous inside his skull, as if it were excelsior. But when the first red colors showed in the east, with the towers of the city against them, he had the blueprint of what should be the complex molecule formed in Murgatroyd's furry body.

He had just begun to realize, vaguely, that his work was done, when twin glaring lights came bouncing and plunging across the empty center of the grid. They were extraordinarily bright in the ruddy darkness. They stopped. A man jumped from the ground-car and ran toward the ship.

Calhoun wearily threw on the outer microphones and speakers.

"What's the matter now?" The man was the younger Walker.

"You're right!" called Walker's voice, strained to the breaking point. "There is sickness! Everywhere! There's an epidemic! It's just beginning! People felt tired and peevish and shut themselves away. Nobody realized! But they've got fevers! They're showing rashes! There's some delirium! The smallest children are worst—they were always quiet—but it's everywhere! We've never had real sickness before! What can we do?"

Calhoun said tiredly:

"I've got the design for an antibody. Murgatroyd made it. It's what he's for. The hospital ships from Phaedra are on the way now. They'll start turning it out in quantity and their doctors will start giving everybody shots of it."

Young Walker cried out fiercely:

"But that would mean they'd land! They'd take over! I can't let them land! I haven't the power! Nobody has! Too many of us would rather die than let them land! They lied to us. It's bad enough to have them hovering outside. If they land, there'll be fighting everywhere and forever! We can't let them help us! We won't! We'll fight—we'll die first!"

Calhoun blinked, owlishly.

"That," he said exhaustedly, "is something you have to figure out for yourself. If you're determined to die, I can't stop you. Die first or die second—it's your choice. You make it. I'm going to sleep!"

He cut off the mike and speakers. He couldn't keep his eyes open.

VII

"... As a strictly practical matter, a man who has to leave a task that he has finished, and wishes it to remain as he leaves it, usually finds it necessary to give the credit for his work to someone who will remain on the spot and will thereby be moved to protect and defend it so long as he lives ..."

Manual, Interstellar Medical Service. Pp. 167–8

Murgatroyd tugged at Calhoun and shrilled anxiously into his ear.

"*Chee-chee!*" he cried frantically. "*Chee-chee-chee!*"

Calhoun blinked open his eyes. There was a crashing sound and the Med Ship swayed upon its landing fins. It almost went over. It teetered horribly, and then slowly swung back past uprightness and tilted nearly as far in the opposite direction. There were crunching sounds as the soil partly gave way beneath one landing fin.

Then Calhoun waked thoroughly. In one movement

he was up and launching himself across the cabin to the control-chair. There was another violent impact. He swept his hand across the row of studs which turned on all sources of information and communication. The screens came on, and the spacephone, and the outside mikes and loud-speakers, and even the planetary communication unit which would have reported had there been any use of the electromagnetic spectrum in the atmosphere of this planet.

Bedlam filled the cabin. From the spacephone speaker a stentorian voice shouted:

"This is our last word! Permit our landing or—"

A thunderous detonation was reported by the outside mikes. The Med Ship fairly bounced. There was swirling white smoke outside the ship. It was midmorning, now, and the giant lacy structure of the landing grid was silhouetted against a deep-blue sky. There were cracklings from some electric storm perhaps a thousand miles away. There were shoutings, also brought in by the outside mikes.

Two groups of figures, fifty or a hundred yards from the Med Ship, labored furiously over some objects on the ground. Smoke billowed out; then a heavy, blastlike *"Boom!"* Something came spinning through the air, end over end, with sputtering sparks trailing behind it. It fell close by the base of the upright Med Ship.

Calhoun struck down the emergency rocket stud as it exploded. The roar of the rocket filled the interior of the ship. The spacephone speaker bellowed again:

"We've got a megaton bomb missile headed down! This is our last word! Permit landing or we come in fighting!"

The object from the crude cannon went off violently. With the emergency rocket flaming to help, it lifted the Med Ship, which jerked upward, settled back—and only two of its fins touched solidity. It began to topple because there was no support for the third.

Once toppled over, it would be helpless. It could be blasted with deliberately placed charges between its hull and the ground. A crater already existed where support for the third landing fin should have been.

Calhoun pushed the stud down full. The ship steadied and lifted. It went swinging across the level center of the landing grid. Its slender, ultra-high-velocity flame knifed down through the sod, leaving a smoking, incandescent slash behind. The figures about the bomb throwers scattered and fled. The Med Ship straightened to an upright position and began to rise.

Calhoun swore. The grid was the planet's defense against landings from space, because it could fling out missiles of any size with perfect aim at any target within some hundred thousand miles—a good twelve planetary diameters. Its operators meant to defy the fleet from Phaedra and had to get rid of the Med Ship before they dared energize its coils. Now they were rid of it. Now they could throw bombs, or boulders, or anything else its force-fields could handle.

The spacephone roared again:

"On the ground there! Our missile is aimed straight for your grid! It carries a megaton fission bomb! Evacuate the area!"

Calhoun swore again. The gang, the guard, the young-warrior group at the grid would be far too self-confident to heed such a threat. If there were wiser heads on Canis III, they could not enforce their commands. A human community has to be complete or it is not workable. The civilization which had existed on Phaedra II was shattered by the coming doom of its sun. The fragments—on Phaedra, in the fleet, in each small occupied community on Canis III—were incomplete and incapable of thinking or acting in concert with any other. Every small group on this planet, certainly, gave only lip-service to the rest. The young world was inherently incapable of organizing itself, save on a miniature scale. And one such miniature group had the grid and would fight with it regardless of the wishes of any other—because that group happened to be composed of instinct-driven members of the young-warrior group.

But he was still within the half-mile-high fence of the grid's steel structure. He strapped himself in his seat. The ship rose and rose. It came level with the top of the colony's one defense against space. The peculiar, corrugated copper lip of that structure, formed into the force-field guide which made it usable, swung toward him. He raised the rocket-thrust and shot skyward.

A deafening bellow came from the speakers:

"Yeah! Go on out and join the old folks! We'll get you!"

Obviously, the voice was from the ground below him. The ship flashed upward. Calhoun rasped into the spacephone mike, himself:

"Med Ship calling fleet! Call back that missile! I've got the antibody structure! This is no time for fighting! Call your missile back!"

Derisive laughter—again from the ground. Then the heavy, growling voice of an older man.

"Keep out of the way, Med Ship! These young fools are destroying themselves. Now they're destroying our grandchildren. If we hadn't been soft-hearted before— if we'd fought them from the beginning—the little ones wouldn't be dying now! Keep out of the way! If you can help us, it'll be after we've won the war."

The sky turned purple, at the height Calhoun had reached. It went black. The sun Canis flamed and flared against a background of ebony space, sprinkled with a thousand million colored stars. The Med Ship continued to rise.

Calhoun felt singularly and helplessly alone. Below him the sunlit surface of a world spread out, its edge already curving, cloud-masses and green-clad plains. There was the blue of ocean, creeping in. The city of the landing-grid was tiny, now. The brown of ploughed fields was no longer divided into rectangular shapes. It was a mere brownish haze between the colorings of as-yet-untouched virgin areas. The colonists of Canis III had so far made only a part of the new world their own. Many times more remained to be turned to human use.

The rear screen showed something coming upward. Masses of stuff, without shape but with terrific velocity. It was inchoate, indefinite stuff. It was plain dirt from the center of the landing-grid's floor, flung upward with the horrible power available for the landing and launching of ships. And, focused upon it, the force-fields of the grid could control it absolutely for a hundred thousand miles.

Calhoun swerved, ever so slightly. His own velocity had reached miles per second, but the formless mass following him was traveling at tens. It would not matter what such a hurtling missile was. At such a velocity it would not strike like a mass, but like a meteor-shower, flaring into incandescence when it touched and vaporizing the Med Ship with itself in the flame of impact.

But the grid would have to let go before it hit. There was monstrous stored power in the ship's Duhanne cells. If so much raw energy were released into anything on which a force-field was focused, it would destroy the source of the field. The grid could control its battering-ram until the very last fraction of a second, but then it must release—and its operator knew it.

Calhoun swung his ship frantically.

The mass of speeding planet-matter raced past no more than hundreds of yards away. It was released. It would go on through empty space for months or years—perhaps forever.

Calhoun swung back to his upward course. Now he sent raging commands before him:

"Pull back that missile! You can't land a bomb on Canis! There are people there! You can't drop a bomb on Canis!"

There was no answer. He raged again:

"Med Ship calling Phaedra fleet! There's disease on Canis! Your children and grandchildren are stricken! You can't fight your way to help them! You can't blast your way to sickbeds! You've got to negotiate! You've got to compromise! You've got to make a bargain or you and they together—"

A snarling voice from the ground said spitefully:

"*Never mind little Med man! Let 'em try to land! Let 'em try to take over and boss us! We listened to them long enough! Let 'em try to land and see what happens! We've got their fleet spotted! We'll take care of them!*"

Then the growling tones Calhoun had come to associate with Phaedra:

"*You keep out of the way, Med Ship. If our young children are sick, we're going to them! We're just beyond the area in which no drive will work. When the grid has been blasted our landing ship will go down and we'll come in! Our missile is only half an hour from target now! We'll begin our landing in three hours or less! Out of the way!*"

Calhoun said very bitter and extremely impolite words. But he faced an absolute emotional stalemate between enemies of whom both were in the wrong. The frantic anger of the adults of Phaedra, barred from the world to which they'd sent their children first so they could stay where doom awaited, was matched by the embittered revolt of the young people who had been worked past endurance and burdened past anyone's power to tolerate. There could be no compromise. It was not possible for either side to confess even partial defeat by the other. The quarrel had to be fought to a finish as between the opposing sides, and then hatred would remain no matter which side won. Such hatred could not be reasoned with.

It could only be replaced by a greater hatred.

Calhoun ground his teeth. The Med Ship hurtled out from the sunlit Canis III. Somewhere—not many thousands of miles away—the fleet of Phaedra clustered. Its crews were raging, but they were sick with anxiety about the enemies they prepared to fight. Aground there was hatred among the older of the colonists—the young-warrior group in particular, because that is the group in which hate is appropriate—and there was no less a sickish disturbance because even in being right they were wrong. Every decent impulse that had been played upon to make them exhaust themselves, before their revolt, now protested the consequences of their revolt. Yet they believed that in revolting they were justified.

Murgatroyd did not like the continued roar of emergency-rockets. He climbed up on Calhoun's lap and protested.

"*Chee!*" he said urgently. "*Chee-chee!*"

Calhoun grunted.

"Murgatroyd," he said, "it is a Med Service rule that a Med Ship man is expendable in case of need. I'm very much afraid that we've got to be expended. Hang on, now! We try some action!"

He turned the Med Ship end for end and fed full

power to the rockets. The ship would decelerate even faster than it had gathered speed. He set the nearest-object indicator to high gain. It showed the now-retreating mass of stone and soil from Canis. Calhoun then set up a scanner to examine a particular part of the sky.

"Since fathers can be insulted," he observed, "they've made a missile to fight its way down through anything that's thrown at it. It'll be remote-controlled for the purpose. It's very doubtful that there's a spaceship on the planet to fight it back. There's been no reference to one, anyhow. So what the missile will have to fight off will be stuff from the landing-grid only. Which is good. Moreover, fathers being what they are, regardless, that missile won't be a high-speed one. They'll want to be able to call it back at the last minute. They'll hope to."

"*Chee!*" said Murgatroyd, insisting that he didn't like the rocket-roar.

"So we will make ourselves as unpopular as possible with the fathers," observed Calhoun, "and if we live through it we will make ourselves even more cordially hated by the sons. And then they will be able to tolerate each other a little, because they both hate us so much. And so the public-health situation on Canis III may be resolved. Ah!"

The nearest-object indicator showed something moving toward the Med Ship. The scanner repeated the information in greater detail. There was a small object headed toward the planet from empty space. Its velocity and course—

Calhoun put on double acceleration to intercept it, while he pointed the ship quartering so he'd continue to lose outward speed.

Ten minutes later the spacephone growled:

"Med Ship! What do you think you're doing?"

"Getting in trouble," said Calhoun briefly.

Silence. The screens showed a tiny pin point of moving light, far away toward emptiness. Calhoun computed his course. He changed it.

"Med Ship!" rasped the spacephone. *"Keep out of the way of our missile! It's a megaton bomb!"*

Calhoun said irrelevantly:

"Those who in quarrels interpose, must often wipe a bloody nose." He added. "I know what it is."

"Let it alone!" rasped the voice. *"The grid on the ground has spotted it. They're sending up rocks to fight it."*

"They're rotten marksmen," said Calhoun. "They missed me!"

He aimed his ship. He knew the capacities of his ship as only a man who'd handled one for a long time could. He knew quite exactly what it could do.

The rocket from remoteness—the megaton-bomb guided missile—came smoking furiously from the stars. Calhoun seemed to throw his ship into a collision course. The rocket swerved to avoid him, though guided from many thousands of miles away. There was a trivial time-lag, too, between the time its scanners picked up a picture and transmitted it, and the transmission reached the Phaedrian fleet and the controlling impulses reached the missile in response. Calhoun counted on that. He had to. But he wasn't trying for a collision. He was forcing evasive action. He secured it. The rocket slanted itself to dart aside, and Calhoun threw the Med Ship into a flip-flop and—it was a hair-raising thing—slashed the rocket lengthwise with his rocket flame. That flame was less than half an inch thick, but it was of the temperature of the surface of a star, and in emptiness it was some hundreds of yards long. It sliced the rocket neatly. It flamed hideously, and even so far, Calhoun felt a cushioned impact from the flame. But that was the missile's rocket fuel. An atom bomb is the one known kind of bomb which will not be exploded by being sliced in half.

The fragments of the guided missile went on toward the planet, but they were harmless.

"All right!" said the spacephone icily—but Calhoun thought there was relief in the voice. *"You've only delayed our landing and lost a good many lives to disease!"*

Calhoun swallowed something he suspected was his heart, come up into his throat.

"Now," he said, "we'll see if that's true!"

His ship had lost its spaceward velocity before it met the missile. Now it was gaining velocity toward the planet. He cut off the rocket to observe. He swung the hull about and gave a couple of short rocket blasts.

"I'd better get economical," he told Murgatroyd. "Rocket fuel is hard to come by, this far out in space. If I don't watch out, we'll be caught in orbit, here, with no way to get down. I don't think the local inhabitants would be inclined to help us."

His lateral dash at the missile had given him something close to orbital speed relative to the planet's surface, though. The Med Ship went floating, with seemingly infinite leisure, around the vast bulge of the embattled world. In less than half an hour it was deep in the blackness of Canis' nighttime shadow. In three-quarters of an hour it came out again at the sunrise edge, barely four hundred miles high.

"Not quite speed enough for a true orbit," he told Murgatroyd critically. "I'd give a lot for a good map!"

He watched alertly. He could gain more height if he needed to, but he was worried about rocket fuel.

It is intended for dire emergencies only. It weighed too much to be carried in quantity.

He spotted the city of Canopolis on the horizon. He became furiously busy. He inverted the little ship and dived down into atmosphere. He killed speed with rocket flames and air friction together, falling recklessly the while. He was barely two miles high when he swept past a ridge of mountains and the city lay ahead and below. He could have crashed just short of it. But he spent more fuel to stay aloft. He used the rockets twice. Delicately.

At a ground speed of perhaps as little as two hundred miles an hour, supported at the end by a jetting, hair-thin rocket flame that was like a rod of electric arc-fire, he swept across the top of the landing grid. The swordlike flame washed briefly over the nearer edge. Very briefly. The flame cut a slash down through steel girders and heavy copper cables together. The rockets roared furiously. That one disabling cut at the grid had been on a downward, darting drift. Now the ship shouted, and swooped up, and on—and it swept above the far side of the grid only yards from the wide strip of copper which guided its force-fields out into space. Here it cut cables, girders, and force-field guide together for better than two hundred feet from the top. The grid was useless until painstaking labor had made the damage good.

Calhoun used nearly the last of his fuel for height while he said crisply on the spacephone:

"Calling fleet! Calling fleet! Med Ship calling fleet! I've disabled the landing grid on Canopolis. You can come in now and take care of the sick. There are no weapons aground to speak of and if you don't get trigger-happy there should be no fighting. I'll be landed off somewhere in the hills to the north of the town. If the local inhabitants don't pack explosives out and crack the ship to get at me, I'll have the facts on the antibody ready for you. In fact, as soon as I get down I'll give them to you by spacephone, just in case."

It was a near thing, though. His rocket fuel was exhausted when he hit the ground. The flame sputtered and stopped when the ship was three feet from touching. It fell over, splintering trees. It was distinctly a rough landing.

Murgatroyd was very indignant about it. He scolded shrilly while Calhoun unstrapped himself from the chair and when he looked out to see where they were.

It was a week later when the Med Ship—brought to the grid for repair and refueling—was ready for space again. The original landing grid still stood, of course. But it was straddled and overwhelmed, huge as it was, by the utterly gigantic flying grid from Phaedra. There were not many ships aground, though. As Calhoun moved toward the control building, now connected by cable to the control quarters in the flying grid, one of the few ships remaining seemed to fall toward the sky. A second ship followed only seconds later.

He went into the control building. Walker the elder, from Phaedra, nodded remotely as he entered. The younger Walker scowled at him. He had been in consultation with his father, and the atmosphere was one of great reserve.

"Hm-m-m," said the elder Walker, gruffly. "What's the report?"

"Fairly good," said Calhoun. "There was one lot of antibody that seems to have been a trifle under strength. But the general situation seems satisfactory. There'll be a few more cases of one thing and another, of course— cases that are incubating now. But they'll do all right on the antibody shots. They have so far, at any rate." He said to the younger Walker, "You did a very good job rounding up the thirteen-to-fifteen-year-olds to escort the fleet doctors and handle the patients for them. They took themselves very seriously. They were ideal for the job. Your young-warrior group—"

"A lot of them," said young Walker dourly, "have taken to the woods. They swear they'll never give in!"

"How about the girls?"

Young Walker shrugged.

"They're fluttering about and beginning to talk about clothes. When older women arrive there'll be dress-making—"

"And the lads in the woods," said Calhoun, "will come out to fascinate, and be fascinated instead. Do you think there'll be really much trouble?"

"No-o-o," said young Walker sourly. "Some of . . . our younger crowd seem relieved to be rid of responsibility."

"But," interposed the older Walker, gruffly, "he wants it. He thrives on it. He'll get it!" He hrrumphed. "The same with the others who showed what they could do here. We oldsters need them. We don't plan any . . . ah . . . reprisals."

Calhoun raised his eyebrows.

"Should I be surprised?"

The older Walker snorted.

"You didn't expect us to fall into each other's arms after what's happened, did you? No! But we are going to try to ignore our . . . differences as much as we can. We won't forget them, though."

"I suspect," said Calhoun, "that they'll be harder to remember than you think. You had a culture that split apart. Its pieces were incomplete—and a society has to be complete to survive. It isn't a human invention. It's something we have an instinct for—as birds have an instinct to build nests. When we build a culture according to our instincts, we get along. When that's impossible—there's trouble." Then he said, "I'm not trying to lecture you."

"Oh," said the elder Walker. "You aren't?"

Calhoun grinned.

"I thought I'd be the most unpopular man on this planet," he said cheerfully. "And I am. I interfered in everybody's business and nobody carried out his plans the way he wanted to. But at least nobody feels like he won. You'll be pleased when I lift the quarantine and take off, won't you?"

The older Walker said scornfully:

"We're paying no attention to your quarantine! Our fleet's loading up our wives on Phaedra, to ferry them here as fast as overdrive will do it. D'you think we'd pay any attention to your quarantine?"

Calhoun grinned again. The younger Walker said painfully:

"I suppose you think we should—" He stopped, and said very carefully: "What you did was for our good, all right, but it hurts us more than it does you. In twenty years, maybe, we'll be able to laugh at ourselves. Then we'll feel grateful. Now we know what we owe you, but we don't like it."

"And that," said Calhoun, "means that everything is back to normal. That's the traditional attitude toward all medical men—owe them a lot and hate to pay. I'll sign the quarantine release and take off as soon as you give me some rocket fuel, just in case of emergency."

"Right away!" said the two Walkers, in unison.

Calhoun snapped his fingers. Murgatroyd swaggered to his side. Calhoun took the little *tormal's* black paw in his hand.

"Come along, Murgatroyd," he said cheerfully. "You're the only person I really treated badly, and you don't mind. I suppose the moral of all this is that a *tormal* is a man's best friend."

PARIAH PLANET

The little Med Ship came out of overdrive and the stars were strange and the Milky Way seemed unfamiliar. Which, of course, was because the Milky Way and the local Cepheid marker-stars were seen from an unaccustomed angle and a not-yet-commonplace pattern of varying magnitudes.

But Calhoun grunted in satisfaction. There was a banded sun off to port, which was good. A breakout at no more than sixty light-hours from one's destination wasn't bad, in a strange sector of the galaxy and after three light-years of journeying blind.

"Arise and shine, Murgatroyd," said Calhoun. "Comb your whiskers. Get set to astonish the natives!"

A sleepy, small, shrill voice said, *"Chee!"*

Murgatroyd the *tormal* came crawling out of the small cubbyhole which was his own. He blinked at Calhoun.

"We're due to land shortly," Calhoun observed. "You will impress the local inhabitants. I will get unpopular. According to the records, there's been no Med Ship inspection here for twelve standard years. And that was practically no inspection, to judge by the report."

Murgatroyd said, *"Chee-chee!"*

He began to make his toilet, first licking his right-hand whiskers and then his left. Then he stood up and shook himself and looked interestedly at Calhoun. *Tormals* are companionable small animals. They are charmed when somebody speaks to them. They find great, deep satisfaction in imitating the actions of humans, as parrots and mynahs and parakeets imitate human speech. But *tormals* have certain valuable, genetically transmitted talents which make them much move valuable than mere companions or pets.

Calhoun got a light-reading for the banded sun. It could hardly be an accurate measure of distance, but it was a guide.

"Hold on to something, Murgatroyd!" he said.

Murgatroyd watched. He saw Calhoun make certain gestures which presaged discomfort. He popped back into his cubbyhole. Calhoun threw the overdrive switch and the Med Ship flicked back into that questionable state of being in which velocities of hundreds of times that of light are possible. The sensation of going into overdrive was unpleasant. A moment later, the sensation of coming out was no less so. Calhoun had experienced it often enough, and still didn't like it.

The sun Weald burned huge and terrible in space. It was close, now. Its disk covered half a degree of arc.

"Very neat," observed Calhoun. "Weald Three is our port, Murgatroyd. The plane of the ecliptic would be . . . Hm . . ."

He swung the outside electron telescope, picked up a nearby bright object, enlarged its image to show details, and checked it against the local star-pilot. He calculated a moment. The distance was too short for even the briefest of overdrive hops, but it would take time to get there on solar-system drive.

He thumbed down the communicator button and spoke into a microphone.

"Med Ship *Aesclipus Twenty* reporting arrival and asking coordinates for landing," he said matter-of-factly. "Purpose of landing is planetary health inspection. Our mass is fifty tons, standard. We should arrive at a landing position in something under four hours. Repeat. Med Ship *Aesclipus Twenty* . . ."

He finished the regular second transmission and made coffee for himself while he waited for an answer. Murgatroyd came out for a cup of coffee himself. Murgatroyd adored coffee. In minutes he held a tiny cup in a furry small paw and sipped gingerly at the hot liquid.

A voice came out of the communicator, "*Aesclipus Twenty*, repeat your identification."

Calhoun went to the control board.

"*Aesclipus Twenty*," he said patiently, "is a Med Ship, sent by the Interstellar Medical Service to make a planetary health inspection on Weald. Check with your public health authorities. This is the first Med Ship visit in twelve standard years, I believe—which is inexcusable. But your health authorities will know all about it. Check with them."

The voice said truculently, "What was your last port?"

Calhoun named it. This was not his home sector, but Sector Twelve had gotten into a very bad situation. Some of its planets had gone unvisited for as long as twenty years, and twelve between inspections was almost commonplace. Other sectors had been called on to help it catch up.

Calhoun was one of the loaned Med Ship men, and

because of the emergency he'd been given a list of half a dozen planets to be inspected one after another, instead of reporting back to sector headquarters after each visit. He'd had minor troubles before with landing-grid operators in Sector Twelve.

So he was very patient. He named the planet last inspected, the one from which he'd set out for Weald Three. The voice from the communicator said sharply, "What port before that?"

Calhoun named the one before the last.

"Don't drive any closer," said the voice harshly, "or you'll be destroyed!"

Calhoun said coldly, "Listen, my fine feathered friend! I'm from the Interstellar Medical Service. You get in touch with planetary health services immediately. Remind them of the Interstellar Medical Inspection Agreement, signed on Tralee two hundred and forty standard years ago. Remind them that if they do not cooperate in medical inspection that I can put your planet under quarantine and your space commerce will be cut off like that.

"No ship will be cleared for Weald from any other planet in the galaxy until there has been a health inspection. Things have pretty well gone to pot so far as the Med Service in this sector is concerned, but it's being straightened up. I'm helping straighten it. I give you twenty minutes to clear this. Then I am coming in, and if I'm not landed a quarantine goes on. Tell your health authorities that!"

Silence. Calhoun clicked off and poured himself another cup of coffee. Murgatroyd held out his cup for a refill. Calhoun gave it to him.

"I hate to put on an official hat, Murgatroyd," he said, annoyed, "but there are some people who demand it. The rule is, never get official if you can help it, but when you must, out-official the official who's officialing you."

Murgatroyd said, *"Chee!"* and sipped at his cup.

Calhoun checked the course of the Med Ship. It bore on through space. There were tiny noises from the communicator. There were whisperings and rustlings and the occasional strange and sometimes beautiful musical notes whose origin is yet obscure, but which, since they are carried by electromagnetic radiation of wildly varying wave lengths, are not likely to be the fabled music of the spheres.

In fifteen minutes a different voice came from the speaker.

"Med Ship *Aesclipus!* Med Ship *Aesclipus!*"

Calhoun answered and the voice said anxiously, "Sorry about the challenge, but we have the blueskin problem always with us. We have to be extremely careful. Will you come in, please?"

"I'm on my way," said Calhoun.

"The planetary health authorities," said the voice, more anxiously still, "are very anxious to be cooperative. We need Med Service help! We lose a lot of sleep over the blueskin! Could you tell us the name of the last Med Ship to land here, and its inspector, and when that inspection was made? We want to look up the record of the event to be able to assist you in every possible way."

"He's lying," Calhoun told Murgatroyd, "but he's more scared than hostile."

He picked up the order folio on Weald Three. He gave the information about the last Med Ship visit.

"What," he asked, "is a blueskin?"

He'd read the folio on Weald, of course, but as the ship swam onward through emptiness he went through it again. The last medical inspection had been only perfunctory. Twelve years earlier—instead of three— a Med Ship had landed on Weald. There had been official conferences with health officials. There was a report on the birth rate, the death rate, the anomaly rate, and a breakdown of all reported communicable diseases. But that was all. There were no special comments and no overall picture.

Presently Calhoun found the word in a Sector dictionary, where words of only local usage were to be found:

> *Blueskin: Colloquial term for a person recovered from a plague which left large patches of blue pigment irregularly distributed over the body. Especially, inhabitants of Dara. The condition is said to be caused by a chronic, nonfatal form of Dara plague and has been said to be noninfectious, though this is not certain. The etiology of Dara plague has not been worked out. The blueskin condition is hereditary but not a genetic modification, as markings appear in non-Mendelian distributions.*

Calhoun puzzled over it. Nobody could have read the entire Sector directory, even with unlimited leisure during travel between solar systems. Calhoun hadn't tried. But now he went laboriously through indices and cross-references while the ship continued to travel onward.

He found no other reference to blueskins. He looked up Dara. It was listed as an inhabited planet, some four hundred years colonized, with a landing grid and, at the time the main notice was written out, a flourishing interstellar commerce. But there was a memo, evidently added to the entry in some change of editions: *"Since plague, special license from Med Service is required for landing."*

That was all. Absolutely all.

The communicator said suavely, "Med Ship *Aesclipus Twenty!* Come in on vision, please."

Calhoun went to the control board and threw on vision.

"Well, what now?" he demanded.

His screen lighted. A bland face looked out at him.

"We have—ah—verified your statements," said the third voice from Weald. "Just one more item. Are you alone in your ship?"

"Of course," said Calhoun, frowning.

"Quite alone?" insisted the voice.

"Obviously!" said Calhoun.

"No other living creature?" insisted the voice again.

"Of—oh!" said Calhoun, annoyed. He called over his shoulder. "Murgatroyd! Come here!"

Murgatroyd hopped to his lap and gazed interestedly at the screen. The bland face changed remarkably. The voice changed even more.

"Very good," it said. "Very, very good! Blueskins do not have *tormals*. You are Med Service! By all means come in! Your coordinates will be . . ."

Calhoun wrote them down. He clicked off the communicator again and growled to Murgatroyd, "So I might have been a blueskin, eh? And you're my passport, because only Med Ships have members of your tribe aboard. What the hell's the matter, Murgatroyd? They act like they think somebody's trying to get down on their planet with a load of plague germs!"

He grumbled to himself for minutes. The life of a Med Ship man is not exactly a sinecure, at best. It means long periods in empty space in overdrive, which is absolute and deadly tedium. Then two or three days aground, checking official documents and statistics, and asking questions to see how many of the newest medical techniques have reached this planet or that, and the supplying of information about such as have not arrived.

Then the lifting out to space for long periods of

tedium, to repeat the process somewhere else. Med Ships carry only one man because two could not stand the close contact without quarreling with each other. But Med Ships do carry *tormals*, like Murgatroyd, and a *tormal* and a man can get along indefinitely, like a man and a dog. It is a highly unequal friendship, but it seems to be satisfactory to both.

Calhoun was very much annoyed with the way the Med Service had been operated in Sector Twelve. He was one of many men at work to correct the results of incompetence in directing Med Service in this sector. But it is always disheartening to have to labor at making up for somebody else's blundering, when there is so much new work that needs to be done.

The condition shown by the landing-grid suspicions was a case in point. Blueskins were people who inherited a splotchy skin pigmentation from other people who'd survived a plague. Weald plainly maintained a one-planet quarantine against them. But a quarantine is normally an emergency measure. The Med Service should have taken over, wiped out the need for a quarantine, and then lifted it. It hadn't been done.

Calhoun fumed to himself.

The world of Weald Three grew brighter and brighter and became a disk. The disk had icecaps and a reasonable proportion of land and water surface. The ship decelerated, voices notifying observation from the surface, and the little ship came to a stop some five planetary diameters out from solidity. The landing grid's force-field locked on to it, and its descent began.

The business of landing was all very familiar, from the blue rim which appeared at the limb of the planet from one diameter out, to the singular flowing-apart of the surface features as the ship sank still lower. There was the circular landing grid, rearing skyward for nearly a mile. It could let down interstellar liners from emptiness and lift them out to emptiness again, with great convenience and economy for everyone.

It landed the Med Ship in its center, and there were officials to greet Calhoun, and he knew in advance the routine part of his visit. There would be an interview with the planet's chief executive, by whatever title he was called. There would be a banquet. Murgatroyd would be petted by everybody. There would be painful efforts to impress Calhoun with the splendid conduct of public health matters on Weald. He would be told much scandal.

He might find one man, somewhere, who passionately labored to advance the welfare of his fellow humans by finding out how to keep them well or, failing that, how to make them well when they got sick. And in two days, or three, Calhoun would be escorted back to the landing grid, and lifted out to space, and he'd spend long empty days in overdrive and land somewhere else to do the whole thing all over again.

It all happened exactly as he expected, with one exception. Every human being he met on Weald wanted to talk about blueskins. Blueskins and the idea of blueskins obsessed everyone. Calhoun listened without asking questions until he had the picture of what blueskins meant to the people who talked of them. Then he knew there would be no use asking questions at random.

Nobody mentioned ever having seen a blueskin. Nobody mentioned a specific event in which a blueskin had at any named time taken part. But everybody was afraid of blueskins. It was a patterned, an inculcated, a stage-directed fixed idea. And it found expression in shocked references to the vileness, the depravity, the monstrousness of the blueskin inhabitants of Dara, from whom Weald must at all costs be protected.

It did not make sense. So Calhoun listened politely

until he found an undistinguished medical man who wanted some special information about gene selection as practiced halfway across the galaxy. He invited that man to the Med Ship, where he supplied the information not hitherto available. He saw his guest's eyes shine a little with that joyous awe a man feels when he finds out something he has wanted long and badly to know.

"Now," said Calhoun, "tell me something? Why does everybody on this planet hate the inhabitants of Dara? It's light-years away. Nobody claims to have suffered in person from them. Why make a point of hating them?"

The Wealdian doctor grimaced.

"They've blue patches on their skins. They're different from us. So they can be pictured as a danger and our political parties can make an election issue out of competing for the privilege of defending us from them. They had plague on Dara, once. They're accused of still having it ready for export."

"Hm," said Calhoun. "The story is that they want to spread contagion here, eh? Doesn't anybody"—his tone was sardonic—"doesn't anybody urge that they be massacred as an act of piety?"

"Yes-s-s-s," admitted the doctor reluctantly. "It's mentioned in political speeches."

"But how's it rationalized?" demanded Calhoun. "What's the argument to make pigment-patches involve moral and physical degradation, as I'm assured is the case?"

"In the public schools," said the doctor, "the children are taught that blueskins are now carriers of the disease they survived—three generations ago! That they hate everybody who isn't a blueskin. That they are constantly scheming to introduce their plague here so most of us will die and the rest will become blueskins.

That's beyond rationalizing. It can't be true, but it's not safe to doubt it."

"Bad business," said Calhoun coldly. "That sort of thing usually costs lives in the end. It could lead to massacre!"

"Perhaps it has, in a way," said the doctor unhappily. "One doesn't like to think about it." He paused. "Twenty years ago there was a famine on Dara. There were crop failures. The situation must have been very bad: They built a spaceship.

"They've no use for such things normally, because no nearby planet will deal with them or let them land. But they built a spaceship and came here. They went in orbit around Weald. They asked to trade for shiploads of food. They offered any price in heavy metals—gold, platinum, iridium, and so on. They talked from orbit by vision communicators. They could be seen to be blueskins. You can guess what happened!"

"Tell me," said Calhoun.

"We armed ships in a hurry," admitted the doctor. "We chased their spaceship back to Dara. We hung in space off the planet. We told them we'd blast their world from pole to pole if they ever dared take to space again. We made them destroy their one ship, and we watched on vision screens as it was done."

"But you gave them food?"

"No," said the doctor ashamedly. "They were blueskins."

"How bad was the famine?"

"Who knows? Any number may have starved. And we kept a squadron of armed ships in their skies for years—to keep them from spreading the plague, we said. And some of us believed it!"

The doctor's tone was purest irony.

"Lately," he said, "there's been a move for economy in our government. Simultaneously, we began to have

a series of overabundant crops. The government had
to buy the excess grain to keep the price up. Retired
patrol ships, built to watch over Dara, were available
for storage space. We filled them up with grain and
sent them out into orbit. They're there now, hundreds
of thousands or millions of tons of grain!"

"And Dara?"

The doctor shrugged. He stood up.

"Our hatred of Dara," he said, again ironically, "has
produced one thing. Roughly halfway between here and
Dara there's a two-planet solar system, Orede. There's
a usable planet there. It was proposed to build an
outpost of Weald there, against blueskins. Cattle were
landed to run wild and multiply and make a reason
for colonists to settle there.

"They did, but nobody wants to move near to
blueskins! So Orede stayed uninhabited until a hunting party, shooting wild cattle, found an outcropping
of heavy-metal ore. So now there's a mine there. And
that's all. A few hundred men work the mine at fabu-
lous wages. You may be asked to check on their health.
But not Dara's!"

"I see," said Calhoun, frowning.

The doctor moved toward the Med Ship's exit port.

"I answered your questions," he said grimly. "But
if I talked to anyone else as I've done to you, I'd be
lucky only to be driven into exile."

"I shan't give you away," said Calhoun. He did not
smile.

When the doctor had gone, Calhoun said deliberately, "Murgatroyd, you should be grateful that you're
a *tormal* and not a man. There's nothing about being
a *tormal* to make you ashamed!"

Then he grimly changed his garments for the full-
dress uniform of the Med Service. There was to be

a banquet at which he would sit next to the planet's chief executive and hear innumerable speeches about the splendor of Weald. Calhoun had his own, strictly Med Service opinion of the planet's latest and most boasted-of achievement. It was a domed city in the polar regions, where nobody ever had to go outdoors.

He was less than professionally enthusiastic about the moving streets, and much less than approving of the dream broadcasts which supplied hypnotic, sleep-inducing rhythms to anybody who chose to listen to them. The price was that while asleep one would hear high praise of commercial products, and might believe them when awake.

But it was not Calhoun's function to criticize when it could be avoided. Med Service had been badly managed in Sector Twelve. So at the banquet Calhoun made a brief and diplomatic address in which he temperately praised what could be praised, and did not mention anything else.

The chief executive followed him. As head of the government he paid some tribute to the Med Service. But then he reminded his hearers proudly of the high culture, splendid health, and remarkable prosperity of the planet since his political party took office. This, he said, despite the need to be perpetually on guard against the greatest and most immediate danger to which any world in all the galaxy was exposed.

He referred to the blueskins, of course. He did not need to tell the people of Weald what vigilance, what constant watchfulness was necessary against that race of deprived and malevolent deviants from the norm of humanity. But Weald, he said with emotion, held aloft the torch of all that humanity held most dear, and defended not alone the lives of its people against blueskin contagion, but their noble heritage of ideals against blueskin pollution.

When he sat down, Calhoun said very politely, "It looks as if some day it should be practical politics to urge the massacre of all blueskins. Have you thought of that?"

The chief executive said comfortably, "The idea's been proposed. It's good politics to urge it, but it would be foolish to carry it out. People vote against blueskins. Wipe them out, and where'd you be?"

Calhoun ground his teeth—quietly.

There were more speeches. Then a messenger, white-faced, arrived with a written note for the chief executive. He read it and passed it to Calhoun. It was from the Ministry of Health. The spaceport reported that a ship had just broken out from overdrive within the Wealdian solar system. Its tape-transmitter had automatically signaled its arrival from the mining planet Orede.

But, having sent off its automatic signal, the ship lay dead in space. It did not drive toward Weald. It did not respond to signals. It drifted like a derelict upon no course at all. It seemed ominous, and since it came from Orede, the planet nearest to Dara of the blueskins, the health ministry informed the planet's chief executive.

"It'll be blueskins," said that astute person firmly. "They're next door to Orede. That's who's done this. It wouldn't surprise me if they'd seeded Orede with their plague, and this ship came from there to give us warning!"

"There's no evidence for anything of the sort," protested Calhoun. "A ship simply came out of overdrive and didn't signal further. That's all!"

"We'll see," said the chief executive ominously. "We'll go to the spaceport. There we'll get the news as it comes in, and can frame orders on the latest information."

He took Calhoun by the arm. Calhoun said sharply, "Murgatroyd!"

During the banquet, Murgatroyd had been visiting with the wives of the higher-up officials. They had enough of their husbands normally, without listening to their official speeches. Murgatroyd was brought, his small paunch distended with cakes and coffee and such delicacies as he'd been plied with. He was half comatose from overfeeding and overpetting, but he was glad to see Calhoun.

Calhoun held the little creature in his arms as the official ground-car raced through traffic with screaming sirens claiming the right of way. It reached the spaceport, where enormous metal girders formed a monster frame of metal lace against a star-filled sky. The chief executive strode magnificently into the spaceport offices. There was no news; the situation remained unchanged.

It seemed to Calhoun that the official handling of the matter accounted for the terror that he could feel building up. The unexplained bit of news was on the air all over the planet Weald. There was nobody awake of all the world's population who did not believe that there was a new danger in the sky. Nobody doubted that it came from blueskins. The treatment of the news was precisely calculated to keep alive the hatred of Weald for the inhabitants of the world Dara.

Calhoun put Murgatroyd into the Med Ship and went back to the spaceport office. A small spaceboat, designed to inspect the circling grain ships from time to time, was already aloft. The landing-grid had thrust it swiftly out most of the way. Now it droned and drove on sturdily toward the enigmatic ship.

Calhoun took no part in the agitated conferences among the officials and news reporters at the spaceport. But he listened to the talk about him. As the investigating small ship drew nearer to the deathly-still cargo vessel, the guesses about the meaning of its breakout and following silence grew more and more wild.

But, singularly, there was no single suggestion that the mystery might not be the work of blueskins. Blueskins were scapegoats for all the fears and all the uneasiness a perhaps over-civilized world developed.

Presently the investigating spaceboat reached the mystery ship and circled it, beaming queries. No answer. It reported the cargo ship dark. No lights anywhere on or in it. There were no induction-surges from even pulsing, idling engines. Delicately, the messenger craft maneuvered until it touched the silent vessel. It reported that microphones detected no motion whatever inside.

"Let a volunteer go aboard," commanded the chief executive. "Let him report what he finds."

A pause. Then the solemn announcement of an intrepid volunteer's name, from far, far away. Calhoun listened, frowning darkly. This pompous heroism wouldn't be noticed in the Med Service. It would be routine behavior.

Suspenseful, second-by-second reports. The volunteer had rocketed himself across the emptiness between the two again separated ships. He had opened the airlock from outside. He'd gone in. He'd closed the outer air-lock door. He's opened the inner. He reported—

The relayed report was almost incoherent, what with horror and incredulity and the feeling of doom that came upon the volunteer. The ship was a bulk-cargo ore-carrier, designed to run between Orede and Weald with cargoes of heavy-metal ores and a crew of no more than five men. There was no cargo in her holds now, though.

Instead, there were men. They packed the ship.

They filled the corridors. They had crawled into every space where a man could find room to push himself. There were hundreds of them. It was insanity. And it had been greater insanity still for the ship to have taken off with so preposterous a load of living creatures.

But they weren't living any longer. The air apparatus had been designed for a crew of five. It would purify the air for possibly twenty or more. But there were hundreds of men in hiding as well as in plain view in the cargo ship from Orede. There were many, many times more than her air apparatus and reserve tanks could possibly have taken care of. They couldn't even have been fed during the journey from Orede to Weald.

But they hadn't starved. Air-scarcity killed them before the ship came out of overdrive.

A remarkable thing was that there was no written message in the ship's log which referred to its take-off. There was no memorandum of the taking on of such an impossible number of passenger.

"The blueskins did it," said the chief executive of Weald. He was pale. All about Calhoun men looked sick and shocked and terrified. "It was the blueskins! We'll have to teach them a lesson!" Then he turned to Calhoun. "The volunteer who went on that ship—he'll have to stay there, won't he? He can't be brought back to Weald without bringing contagion."

Calhoun raged at him.

There was a certain coldness in the manner of those at the Weald spaceport when the Med Ship left next morning. Calhoun was not popular because Weald was scared. It had been conditioned to scare easily, where blueskins might be involved. Its children were trained to react explosively when the word *blueskin* was uttered in their hearing, and its adults tended to say it when anything causing uneasiness entered their minds. So a planet-wide habit of irrational response had formed and was not seen to be irrational because almost everybody had it.

The volunteer who'd discovered the tragedy on the ship from Orede was safe, though. He'd made a completely conscientious survey of the ship he'd volunteered to enter and examine. For his courage, he'd have been doomed but for Calhoun.

The reaction of his fellow citizens was that by entering the ship he might have become contaminated by blueskin infectious material if the plague still existed, and *if* the men in the ship had caught it (but they certainly hadn't died of it), and *if* there had been blueskins on Orede to communicate it (for which there was no evidence), and *if* blueskins were responsible for the tragedy. Which was at the moment pure supposition. But Weald feared he might bring death back to Weald if he were allowed to return.

Calhoun saved his life. He ordered that the guardship admit him to its air-lock, which then was to be filled with steam and chlorine. The combination would sterilize and even partly eat away his spacesuit, after which the chlorine and steam should be bled out to space, and air from the ship let into the lock.

If he stripped off the spacesuit without touching its outer surface, and reentered the investigating ship while the suit was flung outside by a man in another spacesuit, handling it with a pole he'd fling after it, there could be no possible contamination brought back.

Calhoun was quite right, but Weald in general considered that he'd persuaded the government to take an unreasonable risk.

There were other reasons for disapproving of him. Calhoun had been unpleasantly frank. The coming of the death-ship stirred to frenzy those people who believed that all blueskins should be exterminated as a pious act. They'd appeared on every vision screen, citing not only the ship from Orede but other incidents which they interpreted as crimes against Weald.

They demanded that all Wealdian atomic reactors be modified to turn out fusion-bomb materials while a space fleet was made ready for an anti-blueskin crusade. They confidently demanded such a rain of fusion bombs on Dara that no blueskin, no animal, no shred of vegetation, no fish in the deepest ocean, not even a living virus particle of the blueskin plague could remain alive on the blueskin world.

One of these vehement orators even asserted that

Calhoun agreed that no other course was possible, speaking for the Interstellar Medical Service. And Calhoun furiously demanded a chance to deny it by broadcast, and he made a bitter and indiscreet speech from which a planet-wide audience inferred that he thought them fools.

He did.

So he was definitely unpopular when his ship lifted from Weald. He'd curtly given his destination as Orede, from which the death-ship had come. The landing grid locked on, raised the small spacecraft until Weald was a great shining ball below it, and then somehow scornfully cast him off. The Med Ship was free, in clear space where there was not enough of a gravitational field to hinder overdrive.

He aimed for his destination, his face very grim. He said savagely, "Get set, Murgatroyd! Overdrive coming!"

He thumbed down the overdrive button. The universe of stars went out, while everything living in the ship felt the customary sensations of dizziness, of nausea, and of a spiraling fall into nothingness. Then there was silence.

The Med Ship actually moved at a rate which was a preposterous number of times the speed of light, but it felt absolutely solid, absolutely firm and fixed. A ship in overdrive feels exactly as if it were buried deep in the core of a planet. There is no vibration. There is no sign of anything but solidity and, if one looks out a port, there is only utter blackness plus an absence of sound fit to make one's eardrums crack.

But within seconds random tiny noises began. There were recordings to keep the ship from sounding like a grave. The recordings played and the speakers gave off minute creakings, and meaningless hums, and very tiny noises of every imaginable sort, all of which were just above the threshold of the inaudible.

Calhoun fretted. Sector Twelve was in very bad shape. A conscientious Med Service man would never have let the anti-blueskin obsession go unmentioned in a report on Weald. Health is not only a physical affair. There is mental health, also. When mental health goes a civilization can be destroyed more surely and more terribly than by any imaginable war or plague germs. A plague kills off those who are susceptible to it, leaving immunes to build up a world again. But immunes are the first to be killed when a mass neurosis sweeps a population.

Weald was definitely a Med Service problem world. Dara was another. And when hundreds of men jammed themselves into a cargo spaceship which could not furnish them with air to breathe, and took off and went into overdrive before the air could fail ... Orede called for no less of worry.

"I think," said Calhoun dourly, "that I'll have some coffee."

Coffee was one of the words that Murgatroyd recognized. Ordinarily he stirred immediately on hearing it, and watched the coffeemaker with bright, interested eyes. He'd even tried to imitate Calhoun's motions with it, once, and had scorched his paws in the attempt. But this time he did not move.

Calhoun turned his head. Murgatroyd sat on the floor, his long tail coiled reflectively about a chair leg. He watched the door of the Med Ship's sleeping cabin.

"Murgatroyd," said Calhoun. "I mentioned coffee!"

"*Chee!*" shrilled Murgatroyd.

But he continued to look at the door. The temperature was kept lower in the other cabin, and the look of things was different than the control compartment.

The difference was part of the means by which a man was able to be alone for weeks on end—alone save for his *tormal*—without becoming ship-happy.

There were other carefully thought out items in the ship with the same purpose. But none of them should cause Murgatroyd to stare fixedly and fascinatedly at the sleeping cabin door. Not when coffee was in the making!

Calhoun considered. He became angry at the immediate suspicion that occurred to him. As a Med Service man, he was duty-bound to be impartial. To be impartial might mean not to side absolutely with Weald in its enmity to blueskins.

And the people of Weald had refused to help Dara in a time of famine, and had blockaded that pariah world for years afterward. And they had other reasons for hating the people they'd treated badly. It was entirely reasonable for some fanatic on Weald to consider that Calhoun must be killed lest he be of help to the blueskins Weald abhorred.

In fact, it was quite possible that somebody had stowed away on the Med Ship to murder Calhoun, so that there would be no danger of any report favorable to Dara ever being presented anywhere. If so, such a stowaway would be in the sleeping cabin now, waiting for Calhoun to walk in unsuspiciously, only to be shot dead.

So Calhoun made coffee. He slipped a blaster into a pocket where it would be handy. He filled a small cup for Murgatroyd and a large one for himself, and then a second large one.

He tapped on the sleeping cabin door, standing aside lest a blaster-bolt come through it.

"Coffee's ready," he said sardonically. "Come out and join us."

There was a long pause. Calhoun rapped again.

"You've a seat at the captain's table," he said more sardonically still. "It's not polite to keep me waiting!"

He waited, alert for a rush which would be a fanatic's desperate attempt to do murder despite premature discovery. He was prepared to shoot quite ruthlessly, because he was on duty and the Med Service did not approve of the extermination of populations, however justified another population might consider it.

But there was no rush. Instead, there came hesitant footfalls whose sound made Calhoun start. The door of the cabin slid slowly aside. A girl appeared in the opening, desperately white and desperately composed.

"H-how did you know I was there?" she asked shakily. She moistened her lips. "You didn't see me! I was in a closet, and you didn't even enter the room!"

Calhoun said grimly, "I've sources of information. Murgatroyd told me this time. May I present him? Murgatroyd, our passenger. Shake hands."

Murgatroyd moved forward, stood on his hind legs and offered a skinny, furry paw. She did not move. She stared at Calhoun.

"Better shake hands," said Calhoun, as grimly as before. "It might relax the tension a little. And do you want to tell me your story? You have one ready, I'm sure."

The girl swallowed. Murgatroyd shook hands gravely. He said, *"Chee-chee!"* in the shrillest of trebles and went back to his former position.

"The story?" said Calhoun insistently.

"There—there isn't any," said the girl unsteadily. "Just that I—I need to get to Orede, and you're going there. There's no other way to go, now."

"To the contrary," said Calhoun. "There'll undoubtedly be a fleet heading for Orede as soon as it can be assembled and armed. But I'm afraid that as a story yours isn't good enough. Try another."

She shivered a little.

"I'm running away . . ."

"Ah!" said Calhoun. "In that case I'll take you back."

"No!" she said fiercely. "I'll—I'll die first! I'll wreck this ship first!"

Her hand came from behind her. There was a tiny blaster in it. But it shook visibly as she tried to aim it.

"I'll shoot out the controls!"

Calhoun blinked. He'd had to make a drastic change in his estimate of the situation the instant he saw that the stowaway was a girl. Now he had to make another when her threat was not to kill him but to disable the ship. Women are rarely assassins, and when they are they don't use energy weapons. Daggers and poisons are more typical. But this girl threatened to destroy the ship rather than its owner, so she was not actually an assassin at all.

"I'd rather you didn't do that," said Calhoun dryly. "Besides, you'd get deadly bored if we were stuck in a derelict waiting for our air and food to give out."

Murgatroyd, for no reasons whatever, felt it necessary to enter the conversation. *"Chee-chee-chee!"*

"A very sensible suggestion," observed Calhoun. "We'll sit down and have a cup of coffee." To the girl he said, "I'll take you to Orede, since that's where you say you want to go."

"I have a sweetheart there . . ."

"No," he said reprovingly. "Nearly all the mining colony had packed itself into the ship that came into Weald with everybody dead. But not all. And there's been no check of what men were in the ship and what men weren't. You wouldn't go to Orede if it were likely your sweetheart had died on the way to you. Here's your coffee. Sugar or saccho, and do you take cream?"

She trembled a little, but she took the cup.

"I don't understand."

"Murgatroyd and I," explained Calhoun—and he did not know whether he spoke out of anger or something else—"we are do-gooders. We go around trying to keep people from getting sick or dying. Sometimes we even try to keep them from getting killed. It's our profession. We practice it even on our own behalf. We want to stay alive. So since you make such drastic threats, we will take you where you want to go. Especially since we're going there anyhow."

"You don't believe anything I've said!" It was a statement.

"Not a word," admitted Calhoun. "But you'll probably tell us something more believable presently. When did you eat last?"

"Yesterday."

"Would you rather do your own cooking?" asked Calhoun politely. "Or would you permit me to ready a snack?"

"I—I'll do it," she said.

She drank her coffee first, however, and then Calhoun showed her how to punch the readier for such-and-such dishes, to be extracted from storage and warmed or chilled, as the case might be, and served at dialed-for intervals. There was also equipment for preparing food for oneself, in one's own chosen manner—again an item to help make solitude not unendurable.

Calhoun deliberately immersed himself in the Galactic Directory, looking up the planet Orede. He was headed there, but he'd had no reason to inform himself about it before. Now he read with every appearance of absorption.

The girl ate daintily. Murgatroyd watched with highly amiable interest. But she looked acutely uncomfortable.

Calhoun finished with the Directory. He got out the records which contained more information. He was specifically after the Med Service history of all the planets in this sector. He went through the record of every inspection ever made on Weald and on Dara.

But Sector Twelve had not been run well. There was no adequate account of a plague which had wiped out three-quarters of the population of an inhabited planet! It had happened shortly after one Med Ship visit, and was over before another Med Ship came by.

There should have been a painstaking investigation, even after the fact. There should have been a collection of infectious material and a reasonably complete identification and study of the agent. It hadn't been made. There was probably some other emergency at the time, and it slipped by. Calhoun, whose career was not to be spent in this sector, resolved on a blistering report about this negligence and its consequences.

He kept himself casually busy, ignoring the girl. A Med Ship man has resources of study and meditation with which to occupy himself during overdrive travel from one planet to another. Calhoun made use of those resources. He acted as if he were completely unconscious of the stowaway. But Murgatroyd watched her with charmed attention.

Hours after her discovery, she said uneasily, "Please?"

Calhoun looked up.

"Yes?"

"I don't know exactly how things stand."

"You are a stowaway," said Calhoun. "Legally, I have the right to put you out the air-lock. It doesn't seem necessary. There's a cabin. When you're sleepy, use it. Murgatroyd and I can make out quite well out here. When you're hungry, you now know how to get something to eat. When we land on Orede, you'll probably go about whatever business you have there. That's all."

She stared at him.

"But you don't believe what I've told you!"

"No," agreed Calhoun, but didn't add to the statement.

"But—I will tell you," she offered. "The police were after me. I had to get away from Weald! I had to! I'd stolen—"

He shook his head.

"No," he said. "If you were a thief, you'd say anything in the world except that you were a thief. You're not ready to tell the truth yet. You don't have to, so why tell me anything? I suggest that you get some sleep. Incidentally, there's no lock on the cabin door because there's only supposed to be one person on this ship at a time. But you can brace a chair to fasten it somehow or other. Good night."

She rose slowly. Twice her lips parted as if to speak again, but then she went into the other cabin and closed herself in. There was the sound of a chair being wedged against the door.

Murgatroyd blinked at the place where she'd disappeared and then climbed up into Calhoun's lap, with complete assurance of welcome. He settled himself and was silent for moments. Then he said, *"Chee!"*

"I believe you're right," said Calhoun. "She doesn't belong on Weald, or with the conditioning she'd have had, there'd be only one place she'd dread worse than Orede, which would be Dara. But I doubt she'd be afraid to land even on Dara."

"Chee-chee!" Murgatroyd said with conviction.

"Definitely," agreed Calhoun. "She's not doing this for her personal advantage. Whatever she thinks she's doing, it's more important to her than her own life. Murgatroyd . . ."

"*Chee?*" said Murgatroyd in an inquiring tone.

"There are wild cattle on Orede," said Calhoun. "Herds and herds of them. I have a suspicion that somebody's been shooting them. Lots of them. Do you agree? Don't you think that a lot of cattle have been slaughtered on Orede lately?"

Murgatroyd yawned. He settled himself still more comfortably in Calhoun's lap.

"*Chee,*" he said drowsily.

He went to sleep, while Calhoun continued the examination of highly condensed information. Presently he looked up the normal rate of increase, with other data, among herds of *bovis domesticus* in a wild state, on planets where there are no natural enemies.

It wasn't unheard-of for a world to be stocked with useful types of Terran fauna and flora before it was attempted to be colonized. Terran life-forms could play the devil with alien ecological systems—very much to humanity's benefit. Familiar micro-organisms and a standard vegetation added to the practicality of human settlements on otherwise alien worlds. But sometimes the results were strange.

They weren't often so strange, however, as to cause some hundreds of men to pack themselves frantically aboard a cargo ship which couldn't possibly sustain them, so that every man must die while the ship was in overdrive.

Still, by the time Calhoun turned in on a spare pneumatic mattress, he had calculated that as few as a dozen head of cattle, turned loose on a suitable planet, would have increased to herds of thousands or tens or even hundreds of thousands in much less time than had probably elapsed.

❖   ❖   ❖

Next ship-day the girl looked oddly at Calhoun when she appeared in the control-room. Murgatroyd regarded her with great interest. Calhoun nodded politely and went back to what he'd been doing before she appeared.

"Shall I have breakfast?" she asked uncertainly.

"Murgatroyd and I have," he told her. "Why not?"

Silently, she operated the food-readier. She ate. Calhoun gave a very good portrayal of a man who will respond politely when spoken to, but who was busy with activities remote from stowaways.

About noon, ship-time, she asked, "When will we get to Orede?"

Calhoun told her absently, as if he were thinking of something else.

"What—what do you think happened there? I mean, to make that tragedy in the ship."

"I don't know," said Calhoun. "But I disagree with the authorities on Weald. I don't think it was a planned atrocity of the blueskins."

"Wh—what are blueskins?" asked the girl.

Calhoun turned around and looked at her directly.

"When lying," he said mildly, "you tell as much by what you pretend isn't, as by what you pretend is. You know what blueskins are!"

"But what do you think they are?" she asked.

"There used to be a human disease called small-pox," said Calhoun. "When people recovered from it, they were usually marked. Their skin had little scar pits here and there. At one time, back on Earth, it was expected that everybody would catch smallpox sooner or later, and a large percentage would die of it.

"And it was so much a matter of course that if they printed a picture of a criminal they never mentioned if it he were pock-marked. It was no distinction. But if he didn't have the markings, they'd mention that!" He paused. "Those pock-marks weren't hereditary, but otherwise a blueskin is like a man who had them. He can't be anything else!"

"Then you think they're human?"

"There's never yet been a case of reverse evolution," said Calhoun. "Maybe Pithecanthropus had a monkey uncle, but no Pithecanthropus ever went monkey."

She turned abruptly away. But she glanced at him often during that day. He continued to busy himself with those activities which make Med Ship life consistent with retained sanity.

Next day she asked without preliminary, "Don't you believe the blueskins planned for the ship with the dead men to arrive at Weald and spread plague there?"

"No," said Calhoun.

"Why?"

"It couldn't possibly work," Calhoun told her. "With only dead men on board, the ship wouldn't arrive at a place where the landing grid could bring it down. So that would be no good. And plague-stricken living men wouldn't try to conceal that they had the plague. They might ask for help, but they'd know they'd instantly be killed on Weald if they were found to be plague victims. So that would be no good, either! No, the ship wasn't intended to land plague on Weald."

"Are you friendly to blueskins?" she asked uncertainly.

"Within reason," said Calhoun, "I am a well-wisher to all the human race. You're slipping, though. When using the word *blueskin* you should say it uncomfortably, as if it were a word no refined person liked to pronounce. You don't. We'll land on Orede tomorrow, by the way. If you ever intend to tell me the truth, there's not much time left."

She bit her lips. Twice, during the remainder of the day, she faced him and opened her mouth as if to speak, and then turned away again. Calhoun shrugged. He had fairly definite ideas about her, by now. He carefully kept them tentative, but no girl born and raised on Weald would willingly go to Orede, with all of 'Weald believing that a shipload of miners preferred death to remaining there. It tied in, like everything else that was unpleasant, to blueskins. Nobody from Weald would dream of landing on Orede! Not now!

A little before the Med Ship was due to break out from overdrive, the girl said very carefully, "You've been very kind. I'd like to thank you. I—I didn't really believe I would live to get to Orede."

Calhoun raised his eyebrows.

"I wish I could tell you everything you want to know," she added regretfully. "I think you're . . . really decent. But some thing . . ."

Calhoun said caustically, "You've told me a great deal. You weren't born on Weald. You weren't raised there. The people of Dara—notice that I don't say blueskins, though they are—the people of Dara have made at least one spaceship since Weald threatened them with extermination. There is probably a new food shortage on Dara now, leading to pure desperation. Most likely it's bad enough to make them risk landing on Orede to kill cattle and freeze beef to help. They've worked out—"

She gasped and sprang to her feet. She snatched out the tiny blaster in her pocket. She pointed it waveringly at him.

"I have to kill you!" she cried desperately. "I—I have to!"

Calhoun reached out. She tugged despairingly at the blaster's trigger. Nothing happened. Before she could realize that she hadn't turned off the safety,

Calhoun twisted the weapon from her fingers. He stepped back.

"Good girl!" he said approvingly. "I'll give this back to you when we land. And thanks. Thanks very much!"

She wrung her hands. Then she stared at him.

"Thanks? When I tried to kill you?"

"Of course!" said Calhoun. "I'd made guesses. I couldn't know that they were right. When you tried to kill me, you confirmed every one. Now, when we land on Orede I'm going to get you to try to put me in touch with your friends. It's going to be tricky, because they must be pretty well scared about that ship. But it's a highly desirable thing to get done!"

He went to the ships' control board and sat down before it.

"Twenty minutes to breakout," he observed.

Murgatroyd peered out of his little cubbyhole. His eyes were anxious. *Tormals* are amiable little creatures. During the days in overdrive, Calhoun had paid less than the usual amount of attention to Murgatroyd, while the girl was fascinating.

They'd made friends, awkwardly on the girl's part, very pleasantly on Murgatroyd's. But only moments ago there had been bitter emotion in the air. Murgatroyd had fled to his cubbyhole to escape it. He was distressed. Now that there was silence again, he peered out unhappily.

"*Chee?*" he queried plaintively. "*Chee-chee-chee?*"

Calhoun said matter-of-factly, "It's all right, Murgatroyd. If we aren't blasted as we try to land, we should be able to make friends with everybody and get something accomplished."

The statement was hopelessly inaccurate.

III

There was no answer from the ground when breakout came and Calhoun drove the Med Ship to a favorable position for a call. He patiently repeated, over and over again, that the Med Ship *Aesclipus Twenty* notified its arrival and requested coordinates for landing. He added that its mass was fifty standard tons and that the purpose of its visit was a planetary health inspection.

But there was no reply. There should have been a crisp description of the direction from the planet's center at which, a certain time so many hours or minutes later, the force-fields of the grid would find it convenient to lock onto and lower the Med Ship. But the communicator remained silent.

"There is a landing grid," said Calhoun, frowning, "and if they're using it to load fresh meat for Dara, from the herds I'm told about, it should be manned. But they don't seem to intend to answer. Maybe they think that if they pretend I'm not here I'll go away."

He reflected, and his frown deepened.

"If I didn't know what I know, I might. So if I land on emergency rockets the blueskins down below may decide that I come from Weald. And in that case it would be reasonable to blast me before I could land and unload some fighting men. On the other hand, no ship from Weald would conceivably land without impassioned assurance that it was safe. It would drop bombs." He turned to the girl. "How many Darians down below?"

She shook her head.

"You don't know," said Calhoun, "or won't tell, yet. But they ought to be told about the arrival of that ship at Weald, and what Weald thinks about it! My guess is that you came to tell them. It isn't likely that Dara gets news directly from Weald. Where were you put ashore from Dara, when you set out to be a spy?"

Her lips parted to speak, but she compressed them tightly. She shook her head again.

"It must have been plenty far away," said Calhoun restlessly. "Your people would have built a ship, and made fine forged papers for it, and they'd travel so far from this part of space that when they landed nobody would think of Dara. They'd use make-up to cover the blue spots, but maybe it was so far away that blueskins had never been heard of!"

Her face looked pinched, but she did not reply.

"Then they'd land half a dozen of you, with a supply of make-up for the blue patches. And you'd separate, and take ships that went various roundabout ways, and arrive on Weald one by one, to see what could be done there to—" He stopped. "When did you find out positively that there wasn't any plague anymore?"

She began to grow pale.

"I'm not a mindreader," said Calhoun. "But it adds up. You're from Dara. You've been on Weald. It's practically certain that there are other . . . agents, if you

like that word better, on Weald. And there hasn't been
a plague on Weald so you people aren't carriers of it.
But you knew it in advance, I think. How'd you learn?
Did a ship in some sort of trouble land there, on
Dara?"

"Y-yes," said the girl. "We wouldn't let it go again.
But the people didn't catch—they didn't die. They
lived—"

She stopped short.

"It's not fair to trap me!" she cried passionately. "It's
not fair!"

"I'll stop," said Calhoun.

He turned to the control-board. The Med Ship was
only planetary diameters from Orede, now, and the
electron telescope showed shining stars in leisurely
motion across its screen. Then a huge, gibbous shining shape appeared, and there were irregular patches
of that muddy color which is seabottom, and varicol-
ored areas which were plains and forests. Also there
were mountains. Calhoun steadied the image and
squinted at it.

"The mine," he observed, "was found by members
of a hunting party, killing wild cattle for sport."

Even a small planet has many millions of square
miles of surface, and a single human installation on
a whole world will not be easy to find by random
search. But there were clues to this one. Men hunting for sport would not choose a tropic nor an arctic
climate to hunt in. So if they found a mineral deposit,
it would have been in a temperate zone.

Cattle would not be found deep in a mountainous terrain. The mine would not be on a prairie. The
settlement on Orede, then, would be near the edge
of mountains, not far from a prairie such as wild
cattle would frequent, and it would be in a temperate
climate.

Forested areas could be ruled out. And there would be a landing grid. Handling only one ship at a time, it might be a very small grid. It could be only hundreds of yards across and less than half a mile high. But its shadow would be distinctive.

Calhoun searched among low mountains near unforested prairie in a temperate zone. He found a speck. He enlarged it manyfold. It was the mine on Orede. There were heaps of tailings. There was something which cast a long, lacy shadow: the landing grid.

"But they don't answer our call," observed Calhoun, "so we go down unwelcomed."

He inverted the Med Ship and the emergency rockets boomed. The ship plunged planetward.

A long time later it was deep in the planet's atmosphere. The noise of its rockets had become thunderous, with air to carry and to reinforce the sound.

"Hold on to something, Murgatroyd," commanded Calhoun. "We may have to dodge some attack."

But nothing came up from below. The Med Ship again inverted itself, and its rockets pointed toward the planet and poured out pencil-thin, blue-white, high-velocity flames. It checked slightly, but continued to descend. It was not directly above the grid.

It swept downward until almost level with the peaks of the mountains in which the mine lay. It tilted again, and swept onward over the mountaintops, and then tilted once more and went racing up the valley in which the landing grid was plainly visible. Calhoun swung it on an erratic course, lest there be opposition.

But there was no sign. Then the rockets bellowed, and the ship slowed its forward motion, hovered momentarily, and settled to solidity outside the framework of the grid. The grid was small, as Calhoun reasoned. But it reached interminably toward the sky.

The rockets cut off. Slender as the flames had been, they'd melted and bored thin drill-holes deep into the soil. Molten rock boiled and bubbled down below. But there seemed no other sound. There was no other motion. There was absolute stillness all around. But when Calhoun switched on the outside microphones a faint, sweet melange of high-pitched chirpings came from tiny creatures hidden under the vegetation of the mountainsides.

Calhoun put a blaster in his pocket and stood up.

"We'll see what it looks like outside," he said with a certain grimness. "I don't quite believe what the vision screens show."

Minutes later he stepped down to the ground from the Med Ship's exit port. The ship had landed perhaps a hundred feet from what once had been a wooden building. In it, ore from the mines was concentrated and the useless tailings carried away by a conveyer belt to make a monstrous pile of broken stone. But there was no longer a building.

Next to it there had been a structure containing an ore-crusher. The massive machinery could still be seen, but the structure was in fragments. Next to that, again, had been the shaft-head shelters of the mine. They also were shattered practically to matchsticks.

The look of the ground about the building sites was simply and purely impossible. It was a mass of hoof-prints. Cattle by thousands and tens of thousands had trampled everything. Cattle had burst in the wooden sides of the buildings. Cattle had piled themselves up against the beams upholding roofs until the buildings collapsed.

Then cattle had gone plunging over the wrecked buildings until there was nothing left but indescribable chaos. Many, many cattle had died in the crush. There were heaps of dead beasts about the metal girders which were the foundation of the landing grid. The air was tainted by the smell of carrion.

The settlement had been destroyed, positively, by stampeded cattle in tens or hundreds of thousands charging blindly through and over and upon it. Senselessly, they'd trampled each other to horrible shapelessness. The mine shaft was not choked, because enormously strong timbers had fallen across and blocked it. But everything else was pure destruction.

Calhoun said evenly, "Clever. Very clever! You can't blame men when beasts stampede. We should accept the evidence that some monstrous herd, making its way through a mountain pass, somehow went crazy and bolted for the plains. This settlement got in the way and it was too bad for the settlement! Everything's explained, except the ship that went to Weald.

"A cattle stampede, yes. Anybody can believe that. But there was a man stampede. Men stampeded into the ship as blindly as the cattle trampled down this little town. The ship stampeded off into space as insanely as the cattle. But a stampede of men and cattle, in the same place? That's a little too much!"

"But what—"

"How," asked Calhoun directly, "do you intend to get in touch with your friends here?"

"I—I don't know," she said, distressed. "But if the ship stays here, they're bound to come and see why. Won't they? Or will they?"

"If they're sane, they won't," said Calhoun. "The one undesirable thing, here, would be human footprints on top of cattle tracks. If your friends are a meat-getting party from Dara, as I believe, they should cover up their tracks, get off-planet as fast as possible, and pray that no signs of their former presence are ever discovered. That would be their best first move, certainly."

"What should I do?" she asked helplessly.

"I'm far from sure. At a guess, and for the moment, probably nothing. I'll work something out. I've got the devil of a job before me, though. I can't spend but so much time here."

"You can leave me here . . ."

He grunted and turned away. It was naturally unthinkable that he should leave another human being on a supposedly uninhabited planet, with the knowledge that it might actually be uninhabited, and the future knowledge that any visitors would have the strongest of possible reasons to hide themselves away.

He believed that there were Darians here, and the girl in the Med Ship, so he also believed, was also a Darian. But any who might be hiding had so much to lose if they were discovered that they might be hundreds or even thousands of miles from anywhere a spaceship would normally land—if they hadn't fled after the incident of the spaceship's departure with its load of doomed passengers.

Considered detachedly, the odds were that there was again a food shortage on Dara; that blueskins, in desperation, had raided or were raiding or would raid the cattle herds of Orede for food to carry back to their home planet; that somehow the miners on Orede had found that they had blueskin neighbors, and died of the consequences of their terror. It was a risky guess to make on such evidence as Calhoun considered he had, but no other guess was possible.

If his guess was right, he was under some obligation to do exactly what he believed the girl considered her mission—to warn all blueskins that Weald would presently try to find them on Orede, when all hell must break loose upon Dara for punishment. But if there were men here, he couldn't leave a written warning for them in default of friendly contact.

They might not find it, and a search party of

Wealdians might. All he could possibly do was try to
make contact and give warning by such means as would
leave no evidence behind that he'd done so. Weald
would consider a warning sure proof of blueskin guilt.

It was not satisfactory to be limited to broadcasts
which might or might not be picked up, and were
unlikely to be acknowledged. But he settled down with
the communicator to make the attempt.

He called first on a GC wave length and form. It
was unlikely that blueskins would use general communication bands to keep in touch with each other, but
it had to be tried. He broadcast, tuned as broadly as
possible, and went up and down the GC spectrum,
repeating his warning painstakingly and listening without hope for a reply.

He did find one spot on the dial where there was
re-radiation of his message, as if from a tuned receiver.
But he could not get a fix on it: nobody might be
listening. He exhausted the normal communication
pattern. Then he broadcast on old-fashioned amplitude
modulation which a modern communicator would not
pick up at all, and which therefore might be used by
men in hiding.

He worked for a long time. Then he shrugged and
gave it up. He'd repeated to absolute tedium the facts
that any Darians—blueskins—on Orede ought to know.
There'd been no answer. And it was all too likely that
if he'd been received, that those who heard him took
his message for a trick to discover if there were any
hearers.

He clicked off at last and stood up, shaking his head.
Suddenly the Med Ship seemed empty. Then he saw
Murgatroyd staring vexedly at the exit port. The inner
door of that small air-lock was closed. The telltale light
said the outer door was not locked. Someone had gone
out quietly. The girl. Of course.

Calhoun said angrily, "How long ago, Murgatroyd?"

"*Chee!*" said Murgatroyd indignantly.

It wasn't an answer, but it showed that Murgatroyd was vexed that he'd been left behind. He and the girl were close friends, now. If she'd left Murgatroyd in the ship when he wanted to go with her, then she wasn't coming back.

Calhoun swore. He made certain she was not in the ship. He flipped the outside-speaker switch and said curtly into the microphone, "Coffee! Murgatroyd and I are having coffee. Will you come back, please?"

He repeated the call, and repeated it again. Multiplied as his voice was by the speakers, she should hear him within a mile. She did not appear. He went to a small and inconspicuous closet and armed himself. A Med Ship man was not ever expected to fight, but there were blast-rifles available for extreme emergency.

When he'd slung a power-pack over his shoulder and reached the air-lock, there was still no sign of his late stowaway. He stood in the air-lock door for long minutes, staring angrily about. Almost certainly she wouldn't be looking in the mountains for men of Dara come here for cattle. He used a pair of binoculars, first at low-magnification to search as wide an area downvalley as possible, and then at highest power to search the most likely routes.

He found a small, bobbing speck beyond a faraway hill crest. It was her head. It went down below the hilltop.

He snapped a command to Murgatroyd, and when the *tormal* was on the ground outside, he locked the port with that combination that nobody but a Med Ship man was at all likely to discover or use.

"She's an idiot," he told Murgatroyd sourly. "Come along! We've got to be idiots too."

He set out in pursuit.

There was blue sky overhead, as was inevitable on any oxygen-atmosphere planet of a Sol-type yellow sun. There were mountains, as is universal in planets whose surfaces rise and fall and fold and bend from the effects of weather or vulcanism. There were plants, as has come about wherever micro-organisms have broken down rock to a state where it can nourish vegetation. And naturally there were animals.

There were even trees of severely practical design, and underbrush and ground-cover equivalent to grass. There was, in short, a perfectly predictable ecological system on Orede. The organic molecules involved in life here would be made up of the same elements in the same combinations as elsewhere where the same conditions of temperature and moisture and sunshine obtained.

It was a distinctly Earthlike world, as it could not help but be, and it was reasonable for cattle to thrive and increase here. Only men's minds kept it from being a place where humans would thrive, too.

But only Calhoun would have considered the splintered settlement a proof of that last.

The girl had a long start. Twice Calhoun came to places where she could have chosen either of two ways onward. Each time he had to determine which she'd followed. That cost time. Then the mountains abruptly ended and a vast undulating plain stretched away to the horizon. There were at least two large masses and many smaller clumps of what could only be animals gathered together. Cattle.

But here the girl was plainly in view. Calhoun increased his stride. He began to gain on her. She did not look behind.

Murgatroyd said, *"Chee!"* in a complaining tone.

"I should have left you behind," agreed Calhoun dourly, "but there was and is a chance I won't get back. You'll have to keep on hiking."

He plodded on. His memory of the terrain around the mining settlement told him that there was no definite destination in the girl's mind. But she was in no such despair as to want deliberately to be lost. She'd guessed, Calhoun believed, that if there were Darians on the planet, they'd keep the landing grid under observation.

If they saw her leave that area and could see that she was alone, they should intercept her to find out the meaning of the Med Ship's landing. Then she could identify herself as one of them and give them the terribly necessary warning of Weald's suspicions.

"But," said Calhoun sourly, "if she's right, they'll have seen me marching after her now, which spoils her scheme. And I'd like to help it, but the way she's going is too dangerous!"

He went down into one of the hollows of the uneven plain. He saw a clump of a dozen or so cattle a little distance away. The bull looked up and snorted. The cows regarded him truculently. Their air was not one of bovine tranquility.

He was up the farther hillside and out of sight before the bull worked himself up to a charge. Then Calhoun suddenly remembered one of the items in the data about cattle he'd looked into just the other day. He felt himself grow pale.

"Murgatroyd!" he said sharply. "We've got to catch up! Fast! Stay with me if you can, but—" he was jog-trotting as he spoke—"even if you get lost I have to hurry!"

He ran fifty paces and walked fifty paces. He ran fifty and walked fifty. He saw her, atop a rolling of the ground. She came to a full stop. He ran. He saw

her turn to retrace her steps. He flung off the safety
of the blast-rifle and let off a roaring blast at the
ground for her to hear.

Suddenly she was fleeing desperately, toward him.
He plunged on. She vanished down into a hollow.
Horns appeared over the hillcrest she'd just left. Cattle
appeared. Four, a dozen, fifteen, twenty! They moved
ominously in her wake.

He saw her again, running frantically over another
upward swell of the prairie. He left off another blast
to guide her. He ran on at top speed with Murgatroyd
trailing anxiously behind. From time to time
Murgatroyd called *"Chee-chee-chee!"* in frightened
pleading not to be abandoned.

More cattle appeared against the horizon. Fifty or
a hundred. They came after the first clump. The first
group of a bull and his harem were moving faster, now.
The girl fled from them, but it is the instinct of beef
cattle on the open range—Calhoun had learned it only
two days before—to charge any human they find on
foot. A mounted man to their dim minds is a creature to be tolerated or fled from, but a human on foot
is to be crushed and stamped and gored.

Those in the lead were definitely charging now, with
heads bent low. The bull charged furiously with shut
eyes, as bulls do, but the cows, many times more
deadly, charged with their eyes wide open and wick-
edly alert, and with a lumbering speed much greater
than the girl could manage.

She came up over the last rise, chalky-white and
gasping, her hair flying, in the last extremity of terror. The nearest of the pursuing cattle were within ten
yards when Calhoun fired from twenty yards beyond.
One creature bellowed as the blast-bolt struck.

It went down and others crashed into it and swept
over it, and more came on. The girl saw Calhoun now,

and ran toward him, panting. He knelt very deliberately and began to check the charge by shooting the leading animals.

He did not succeed. There were more cattle following the first, and more and more behind them. It appeared that all the cattle on the plain joined in the blind and senseless charge. The thudding of hoofs became a mutter and then a rumble and then a growl.

Plunging, clumsy figures rushed past on either side. But horns and heads heaved up over the mound of animals Calhoun had shot. He shot them too. More and more cattle came pounding past the rampart of his victims, but always, it seemed, some elected to climb the heap of their dead and dying fellows, and Calhoun shot and shot . . .

But he split the herd. The foremost animals had been charging a sighted human enemy. Others had followed because it is the instinct of cattle to join their running fellows in whatever crazed urgency they feel. There was a dense, pounding, wailing, grunting, puffing, raising thick and impenetrable clouds of dust which hid everything but galloping beasts going past on either side.

It lasted for minutes. Then the thunder of hoofs diminished. It ended abruptly, and Calhoun and the girl were left alone with the gruesome pile of animals which had divided the charging herd into two parts. They could see the rears of innumerable running animals, stupidly continuing the charge, hardly different, now, from a stampede, whose original objective none remembered.

Calhoun thoughtfully touched the barrel of his blast-rifle and winced at its scorching heat.

"I just realized," he said coldly, "that I don't know your name. What is it?"

"Maril," said the girl. She swallowed. "Th—thank you."

"Maril," said Calhoun, "you are an idiot! It was half-witted at best to go off by yourself. You could have been lost! You could have cost me days of hunting for you, days badly needed for more important matters."

He stopped and took breath. "You may have spoiled what little chance I've got to do something about the plans Weald's already making. You have just acted with the most concentrated folly, and the most magnificent imbecility that you or anybody else could manage!"

He said more bitterly still, "And I had to leave Murgatroyd behind to get to you in time! He was right in the path of that charge!"

He turned away from her and said dourly, "All right! Come on back to the ship. We'll go to Dara. We'd have to, anyhow. But Murgatroyd—"

Then he heard a very small sneeze. Out of a rolling wall of still-roiling dust, Murgatroyd appeared forlornly. He was dust-covered, and draggled, and his tail dropped, and he sneezed again. He moved as if he could barely put one paw before another, but at sight of Calhoun he sneezed yet again and said, *"Chee!"* in a disconsolate voice. Then he sat down and waited for Calhoun to come and pick him up.

When Calhoun did so, Murgatroyd clung to him pathetically and said, *"Chee-chee!"* and again, *"Chee-chee!"* with the intonation of one telling of incredible horrors and disasters endured. And as a matter of fact the escape of a small animal like Murgatroyd was remarkable. He'd escaped the trampling hoofs of at least hundreds of charging animals. Luck must have played a great part in it, but an hysterical agility in dodging must have been required, too.

Calhoun headed back for the valley where the settlement had been, and the Med Ship was. Murgatroyd clung to his neck. The girl Maril followed discouragedly. She was at that age when girls—and men of corresponding type—can grow most passionately devoted to ideals or causes in default of a promising personal romance. When concerned with such causes they become splendidly confident that whatever they decide to do is sensible if only it is dramatic. But Maril was shaken, now.

Calhoun did not speak to her again. He led the way. A mile back toward the mountains, they began to see stragglers from the now-vanished herd. A little farther, those stragglers began to notice them. It would have been a matter of no moment if they'd been domesticated dairy cattle, but these were range cattle gone wild. Twice, Calhoun had to use his blast-rifle to discourage incipient charges by irritated bulls or even more irritated cows. Those with calves darkly suspected Calhoun of designs upon their offspring.

It was a relief to enter the valley again. But it was two miles more to the landing grid with the Med Ship beside it and the reek of carrion in the air.

They were perhaps two hundred feet from the ship when a blast-rifle crashed and its bolt whined past Calhoun so close that he felt the monstrous heat. There had been no challenge. There was no warning. There was simply a shot which came horribly close to ending Calhoun's career in a completely arbitrary fashion.

IV

Five minutes later Calhoun had located one would-be killer behind a mass of splintered planking that once had been a wall. He set the wood afire by a blaster-bolt and then viciously sent other bolts all around the man it had sheltered when he fled from the flames. He could have killed him ten times over, but it was more desirable to open communication. So he missed intentionally.

Maril had cried out that she came from Dara and had word for them, but they did not answer. There were three men with heavy-duty blast-rifles. One was the one Calhoun had burned out of his hiding place. That man's rifle exploded when the flames hit it. Two remained.

One—so Calhoun presently discovered—was working his way behind underbrush to a shelf from which he could shoot down at Calhoun. Calhoun had dropped into a hollow and pulled Maril to cover at the first shot. The second man happily planned to get to a point where he could shoot him like a fish in a barrel.

The third man had fired half a dozen times and then disappeared. Calhoun estimated that he intended to get around to the rear, hoping there was no protection from that direction for Calhoun. It would take some time for him to manage it.

So Calhoun industriously concentrated his fire on the man trying to get above him. He was behind a boulder, not too dissimilar to Calhoun's breastwork. Calhoun set fire to the brush at the point at which the other man aimed. That, then, made his effort useless.

Then Calhoun sent a dozen bolts at the other man's rocky shield. It heated up. Steam rose in a whitish mass and blew directly away from Calhoun. He saw that antagonist flee. He saw him so clearly that he was positive that there was a patch of blue pigment on the right-hand side of the back of his neck.

He grunted and swung to find the third. That man moved through thick undergrowth, and Calhoun set it on fire in a neat pattern of spreading flames. Evidently, these men had had no training in battle tactics with blast-rifles. The third man also had to get away. He did. But something from him arched through the smoke. It fell to the ground directly upwind from Calhoun. White smoke puffed up violently.

It was instinct that made Calhoun react as he did. He jerked the girl Maril to her feet and rushed her toward the Med Ship. Smoke from the flung bomb upwind barely swirled around him and missed Maril altogether. Calhoun, though, got a whiff of something strange, not scorched or burning vegetation at all. He ceased to breathe and plunged onward. In clear air he emptied his lungs and refilled them. They were then halfway to the ship, with Murgatroyd prancing on ahead.

But then Calhoun's heart began to pound furiously.

His muscles twitched and tensed. He felt extraordinary symptoms like an extreme of agitation. He swore, but a Med Ship man would not react to such symptoms as a non-medically trained man would have done. Calhoun was familiar enough with tear gas, used by police on some planets.

But this was different and worse. Even as he helped and urged Maril onward, he automatically considered his sensations, and had it—panic gas. Police did not use it because panic is worse than rioting. Calhoun felt all the physical symptoms of fear and of gibbering terror.

A man whose mind yields to terror experiences certain physical sensations: wildly beating heart, tensed and twitching muscles, and a frantic impulse to convulsive action. A man in whom those physical sensations are induced by other means will, ordinarily, find his mind yielding to terror.

Calhoun couldn't combat his feelings, but his clinical attitude enabled him to act despite them. The three from Weald reached the base of the Med Ship. One of their enemies had lost his rifle and need not be counted. Another had fled from flames and might be ignored for some moments, anyhow. But a blast-bolt struck the ship's metal hull only feet from Calhoun, and he whipped around to the other side and let loose a staccato rat-tat-tat of fire which emptied the rifle of all its charges.

Then he opened the air-lock door, hating the fact that he shook and trembled. He urged the girl and Murgatroyd in. He slammed the outer air-lock door just as another blast-bolt hit.

"They—they don't realize," said Maril desperately. "If they only knew . . ."

"Talk to them, if you like," said Calhoun. His teeth chattered and he raged, because the symptom was of terror he denied.

He pushed a button on the control-board. He pointed to a microphone. He got at an oxygen bottle and inhaled deeply. Oxygen, obviously, should be an antidote for panic, since the symptoms of terror act to increase the oxygenation of the bloodstream and muscles, and to make superhuman exertion possible if necessary.

Breathing ninety-five percent oxygen produced the effect the terror-inspiring gas strove for, so his heart slowed nearly to normal and his body relaxed. He held out his hand and it did not tremble. He'd been affronted to see it shake uncontrollably when he pushed the microphone button for Maril.

He turned to her. She hadn't spoken into the mike.

"They may not be from Dara!" she said shakily. "I just thought! They could be somebody else, maybe criminals who planned to raid the mine for a shipload of its ore."

"Nonsense," said Calhoun. "I saw one of them clearly enough to be sure. But they're skeptical characters. I'm afraid there may be more on the way here from wherever they keep themselves. Anyhow, now we know some of them are in hearing. I'll take advantage of that and we'll go on."

He took the microphone. An instant later his voice boomed in the stillness outside the ship, cutting through the thin shrill whirring of invisible small creatures.

"This is the Med Ship *Aesclipus Twenty*," said Calhoun's voice, amplified to a shout. "I left Weald four days ago, one day after the cargo ship from here arrived with everybody on board dead. On Weald they don't know how it happened, but they suspect blueskins. Sooner or later they'll search here.

"Get away! Cover up your tracks! Hide all signs that you've ever been here! Get the hell away, fast! One

more warning: There's talk of fusion-bombing Dara.
They're scared! If they find your traces, they'll be still
more scared. So cover up your tracks and get away
from here!"

The many-times-multiplied voice rolled and echoed
among the hills. But it was very clear. Where it could
be heard it could be understood, and it could be heard
for miles.

But there was no response to it. Calhoun waited a
reasonable time. Then he shrugged and seated himself at the control-board.

"It isn't easy," he observed, "to persuade desperate
men that they've outsmarted themselves. Hold hard,
Murgatroyd!"

The rockets bellowed. Then there was a tremendous
noise to end all noises, and the ship began to climb.
It sped up and up and up. By the time it was out of
atmosphere it had velocity enough to coast to clear
space and Calhoun cut the rockets altogether.

He busied himself with those astrogational chores
which began with orienting oneself to galactic directions
after leaving a planet which rotates at its own individual
speed. Then one computes the overdrive course to
another planet, from the respective coordinates of the
world one is leaving and the one one aims for.

Then, in this case at any rate, there was the very
finicky task of picking out a fourth-magnitude star of
whose planets one was his destination. He aimed for
it with ultra-fine precision.

"Overdrive coming," he said presently. "Hold on!"

Space reeled. There was nausea and giddiness and
a horrible sensation of falling in a wildly unlikely spiral.
Then stillness, and solidity, and the blackness outside
the Med Ship. The little craft was in overdrive again.

After a long while, the girl Maril said uneasily, "I
don't know what you plan now—"

"I'm going to Dara," said Calhoun. "On Orede I tried to get the blueskins there to get going, fast. Maybe I succeeded. I don't know. But this thing's been mishandled! Even if there's a famine people shouldn't do things out of desperation. Being desperate jogs the brain off-center. One doesn't think straight!"

"I know now that I was . . . very foolish."

"Forget it," commanded Calhoun. "I wasn't talking about you. Here I run into a situation that the Med Service should have caught and cleaned up generations ago. But it's not only a Med Service obligation; it's a current mess! Before I could begin to get at the basic problem, those idiots on Orede—it'd happened before I reached Weald! An emotional explosion triggered by a ship full of dead men that nobody intended to kill."

Maril shook her head.

"Those Darian characters," said Calhoun, annoyed, "shouldn't have gone to Orede in the first place. If they went there, they should at least have stayed on a continent where there were no people from Weald digging a mine and hunting cattle for sport on their off days. They could be spotted. I believe they were.

"And again, if it had been a long way from the mine installation, they could probably have wiped out the people who sighted them before they could get back with the news. But it looks like miners saw men hunting, and got close enough to see they were blueskins, and then got back to the mine with the news."

She waited for him to explain.

"I know I'm guessing, but it fits," he said distastefully. "So something had to be done. Either the mining settlement had to be wiped out or the story that blueskins were on Orede had to be discredited. The blueskins tried for both. They used panic gas on a herd of cattle and it made them crazy and they charged the settlement like the four-footed lunatics they are!

"And the blueskins used panic gas on the settlement itself as the cattle went through. It should have settled the whole business nicely. After it was over every man in the settlement would believe he'd been out of his head for a while, and he'd have the crazy state of the settlement to think about.

"He wouldn't be sure of what he'd seen or heard beforehand. They might try to verify the blueskin story later, but they wouldn't believe anything with certainty. It should have worked!"

Again she waited.

"Unfortunately, when the miners panicked, they stampeded into the ship. Also unfortunately, panic gas got into the ship with them. So they stayed panicked while the astrogator—in panic!—took off. They headed for Weald and threw on the overdrive—which would be set for Weald anyhow—because that would be the fastest way to run away from whatever he imagined he feared. But he and all the men on the ship were still crazy with panic from the gas they kept breathing until they died!"

Silence. After a long interval, Maril asked, "You don't think the Darians intended to kill?"

"I think they were stupid!" said Calhoun angrily. "Somebody's always urging the police to use panic gas in case of public tumult. But it's too dangerous. Nobody knows what one man will do in a panic. Take a hundred or two or three and panic them all, and there's no limit to their craziness! The whole thing was handled wrong."

"But you don't blame them?"

"For being stupid, yes," said Calhoun fretfully. "But if I'd been in their place, perhaps—"

"Where were you born?" asked Maril suddenly.

Calhoun jerked his head around. "No! Not where you're guessing, or hoping. Not on Dara. Just because I act as if Darians were human doesn't mean I have to be one. I'm a Med Service man, and I'm acting as I think I should." His tone became exasperated.

"Dammit, I'm supposed to deal with health situations, actual and possible causes of human deaths! And if Weald thinks it finds proof that blueskins are in space again and caused the death of Wealdians, it won't be healthy. They're halfway set anyhow to drop fusion-bombs on Dara to wipe it out."

Maril said fiercely, "They might as well drop bombs. It'll be quicker than starvation, at least!"

Calhoun looked at her, more exasperated than before.

"It is a crop failure again?" he demanded. When she nodded he said bitterly, "Famine conditions already?" When she nodded again he said drearily, "And of course famine is the great-grandfather of health problems. And that's right in my lap with all the rest!"

He stood up. Then he sat down again.

"I'm tired," he said flatly. "I'd like to get some sleep. Would you mind taking a book or something and going into the other cabin? Murgatroyd and I would like a little relaxation from reality. With luck, if I go to sleep, I may only have a nightmare. It'll be a terrific improvement on what I'm in now."

Alone in the control-compartment, he tried to relax, but it was not possible. He flung himself into a comfortable chair and brooded. There is brooding and brooding. It can be a form of wallowing in self-pity, engaged in for emotional satisfaction. But it can be, also, a way of bringing out unfavorable factors in a situation. A man in an optimistic mood can ignore them. But no awkward situation is likely to be remedied while any of its elements are neglected.

Calhoun dourly considered the situation of the
people of the planet Dara, which it was his job as
a Med Service man to remedy or at least improve.
Now there was famine on Dara for the second time,
and they were of no mind to starve quietly. There
was food on the planet Orede, monstrous herds of
cattle without owners. It was natural enough for
Darians to build a ship or ships and try to bring food
back to its starving people. But that desperately
necessary enterprise had now roused Weald to a
frenzy of apprehension.

Weald was, if possible, more hysterically afraid of
blueskins than ever before, and even more implaca-
bly the enemy of the starving planet's population.
Weald itself prospered. Ironically, it had such an excess
of foodstuffs that it stored them in unneeded spaceships in orbits about itself.

Hundreds of thousands of tons of grain circled
Weald in sealed-tight hulks, while the people of Dara
starved and only dared try to steal—if it could be called
stealing—some of the innumerable wild cattle of
Orede.

The blueskins on Orede could not trust Calhoun,
so they pretended not to hear. Or maybe they didn't
hear. They'd been abandoned and betrayed by all of
humanity off their world. They'd been threatened and
oppressed by guardships in orbit about them, ready
to shoot down any spacecraft they might send aloft . . .

So Calhoun brooded, while Murgatroyd presently
yawned and climbed to his cubbyhole and curled up
to sleep with his furry tail carefully adjusted over his
nose.

A long time later Calhoun heard small sounds which
were not normal on a Med Ship in overdrive. They
were not part of the random noises carefully gener-
ated to keep the silence of the ship endurable. Calhoun

raised his head. He listened sharply. No sound could come from outside.

He knocked on the door of the sleeping cabin. The noises stopped instantly.

"Come out," he commanded through the door.

"I'm—I'm all right," said Maril's voice. But it was not quite steady. She paused. "Did I make a noise? I was having a bad dream."

"I wish," said Calhoun, "that you'd tell me the truth just occasionally. Come out, please!"

There were stirrings. After a little it opened and Maril appeared. She looked as if she'd been crying. She said, quickly, "I probably look queer, but it's because I was asleep."

"To the contrary," said Calhoun, fuming. "You've been lying awake crying. I don't know why. I've been out here wishing I could, because I'm frustrated. But since you aren't asleep maybe you can help me with my job. I've figured some things out. For some others I need facts. Will you give them to me?"

She swallowed. "I'll try."

"Coffee?" he asked.

Murgatroyd popped his head out of his miniature sleeping cabin.

"*Chee?*" he asked interestedly.

"Go back to sleep!" snapped Calhoun.

He began to pace back and forth.

"I need to know something about the pigment patches," he said jerkily. "Maybe it sounds crazy to think of such things now—first things first, you know. But this is a first thing! So long as Darians don't look like the people of other worlds, they'll be believed to be different. If they look repulsive, they'll be believed to be evil.

"Tell me about those patches. They're different sizes and different shapes and they appear in different places. You've none on your face or hands, anyhow."

"I haven't any at all," said the girl reservedly.

"I thought—"

"Not everybody," she said defensively. "Nearly, yes. But not all. Some people don't have them. Some people are born with bluish splotches on their skin, but they fade out while they're children. When they grow up they're just like the people of Weald or any other world. And their children never have them."

Calhoun stared.

"You couldn't possibly be proved to be a Darian, then?"

She shook her head. Calhoun remembered, and started the coffee.

"When you left Dara," he said, "you were carried a long, long way, to some planet where they'd practically never heard of Dara, and where the name meant nothing. You could have settled there, or anywhere else and forgotten about Dara. But you didn't. Why not, since you're not a blueskin?"

"But I am!" she said fiercely. "My parents, my brothers and sister, and Korvan—"

Then she bit her lip. Calhoun took note but did not comment on the name she'd mentioned.

"Then your parents had the splotches fade, so you never had them," he said absorbedly. "Something like that happened on Tralee, once. There's a virus, a whole group of virus particles. Normally we humans are immune to them. One has to be in terrifically bad physical condition for them to take hold and produce whatever effects they do. But once they're established they're passed on from mother to child. And when they die out it's during childhood, too."

He poured coffee for the two of them. Murgatroyd

swung down to the floor and said, impatiently, *"Chee! Chee! Chee!"*

Calhoun absently filled Murgatroyd's tiny cup and handed it to him.

"But this is marvelous!" he said exuberantly. "The blue patches appeared after the plague, didn't they? After people recovered—when they recovered?"

Maril stared at him. His mind was filled with strictly professional considerations. He was not talking to her as a person. She was purely a source of information.

"So I'm told," said Maril reservedly. "Are there any more humiliating questions you want to ask?"

He gaped at her. Then he said ruefully, "I'm stupid, Maril, but you're touchy. There's nothing personal—"

"There is to me!" she said fiercely. "I was born among blueskins, and they're of my blood, and they're hated and I'd have been killed on Weald if I'd been known as . . . what I am! And there's Korvan, who arranged for me to be sent away as a spy and advised me to do just what you said: abandon my home world and everybody I care about! Including him! It's personal to me!"

Calhoun wrinkled his forehead helplessly.

"I'm sorry," he repeated. "Drink your coffee!"

"I don't want it," she said bitterly. "I'd like to die!"

"If you stay around where I am," Calhoun told her, "you may get your wish. All right, there'll be no more questions."

She turned and moved toward the door to the cabin. Calhoun looked after her.

"Maril."

"What?"

"Why were you crying?"

"You wouldn't understand," she said evenly.

Calhoun shrugged his shoulders almost up to his

ears. He was a professional man. In his profession he
was not incompetent. But there is no profession in
which a really competent man tries to understand
women. Calhoun, annoyed, had to let fate or chance
or disaster take care of Maril's personal problems. He
had larger matters to cope with.

But he had something to work on, now. He hunted
busily in the reference tapes. He came up with an
explicit collection of information on exactly the subject he needed. He left the control-room to go down
into the storage areas of the Med Ship's hull. He found
an ultra frigid storage box, whose contents were kept
at the temperature of liquid air.

He donned thick gloves, used a special set of tongs,
and extracted a tiny block of plastic in which a sealed-
tight phial of glass was embedded. It frosted instantly
he took it out, and when the storage box was closed
again the block was covered with a thick and opaque
coating of frozen moisture.

He went back to the control-room and pulled
down the panel which made available a small-scale
but surprisingly adequate biological laboratory. He set
the plastic block in a container which would raise
it very, very gradually to a specific temperature and
hold it there. It was, obviously, a living culture from
which any imaginable quantity of the same culture
could be bred. Calhoun set the apparatus with great
exactitude.

"This," he told Murgatroyd, "may be a good day's
work. Now I think I can rest."

Then, for a long while, there was no sound or
movement in the Med Ship. The girl may have slept,
or maybe not. Calhoun lay relaxed in a chair which
at the touch of a button became the most comfortable of sleeping places. Murgatroyd remained in his
cubbyhole, his tail curled over his nose.

There were comforting, unheard, easily dismissable murmurings now and again. They kept the feeling of life alive in the ship. But for such infinitesimal stirrings of sound, carefully recorded for this exact purpose, the feel of the ship would have been that of a tomb.

But it was quite otherwise when another ship-day began with the taped sounds of morning activities as faint as echoes but nevertheless establishing an atmosphere of their own.

Calhoun examined the plastic block and its contents. He read the instruments which had cared for it while he slept. He put the block—no longer frosted—in the culture microscope and saw its enclosed, infinitesimal particles of life in the process of multiplying on the food that had been frozen with them when they were reduced to the spore condition. He beamed. He replaced the block in the incubation oven and faced the day cheerfully.

Maril greeted him with great reserve. They breakfasted, with Murgatroyd eating from his own platter on the floor, a tiny cup of coffee alongside.

"I've been thinking," said Maril evenly. "I think I can get you a hearing for whatever ideas you may have to help Dara."

"Kind of you," murmured Calhoun.

In theory, a Med Service man had all the authority needed for this or any other emergency. The power to declare a planet in quarantine, so cutting it off from all interstellar commerce, should be enough to force cooperation from any world's government. But in practice Calhoun had exactly as much power as he could exercise.

And Weald could not think straight where blueskins were concerned, and certainly the authorities on Dara could not be expected to be level-headed. They had a history of isolation and outlawry, and long experience of being regarded as less than human. In cold fact, Calhoun had no power at all.

"May I ask whose influence you'll exert?" asked Calhoun.

"There's a man," said Maril reservedly, "who thinks a great deal of me. I don't know his present official position, but he was certain to become prominent. I'll tell him how you've acted up to now, and your attitude, and of course that you're Med Service. He'll be glad to help you, I'm sure."

"Splendid!" said Calhoun, nodding. "That will be Korvan."

She stared. "How did you know?"

"Intuition," said Calhoun dryly. "All right. I'll count on him."

But he did not. He worked in the tiny biological lab all that ship-day and all the next. The girl was very quiet. Murgatroyd tried to enter into pretended conversation with her, but she was not able to match his pretense.

On the ship-day after, the time for breakout approached. While the ship was practically a world all by itself, it was easy to look forward with confidence to the future. But when contact and, in a fashion, conflict with other and larger worlds loomed nearer, prospects seemed less bright. Calhoun had definite plans, now, but there were so many ways in which they could be frustrated.

Calhoun sat down at the control-board and watched the clock.

"I've got things lined up," he told Maril, "if only they work out. If I can make somebody on Dara listen, which is unlikely, and follow my advice, which they probably won't; and if Weald doesn't get the ideas it probably will get; and isn't doing what I suspect it is—why, maybe something can be done."

"I'm sure you'll do your best," said Maril politely.

Calhoun managed to grin. He watched the clock. There was no sensation attached to overdrive travel except at the beginning and the end. It was now time for the end. He might find most anything having happened. His plans might immediately be seen to be hopeless. Weald could have sent ships to Dara, or Dara might be in such a state of desperation . . .

As it turned out, Dara was desperate. The Med Ship came out nearly a light-month from the sun about which the planet Dara revolved. Calhoun went into a short hop toward it. Then Dara was on the other side of the blazing yellow star. It took time to reach it.

He called down, identifying himself and the ship and asking for coordinates so his ship could be brought to ground. There was confusion, as if the request were so unusual that the answers were not ready. The grid, too, was on the planet's night side. Presently the ship was locked onto by the grid's force-fields. It went downward.

Calhoun saw that Maril sat tensely, twisting her fingers within each other, until the ship actually touched ground.

Then he opened the exit port—and faced armed men in the darkness, with blast-rifles trained on him. There was a portable cannon trained on the Med Ship itself.

"Come out!" rasped a voice. "If you try anything you get blasted! Your ship and its contents are seized by the planetary government!"

V

It seemed that the smell of hunger was in the air. The armed men were emaciated. Lights came on, and stark, harsh shadows lay black upon the ground. Calhoun's captors were uniformed, but the uniforms hung loosely upon them. Where the lights struck upon their faces, their cheeks were hollow. They were cadaverous. And there were the splotches of pigment of which Calhoun had heard.

The man nearest the Med Ship's port had a monstrous, irregular dull-blue marking over half of one side of his face and up upon his forehead. The man next to him had a blue throat. The next man again was less marked, but his left ear was blue and there was what seemed a splashing of the same color on the skin under his hair.

The leader of the truculent group—it might have been a firing squad—made an imperious gesture with his hand. It was blue, except for two fingers which in the glaring illumination seemed whiter than white.

"Out!" said that man savagely. "We're taking over

your stock of food. You'll get your share of it, like everybody else, but—"

Maril spoke over Calhoun's shoulder. She uttered a cryptic sentence or two. It should have amounted to identification but there was skepticism in the armed party.

"Oh, you're one of us, eh?" said the guard leader sardonically. "You'll have a chance to prove that. Come out of there!"

Calhoun spoke abruptly. "This is a Med Ship," he said. "There are medicines and bacterial culture inside it. They shouldn't be meddled with. Here on Dara you've had enough of plagues!"

The man with the blue hand said as sardonically as before, "I said the government was taking over your ship! It won't be looted. But you're not taking a full cargo of food away. In fact, it's not likely you're leaving."

"And I want to speak to someone in authority," snapped Calhoun. "We've just come from Weald." He felt bristling hatred all about him as he named Weald. "There's tumult there. They're talking about dropping fusion-bombs here. It's important that I talk to somebody with the authority to take a few sensible precautions!"

He descended to the ground. There was a panicky *"Chee! Chee!"* from behind him, and Murgatroyd came dashing to swarm up his body and cling apprehensively to his neck.

"What's that?"

"A *tormal*," said Calhoun. "He's not a pet. Your medical men will know something about him. This is a Med Ship and I'm a Med Ship man, and he's an important member of the crew. He's a Med Ship *tormal* and he stays with me!"

The man with the blue hand said harshly, "There's somebody waiting to ask you questions. Here!"

A ground-car came rolling out from the side of the landing-grid enclosure. The ground-car ran on wheels, and wheels were not much used on modern worlds. Dara was behind the times in more ways than one.

"This car will take you to Defense and you can tell them anything you want. But don't try to sneak back in this ship. It'll be guarded."

The ground-car was enclosed, with room for a driver and the three from the Med Ship. But armed men festooned themselves about its exterior and it went bumping and rolling to the massive ground-layer girders of the grid. It rolled out under them and onto a paved highway. It picked up speed.

There were buildings on either side of the road, but few showed lights. This was night, and the men at the landing grid had set a pattern of hunger, so that the silence and the dark buildings did not seem a sign of tranquility and sleep, but of exhaustion and despair.

The highway lamps were few, by comparison with other inhabited worlds, and the ground-car needed lights of its own to guide its driver over a paved surface that needed repair. By those moving lights other depressing things could be seen: untidiness, buildings not kept up to perfection, evidences of apathy, the road, which hadn't been cleaned lately, litter here and there.

Even the fact that there were no stars added to the feeling of wretchedness and gloom and, ultimately, of hunger.

Maril spoke nervously to the driver.

"The famine isn't any better?"

He moved his head in negation, but did not speak. There was a splotch of blue pigment at the back of his neck. It extended upward into his hair.

"I left two years ago," said Maril. "It was just beginning then. Rationing hadn't started."

The driver said evenly, "There's rationing now."

The car went on and on. A vast open space appeared ahead. Lights about its perimeter seemed few and pale.

"Everything seems worse. Even the lights."

"Using all the power," said the driver, "to warm up ground to grow crops where it ought to be winter. Not doing too well, either."

Calhoun knew, somehow, that Maril moistened her lips.

"I was sent," she explained to the driver, "to go ashore on Trent and then make my way to Weald. I mailed reports of what I found out back to Trent. Somebody got them back to here whenever it was possible."

The driver said, "Everybody knows the man on Trent disappeared. Maybe he got caught, maybe somebody saw him without make-up. Or maybe he just quit being one of us. What's the difference? No use!"

Calhoun found himself wincing a little. The driver was not angry. He was hopeless. But men should not despair. They shouldn't accept hostility from those about them as a device of fate for their destruction.

Maril said quickly to Calhoun, "You understand? Dara's a heavy-metals planet. There aren't many light elements in our soil. Potassium is scarce. So our ground isn't very fertile. Before the plague we traded metals and manufactured products for imports of food and potash. But since the plague we've had no off-planet commerce. We've been quarantined."

"I gathered as much," said Calhoun. "It was up to Med Service to see that that didn't happen. It's up to Med Service now to see that it stops."

"Too late now for anything," said the driver. "Whatever Med Service may be! They're talking about cutting down our population so there'll be food enough for some to live. There are two questions about it. One is who's to be kept alive, and the other is why."

The ground-car aimed now for a cluster of faintly
brighter lights on the far side of the great open space.
They enlarged as they grew nearer. Maril said hesitantly, "There was someone, Korvan—" Calhoun didn't
catch the rest of the name. Maril said hesitantly, "He
was working on food plants. I thought he might accomplish something . . ."

The driver said caustically, "Sure. Everybody's heard
about him. He came up with a wonderful thing! He
and his outfit worked out a way to process weeds so
they can be eaten. And they can. Yo can fill your belly
and not feel hungry, but it's like eating hay. You starve
just the same. He's still working. Head of a government division."

The ground-car passed through a gate. It stopped
before a lighted door. The armed men hanging to its
outside dropped off. They watched Calhoun closely as
he stepped out with Murgatroyd riding on his shoulder.

Minutes later they faced a hastily summoned group
of officials of the Darian government. For a ship to
land on Dara was so remarkable an event that it called
practically for a cabinet meeting. And Calhoun noted
that they were no better fed than the guards at the
spaceport.

They regarded Calhoun and Maril with oddly burning eyes. It was, of course, because the two of them
showed no signs of hunger. They obviously had not
been on short rations. Darians had this, now, to
increase a hatred which was inevitable anyhow, directed
at all peoples off their own pl net.

"My name is Calhoun," said Calhoun briskly. "I've
the usual Med Service credentials. Now—"

He did not wait to be questioned. He told them
of the appalling state of things in the Twelfth Sector
of the Med Service, so that men had been borrowed
from other sectors to remedy the intolerable, and he

was one of them. He told of his arrival at Weald and what had happened there, from the excessively cautious insistence that he prove he was not a Darian, to the arrival of the death-ship from Orede.

He was giving them the news affecting them, as they had not heard it before. He went on to tell of his stop at Orede and his purpose, and his encounter with the men he found there. When he finished there was silence. He broke it.

"Now," he said, "Maril's an agent of yours. She can add to what I've told you. I'm Med Service. I have a job to do here to carry out what wasn't done before. I should make a planetary health inspection and make recommendations for the improvement of the state of things. I'll be glad if you'll arrange for me to talk to your health officials. Things look bad, and something should be done."

Someone laughed without mirth.

"What will you recommend for long-continued undernourishment?" he asked derisively. "That's our health problem!"

"I recommend food," said Calhoun.

"Where'll you fill the prescription?"

"I've the answer to that, too," said Calhoun curtly. "I'll want to talk to any space pilots you've got. Get your astrogators together and I think they'll approve my idea."

The silence was totally skeptical.

"Orede—"

"Not Orede," said Calhoun. "Weald will be hunting that planet over for Darians. If they find any, they'll drop bombs here."

"Our only space pilots," said a tall man, presently, "are on Orede now. If you've told the truth, they'll probably head back because of your warning. They should bring meat."

His mouth worked peculiarly, and Calhoun knew that it was at the thought of food.

"Which," said another man sharply, "goes to the hospitals! I haven't tasted meat in two years."

"Nobody has," growled another man still. "But here's this man Calhoun. I'm not convinced he can work magic, but we can find out if he lies. Put a guard on his ship. Otherwise let our health men give him his head. They'll find out if he's from this Medical Service he tells of. And this Maril . . ."

"I can be identified," said Maril. "I was sent to gather information and sent it in secret writing to one of us on Trent. I have a family here. They'll know me! And I—there was someone who was working on foods, and I believe he made it possible to use . . . all sorts of vegetation for food. He will identify me."

Someone laughed harshly.

Maril swallowed.

"I'd like to see him," she repeated. "And my family."

Some of the blue-splotched men turned away. A broad-shouldered man said bluntly, "Don't look for them to be glad to see you. And you'd better not show yourself in public. You've been well fed. You'll be hated for that."

Maril began to cry. Murgatroyd said bewilderedly, *"Chee! Chee!"*

Calhoun held him close. There was confusion. And Calhoun found the Minister of Health at hand. He looked most harried of all the officials gathered to question Calhoun. He proposed that he get a look at the hospital situation right away.

It wasn't practical. With all the population on half rations or less, when night came people needed to sleep. Most people, indeed, slept as many hours out of the traditional twenty-four as they could manage.

It was much more pleasant to sleep than to be awake and constantly nagged at by continued hunger.

And there was the matter of simple decency. Continuous gnawing hunger had an embittering effect upon everyone. Quarrelsomeness was a common experience. And people who would normally be the leaders of opinion felt shame because they were obsessed by thoughts of food. It was best when people slept.

Still, Calhoun was in the hospitals by daybreak. What he found moved him to savage anger. There were too many sick children. In every case undernourishment contributed to their sickness. And there was not enough food to make them well. Doctors and nurses denied themselves food to spare it for their patients. And most of that self-denial was doubtless voluntary, but it would not be discreet for anybody on Dara to look conspicuously better fed than his fellows.

Calhoun brought out hormones and enzymes and medicaments from the Med Ship while the guard in the ship looked on. He demonstrated the processes of synthesis and autocatalysis that enabled such small samples to be multiplied indefinitely. He was annoyed by a clamorous appetite. There were some doctors who ignored the irony of medical techniques being taught to cure nonnutritional disease, when everybody was half-fed, or less. They approved of Calhoun. They even approved of Murgatroyd when Calhoun explained his function.

The tragedy for Dara was, of course, that no Med Ship had come to Dara three generations ago, when the Dara plague raged. Worse, after the plague Weald was able to exert pressure which only a criminally incompetent Med Service director would have permitted. But criminal incompetence and its consequences was what Calhoun had been loaned to Sector Twelve to help remedy. He was not at ease, though. No ship arrived from Orede to bear out his account of an attempt to get that lonely world evacuated before Weald discovered it had blueskins on it. Maril had vanished, to visit or return to her family, or perhaps to consult with the mysterious Korvan who'd arranged for her to leave Dara to be a spy, and had advised her simply to make a new life somewhere else, abandoning a famine-ridden, despised, and outcaste world.

Calhoun had learned of two achievements the same Korvan had made for his world. Neither was remarkably constructive. He'd offered to prove the value of the second by dying of it. Which might make him a very admirable character, or he could have a passion for martyrdom, which is much more common than most people think. In two days Calhoun was irritable enough from unaccustomed hunger to suspect the worst of him.

Meanwhile Calhoun worked doggedly; in the hospitals while the patients were awake and in the Med Ship, under guard, afterward. He had hunger cramps now, but he tested a plastic cube with a thriving biological culture in it.

He worked at increasing the store of it. He'd snipped samples of pigmented skin from dead patients in the hospitals, and examined the pigmented areas, and very, very painstakingly verified a theory. It took an electron microscope to do it, but he found a virus in the blue patches which matched the type discovered on Tralee.

The Tralee viruses had effects which were passed on from mother to child, and heredity had been charged with the observed results of quasi-living viral particles. And then Calhoun very, very carefully introduced into a virus culture the material he had been growing in a plastic cube. He watched what happened.

He was satisfied, so much so that immediately

afterward he yawned and yawned and barely managed to stagger off to bed. The watching guard in the Med Ship watched him in amazement.

That night the ship from Orede came in, packed with frozen bloody carcasses of cattle. Calhoun knew nothing of it. But next morning Maril came back. There were shadows under her eyes and her expression was of someone who has lost everything that had meaning in her life.

"I'm all right," she insisted, when Calhoun commented. "I've been visiting my family. I've seen Korvan. I'm quite all right."

"You haven't eaten any better than I have," Calhoun observed.

"I couldn't!" admitted Maril. "My sisters, my little sisters so thin . . . There's rationing for everybody and it's all efficiently arranged. They even had rations for me. But I couldn't eat. I gave most of my food to my sisters and they—they squabbled over it!"

Calhoun said nothing. There was nothing to say. Then she said, in a no less desolate tone, "Korvan said I was foolish to come back."

"He could be right," said Calhoun.

"But I had to!" protested Maril. "And now I—I've been eating all I wanted to, in Weald and in the ship, and I'm ashamed because they're half-starved and I'm not. And when you see what hunger does to them . . . It's terrible to be half-starved and not able to think of anything but food!"

"I hope," said Calhoun, "to do something about that. If I can get hold of an astrogator or two—"

"The ship that was on Orede came in during the night," Maril told him shakily. "It was loaded with frozen meat, but one load's not enough to make a difference on a whole planet. And if Weald hunts for us on Orede, we daren't go back for more meat."

She said abruptly, "There are some prisoners. They were miners. They were crowded out of the ship. The Darians who'd stampeded the cattle took them prisoners. They had to!"

"True," said Calhoun. "It wouldn't have been wise to leave Wealdians around on Orede with their throats cut. Or living, either, to tell about a rumor of blueskins. Even if their throats will be cut now. Is that the program?"

Maril shivered.

"No. They'll be put on short rations like everybody else. And people will watch them. The Wealdians expect to die of plague any minute because they've been with Darians. So people look at them and laugh. But it's not very funny."

"It's natural," said Calhoun, "but perhaps lacking in charity. Look there! How about those astrogators? I need them for a job I have in mind."

Maril wrung her hands.

"C—come here," she said in a low tone.

There was an armed guard in the control-room of the ship. He'd watched Calhoun a good part of the previous day as Calhoun performed his mysterious work. He'd been off-duty and now was on duty again. He was bored. So long as Calhoun did not touch the control-board, though, he was uninterested. He didn't even turn his head when Maril led the way into the other cabin and slid the door shut.

"The astrogators are coming," she said swiftly. "They'll bring some boxes with them. They'll ask you to instruct them so they can handle our ship better. They lost themselves coming back from Orede. No, they didn't lose themselves, but they lost time, enough time almost to make an extra trip for meat. They need to be experts. I'm to come along, so they can be sure that what you teach them is what you've been doing right along."

Calhoun said, "Well?"

"They're crazy!" said Maril vehemently. "They knew Weald would do something monstrous sooner or later. But they're going to try to stop it by being more monstrous sooner! Not everybody agrees, but there are enough. So they want to use your ship—it's faster in overdrive and so on. And they'll go to Weald in this ship and—they say they'll give Weald something to keep it busy without bothering us!"

Calhoun said dryly, "This pays me off for being too sympathetic with blueskins! But if I'd been hungry for a couple of years, and was despised to boot by the people who kept me hungry, I suppose I might react the same way. No," he said curtly as she opened her lips to speak again, "don't tell me the trick. Considering everything, there's only one trick it could be. But I doubt profoundly that it would work. All right."

He slid the door back and returned to the control-room. Maril followed him. He said detachedly, "I've been working on a problem outside of the food one. It isn't the time to talk about it right now, but I think I've solved it."

Maril turned her head, listening. There were footsteps on the tarmac outside the ship. Both doors of the air-lock were open. Four men came in. They were young men who did not look quite as hungry as most Darians, but there was a reason for that. Their leader introduced himself and the others. They were the astrogators of the ship Dara had built to try to bring food from Orede. They were not, said their self-appointed leader, good enough. They'd overshot their destination. They came out of overdrive too far off line. They needed instruction.

Calhoun nodded, and observed that he'd been asking for them. They were, of course, blueskins. On one the only visible disfigurement was a patch of blue upon his wrist. On another the appearance of a blue birth-mark appeared beside his eye and went back and up his temple. A third had a white patch on his temple, with all the rest of his face a dull blue. The fourth had blue fingers on one hand.

"We've got orders," said their leader, steadily, "to come on board and learn from you how to handle this ship. It's better than the one we've got."

"I asked for you," repeated Calhoun. "I've an idea I'll explain as we go along . . . Those boxes?"

Someone was passing in iron boxes through the air-lock. One of the four very carefully brought them inside.

"They're rations," said a second young man. "We don't go anywhere without rations, except Orede."

"Orede, yes. I think we were shooting at each other there," said Calhoun pleasantly. "Weren't we?"

"Yes," said the young man.

He was neither cordial nor antagonistic. He was impassive. Calhoun shrugged.

"Then we can take off immediately. Here's the communicator and there's the button. You might call the grid and arrange for us to be lifted."

The young man seated himself at the control-board. Very professionally, he went through the routine of preparing to lift by landing grid, which routine has not changed in two hundred years. He went briskly ahead until the order to lift. Then Calhoun stopped him.

"Hold it!"

He pointed to the air-lock. Both doors were open. The young man at the control-board flushed vividly. One of the others closed and dogged the doors.

The ship lifted. Calhoun watched with seeming negligence. But he found occasion for a dozen corrections of procedure. This was presumably a training voyage of his own suggestion. Therefore, when the blueskin pilot would have flung the Med Ship into undirected overdrive, Calhoun grew stern. He insisted on a destination. He suggested Weald.

The young men glanced at each other and accepted the suggestion. He made the acting pilot look up the intrinsic brightness of its sun and measure its apparent brightness from just off Dara. He made him estimate the change in brightness to be expected after so many hours in overdrive, if one broke out to measure.

The first blueskin student pilot ended a Calhoun-determined tour of duty with more respect for Calhoun than he'd had at the beginning. The second was anxious to show up better than the first. Calhoun drilled him in the use of brightness-charts, by which the changes in apparent brightness of stars between overdrive hops could be correlated with angular changes to give a three-dimensional picture of the nearer heavens.

It was a highly necessary art which had not been worked out on Dara, and the prospective astrogators became absorbed in this and other fine points of space-piloting. They'd done enough, in a few trips to Orede, to realize that they needed to know more. Calhoun showed them.

Calhoun did not try to make things easy for them. He was hungry and easily annoyed. It was sound training tactics to be severe, and to phrase all suggestions as commands. He put the four young men in command of the ship in turn, under his direction. He continued to use Weald as a destination, but he set up problems in which the Med Ship came out of overdrive pointing in an unknown direction and with a precessory motion.

He made the third of his students identify Weald in the celestial globe containing hundreds of millions of stars, and get on course in overdrive toward it. The

fourth was suddenly required to compute the distance
to Weald from such data as he could get from observation, without reference to any records.

By this time the first man was chafing to take a
second turn. Calhoun gave each of them a second
grueling lesson. He gave them, in fact, a highly condensed but very sound course in the art of travel in
space. His young students took command in four-hour
watches, with at least one breakout from overdrive in
each watch.

He built up enthusiasm in them. They ignored the
discomfort of being hungry—though there had been
no reason for them to stint on food on Orede—in
growing pride in what they came to know.

When Weald was a first-magnitude star, the four
were not highly qualified astrogators, to be sure, but
they were vastly better spacemen than at the beginning. Inevitably, their attitude toward Calhoun was
respectful. He'd been irritable and right. To the young,
the combination is impressive.

Maril had served as passenger only. In theory she
was to compare Calhoun's lessons with his practice
when alone. But he did nothing on this journey which,
teaching considered, was different from the two interstellar journeys Maril had made with him.

She occupied the sleeping cabin during two of the
six watches of each ship-day. She operated the food-
readier, which was almost completely emptied of its
original store of food, it having been confiscated by
the government of Dara. That amount of food would
make no difference to the planet, but it was wise for
everyone on Dara to be equally ill-fed.

On the sixth day out from Dara, the sun of Weald
had a magnitude of minus five-tenths. The electron
telescope could detect its larger planets, especially a
gas-giant fifth-orbit world of high albedo. Calhoun had

his four students estimate its distance again, pointing out the difference that could be made in breakout position if the Med Ship were mis-aimed by as much as one second of arc.

"And now," he said briskly, "we'll have coffee. I'm going to graduate you as pilots. Maril, four cups of coffee, please."

Murgatroyd said, *"Chee?"* The Med Ship was badly crowded with six humans and Murgatroyd in a space intended for Calhoun and Murgatroyd alone. The little *tormal* had spent most of his time in his cubbyhole, watching with beady eyes as so many people moved about on what had been a spacious ship before.

"No coffee for you, Murgatroyd," said Calhoun. "You didn't do your lessons. This is for the graduating class only."

Murgatroyd came out of his miniature den. He found his little cup and offered it insistently, saying, *"Chee! Chee! Chee!"*

"No!" said Calhoun firmly. He regarded his class of four young men with their blueskin markings. "Drink it down!" he commanded. "That's the last order I'll give you. You're graduate pilots, now!"

They drank the coffee with a flourish. There was not one who did not admire Calhoun for having made them admire themselves. They were, actually, almost as much better pilots as they believed.

"And now," said Calhoun, "I suppose you'll tell me the truth about those boxes you brought on board. You said they were rations, but they haven't been opened in six days. I have an idea what they mean, but you tell me."

The four looked uncomfortable. There was a long pause.

"They could be," said Calhoun detachedly, "cultures to be dumped on Weald. Weald is making plans to wipe out Dara. So some fool has decided to get Weald too busy fighting a plague of its own to bother with you. Is that right?"

The young men stirred unhappily. Young men can very easily be made into fanatics. But they have to be kept stirred up. They can't be provided with sound reason for self-respect. On the Med Ship there'd not been a single reference to Weald except as an object toward which the Med Ship was being astrogated. There'd been no reference to blueskins or enemies or threats or anything but space-piloting. The four young men were now fanatical about the proper handling of a ship in emptiness.

"Well, sir," said one of them, unhappily, "that's what we were ordered to do."

"I object," said Calhoun. "It wouldn't work. I just left Weald a little while back, remember. They've been telling themselves that some day Dara might try that. They've made preparations to fight any imaginable contagion you could drop on them. Every so often somebody claims it's happening. It wouldn't work. I object!"

"But—"

"In fact," said Calhoun, "I forbid it. I shall prevent it. You shan't do anything of the kind."

One of the young men, staring at Calhoun, nodded suddenly. His eyes closed. He jerked his head erect and looked bewildered. A second sank heavily into a chair. He said remotely, "Thish sfunny!" and abruptly went to sleep. The third found his knees giving way. He paid elaborate attention to them, stiffening them. But they yielded like rubber and he went slowly down to the floor. The fourth said thickly and reproachfully, "Thought y'were our frien'!"

He collapsed.

Calhoun very soberly tied them hand and foot and

laid them out comfortably on the floor. Maril watched, white-faced, her hand to her throat. Murgatroyd looked agitated. He said anxiously, *"Chee? Chee?"*

"No," said Calhoun. "They'll wake up presently."

Maril said in a tense and desperate whisper, "You're betraying us! You're going to take us to Weald!"

"No," said Calhoun. "We'll only orbit around it. First, though, I want to get rid of those damned packed-up cultures. They're dead, by the way. I killed them with supersonics a couple of days ago, while a fine argument was going on about distance-measurements by variable Cepheids of known period."

He put the four boxes carefully in the disposal unit. He operated it. The boxes and their contents streamed out to space in the form of metallic and other vapors. Calhoun sat at the control desk.

"I'm a Med Service man," he said detachedly. "I couldn't cooperate in the spread of plagues, anyhow, though a useful epidemic might be another matter. But the important thing right now is not keeping Weald busy with troubles to increase their hatred of Dara. It's getting some food for Dara. And driblets won't help. What's needed is thousands of tons, or tens of thousands." Then he said, "Overdrive coming, Murgatroyd! Hold fast!"

The universe vanished. The customary unpleasant sensations accompanied the change. Murgatroyd burped.

VI

A large part of the firmament was blotted out by the blindingly bright half-disk of Weald, as it shone in the sunshine. The Med Ship floated free, and Calhoun fretfully monitored all the beacon frequencies known to man.

There was relative silence inside the ship. Maril watched Calhoun in a sort of despairing indecision. The four young blueskins still slept, still bound hand and foot upon the control-room floor. Murgatroyd regarded them, and Maril, and Calhoun in turn, and his small and furry forehead wrinkled helplessly.

"They can't have landed what I'm looking for!" protested Calhoun as his search had no result. "They can't. It would be too sensible for them to have done it!"

Murgatroyd said, *"Chee!"* in a subdued voice.

"But where the devil did they put them?" demanded Calhoun. "A polar orbit would be ridiculous! They—" Then he grunted in disgust. "Oh! Of course! Now, where's the landing grid?"

He worked busily for minutes, checking the position of the Wealdian landing grid, which was mapped in the Sector Directory, against the look of continents and seas on the half-disk so plainly visible outside. He found what he wanted. He put on the ship's solar system drive.

"I wish," he complained to Maril, "I wish I could think straight the first time. And it's so obvious! If you want to put something out in space, and not have it interfere with traffic, in what sort of orbit and at what distance will you put it?"

Maril did not answer.

"Obviously," said Calhoun, "you'll put it as far as possible from the landing pattern of ships coming in to the spaceport. You'll put it on the opposite side of the planet. And you'll want it to stay out of the way, where anybody can know where it is at any time of the day or night without having to calculate anything.

"So you'll put it out in orbit so it will revolve around Weald in exactly one day, neither more nor less, and you'll put it above the equator. And then it will remain quite stationary above one spot on the planet, a hundred and eighty degrees longitude away from the landing grid and directly over the equator."

He scribbled for a moment.

"Which means forty-two thousand miles high, give or take a few hundred, and—here! And I was hunting for it in a close-in orbit!"

He grumbled to himself. He waited while the solar system drive pushed the Med Ship a quarter of the way around the bright planet below. The sunset line vanished and the planet's disk became a complete circle. Then Calhoun listened to the monitor earphones again, and grunted once more, and changed course, and presently made a noise indicating satisfaction.

He abandoned instrument control and peered directly out of a port, handling the solar system drive with great care. Murgatroyd said depressedly, *"Chee!"*

"Stop worrying," commanded Calhoun. "We haven't been challenged, and there is a beacon transmitter at work, just to make sure that nobody bumps into what we're looking for. It's a great help, because we do want to bump, but gently."

Stars swung across the port out of which he looked. Something dark appeared, and then straight lines and exact curvings. Even Maril, despairing and bewildered as she was, caught sight of something vastly larger than the Med Ship, floating in space. She stared. The Med Ship maneuvered very cautiously. She saw another large object. A third. A fourth. There seemed to be dozens of them.

They were spaceships, huge by comparison with *Aesclipus Twenty*. They floated as the Med Ship did. They did not drive. They were not in formation. They were not at even distances from each other. They did not point in the same direction. They swung in emptiness like derelicts.

Calhoun jockeyed his small ship with infinite care. Presently there came the gentlest of impacts and then a clanking sound. The appearance out the vision port became stationary, but still unbelievable. The Med Ship was grappled magnetically to a vast surface of welded metal.

Calhoun relaxed. He opened a wall panel and brought out a vacuum suit. He began briskly to get it on.

"Things moving smoothly," he commented. "We weren't challenged. So it's extremely unlikely that we were spotted. Our friends on the floor ought to begin to come to shortly. And I'm going to find out now whether I'm a hero or in sure-enough trouble!"

Maril said drearily, "I don't know what you've done, except—"

Calhoun blinked at her, in the act of hauling the vacuum suit up his chest and over his shoulders.

"Isn't it self-evident?" he demanded. "I've been giving astrogation lessons to these characters. I certainly didn't do it to help them dump germ cultures on Weald! I brought them here! Don't you see the point? These are spaceships. They're in orbit around Weald. They're not manned and they're not controlled. In fact, they're nothing but sky-riding storage bins."

He seemed to consider the explanation complete. He wriggled his arms into the sleeves and gloves of the suit. He slung the air tanks over his shoulder and hooked them to the suit.

"I'll be back," he said. "I hope with good news. I've reason to be hopeful, though, because these Wealdians are very practical men. They have things all prepared and tidy. I suspect I'll find these ships with stores of air and fuel, maybe even food, so that if Weald should manage to make a deal for the stuff stored out here in them, they'd only have to bring out crews."

He lifted the space helmet down from its rack and put it on. He tested it, reading the tank air-pressure, power-storage, and other data from the lighted miniature instruments visible through pinholes above his eye-level. He fastened a space rope about himself, speaking through the helmet's opened faceplate.

"If our friends should wake up before I get back," he added, "please restrain them. I'd hate to be marooned."

He went waddling into the air-lock with the coil of space rope over one vacuum-suited arm. The inner lock door closed behind him. A little later Maril heard the outer lock open. Then silence.

Murgatroyd whimpered a little. Maril shivered.

Calhoun had gone out of the ship to nothingness. He'd said that what he was looking for, and what he'd found, was forty-two thousand miles from Weald. One could imagine falling forty-two thousand miles, where one couldn't imagine falling a light-year.

Calhoun was walking on the steel plates of a gigantic spaceship which floated among dozens of its fellows, all seeming derelicts and seemingly abandoned. He was able to walk on the nearest because of magnetic-soled shoes. He trusted his life to them and to a flimsy space rope which trailed after him out the Med Ship's air-lock.

Time passed. A clock ticked in that hurried tempo of five ticks to the second which has been the habit of clocks since time immemorial. Very small and trivial noises came from the background tape, preventing utter silence from hanging intolerably in the ship.

Maril found herself listening tensely for something else. One of the four bound blueskins snored, and stirred, and slept again. Murgatroyd gazed about unhappily, and swung down to the control-room floor, and then paused for lack of any place to go or anything to do. He sat down and began half-heartedly to lick his whiskers. Maril stirred.

Murgatroyd looked at her hopefully.

"Chee?" he asked shrilly.

She shook her head. It became a habit to act as if Murgatroyd were a human being. "No," she said unsteadily. "Not yet."

More time passed. An unbearably long time. Then there was the faintest of clankings. It repeated. Then, abruptly, there were noises in the air-lock. They continued. They were fumbling noises.

The outer air-lock door closed. The inner door opened. Dense white fog came out of it. There was motion. Calhoun followed the fog out of the lock. He carried objects which had been weightless, but were suddenly heavy in the ship's gravity-field. There were two spacesuits and a curious assortment of parcels. He spread them out, flipped aside his faceplate, and said briskly, "This stuff is cold! Turn a heater on it, will you, Maril?"

He began to work his way out of his own vacuum-suit.

"Item," he said. "The ships are fueled *and* provisioned. A practical tribe, the Wealdians! The ships are ready to take off as soon as they're warmed up inside. A half-degree sun doesn't radiate heat enough to keep a ship warm, when the rest of the cosmos is effectively near zero Kelvin. Here, point the heaters like this."

He adjusted the radiant-heat dispensers. The fog disappeared where their beams played. But the metal spacesuits glistened and steamed, and the steam disappeared within inches. They were so completely and utterly cold that they condensed the air about them as a liquid, which re-evaporated to make fog, which warmed up and disappeared and was immediately replaced.

"Item," said Calhoun again, getting his arms out of the vacuum-suit sleeves. "The controls are pretty nearly standard. Our sleeping friends will be able to astrogate them back to Dara without trouble, provided only that nobody comes out here to bother us before they leave."

He shed the last of the spacesuit, stepping out of its legs.

"And," he finished wryly, "I brought back an emergency supply of ship provisions for everybody concerned, but find that I'm idiot enough to feel that they'll choke me if I eat them while Dara's still starving."

Maril said, "But there isn't any hope for Dara! No real hope!"

He gaped at her.

"What do you think we're here for?"

He set to work to restore his four recent students to consciousness. It was not a difficult task. The dosage mixed in the coffee given them as a graduation ceremony—the ceremony which had consisted solely of drinking coffee and passing out—allowed for waking-up processes. Calhoun took the precaution of disarming them first, but presently four hot-eyed young men glared at him.

"I'm calling," said Calhoun, holding a blaster negligently in his hand, "I'm calling for volunteers. There's a famine on Dara. There've been unmanageable crop surpluses on Weald. On Dara, the government grimly rations every ounce of food. On Weald, the government has been buying surplus grain to keep the price up.

"To save storage costs, it's loaded the grain into out-of-date spaceships it once used to stand sentry over Dara to keep it out of space when there was another famine there. Those ships have been put out in orbit, where we're hooked on to one of them.

"It's loaded with half a million bushels of grain. I've brought spacesuits from it, I've turned on the heaters in its interior, and I've set its overdrive unit for a hop to Dara. Now I'm calling for volunteers to take half a million bushels of grain to where it's needed. Do I get any volunteers?"

He got four. Not immediately, because they were ashamed that he'd made it impossible to carry out their original fanatic plan, and now offered something much better to make up for it. They raged. But half a million bushels of grain meant that people who must otherwise die might live.

Ultimately, truculently, first one and then another angrily agreed.

"Good!" said Calhoun. "Now, how many of you dare risk the trip alone? I've got one grain ship warming up. There are plenty of others around us. Every one of you can take a ship and half a million bushels to Dara, if you have the nerve!"

The atmosphere changed. Suddenly they clamored for the task he offered them. They were still acutely uncomfortable. He'd bossed them and taught them until they felt capable and glamorous and proud. Then he'd pinned their ears back. But if they returned to Dara with four enemy ships and unimaginable quantities of food with which to break the famine . . .

There was work to be done first, of course. Only one ship was so far warming up. Three more had to be entered, in spacesuits, and each had to have its interior warmed so breathable air could exist inside it, and at least part of the stored provisions had to be brought up to reasonable temperature for use on the journey.

Then the overdrive unit had to be inspected and set for the length of journey that a direct overdrive hop to Dara would mean, and Calhoun had to make sure again that each of the four could identify Dara's sun under all circumstances and aim for it with the requisite high precision, both before going into overdrive and after breakout. When all that was accomplished, Calhoun might reasonably hope that they'd arrive. But it wasn't a certainty.

Still, presently his four students shook hands with him, with the fine tolerance of young men intending much greater achievements than their teacher. They wouldn't speak on communicator again, because their messages might be picked up on Weald.

Of course, for this high heroic action to be successful, it had to be performed with the stealth of sneak-thieves.

What seemed a long time passed. Then one ship turned slowly upon some unseen axis. It wavered back and forth, seeking a point of aim. A second twisted in its place. A third put on the barest trace of solar system drive to get clear of the rest. The fourth—

One ship vanished. It had gone into overdrive, heading for Dara at many times the speed of light. Another. Two more.

That was all. The remainder of the fleet hung clumsily in emptiness. And Calhoun worriedly went over in his mind the lessons he'd given in such a pathetically small number of days. If the four ships reached Dara, their pilots would be heroes. Calhoun had presented them with that estate over their bitter objection. But they would glory in it—if they reached Dara.

Maril looked at him with very strange eyes.

"Now what?" she asked.

"We hang around," said Calhoun, "to see if anybody comes up from Weald to find out what's happened. It's always possible to pick up a sort of signal when a ship goes into overdrive. Usually it doesn't mean a thing. Nobody pays any attention. But if somebody comes out here . . ."

"What?"

"It'll be regrettable," said Calhoun. He was suddenly very tired. "It'll spoil any chance of our coming back and stealing some more food, like interstellar mice. If they find out what we've done they'll expect us to try it again. They might get set to fight. Or they might simply land the rest of these ships."

"If I'd realized what you were about," said Maril, "I'd have joined in the lessons. I could have piloted a ship."

"You wouldn't have wanted to," said Calhoun. He yawned. "You wouldn't want to be a heroine. No normal girl does."

"Why?"

"Korvan," said Calhoun. He yawned again. "I've asked about him. He's been trying very desperately to deserve well of his fellow blueskins. All he's accomplished is develop a way to starve painlessly. He wouldn't feel comfortable with a girl who'd helped make starving unnecessary. He'd admire you politely, but he'd never marry you. And you know it."

She shook her head, but it was not easy to tell whether she denied the reaction of Korvan, whom Calhoun had never met, or denied that he was more important to her than anything else. The last was what Calhoun plainly implied.

"You don't seem to be trying to be a hero!" she protested.

"I'd enjoy it," admitted Calhoun, "but I have a job to do. It's got to be done. It's more important than being admired."

"You could take another ship back," she told him. "It would be worth more to Dara than the Med Ship is. And then everybody would realize that you'd planned everything."

"Ah," said Calhoun, "but you've no idea how much this ship matters to Dara!"

He seated himself at the controls. He slipped headphones over his ears. He listened. Very, very carefully, he monitored all the wave lengths and wave forms he could discover in use on Weald. There was no mention of the oddity of behavior of shiploads of surplus grain aloft. There was no mention of the ships at all. There was plenty of mention of Dara, and blueskins, and of the vicious political fight now going on to see which political party could promise the most complete protection against blueskins.

After a full hour of it, Calhoun flipped off his

receptor and swung the Med Ship to an exact, painstakingly precise aim at the sun around which Dara
rolled. He said, "Overdrive coming, Murgatroyd!"

Murgatroyd grabbed. The stars went out and the
universe reeled and the Med Ship became a sort of
cosmos all its own, into which no signal could come, no
danger could enter, and in which there could be no
sound except those minute ones made to prevent silence.

Calhoun yawned again.

"Now there's nothing to be done for a day or two,"
he said wearily, "and I'm beginning to understand why
people sleep all they can, on Dara. It's one way not
to feel hungry. And one dreams such delicious meals!
But looking hungry is a social requirement, on Dara."

Maril said tensely, "You're going back? After they
took the ship from you?"

"The job's not finished," he explained. "Not even
the famine's ended, and the famine's a second-order
effect. If there were no such thing as a blueskin,
there'd be no famine. Food could be traded for. We've
got to do something to make sure there are no more
famines."

She looked at him oddly.

"It would be desirable," she said with irony. "But
you can't do it."

"Not today, no," he admitted. Then he said long-
ingly, "I didn't get much sleep on the way here, while
running a seminar on astrogation. I think I'll take a
nap."

She rose and almost ostentatiously went into the
other cabin to leave him alone. He shrugged. He
settled down into the chair which, to let a Med Ship
man break the monotony of life in unchanging surroundings, turned into a comfortable sleeping arrangement. He fell instantly asleep.

❖   ❖   ❖

On the second ship-day Calhoun labored painstakingly and somewhat distastefully at the little biological laboratory. Maril watched him in a sort of brooding silence. Murgatroyd slept much of the time, with his furry tail wrapped meticulously across his nose.

Toward the end of the day Calhoun finished his task. He had a matter of six or seven cubic centimeters of clear liquid as the conclusion of a long process of culturing, and examination by microscope, and again culturing plus final filtration. He looked at a clock and calculated time.

"Better wait until tomorrow," he observed, and put the bit of clear liquid in a temperature-controlled place of safekeeping.

"What is it?" asked Maril. "What's it for?"

"It's part of a job I have on hand," said Calhoun. He considered. "How about some music?"

She looked astonished. But he set it up and settled back to listen. Then there was music such as she had never heard before. It was another device to counteract isolation and monotonous between-planet voyages. To keep it from losing its effectiveness, Calhoun rationed himself on music, as on other things.

Any indulgence frequently repeated would become a habit, in the sense that it would give no special pleasure when indulged in, but would make for stress if it were omitted. Calhoun deliberately went for weeks between uses of his recordings, so that music was an event to be looked forward to and cherished.

When he tapered off the stirring symphonies of Kun Gee with tranquilizing, soothing melodies from the Rim School of composers, Maril regarded him with a very peculiar gaze indeed.

"I think I understand now," she said slowly, "why you don't act like other people. Toward me, for example. The way you live gives you what other

people have to get in crazy ways—making their work
feed their vanity, and justify pride, and make them
feel significant. But you can put your whole mind
on your work."

He thought it over.

"Med Ship routine is designed to keep one healthy
in his mind," he admitted. "It works pretty well. It
satisfies all my mental appetites. But there are
instincts . . ."

She waited. He did not finish.

"What do you do about the instincts that work and
music and such things can't satisfy?"

Calhoun grinned wryly, "I'm stern with them. I have
to be."

He stood up and plainly expected her to go into the
other cabin for the night. She went.

It was after breakfast time of the next ship-day when
he got out the sample of clear liquid he'd worked so
long to produce.

"We'll see how it works," he observed. "Murgatroyd's
handy in case of a slip-up. It's perfectly safe so long
as he's aboard and there are only the two of us."

She watched as he injected half a cc. under his own
skin. Then she shivered a little.

"What will it do?"

"That remains to be seen." He paused a moment.
"You and I," he said with some dryness, "make a
perfect test for anything. If you catch something from
me, it will be infectious indeed!"

She gazed at him utterly without comprehension.

He took his own temperature. He brought out the
folios which were his orders, covering each of the
planets he should give a standard Medical Service
inspection. Weald was there. Dara wasn't. But a Med
Service man has much freedom of action, even when

only keeping up the routine of normal Med Service. When catching up on badly neglected operations, he necessarily has much more. Calhoun went over the folios.

Two hours later he took his temperature again. He looked pleased. He made an entry in the ship's log. Two hours later yet he found himself drinking thirstily and looked more pleased still.

He made another entry in the log and matter-of-factly drew a small quantity of blood from his own vein and called to Murgatroyd. Murgatroyd submitted amiably to the very trivial operation Calhoun carried out. Calhoun put away the equipment and saw Maril staring at him with a certain look of shock.

"It doesn't hurt him," Calhoun explained. "Right after he's born there's a tiny spot on his flank that has the pain-nerves desensitized. Murgatroyd's all right. That's what he's for."

"But he's your friend!" said Maril.

Murgatroyd, despite his small size and furriness, had all the human attributes an animal which lives with humans soon acquires. Calhoun looked at him with affection.

"He's my assistant. I don't ask anything of him that I can do myself. But we're both Med Service. And I do things for him that he can't do for himself. For example, I make coffee for him."

Murgatroyd heard the familiar word. He said, *"Chee!"*

"Very well," agreed Calhoun. "We'll all have some."

He made coffee. Murgatroyd sipped at the cup especially made for his little paws. Once he scratched at the place on his flank which had no pain nerves. It itched. But he was perfectly content. Murgatroyd would always be contented when he was somewhere near Calhoun.

Another hour went by. Murgatroyd climbed up into Calhoun's lap and with a determined air went to sleep there. Calhoun disturbed him long enough to get an instrument out of his pocket. He listened to Murgatroyd's heartbeat, while Murgatroyd dozed.

"Maril," he said. "Write down something for me. The time, and ninety-six, and one-twenty over ninety-four."

She obeyed, not comprehending. Half an hour later, still not stirring to disturb Murgatroyd, he had her write down another time and sequence of figures, only slightly different from the first. Half an hour later still, a third set. But then he put Murgatroyd down, well satisfied.

He took his own temperature. He nodded.

"Murgatroyd and I have one more chore to do," he told her. "Would you go in the other cabin for a moment?"

Disturbed, she went into the other cabin. Calhoun drew a small sample of blood from the insensitive area on Murgatroyd's flank. Murgatroyd submitted with complete confidence in the man. In ten minutes Calhoun had diluted the sample, added an anticoagulant, shaken it up thoroughly, and filtered it to clarity with all red and white corpuscles removed. Another Med Ship man would have considered that Calhoun had had Murgatroyd prepare a splendid small sample of antibody-containing serum, in case something got out of hand. It would assuredly take care of two patients.

But a Med Ship man would also have known that it was simply one of those scrupulous precautions a Med Ship man takes when using cultures from store.

Calhoun put the sample away and called Maril back.

"It was nothing," he explained, "but you might have felt uncomfortable. We simply had a bit of Med

Service routine that had to be gone through. It's all right now."

He offered no further explanation. She said, "I'll fix lunch." She hesitated. "You brought some food from the first Weald ship. Do you want to—"

He shook his head.

"I'm squeamish," he admitted. "The trouble on Dara is Med Service fault. Before my time, but still . . . I'll stick to rations until everybody eats."

He watched her unobtrusively as the day went on. Presently he considered that she was slightly flushed. Shortly after the evening meal of singularly unappetizing Darian rations, she drank thirstily. He did not comment. He brought our cards and showed her a complicated game of solitaire in which mental arithmetic and expert use of probability increased one's chances of winning.

By midnight she'd learned the game and played it absorbedly. Calhoun was able to scrutinize her without appearing to do so, and he was satisfied again. When he mentioned that the Med Ship should arrive off Dara in eight hours more, she put the cards away and went into the other cabin.

Calhoun wrote up the log. He added the notes that Maril had made for him, of Murgatroyd's pulse and blood pressure after the injection of the same culture that produced fever and thirstiness in himself and later, without contact with him or the culture, in Maril. He put a professional comment at the end:

The culture seems to have retained its normal characteristics during long storage in the spore state. It revived and reproduced rapidly. I injected .5 cc. under my skin and in less than one hour my temperature was 30.8° C. An hour later it was 30.9° C. This was its peak. It immediately

*returned to normal. The only other observable
symptom was slightly increased thirst. Blood-
pressure and pulse remained normal. The other
person in the Med Ship displayed the same symptoms, in prompt and complete repetition, without physical contact.*

He went to sleep, with Murgatroyd curled up in his
cubbyhole, his tail draped carefully over his nose.

The Med Ship broke out of overdrive at 1300 hours,
ship-time. Calhoun made contact with the grid and was
promptly lowered to the ground.

It was almost two hours later, at 1500 hours ship-
time, when the people of Dara were informed by
broadcast that Calhoun was to be executed immediately.

VII

From the viewpoint of Darians, who were also blueskins, the decision of Calhoun's guilt and the decision to execute him were reasonable enough. Maril protested fiercely, and her testimony agreed with Calhoun's in every respect, but from a blueskin viewpoint their own statements were damning.

Calhoun had taken four young astrogators to space. They were the only semiskilled space pilots Dara had. There were no fully qualified men. Calhoun had asked for them, and take them out to emptiness, and there he had instructed them in modern guidance methods for ships of space.

So far there was no disagreement. He'd proposed to make them more competent pilots; more capable of driving a ship to Orede, for example, to raid the enormous cattle herds there. And he'd had them drive the Med Ship to Weald, against which there could be no objection.

But just before arrival he had tricked all four of them by giving them drugged coffee. He'd destroyed the lethal bacterial cultures they'd been ordered to dump on Weald. Then he'd sent the four student pilots off separately, so he and Maril claimed, in huge ships crammed with grain. But those ships were not to be believed in, anyhow.

Nobody believed in shiploads of grain to be had for the taking. They did know that the only four partially experienced space pilots on Dara had been taken away and by Calhoun's own story sent out of the ship after they'd been drugged.

Had they been trained, and had they been helped or even permitted to sow the seeds of plague on Weald, and had they come back prepared to pass on training to other men to handle other spaceships now feverishly being built in hidden places on Dara, then Dara might have a chance of survival.

But a space battle with only partly trained pilots would be hazardous at best. With no trained pilots at all, it would be hopeless. So Calhoun, by his own story, appeared to have doomed every living being on Dara to massacre from the bombs of Weald.

It was this last angle which destroyed any chance of anybody believing in such fairy-tale objects as ships loaded down with grain. Calhoun had shattered Dara's feeble hope of resistance. Weald had some ships and could build or buy others faster than Dara could hope to construct them.

Equally important, Weald had a plentitude of experienced spacemen to man some ships fully and train the crews of others. If it had become desperately busy fighting plague, then a fleet to exterminate life on Dara would be delayed. Dara might have gained time at least to build ships which could ram their enemies and destroy them that way.

But Calhoun had made it impossible. It he told the truth and Weald already had a fleet of huge ships which only needed to be emptied of grain and filled with guns and men, then Dara was doomed. But if he did not tell the truth it was equally doomed by his actions. So Calhoun would be killed.

His execution was to take place in the open space of the landing grid, with vision cameras transmitting the sight over all the blueskin planet. Half-starved men with grisly blue blotches on their skins, marched him to the center of the largest level space on the planet which was not desperately being cultivated. Their hatred showed in their expressions. Bitterness and fury surrounded Calhoun like a wall. Most of Dara would have liked to have seen him killed in a manner as atrocious as his crime, but no conceivable death would be satisfying.

So the affair was coldly businesslike, with not even insults offered to him. He was left to stand alone in the very center of the landing-grid floor. There were a hundred blasters which would fire upon him at the same instant. He would not only be killed; he would be destroyed. He would be vaporized by the blue-white flames poured upon him.

His death was remarkably close, nothing remaining but the order to fire, when loudspeakers from the landing-grid froze everything. One of the grain ships from Weald had broken out of overdrive and its pilot was triumphantly calling for landing coordinates. The grid office relayed his call to loudspeaker circuits as the quickest way to get it on the communication system of the whole planet.

"Calling ground," boomed the triumphant voice of the first of the student pilots Calhoun had trained. "Calling ground! Pilot Franz in captured ship requests coordinates for landing! Purpose of landing is to deliver half a million bushels of grain captured from the enemy!"

At first, nobody dared believe it. But the pilot could be seen on vision. He was known. No blueskin would be left alive long enough to be used as a decoy by the men of Weald! Presently the giant ship on its second voyage to Dara—the first had been a generation ago, when it threatened death and destruction—appeared as a dark pinpoint in the sky. It came down and down, and presently it hovered over the center of the tarmac, where Calhoun composedly stood on the spot where he was to have been executed.

The landing-grid crew shifted the ship to one side, and only then did Calhoun stroll in a leisurely fashion toward the Med Ship by the grid's metal-lace wall.

The big ship touched ground, and its exit port revolved and opened, and the student pilot stood there grinning and heaving out handfuls of grain. There was a warming, yelling, deliriously triumphant crowd, then, where only minutes before there'd been a mob waiting to rejoice when Calhoun's living body exploded into flame.

They no longer hated Calhoun, but he had to fight his way to the Med Ship, nevertheless. He was surrounded by ecstatically admiring citizens of Dara. They shouted praise and rejoicing in his ears until he was half-deafened, and they almost tore his clothing from him in their desire to touch, to pat, to assure him of their gratitude and affection, minutes since they'd thirsted for his blood.

Two hours after the first ship, a second landed. Dara went wild again. Four hours later still, the third arrived. The fourth came down to ground on the following day.

When Calhoun faced the executive and cabinet of Dara for the second time his tone and manner were very dry.

"Now," he said curtly, "I would like a few more

astrogators to train. I think it likely that we can raid the Wealdian grain fleet one more time, and in so doing get the beginning of a fleet for defense. I insist, however, that it must not be used in combat. We might as well be sensible about this situation. After all, four shiploads of grain won't break the famine. They'll help a lot, but they're only the beginning of what's needed for a planetary population."

"How much grain can we hope for?" demanded a man with a blue mark covering all his chin.

Calhoun told him.

"How long before Weald can have a fleet overhead, dropping fusion-bombs?" demanded another, grimly.

Calhoun named a time. But then he said, "I think we can keep them from dropping bombs if we can get the grain fleet and some capable astrogators."

"How?"

He told them. It was not possible to tell the whole story of what he considered sensible behavior. An emotional program can be presented and accepted immediately. A plan of action which is actually intelligent, considering all elements of a situation, has to be accepted piecemeal. Even so, the military men growled.

"We've plenty of heavy elements," said one. "If we'd used our brains, we'd have more bombs than Weald can hope for! We could turn that whole planet into a smoking cinder!"

"Which," said Calhoun acidly, "would give you some satisfaction but not an ounce of food! And food's more important than satisfaction. Now, I'm going to take off for Weald again. I'll want somebody to build an emergency device for my ship, and I'll want the four pilots I've trained and twenty more candidates. And I'd like to have some decent rations. The last trip brought back two million bushels of grain. You can certainly spare adequate food for twenty men for a few days!"

It took some time to get the special device constructed, but the Med Ship lifted in two days more. The device for which it had waited was simply a preventive of the disaster overtaking the ship from the mine on Orede. It was essentially a tank of liquid oxygen, packed in the space from which stores had been taken away. When the ship's air supply was pumped past it, first moisture and then CO_2 froze out.

Then the air flowed over the liquefied oxygen at a rate to replace the CO_2 with more useful breathing material. Then the moisture was restored to the air as it warmed again. For so long as the oxygen lasted, fresh air for any number of men could be kept purified and breathable. The Med Ship's normal equipment could take care of no more than ten. But with this it could journey to Weald with almost any complement on board.

Maril stayed on Dara when the Med Ship left. Murgatroyd protested shrilly when he discovered her about to be closed out by the closing air-lock.

"Chee!" he said indignantly. *"Chee! Chee!"*

"No," said Calhoun. "We'll be crowded enough anyhow. We'll see her later."

He nodded to one of the first four student pilots, who crisply made contact with the landing-grid office, and very efficiently supervised as the grid took the ship up. The other three of the four first-trained men explained every move to sub-classes assigned to each. Calhoun moved about, listening and making certain that the instruction was up to standard.

He felt queer, acting as the supervisor of an educational institution in space. He did not like it. There were twenty-four men beside himself crowded into the Med Ship's small interior. They got in each other's way.

They trampled on each other. There was always some-body eating, and always somebody sleeping, and there was no need whatever for the background recording to keep the ship from being intolerably quiet. But the air system worked well enough, except once when the reheating unit quit and the air inside the ship went down below freezing before the trouble could be found and corrected.

The journey to Weald, this time, took seven days because of the training program in effect. Calhoun bit his nails over the delay. But it was necessary for each of the students to make his own line-ups on Weald's sun, and compute distances, and for each of them to practice maneuverings that would presently be called for. Calhoun hoped desperately that preparations for active warfare did not move fast on Weald.

He believed, however, that in the absence of direct news from Dara, Wealdian officials would take the normal course of politicos. They had proclaimed the ship from Orede an attack from Dara. Therefore, they would specialize on defensive measures before plump-ing for offense. They'd get patrol ships out to spot invasion ships long before they worked on a fleet to destroy the blueskins. It would meet the public demand for defense.

Calhoun was right. The Med Ship made its final approach to Weald under Calhoun's own control. He'd made brightness-measurements on his previous jour-ney and he used them again. They would not be strictly accurate, because a sunspot could knock all meaning out of any reading beyond two decimal places. But the first breakout was just far enough from the Wealdian system for Calhoun to be able to pick out its planets with the electron telescope at maximum magnification. He could aim for Weald itself, allowing, of course, for the lag in the apparent motion of its image because of the limited speed of light. He tried the briefest of overdrive hops, and came out within the solar system and well inside any watching patrol.

That was pure fortune. It continued. He'd broken through the screen of guard ships in undetectable overdrive. He was within half an hour's solar system drive of the grain fleet. There was no alarm, at first. Of course radars spotted the Med Ship as an object, but nobody paid attention. It was not headed for Weald. It was probably assumed to be a guard boat itself. Such mistakes do happen.

Again from the storage space from which supplies had been removed, Calhoun produced vacuum suits. The first four students went out, each escorting a less-accustomed neophyte and all fastened firmly together with space ropes. They warmed the interiors of four ships and went on to others. Presently there were eight ships making ready for an interstellar journey, each with a scared but resolute new pilot familiarizing himself with its controls. There were sixteen ships. Twenty. Twenty-three.

A guard ship came humming out from Weald. It would be armed, of course. It came droning, droning up the forty-odd thousand miles from the planet. Calhoun swore. He could not call his students and tell them what was toward. The guard ship would overhear. He could not trust untried young men to act rationally if they were unaware and the guard ship arrived and matter-of-factly attempted to board one of them.

Then he was inspired. He called Murgatroyd, placed him before the communicator, and set it at voice-only transmission. This was familiar enough, to Murgatroyd. He'd often seen Calhoun use a communicator.

"Chee!" shrilled Murgatroyd. *"Chee-chee!"*

A startled voice came out of the speaker, "What's that?"

"*Chee*," said Murgatroyd zestfully.

The communicator was talking to him. Murgatroyd adored three things, in order. One was Calhoun. The second was coffee. The third was pretending to converse like a human being. The speaker said explosively, "You there, identify yourself!"

"*Chee-chee-chee-chee!*" observed Murgatroyd. He wriggled with pleasure and added, reasonably enough, "*Chee!*"

The communicator bawled, "Calling ground! Calling ground! Listen to this! Something that ain't human's talking at me on a communicator! Listen in an' tell me what to do!"

Murgatroyd interposed with another shrill, "*Chee!*"

Then Calhoun pulled the Med Ship slowly away from the clump of still-lifeless grain ships. It was highly improbable that the guard boat would carry an electron telescope. Most likely it would have only an echo-radar, and so could determine only that an object of some sort moved of its own accord in space. Calhoun let the Med Ship accelerate. That would be final evidence. The grain ships were between Weald and its sun. Even electron telescopes on the ground—and electron telescopes were ultimately optical telescopes with electronic amplification—could not get a good image of the ship through sunlit atmosphere.

"*Chee?*" asked Murgatroyd solicitously. "*Chee-chee-chee?*"

"Is it blueskins?" shakily demanded the voice from the guard boat. "Ground! Ground! Is it blueskins?"

A heavy, authoritative voice came in with much greater volume. "That's no human voice," it said harshly. "Approach its ship and send back an image. Don't fire first unless it heads for ground."

The guard ship swerved and headed for the Med Ship. It was still a very long way off.

"*Chee-chee,*" said Murgatroyd encouragingly.

Calhoun changed the Med Ship's course. The guard ship changed course too. Calhoun let it draw nearer, but only a little. He led it away from the fleet of grain ships. He swung his electron telescope on them. He saw a space-suited figure outside one, safely roped, however. It was easy to guess that someone had meant to return to the Med Ship for orders or to make a report, and found the Med Ship gone. He'd go back inside and turn on a communicator.

"*Chee!*" said Murgatroyd.

The heavy voice boomed. "You there! This is a human-occupied world! If you come in peace, cut your drive and let our guard ship approach!"

Murgatroyd replied in an interested but doubtful tone. The booming voice bellowed. Another voice of higher authority took over. Murgatroyd was entranced that so many people wanted to talk to him. He made what for him was practically an oration. The last voice spoke persuasively and suavely.

"*Chee-chee-chee-chee,*" said Murgatroyd.

One of the grain ships flickered and ceased to be. It had gone into overdrive. Another. And another. Suddenly they began to flick out of sight by twos and threes.

"*Chee,*" said Murgatroyd with a note of finality.

The last grain ship vanished.

"Calling guard ship," said Calhoun dryly. "This is Med Ship *Aesclipus Twenty*. I called here a couple of weeks ago. You've been talking to my *tormal*, Murgatroyd."

A pause. A blank pause. Then profanity of deep and savage intemperance.

"I've been on Dara," said Calhoun.

Dead silence fell.

"There's a famine there," said Calhoun deliberately.

"So the grain ships you've had in orbit have been taken away by men from Dara—blueskins if you like—to feed themselves and their families. They've been dying of hunger and they don't like it."

There was a single burst of the unprintable. Then the formerly suave voice said waspishly, "Well? The Med Service will hear of your interference!"

"Yes," said Calhoun. "I'll report it myself. I have a message for you. Dara is ready to pay for every ounce of grain and for the ships it was stored in. They'll pay in heavy metals—iridium, uranium, that sort of thing."

The suave voice fairly curdled.

"As if we'd allow anything that was ever on Dara to touch ground here!"

"Ah! But there can be sterilization. To begin with metals, uranium melts at 1150° centigrade, and tungsten at 3370° and iridium at 2350°. You could load such things and melt them down in space and then tow them home. And you can actually sterilize a lot of other useful materials!"

The suave voice was infuriated. "I'll report this! You'll suffer for this!"

Calhoun said pleasantly, "I'm sure that what I say is being recorded, so that I'll add that it's perfectly practical for Wealdians to land on Dara, take whatever property they think wise—to pay for damage done by blueskins, of course—and get back to Wealdian ships with absolutely no danger of carrying contagion. If you'll make sure the recording's clear . . ."

He described, clearly and specifically, exactly how a man could be outfitted to walk into any area of any conceivable contagion, do whatever seemed necessary in the way of looting—but Calhoun did not use the word—and then return to his fellows with no risk whatever of bringing back infection. He gave exact details.

Then he said, "My radar says you've four ships converging on me to blast me out of space. I sign off."

The Med Ship disappeared from normal space, and entered that improbably stressed area of extension which it formed about itself and in which physical constants were wildly strange. For one thing, the speed of light in overdrive-stressed space had not been measured yet. It was too high. For another, a ship could travel very many times 186,000 miles per second in overdrive.

The Med Ship did just that. There was nobody but Calhoun and Murgatroyd on board. There was companionable silence, with only the small threshold-of-perception sounds which one did not often notice.

Calhoun luxuriated in regained privacy. For seven days he'd had twenty-four other human beings crowded into the two cabins of the ship, with never so much as one yard of space between himself and someone else. One need not be snobbish to wish to be alone sometimes!

Murgatroyd licked his whiskers thoughtfully.

"I hope," said Calhoun, "that things work out right. But they may remember on Dara that I'm responsible for some ten million bushels of grain reaching them. Maybe, just possibly, they'll listen to me and act sensibly. After all, there's only one way to break a famine. Not with ten million bushels for a whole planet! And certainly not with bombs!"

Driving direct, without pausing for practicing, the Med Ship could arrive at Dara in a little more than five days. Calhoun looked forward to relaxation. As a beginning he made ready to give himself an adequate meal for the first time since first landing on Dara. Then, presently, he sat down to a double meal of Darian famine-rations, which were far from appetizing. But there wasn't anything else on board.

He had some pleasure later, though, envisioning what went on in the normal, non-overdrive universe. Suns flared, and comets hurtled on their way, and clouds formed and dropped down rain, and all sorts of celestial and meteorological phenomena took place. On Weald, obviously, there would be purest panic.

The vanishing of the grain fleet wouldn't be charged against twenty-four men. A Darian fleet would be suspected, and with the suspicion would come terror, and with terror a governmental crisis. Then there'd be a frantic seizure of any craft that could take to space, and the agitated improvisation of a space fleet.

But besides that, biological-warfare technicians would examine Calhoun's instructions for equipment by which armed men could be landed on a plague-stricken planet and then safely taken off again. Military and governmental officials would come to the eminently sane conclusion that while Calhoun could not well take active measures against blueskins, as a sane and proper citizen of the galaxy he would be on the side of law and order and propriety and justice—in short, of Weald. So they ordered sample anticontagion suits made according to Calhoun's directions, and they had them tested. They worked admirably.

On Dara, while Calhoun journeyed placidly back to it, grain was distributed lavishly, and everybody on the planet had their cereal ration almost doubled. It was still not a comfortable ration, but the relief was great. There was considerable gratitude felt for Calhoun, which as usual included a lively anticipation of further favors to come. Maril was interviewed repeatedly, as the person best able to discuss him, and she did his reputation no harm. That was all that happened on Dara . . .

No. There was something else. A very curious thing,

too. There was a spread of mild symptoms which nobody could exactly call a disease. They lasted only a few hours. A person felt slightly feverish, and ran a temperature which peaked at 30.9° centigrade, and drank more water than usual. Then his temperature went back to normal and he forgot all about it. There have always been such trivial epidemics. They are rarely recorded, because few people think to go to a doctor. That was the case here.

Calhoun looked ahead a little, too. Presently the fleet of grain ships would arrive and unload and lift again for Orede, and this time they would make an infinity of slaughter among wild cattle herds, and bring back incredible quantities of fresh-slaughtered frozen beef. Almost everybody would get to taste meat again, which would be most gratifying.

Then, the industries of Dara would labor at government-required tasks. An astonishing amount of fissionable material would be fashioned into bombs— a concession by Calhoun—and plastic factories would make an astonishing number of plastic sag-suits. And large shipments of heavy metals in ingots would be made to the planet's capital city and there would be some guns and minor items.

Perhaps somebody could have predicted any of these items in advance, but it was unlikely that anyone did. Nobody but Calhoun, however, would ever have put them together and hoped very urgently that things would work out. He could see a promising total result. In fact, in the Med Ship hurtling through space, on the fourth day of his journey, he thought of an improvement that could be made in the sum of all those happenings when they got mixed together.

He got back to Dara. Maril came to the Med Ship. Murgatroyd greeted her with enthusiasm.

"Something strange has happened," said Maril, very

much subdued. "I told you that sometimes blueskin markings fade out on children, and then neither they nor their children ever have markings again."

"Yes," said Calhoun. "I remember that you told me."

"And you were reminded of a group of viruses on Tralee. You said they only took hold of people in terribly bad physical condition, but then they could be passed on from mother to child, until sometimes they died out."

Calhoun blinked.

"Yes?"

"Korvan," said Maril very carefully, "has worked out an idea that that's what happens to the blueskin markings on Darians. He thinks that people almost dead of the plague could get the virus, and if they recovered from the plague pass the virus on and be blueskins."

"Interesting," said Calhoun, noncommittally.

"And when we went to Weald," said Maril very carefully indeed, "you were working with some culture material. You wrote quite a lot about it in the ship's log. You gave yourself an injection. Remember? And Murgatroyd? You wrote down your temperature, and Murgatroyd's?" She moistened her lips. "You said that if infection passed between us, something would be very infectious indeed?"

"This is a long discussion," said Calhoun. "Does it arrive at a point?"

"It does," said Maril. "Thousands of people are having their pigment-spots fade away. Not only children but grownups. And Korvan has found out that it always seems to happen after a day when they felt feverish and very thirsty, and then felt all right again. You tried out something that made you feverish and thirsty. I had it too, in the ship. Korvan thinks there's been an epidemic of something that is obliterating the

blue spots on everybody that catches it. There are
always trivial epidemics that nobody notices. Korvan's
found evidence of one that's making *blueskin* no longer
a word with any meaning."

"Remarkable!" said Calhoun.

"Did you do it?" asked Maril. "Did you start a
harmless epidemic that wipes out the virus that makes
blueskins?"

Calhoun said in feigned astonishment, "How can you
think such a thing, Maril?"

"Because I was there," said Maril. She said, somehow desperately, "I know you did it! But the question
is, are you going to tell? When people find they're not
blueskins any longer, when there's no such thing as a
blueskin any longer, will you tell them why?"

"Naturally not," said Calhoun. "Why?" Then he
guessed. "Has Korvan—"

"He thinks," said Maril, "that he thought it up all
by himself. He's found the proof. He's very proud. I'd
have to tell him how the ideas got into his head if you
were going to tell. And he'd be ashamed and angry."

Calhoun considered, staring at her.

"How it happened doesn't matter," he said at last.
"The idea of anybody doing it deliberately would be
disturbing, too. It shouldn't get about. So it seems
much the best thing for Korvan to discover what's
happened to the blueskin pigment, and how it happened. But not why."

She read his face carefully.

"You aren't doing it as a favor to me," she decided.
"You'd rather it was that way."

She looked at him for a long time, until he
squirmed. Then she nodded and went away.

An hour later the Wealdian space fleet was reported
massed in space and driving for Dara.

VIII

There were small scout ships which came on ahead
of the main fleet. They'd originally been guard boats,
intended for solar system duty only and quite incapable
of overdrive. They'd come from Weald in the cargo
holds of the liners now transformed into fighting ships.
The scouts swept low, transmitting fine-screen images
back to the fleet, of all they might see before they were
shot down. They found the landing grid. It contained
nothing larger than Calhoun's Med Ship, *Aesclipus
Twenty*.

They searched here and there. They flittered to and
fro, scanning wide bands of the surface of Dara. The
planet's cities and highways and industrial centers were
wholly open to inspection from the sky. It looked as
if the scouts hunted most busily for the fleet of former
grain ships which Calhoun had said the blueskins had
seized and rushed away. If the scouts looked for them,
they did not find them.

Dara offered no opposition to the ships. Nothing
rose to space to oppose or to resist their search. They

went darting over every portion of the hungry planet, land and seas alike, and there was no sign of military preparedness against their coming. The huge ships of the main fleet waited while the scouts reported monotonously that they saw no sign of the stolen fleet. But the stolen fleet was the only means by which the planet could be defended. There could be no point in a pitched battle in emptiness. But a fleet with a planet to back it might be dangerous.

Hours passed. The Wealdian main fleet waited. There was no offensive movement by the fleet. There was no defensive action from the ground. With fusion-bombs certain to be involved in any actual conflict, there was something like an embarrassed pause. The Wealdian ships were ready to bomb. They were less anxious to be vaporized by possible suicide dashes of defending ships which might blow themselves up near contact with their enemies.

But a fleet cannot travel some light-years through space to make a mere threat. And the Wealdian fleet was furnished with the material for total devastation. It could drop bombs from hundreds, or thousands, or even tens of thousands of miles away. It could cover the world of Dara with mushroom clouds springing up and spreading to make a continuous pall of atomic-fusion products. And they could settle down and kill every living thing not destroyed by the explosions themselves. Even the creatures of the deepest oceans would die of deadly, purposely contrived fallout particles.

The Wealdian fleet contemplated its own destructiveness. It found no capacity for defense on Dara. It moved forward.

But then a message went out from the capital city of Dara. It said that a ship in overdrive had carried word to a Darian fleet in space. The Darian fleet now hurtled toward Weald. It was a fleet of thirty-seven giant ships. They carried such-and-such bombs in such-and-such quantities. Unless its orders were countermanded, it would deliver those bombs on Weald, set to explode. If Weald bombed Dara, the orders could not be withdrawn. So Weald could bomb Dara. It could destroy all life on the pariah planet. But Weald would die with it.

The fleet ceased its advance. The situation was a stalemate with pure desperation on one side and pure frustration on the other. This was no way to end the war. Neither planet could trust the other, even for minutes. If they did not destroy each other simultaneously, as now was possible, each would expect the other to launch an unwarned attack at some other moment. Ultimately one or the other must perish, and the survivor would be the one most skilled in treachery.

But then the pariah planet made a new proposal. It would send a messenger ship to stop its own fleet's bombardment if Weald would accept payment of the grain ships and their cargoes. It would pay in ingots of iridium and uranium and tungsten, and gold if Weald wished it, for all damages Weald might claim.

It would even pay indemnity for the miners of Orede, who had died by accident but perhaps in some sense through its fault. It would pay. But if it were bombed, Weald must spout atomic fire and the fleet of Weald would have no home planet to return to.

This proposal seemed both craven and foolish. It would allow the fleet of Weald to loot and then betray Dara. But it was Calhoun's idea. It seemed plausible to the admirals of Weald. They felt only contempt for blueskins. Contemptuously, they accepted the semi-surrender.

The broadcast waves of Dara told of agreement, and wild and fierce resentment filled the pariah planet's

people. There was almost revolution to insist upon
resistance, however hopeless and however fatal. But
not all of Dara realized that a vital change had come
about in the state of things on Dara. The enemy fleet
had not a hint of it.

In menacing array, the invading fleet spread itself
about the skies of Dara, well beyond the atmosphere.
Harsh voices talked with increasing arrogance to the
landing-grid staff. A monster ship of Weald came
heavily down, riding the landing grid's force-fields. It
touched gently. Its occupants were apprehensive, but
hungry for the loot they had been assured was theirs.
The ship's outer hull would be sterilized before it
returned to Weald, of course. And there was adequate
protection for the landing party.

Men came out of the ship's ports. They wore the
double, transparent sag-suits Calhoun had suggested,
which had been painstakingly tested, and which were
perfect protection against contagion. They were double
garments of plastic, with air tanks inside the inner
flexible envelope.

Men wearing such sag-suits could walk about on
Dara. They could work on Dara. They could loot with
impunity and all contamination must remain outside
the suits, and on their return to their ships they would
simply stand in the air-locks while corrosive gases
swirled around them, killing any possible organism of
disease. Then, for extra assurance, when air from
Weald filled the air-lock again, the men would burn
the outer plastic covering and step into the ship without ever having come within two layers of plastic of
infection.

What loot they gathered, obviously, could be decon-
taminated before it was returned to Weald. Metals
could be melted, if necessary. Gems could be sterilized. It was a most satisfactory discovery, to realize that

blueskins could be not only scorned but robbed. There
was only one bit of irrelevant information the space
fleet of Weald did not have.

That information was that the people of Dara
weren't blueskins any longer. There'd been a trivial
epidemic . . .

The sag-suited men of Weald went zestfully about
their business. They took over the landing grid's operation, driving the Darian operators away. For the first
time in history the operators of a landing grid wore
make-up to look like they did have blue pigment in
their skins. They didn't. The Wealdian landing party
tested the grid's operation. They brought down another
giant ship. Then another. And another.

Parties in the shiny sag-suits spread through the city.
There were the huge stockpiles of precious metals,
brought in readiness to be surrendered and carried
away. Some men set to work to load these into the
holds of the ships of Weald. Some went forthrightly
after personal loot.

They came upon very few Darians. Those they saw
kept sullenly away from them. They entered shops and
took what they fancied. They zestfully removed the
treasure of banks.

Triumphant and scornful reports went up to the
hovering great ships. The blueskins, said the reports,
were spiritless and cowardly. They permitted themselves to be robbed. They kept out of the way. It had
been observed that the population was streaming out
of the city, fleeing because they feared the ships'
landing parties. The blueskins had abjectly produced
all they'd promised of precious metals, but there was
more to be taken.

More ships came down, and more. Some of the first,
heavily loaded, were lifted to emptiness again and the
process of decontamination of their hulls began. There

was jealousy among the ships in space for those upon
the ground. The first landed ships had had their choice
of loot. There were squabblings about priorities, now
that the navy of Weald plainly had a license to steal.
There was confusion among the members of the landing
parties. Discipline disappeared. Men in plastic sag-suits
roved about as individuals, seeking what they might loot.

There were armed and alerted landing parties
around the grid itself, of course, but the capital city
of Dara lay open. Men coming back with loot found
their ships already lifted off to make room for others.
They were pushed into re-embarking parties of other
ships. There were more and more men to be found
on ships where they did not belong, and more and
more not to be found where they did.

By the time half the fleet had been aground, there
was no longer any pretense of holding a ship down
until all its crew returned. There were too many other
ships' companies clamoring for their turn to loot. The
rosters of many ships, indeed, bore no particular relationship to the men actually on board.

There were less than fifteen ships whose to-be-
fumigated holds were still emptied, when the watch-
ful government of Dara broadcast a new message to
the invaders. It requested that the looting stop. No
matter what payment Weald claimed, it had taken
payment five times over. Now was time to stop.

It was amusing. The space admiral of Weald ordered
his ships alerted for action. The message ship, ordering
the Darian fleet away from Weald, had been sent off
long since. No other ship could get away now! The
Darians could take their choice: accept the consequences of surrender, or the fleet would rise to throw
down bombs.

Calhoun was asking politely to be taken to the
Wealdian admiral when the trouble began. It wasn't

on the ground, at all. Everything was under splendid control where a landing force occupied the grid and all the ground immediately about it. The space admiral had headquarters in the landing-grid office. Reports came in, orders were issued, admirably crisp salutes were exchanged among sag-suited men. Everything was in perfect shape there.

But there was panic among the ships in space. Communicators gave off horrified, panic-stricken yells. There were screamings. Intelligible communications ceased. Ships plunged crazily this way and that. Some vanished in overdrive. At least one plunged at full power into a Darian ocean.

The space admiral found himself in command of fifteen ships only out of all his former force. The rest of the fleet went through a period of hysterical madness. In some ships it lasted for minutes only. In others it went on for half an hour or more. Then they hung overhead, but did not reply to calls.

Calhoun arrived at the spaceport with Murgatroyd riding on his shoulder. A bewildered officer in a sag-suit halted him.

"I've come," said Calhoun, "to speak to the admiral. My name is Calhoun and I'm Med Service, and I think I met the admiral at a banquet a few weeks ago. He'll remember me."

"You'll have to wait," protested the officer. "There's some trouble—"

"Yes," said Calhoun. "I know about it. I helped design it. I want to explain it to the admiral. He needs to know what's happened, if he's to take appropriate measures."

There were jitterings. Many men in sag-suits had still no idea that anything had gone wrong. Some appeared, brightly carrying loot. Some hung eagerly around the air-locks of ships on the grid tarmac, waiting their turns to stand in corrosive gases for the decontamination of their suits, when they would burn the outer layers and step, asceptic and happy, into a Wealdian ship again. There they could think how rich they were going to be back on Weald.

But the situation aloft was bewildering and very, very ominous. There was strident argument. Presently Calhoun stood before the Wealdian admiral.

"I came to explain something," said Calhoun pleasantly. "The situation has changed. You've noticed it, I'm sure."

The admiral glared at him through two layers of plastic, which covered him almost like a gift-wrapped parcel.

"Be quick!" he rasped.

"First," said Calhoun, "there are no more blueskins. An epidemic of something or other has made the blue patches on the skins of Darians fade out. There have always been some who didn't have blue patches. Now nobody has them."

"Nonsense!" rasped the admiral. "And what has that got to do with this situation?"

"Why, everything," said Calhoun mildly. "It seems that Darians can pass for Wealdians whenever they please. That they *are* passing for Wealdians. That they've been mixing with your men, wearing sag-suits exactly like the one you're wearing now. They've been going aboard your ships in the confusion of returning looters. There's not a ship now aloft, which has been aground today, which hasn't from one to fifteen Darians—no longer blueskins—on board."

The admiral roared. Then his face turned gray.

"You can't take your fleet back to Weald," said Calhoun gently, "if you believe its crews have been exposed to carriers of the Dara plague. You wouldn't be allowed to land, anyhow."

The admiral said through stiff lips, "I'll blast—"

"No," said Calhoun, again gently. "When you ordered all ships alerted for action, the Darians on each ship released panic gas. They only needed tiny, pocket-sized containers of the gas for the job. They had them. They only needed to use air tanks from their sag-suits to protect themselves against the gas. They kept them handy.

"On nearly all your ships aloft your crews are crazy from panic gas. They'll stay that way until the air is changed. Darians have barricaded themselves in the control-rooms of most if not all your ships. You haven't got a fleet. The few ships who will obey your orders— if they drop one bomb, our fleet off Weald will drop fifty.

"I don't think you'd better order offensive action. Instead, I think you'd better have your fleet medical officers come and learn some of the facts of life. There's no need for war between Dara and Weald, but if you insist . . ."

The admiral made a choking noise. He could have ordered Calhoun killed, but there was a certain appalling fact. The men aground from the fleet were breathing Wealdian air from tanks. It would last so long only. If they were taken on board the still obedient ships overhead, Darians would unquestionably be mixed with them. There was no way to take off the parties now aground without exposing them to contact with Darians, on the ground or in the ships. There was no way to sort out the Darians.

"I—I will give the orders," said the admiral thickly. "I do not know what you devils plan, but—I do not know how to stop you."

"All that's necessary," said Calhoun warmly, "is an open mind. There's a misunderstanding to be cleared up, and some principles of planetary health practices

to be explained, and a certain amount of prejudice that
has to be thrown away. But nobody need die of changing their minds. The Interstellar Medical Service has
proved that over and over!"

Murgatroyd, perched on his shoulder, felt that it was
time to take part in the conversation. He said, *"Chee-
chee!"*

"Yes," agreed Calhoun. "We do want to get the job
done. We're behind schedule now."

It was not, of course, possible for Calhoun to leave
immediately. He had to preside at various meetings
of the medical officers of the fleet and the health officials of Dara. He had to make explanations, and correct misapprehensions, and delicately suggest such
biological experiments as would prove to the doctors
of Weald that there was no longer a plague on Dara,
whatever had been the case three generations before.

He had to sit by while an extremely self-confident
young Darian doctor—one of his names was Korvan—
rather condescendingly demonstrated that the former
blue pigmentation was a viral product quite uncon-
nected with the plague, and that it had been wiped
out by a very trivial epidemic of such and such.

Calhoun regarded that young man with a detached
interest. Maril thought him wonderful, even if she had
to give him the material for his work. He agreed with
her that he was wonderful. Calhoun shrugged and went
on with his own work.

The return of loot, mutual, full, and complete agreement that Darians were no longer carriers of plague,
if they had ever been—unless Weald convinced other
worlds of this, Weald itself would join Dara in isolation from neighboring worlds. A messenger ship had
to recall the twenty-seven ships once floating in orbit
about Weald. Most of them would be used for some

time, to bring beef from Orede. Some would haul more grain from Weald. It would be paid for. There would be a need for commercial missions to be exchanged between Weald and Dara. There would have to be . . .

It was a full week before he could go to the little Med Ship and prepare for departure. Even then there were matters to be attended to. All the food-supplies that had been removed could not be replaced. There were biological samples to be replaced and some to be destroyed.

Maril came to the Med Ship again when he was almost ready to leave. She did not seem comfortable.

"I wanted you to meet Korvan," she said regretfully.

"I met him," said Calhoun. "I think he will be a most prominent citizen, in time. He has all the talents for it."

Maril smiled very faintly.

"But you don't admire him."

"I wouldn't say that," protested Calhoun. "After all, he is desirable to you, which is something I couldn't manage."

"You didn't try," said Maril. "Just as I didn't try to be fascinating to you. Why?"

Calhoun spread out his hands. But he looked at Maril with respect. Not every woman could have faced the fact that a man did not feel impelled to make passes at her. It is simply a fact that has nothing to do with desirability or charm or anything else.

"You're going to marry him," he said. "I hope you'll be very happy."

"He's the man I want," said Maril frankly. "And I doubt he'll ever look at another woman. He looks forward to splendid discoveries. I wish he didn't."

Calhoun did not ask the obvious question. Instead, he said thoughtfully, "There's something you could do. It needs to be done. The Med Service in this sector has been badly handled. There are a number of discoveries that need to be made. I don't think your Korvan would relish having things handed to him on a visible silver platter. But they should be known . . ."

Maril said, "I can guess what you mean. I dropped hints about the way the blueskin markings went away, yes. You've got books for me."

Calhoun nodded. He found them.

"If we had only fallen in love with each other, Maril, we'd be a team! Too bad! These are a wedding present you'll do well to hide."

She put her hands in his.

"I like you almost as much as I like Murgatroyd! Yes! Korvan will never know, and he'll be a great man." Then she added defensively, "But I don't think he'll only discover things from hints I drop him. He'll make wonderful discoveries."

"Of which," said Calhoun, "the most remarkable is you. Good luck, Maril!"

She went away smiling. But she wiped her eyes when she was out of the ship.

Presently the Med Ship lifted. Calhoun aimed it for the next planet on the list of those he was to visit. After this one more he'd return to sector headquarters with a biting report to make on the way things had been handled before him.

"Overdrive coming, Murgatroyd!"

Then the stars went out and there was silence, and privacy, and a faint, faint, almost unhearable series of background sounds which kept the Med Ship from being totally unendurable.

Long, long days later the ship broke out of overdrive and Calhoun guided it to a round and sunlit world. In due time he thumbed the communicator button.

"Calling ground," he said crisply. "Calling ground!

Med Ship *Aesclipus Twenty* reporting arrival and asking coordinates for landing. Purpose of landing is planetary health inspection. Our mass is fifty standard tons."

There was a pause while the beamed message went many, many thousands of miles. Then the speaker said, "*Aesclipus Twenty*, repeat your identification!"

Calhoun repeated it patiently. Murgatroyd watched with bright eyes. Perhaps he hoped to be allowed to have another long conversation with somebody by communicator.

"You are warned," said the communicator sternly, "that any deceit or deception about your identity or purpose in landing will be severely punished. We take few chances, here! If you wish to land notwithstanding this warning—"

"I'm coming in," said Calhoun. "Give me the coordinates."

He wrote them down. His expression was slightly pained. The Med Ship drove on, in solar system drive. Murgatroyd said, "*Chee-chee? Chee?*"

Calhoun sighed.

"That's right, Murgatroyd. Here we go again!"

Editors' Afterword

To modern science fiction readers, the "dean of science fiction" is a reference to Robert Heinlein. But the phrase was actually first applied to Murray Leinster, and the unofficial title was one he carried for many years.

There were three reasons he enjoyed that accolade.

The first is simply his longevity as a writer. Leinster's first science fiction story, "The Runaway Skyscraper," was published in *Argosy* magazine in February of 1919. And he continued to publish science fiction stories for half a century thereafter.

The second reason is that Leinster, to a large degree, set the basic parameters for science fiction. He was the first writer—or, at least, the most important one—to establish such fundamental themes as "first contact" and "alternate history" and a number of other basic story lines in the genre.

In fact, in the stories which are collected in this volume, *Med Ship*, Leinster established the sub-genre of the "science fiction doctor story." That sub-genre, as with so many others which Leinster created, would be explored and expanded on by later writers. Alan Nourse's *Star Surgeon* and James White's very popular *Sector General* series are the direct lineal descendants of these stories—as is the current *Stardoc* series by S.L. Viehl.

The third reason he was called "the dean of science fiction writers," however, is the most important. Without it, the first two would be of only academic interest. Leinster was one of a handful of early science fiction writers who placed telling a *story* at the center of the stage, not "illustrating science in fiction." He, probably more than any other writer in the first decades of the twentieth century, transformed science fiction into a real genre of fiction. And that is why his work survives, and why we are re-issuing these volumes.

We began with his Med Ship stories, because those are probably the best known of his works to the modern audience. This edition, for the first time, contains all eight of the stories which Leinster wrote in that setting. In the next volume, *Planets of Adventure,* we will present more of the best stories which Leinster wrote. As the title suggests, these all have a common theme: adventures on other planets.

It seems a fitting title. By and large, it's fair to say that Leinster created *that* sub-genre also. Granted, Edgar Rice Burroughs' Barsoom novels were already coming into print when Leinster was still a teenager. But Barsoom, although it claims to be Mars, is not really a planet so much as the setting for a fantasy adventure. Leinster's planets—such as the planet on which Burl struggles against giant mutated insects in *The Forgotten Planet*, or the ones on which Colonial Survey Officer Bordman has his adventures—are those of a science fiction writer, not a fantasist.

In truth, it's hard to think of *any* branch of science

fiction which Murray Leinster didn't pioneer. And write wonderfully entertaining stories in the process.

Think of him as "the dean of science fiction *emeritus*," if you wish. Or simply, as we do, as one of science fiction's all-time greatest story-tellers.

—Eric Flint
—Guy Gordon